The Crime Writer

For Stephen F. Breimer,
with great affection and gratitude

The Crime Writer

I woke up with IVs taped to my arms, a feeding tube shoved through my nose, and my tongue pushed against my teeth, dead and thick as a sock. My mouth was hot and tasted of copper, and my molars felt loose, jogged in their beds from grinding. I blinked against the harsh light and squinted into a haze of face too close for casual—a man straddling a backward chair, strong forearms overlapped, a sheet of paper drooping from one square fist. Another guy behind him, dressed the same—rumpled sport coat, loose tie offset from open collar, glint at the hip. Downgraded to bystander, a doctor stood by the door, ignoring the electronic blips and bleeps. I was in a hospital room.

With consciousness came pain. No tunnels of light, no bursts or fireworks or other page-worn clichés, just pain, mindless and dedicated, a rottweiler working a bone. A creak of air moved through my throat.

"He's up," said the doctor from far away. A nurse materialized and fed a needle into the joint in my IV. A second later the warmth rode through my veins and the rottweiler paused to catch his breath.

I raised an arm trailing IV lines and fingered my head where it tingled. Instead of hair, a seam of stubble and stitches cactused my palm. Light-headedness and nausea compounded my confusion. As my hand drifted back to my chest, I noticed dark crescents caking the undersides of my nails.

I'd dug myself out of somewhere?

The cop in the chair flipped the piece of paper over, and I saw that it was an eight-by-ten.

A crime-scene photo.

A close-up of a woman's midsection, the pan of the abdomen crusted with dark blood. A narrow puncture below the ribs faded into blackness, as if a stronger flashbulb were required to sound its depths.

I raised a hand as if to push away the image, and in the dead blue fluorescence I saw that the grime under my nails carried a tinge of crimson. Whether from the drugs or the pain, I felt my gorge rise and push at the back of my throat. It took two tries, and still my voice came out a rasp, barely audible around the plastic tube. "Who is that?"

"Your ex-fiancée."

"Who . . . who *did* that to her?"

The detective's jaw shifted once, slowly, left to right. "You did."

My car occupied slot 221 in the impound lot. A Toyota Highlander, the hybrid model selected so I could drive an SUV and still think highly of myself. I turned over the engine and sat with my hands on the wheel, readjusting to the familiarity of this object that was mine. My head hummed; my scar, largely hidden by grown-back hair, prickled. I felt pressure beneath my face, as if I wanted to cry but my tears had forgotten the pathways. My radio had been left on, Springsteen still going down to the river despite the fact that it had yielded nothing but blue-collar heartache for three decades now. I wondered if I'd left the radio on myself or if somewhere along its towed journey someone had smacked the button. Had I been listening to music on my last nighttime drive? Had I been behind the wheel? Alone?

Of course, I had to pay a vehicle storage fee, six hundred–some bucks. I used a credit card that my keepers had been considerate enough to leave in my wallet while they'd safeguarded it for me. Driving home, I passed a flickering yellow sign and felt a sting of excitement as I parked, the promise of a new liquor store.

"I'm looking for bourbon. You got Blanton's?"

"Nope." The guy at the counter didn't look up from a black-and-white television the size of a clock radio. A cigarette dangled from his lips, supporting an impossible length of ash. I couldn't see the screen, but a reporter was providing updates about some schmuck who had the same name as me.

"Knob Creek?" I asked. He shook his head. "Maker's?"

His eyes pulled over to me, snagged for a beat. "Jack Daniel's."

I could've pointed out that Jack Daniel's is Tennessee sour mash, not bourbon, but I figured that my first stand back in the world should be over something of greater consequence. Box wine, maybe.

"Single-barrel?"

"Yeah, we got the single-barrel."

I felt his stare on my back as I left the store.

Two minutes later I was on Mulholland Drive. The asphalt vine clings to the ridgeline of the Santa Monicas, shooting tendrils north through the Valley to the Santa Anas and south into the L.A. Basin. On its eastern stretch, tourists pull over to snap shots of Hollywood writ large in white block letters. Persian palaces and mutant Pueblo Revivals perch along crests and hillsides, hiding behind gates and rock walls. It's a dangerous road, soaked in affluence and romance, home to the breached guardrail, the meandering Marlowe, the David Lynch fantasy, the 2:00 A.M. drunken head-on. You'll drive it too fast and be glad you did.

Tonight I went the speed limit, figuring I'd had my fill of problems. I rode Mulholland west, banking downslope just before the 405 and easing right off the stop sign. My cul-de-sac was as it always was, pinprick lit with porch lamps and walkway goosenecks, the freeway distant enough to sound like sighing waves. My house was unlit, but I paused to recognize its contours. Despite my absence, it looked the same—Richard Neutra on a budget, a steel, glass, and concrete rise of intersecting planes and right angles that came together nicely but fell short of elegant. After my third book deal, I'd begged, borrowed, and borrowed to catch the lip of the ever-receding tide that is L.A.'s real-estate market. I'd paid too much, but the million-dollar view tacked on to the abrupt backyard consoled me in that. If I couldn't afford it before the trial, I sure as hell couldn't now.

There were no news crews camped on my front lawn. No paparazzi hiding in seedy cars. No Geraldo Rivera in camo gear and full mustache, ready to pounce.

I pulled in to the garage, plucked the jar from the cup holder and the brown paper bag from the backseat, and headed inside. It felt odd to be carrying so little after so long. No suitcases, no carry-on, just the clothes I was wearing, a bottle in a bag, and a brain tumor in a jar.

I'd been gone four months, but the familiarity was undiminished. The catch of the opening door as the weatherboard scraped the threshold. The particular scent of the interior, a layered blend of carpet and tile, coffee and candle wax. Objects I'd bought, choices I'd made. The emotion rising through my chest broke the instant the door closed behind me. Alone in my house, I finally wept, standing, head bowed, tears dotting the floor at my feet despite the hand I'd clamped over my eyes in a futile attempt to keep the anguish from flooding out. I don't know how long I stood there shuddering, but when I removed my hand, the overhead light made me squint.

I trudged through my kitchen with its stainless appliances and teak cabinets, through the entryway with its repetitive Warhols that even I'd tired of long ago, past the wide staircase. Everything in the house was cold and sharp—flagstone underfoot, marble corners on countertops, pointy knobs on drawers. The ambience now felt affected, hubristic. I supposed I should have been relieved to be home, even happy, but all I felt was unsure of myself.

I went to the only worn-in piece of furniture in the house, the club chair in the family room. Distressed leather, brass studs, matching ottoman—displayed curbside at a garage sale near Melrose, it had brought my Highlander to a screeching halt. I seated Jack Daniel's and the brain tumor together on the coffee table, figuring they could swap trade secrets, collapsed into the chair, and felt my shoulders go limp for the first time in four months.

Deep breath. Longer exhale than seemed possible.

Nothing I'd written could compare to this. And I'd had ample opportunity for contrivance. I'd published five books, three of them optioned by the studios, one of which was actually made into a movie, albeit unrecognizable to my readers—the three who saw it—

and myself despite the fact that I'd written the first draft. The produced script, about a priest bounty hunter, was named, I'm ashamed
to admit, *Hunter Pray,* and it starred a crossover TV star who didn't
cross over. My books feature Derek Chainer of LAPD's Homicide
Special (unhappily converted into Father Chainer for aforemen-
tioned flop). In them, pain causes white bursts before the eyes and
anger makes the head throb with rage. What my books *don't* do is
capture the feeling of seeing your ex-fiancée's mutilated body in
crime-scene photos. Or how hard it is to scrape dried blood from
under your fingernails.

I'd thought I knew this world. But I'd known only the outside of
it. Once I got in the belly of the beast, once the digestive juices went
to work on me, I discovered I knew nothing at all. I'd been merely a
tourist on the dark side, watching through binoculars as the crea-
tures stalked and feasted.

My gaze drifted across the room to the row of my titles—
hardcovers, paperbacks, foreign editions—and it struck me how I'd
overestimated even the minor importance I'd ascribed them. I felt
abruptly ill-equipped to take the world at its word, hard-pressed to
believe that there was *any* fundamental merit underlying its designa-
tions of failure and success. My yard-sale chair, solid and comforting
beneath me, seemed invaluable. But my name, embossed on five
glossy spines? One day I'd be a faint reminiscence, me and other
low-grade celebs, joining the dusty ranks of brush-with-famers past.
Years hence, some blowhard grasping for conversation at a dinner
party would have his memory tripped by a turn of phrase. And others might nod their heads and lie kindly. *Andrew Danner. Rings a
bell. Remind me.*

And what would be our blowhard's response? A mystery plot retrieved from the thickets of senility? A response sensitive to legal in-
tricacies? Or a simple tabloid reckoning? *He was a murderer.*

As always, I had difficulty keeping my fingertips from my head,
from that ridge of hardening tissue, the one known entity I'd carried

out of my amnesic fog. The scar where they'd dug into my brain rose straight from my left ear just behind the hairline, then curved slightly toward my forehead. By now I'd memorized each millimeter of the pink seam by touch, as if its bumps and edges held answers written in Braille.

I turned on the TV just to get away from myself, but there I was. My shell-shocked reaction when the verdict was intoned. A *Brady Bunch* split screen of DAs and victims'-rights activists and Alan Dershowitzes. An interview with my seventh-grade teacher. The same old helicopter footage of Genevieve's house. A witty cable anchor had Photoshopped courthouse pictures to depict me miming the see-no, hear-no, speak-no monkeys.

I had achieved some success as a novelist, but fame had come to me as a killer. Squeaky Fromme, Johnny Stompanato, O.J., the Menendez brothers. I was one of them now. A tale of fate and shame, bent to a classical model. Another modern slant on an ancient story from those funny people with olive laurels and knobby knees. Silly Pandora couldn't keep her box closed. Crazy dude, whacked his dad and humped his mom. Did you hear the one about the guy, woke up and didn't even know he'd killed his ex? I was Starbucks chatter, Jamba jive, a drive-time-radio punch line.

I clicked off the TV and sat in the piercing silence.

What would *I* think if I didn't know me? Motive. Means. Opportunity. How's gut instinct stack up against those?

What had I said on the stand? *I believe that anyone is capable of anything.*

But, unfortunately, I was my own unreliable narrator. What I needed were some hard facts to slap on the table beside the sour mash and that handsome tumor of mine.

The neighbor's kid, a chubby, bespectacled tyrant out of a Gary Larson sketch, was at it again with his trumpet, practicing "Whistle While You Work" off tempo and key. *And CHEERfully toGETHER we can TIDY up the PLACE.*

I rose and padded around the house, reacquainting myself. On the wobbly kitchen table, beside two grocery bags filled with mail, sat my block of Shun cutlery, sealed in a clear evidence bag. It stopped me cold. A welcome-home gift from the prosecution or the cops, calculated to throw me in case I was entertaining any thoughts about getting my life back to normal. The forged stainless-steel set had been a passive-aggressive gift from Genevieve, a tenfold upgrade on my sorry plastic-handled Target crap. The same expensive set she owned, a perfect match. My knives had made a cameo appearance in the trial, a nice bit of theater. See, jury, he has a set just like hers, all shiny and bristling, and a present from the victim herself! The inspiration for the crime!

The boning knife from Genevieve's set had been a key piece of evidence. It was what I had been told I'd plunged into her abdomen.

I got scissors from the drawer and sliced the bag open. With odd ceremoniousness I transferred the block to its place on the counter. I balled the evidence bag and threw it away and then leaned against the counter for a moment.

I tried to refocus, to remember how to care for myself. The last thing I needed was a postoperative seizure, so I fought my pills out of my pocket and popped a Dilantin, washing it down with a handful of water from the tap. What a pathetic homecoming.

In the sink rested an empty glass and a white bowl holding a dried orange paisley—incontrovertible evidence of cantaloupe. Breakfast, September 23. The last concrete presurgery event I remembered. The dishes carried the weight of archaeological relics. I rinsed them out and put them away, then trudged upstairs, toting the bags of mail and my tumor, and down the floating hall my Realtor referred to as a catwalk.

More industrious cheer from next door—*put ON that GRIN and START right in to WHISTLE loud and LONG.*

My office has the best view in the house. The soundproofed French doors that let into the master were now closed. My chair lay on its back, toppled over; it drew into view eerily, like a body, as I came off the stairs. I stared down at it a few minutes before righting it. Knocked over by a cop during the search? An intruder? Yours truly, lost in my brain-tumor blackout?

Crumpled in my office wastepaper basket were a faxed offer from an Italian publisher, stubs from Dodgers tickets, and a few pieces of junk mail. Remnants of an ordinary day in oblivious progress. I checked my PalmPilot, clicking backward through all the appointments and meetings I'd missed, until I arrived at September 23. The screen was appropriately blank. As I reseated the Palm in its cradle, I was hit by the bizarreness of investigating myself. I was an intruder in my own house.

I tapped the speaker button on my telephone and reached to dial, figuring I should order takeout in case my appetite ever returned, but after three digits realized that no tones issued forth. I dug through the grocery bags, unearthing a handful of disconnection notices. My other services, fortunately, autowithdrew from my diminishing checking account, like my cell phone dutifully charging on the file cabinet. I stuck my headset into my Motorola and dialed.

As Pac Bell's hold music competed with Snow White, still squalling from next door, I retrieved my e-mail. Expressions of support from friends and readers, a few nastygrams from others convinced of my guilt, a surfeit of Viagra and penis-enlargement offerings that I elected to regard as spam rather than targeted marketing. When I scrolled down to the days around Genevieve's death, I was simultaneously disappointed and relieved to note nothing unusual.

I logged out of the e-mail account and stared at the blank screen. The thought of writing anything soon—or ever again, for that matter—was daunting. Nothing like a little old-fashioned trauma to bring the self-indulgence of my job to the surface. The impracticality, too. I wished I had a surgery to scrub in for or, failing that, an orphan to mend. Something aside from confronting a monitor and pretending that what I could think up would be of interest to hundreds of thousands of people, most of whom performed jobs that were actually useful.

Serge finally came on the line asking how he might provide me excellent service. I explained that I'd lapsed in paying my phone bill but would do so now, and that I needed my service restored. After he finished lambasting me with outstanding penalties and reconnect charges, all of which I contritely pledged to pay, he sighed with disappointment and took down my credit-card number.

"Can I keep my phone number?" I asked, anxious to retain anything familiar.

"Your service wasn't disconnected, just interrupted," Serge said, "so yeah. We'll send a guy out to reconnect the line."

"When?"

"By next Thursday."

"Can't you get anyone here sooner?"

"Maybe. But next Thursday's the first we can guarantee."

This didn't strike me as excellent service.

"Listen," I said, "I can't not have a phone right now."

"Then maybe it was a bad idea to ignore your bill for four months?"

"Did I reach the call center in India?"

A brief pause, and then he said, "Oh, *right*. Andrew Danner. You were otherwise detained."

But while extenuating circumstances had granted me my freedom, they were no match for the phone company. Serge remained unmoved, so I flipped my cell phone shut and powered off my computer, leaving the office in peace.

The bedroom told a story of its own, the tale of April's departure. Door ajar. Sheets thrown back. A few of my toiletries knocked over on the bathroom counter as she'd scrambled to pack up her overnight bag. Pink razor overlooked in the shower. Maybe I'd give it a try later for old times' sake. April had dropped one of her socks by the sink in her haste to leave.

We'd still been in the first flush of romance. An orthopedist with neat, pretty features and an even temperament I'd enviously put down to a midwestern upbringing, April had seen me after I'd snapped a collarbone playing pickup ball at Balboa Park. The firm medical touch, the caring tempered by reason, the proximity of our faces as she manipulated my arm through this test or that—I hadn't stood a chance. We were three months new, full of imaginings that seemed youthful for a couple of hunkered-down thirty-eight-year-olds. Good-night calls. Ice cream from the carton in bed. Howard Hawks classics and Fabrocini's pizza. The occasional sleepover, just for practice. Then a brutal killing.

That interrupted a kind of levity and hopefulness I'd doubted I would feel again after Genevieve and I had gone our separate, bemused ways half a year before. Or, according to the prosecution and the cable anchors, our bitter, vituperative ways.

I picked up April's sock, feeling the emotion rising again before deciding I wouldn't allow myself to get all blubbery over footwear. I set my tumor on the nightstand, made the bed, then sat on top of the sheets, wondering what kind of loneliness we were in for. Me and my tumor.

Gazing at that suspended mass of brown cells, my mind pulled again to Genevieve, the horror of her death, the greater horror of my unknown implication in it. She'd brought a tinge of the exotic to her tastes, to her pronouncements, that I'd found irresistible. Most of her I found attractive. The finality of her judgments. The sureness of her passions. She was a big woman, thick around the thighs and hips, and refreshingly comfortable—no, *confident*—in her body and in what it could do. I remembered her mostly as a collection of sensations. The smoothness of a cheek brushing my chest. Traces of Petite Cherie on the pillowcase. Beads of sweat on her alabaster back. Her sleeping face—smooth as a child's. She had no bad angles, Genevieve, and no bad-face days. It's much harder to resent someone when she has no bad angles. It takes a measure more of behavioral ugliness. But while I took my time getting there, she raced ahead, re-senting her moods enough for us both. I was in love with her, cer-tainly, but more in love with holding her together, and she was the only one of us perceptive enough to grasp that complexity.

The night of our breakup, she'd run her full gamut. I'd emerged from my office in the evening to find her sitting in my bedroom, watching *The Bachelor*'s rose ceremony, pint of Chunky Monkey in her lap. She'd held up the spoon in my direction to prevent me from distracting her from the TV. "Jane's a vile cow, and she needs to go *home*." The trace of French accent undercut the prosaic declaration, making me suppress a smile. Then later, with a devilish giggle: "Let's grab a bite. If we stay in, we'll just fight or fuck." She'd held my hand across the restaurant table, face soft with ecstasy, while she named the spices in the merguez. We'd gone home and made love, sweaty in the hot breeze through the screen. That night I'd lost her into an-other dark mood, coming upon her sobbing in the shower. "There's no dignity in anything anymore. It's all so *cheap*."

She was sitting on the tile, water pounding her chest. I'd crouched, feeling the familiar helplessness, the streams striking my sleeve. "What is?"

"All of it. TV. Nothing. I'm sorry. My head's not right. It's one of those . . . I'm sorry. This isn't fair to you. I should go."

Later I'd awakened somewhere in the early-morning hours to find my hand clasped between her clammy palms, her front teeth worrying a pale lower lip, her eyes seeking comfort even as she said, "It's not going to work with us." I didn't have the energy to talk her around anymore. She packed up the few belongings she kept here, plugged in to opera on her iPod so we wouldn't argue as an excuse to lose nerve.

All the media confabulations about her made me realize how dif-ficult she'd been to know. Despite her vague claims of managing a portion of the family real-estate portfolio, she hadn't worked. She read a lot. She went to matinees. She knew good bakeries. She hadn't asked a lot of life, and, in the end, it had given her less. I couldn't help but think now of the experiences she'd never get to have. The whole world denied to her, irrevocably.

I wanted to shake off the past four months like an unsettling dream. But certain facts are like boulders. They get in your way. They've got sharp edges that cut you when you try to move them. For weeks after my mother died, I awoke in the morning, reduced to the most basic, childlike thoughts. *I want this not to be true. I want it not to have happened.* I just couldn't bend my brain around it. My father's death a year and a half later was equally painful, though by then at least I'd had some practice. But where to file Genevieve with the gash through the solar plexus?

"I didn't do it," I said to the tumor.

It gazed back indifferently.

I headed downstairs, opened the Jack Daniel's, and inhaled the rich, satisfying aroma. Then I walked over to the kitchen sink and poured the smoky single-barrel down the drain. The Jews leave a glass of wine for Elijah; the Buddhists offer fruit; the gangbangers pour one out for their dead homeys. You've got to feed the gods. Or the gods feed on you.

Not that they won't feed on you anyway.

A brass-plated cappuccino maker overcrowded the counter like a perched Labrador. I'd picked it up for Genevieve in the five-minute period when things were going smoothly between us, and it had put out fifteen shots of sludgelike espresso at a cost of $147 a cup. The refrigerator held three bottled waters and a dark chocolate bar, half eaten by April. Walking over to the cupboard, I removed the juice glass and white bowl that I'd just put away. I set them on the counter and stared at them as if I expected them to start talking.

Breakfast, September 23. My last memory before waking up in the recovery room.

I couldn't stop my gaze from moving to the knives resting in the wooden block on the counter. A dark curiosity stirred in the pit of my gut. It felt like a blue-hot flame. Like a twenty-year scotch hitting the blood after a two-hour jog. I walked over to the wooden block, guessing correctly at which was the boning knife. I bounced it, feeling its heft. Stainless gleam, Japanese character on the blade. I'd used my knives maybe four or five times. Why had my hand found the boning knife so easily?

I stared at my hands for a good long time, then at my reflection in the window above the sink, some guy holding a knife, a notched line of hair over his scar. The sight made me shudder.

I visited my humidor, then went out to a deck chair, put my feet on the railing, and smoked a cigar down to the yellow speckled band. My sole remaining vice. Except writing.

If I ever actually wrote again.

The night was dark and January-sharp. People forget how cool L.A. can be in the winter—Pacific breeze, Santa Ana winds, angry spates of rain with half-assed lightning, like a constipated monsoon trying to find relief.

A view heals all woes. A view makes you feel as if you own something bigger than yourself, as if you own a place on the planet.

I watched the Valley twinkle in the heat below, like the ocean only prettier, because it was a sea of lights, because it was movement and life, because it let me be separate but connected to a thousand people in a thousand houses with a thousand stories, many sadder than my own. The mainline of Sepulveda charging north into worsening demographics. Van Nuys, beautiful only from a distance, where Mexicans play soccer workday mornings, crossing themselves before kickoff as if God cares about the outcome of a hungover pickup game. The 405, a curved waterfall of white headlights. Ventura moving east past the by-the-hour motels with glam studio names where johns bring broken street kids or vice versa. And around the Cahuenga Pass, where the city waits, an insatiable and inscrutable mistress, spread on a bed of neon with a sphinx smile, her just-pounced paws set down on punctured dreams.

I closed my eyes, cruising through Hollywood of the hipsters and wannabes, the culture consumers with brand names Roman-lettered across ass velour. Drifted behind the honk-oblivious Cutlass with Arkansas plates doing five miles per hour down the boulevard as heads inside craned on substantial southern necks, past black kids rat-a-tat-tatting on overturned white buckets, past peeling German noses, the sticky smell of suntan lotion, intoxicating smog, silver hoops piercing bronze belly buttons, Gap billboards of pop sensations in floppy hats, and up the alleys into real Hollywood, where hookers kneel over pools of vomit and junkies stumble from doorways, scratching their shoulders, mumbling their nighttime song, *Gotta get well, gotta get well.*

Through the run of comedy clubs, where husbands from Wichita laugh at Jesus jokes despite sideways glances from prim-mouthed housewives, where amateurs sweat through sets and maybe, just maybe, after the heard-it-all waitresses clear the second empty glass of the two-drink minimum, that big-name sitcom actor will pop in to work out some new material. Then west to Boys Town, where gay couples come in shapes and sizes to defy the limited straight imagination, where soft-porn billboards overlook studded leather window treatments, glowing tarot cards, and tattoo parlors, where lovers sip coffee within screamshot of porn palaces with purple polystyrene, and parking signs totem pole atop one another, impervious to comprehension. Past the Urth Café, where washed-up divorcées munch organic lettuce, faces caved from pills and swollen with collagen, a war of fleshy attrition. Down the slick snake of Sunset with its old mansions, its bright and brazen Hustler store, its Carnation lights at the holidays. Through Beverly Hills' runs of palms oft filmed but never captured, leisure suits riding Segways to Valentino, celebutantes strolling with purse dogs, agents with their invisible cell-phone earpieces mumbling solo outside restaurants and at stoplights, the nattering dispossessed.

Come Westwood, come Brentwood, where 310 moms push symmetrical children in designer strollers through farmer's markets and wax dreamily about Bali hotels. Onward to the Palisades, Santa Monica Canyon, and Malibu, up the sparkling coastline reeking of exhaust and covered with seagull guano, then through the runs of canyons, deep russet pleats like streaks of ore or a woman's folds, the air startlingly crisp and tinged with salt.

My cheeks were wet with the breeze and the swell of my heart for the lights below. Los Angeles. A mirage of a town that sprang up like a cold sweat on the backs of gold diggers and railroad workers, and took form when pirate film distributors, fleeing Edison's patents, took a train and a gamble backed by East Coast muscle.

Los Angeles, land of endless promise. And endless failure. Los Angeles of the petty cruelties. Los Angeles of the instant hierarchy, the spray-on tan, the copped feel. L.A. of the bandaged, postoperative nose, the chai menu, the slander lawsuit. Of the hyphenated job title. The two-SUV garage. L.A. with its wide-open minds and well-formed opinions. L.A. of the high-octane sunset, the warm night air that leaves you drunk. L.A. of the prolonged adolescence, the slow-motion seduction, the ageless, replaceable blonde. L.A., where a porn star runs for governor and an action figure wins. L.A., where anything can happen at any time to some poor schmuck or lucky bastard. Where anything can happen to you.

Where anything had happened to me.

2

I am in the Highlander, driving up a sharp grade, the only illumination coming from my headlights and a branch-occluded streetlight. Sweat runs down my forehead, stings my eyes. An acrid smell, like smoldering rubber, lingers in my nostrils. I am driving fast. The street is absurdly narrow, and I swerve to dodge parked cars. I know this street. I negotiate a hairpin with a screech, and there it is, drawing into view.

Genevieve's house.

It looms darkly overhead, a wooden face staring out from the cliff wall. The stilts reach down into the earth like tentacles. Ivy crawls up the clapboards, fluttering.

The dashboard clock glows 1:21 A.M.

A spasm of fear seizes my chest. I pull over too hard, a front tire jumping the curb and snapping a sprinkler at the edge of the modest strip of lawn. I throw open my car door, run up the steep walk, concrete pavers shifting underfoot. The bitter smell grows stronger, almost unbearably so. Behind me the open car door dings, competing with the crickets.

I nearly trip over the last step and stumble up onto the porch. I hear music—something classical and majestic. In my head?

The philodendron quivers in the breeze. I lean forward, grasp the terra-cotta pot with sweaty hands as glossy leaves brush my face. The plant tilts easily but slips back through my hands, cracking the clay saucer in a lightning bolt that almost reaches the lip. I wipe my palms on my jeans, angle back the pot again, and there, glittering in the grime, lies the brass key.

My head screaming, I came awake in a tangle of sheets, lost in clammy, adrenalized panic. Heat raged along my scar, so intense that when I fingered the line I thought for a moment it was wet. It took a few moments for me to get my bearings. My bed. First night home. My window had split into two floating rectangles. I squinted hard, fighting to bring the wavering panes back into one. My tongue tasted bitter, like the rind of a hard fruit. 11:23 P.M. stared back at me from my bedside clock.

I tried to slow my breathing, but my dream kept cycling through my head, a disorienting loop of agitation. It felt different from any nightmare I'd had. More real and more surreal at the same time. Had I recaptured a segment of time? Myself driving over to Genevieve's the night of September 23? Earlier tonight? Or was it just Freud in overdrive, fantasies at play while the censors took a coffee break?

In the dream my car tire had snapped a sprinkler. And the terra-cotta pot had slipped through my hands, cracking the saucer beneath. The images meant nothing. But what if that sprinkler and saucer really *were* broken? At last—something concrete I could confirm with my own eyes.

I threw off the sheets and rolled out of bed, drowsy, feeling as though I were walking underwater. The air was inexplicably cold, and suddenly I had a sense of movement downstairs. I trudged onto the catwalk and peered over the railing into the living room.

Resting on the carpet downstairs was a four-foot metal rod. In my grogginess it took me a moment to identify it as the security bar that fits into the track of the sliding glass door opening to the back-yard. I heard the wind suck against the frame, out of view, and became aware, again, of the cold air rising to my bare skin. The sound of traffic down on the freeway was faint but unmuted.

Standing there, I tried to unfreeze myself, to find logic. I'd proba-bly come in from the deck, exhausted, and neglected to close up. After all, I'd just come off four months of having no control over when the doors opened or closed. But doubt nagged. The security bar maybe I would've overlooked, but forgetting to slide the door closed behind me? With the chill that had settled in out there?

I crept down the stairs. The sliding glass door was indeed wide open. A few leaves had blown in, great yellow husks wagging on the carpet. I stared at the black square of the deck, steeling myself, then headed for it. I collected the leaves and slipped outside. The deck was empty, as was the modest patch of lawn to the right, before the ivied slope. A noise to the side of the house drew my attention, the fence rattling in the wind perhaps, and I stepped around the corner and peered back toward the street. The walkway lights of the facing house flickered, one after another, as if a form were moving across them, though how could I be certain? I was glad I'd kept the lights off, preserving my night vision, but the moon, lost behind the Johnsons' sycamore, gave me little aid. I jogged down the side run. The gate clinked—the sound from earlier—its latch undone. I passed through and walked down my stone-paved driveway to the middle of the street, rotating, bewildered, in my boxers. No sign of anyone, no sound of an engine turning over.

I retraced my steps, reentering the house and securing the sliding glass door behind me. On the carpet, made barely visible by the glow of distant city lights, was tracked dirt. A C-shaped repeat, stamped perhaps by the edge of a shoe.

Telephone out. Cell phone upstairs. Media-darling me in my underwear, sound of mind and beloved by local law enforcement.

I moved silently along the trail and into the kitchen. Keeping my eyes on the doorway, I grasped the ten-inch chef's knife and slid it out of the block. My knuckles sensed an emptiness, and I glanced down. Among the protruding handles, a black slit.

The boning knife was missing.

3

A faultless member of the city's prominent French community, her life cut short by an upwardly mobile crime novelist who'd ceased moving upward. Six months after she'd dumped him, he'd broken into her house at one-thirty in the morning. Entering her kitchen, he'd seized a boning knife, the twin of the one in the matching set she'd bought for him. He crept to the bedroom where he was no longer welcome and stabbed her. He'd been discovered red-handed—literally—over the body. By the time the cops arrived, she was dead and he was having a seizure. He'd been rushed to the hospital, where the doctors had discovered the brain tumor and performed an emergency resection. When he'd awakened the next morning, the tumor had been removed, and with it—he claimed—his memory of everything after breakfast on the previous day. Convenient amnesia, that old dime-store-novel standby. The kind of defense that could work only in Los Angeles.

That's how the *Enquirer* told it. And the *L.A. Times*, Fox News, and even *Vanity Fair*. The story's all wrong, in detail and nuance, but they tell it with a tabloid fervor.

I can only tell it like me.

I spent the first night of my incarceration vomiting into the stainless-steel basin until my stomach lining felt as threadbare as the narrow mattress on its bolted base. After nearly forty-eight hours in the Sheriff's ward at USC Medical, I'd landed in a protective-isolation cell on the seventh floor of Twin Towers Correctional Facility. The unit was cramped and metal and had a square vent through which wafted the pristine air of downtown Los Angeles. I missed my own bed, the framed cigarette cards of Shakespeare characters hanging beside my closet. I missed my mother and father. I'd passed plenty of sleepless nights in my time, not to mention the restless small hours during both of my parents' deteriorations, my mother after a series of debilitating strokes in her early sixties, my father, eighteen months later and less cruelly, to an aneurysm. But nothing—*nothing*—that I had encountered could raise a candle against that night's utter blackness.

Night after day the guards commanded prisoners through what I assumed was a narrow alley below, and rising up the chamber of gray walls came the clinking of leg restraints and disembodied voices, strong and cracked, black and white, most of them complaining. Singing their inmate tunes.

Wudn't me.

Some motherfucker framed *me.*

I'm innocent. I was just minding my own bidness when . . .

Up in that cold box, far from the levers of power, it seemed wise not to add my voice to the chorus. But I knew I hadn't done it. I knew that I could not have murdered Genevieve, even as I grew terrified that I had.

Chic had come first, of course, as soon as they allowed it.

I was led down a harshly lit corridor that smelled of ammonia into a private interview room used for prisoners kept out of general pop for their own protection. Battle-scarred wooden chair, Plexiglas shield, obscenities finger-smudged on the metal desktop—high school all over again.

The guard pronounced his name incorrectly, like the French appraisal of a hairdo, though Chic is anything but. He was dressed as he always was, as if he'd just gone shopping for the first time without his mother. Denim shorts that stretched below the knee. Oversize silk shirt, olive green, buttoned across his vast chest. A bling chain necklace matched the chunk of gold on the left-hand ring finger.

He shifted his big frame around, trying to get comfortable on a chair not designed for professional athletes. Seeing him made my eyes well at the ways in which my life had unraveled since the last time I'd seen him. A week? Eight days?

Chic placed a surprisingly white palm on the Plexiglas. I matched it with my own—it felt surreal to mimic the gesture I knew only from movies.

"What do you need?" he asked.

My voice, little used, sounded as hoarse as those that floated up the walls. "I didn't do this."

He gave me a calming gesture, hands spread, head tilted and slightly lowered. "Don't you cry, Drew-Drew," he said softly. "Not in here. Don't give 'em that."

I wiped my eyes with the hem of my prison-issue shirt. "I know. I'm not."

Chic looked like he wanted to break through the glass and fight a few fights for me to make sure the bullies gave me wide berth. "What can I do?"

"Just being here."

He bridled a bit, indicating, I guessed, his desire for a task, for some better way to help. Philly born, Chic is East Coast loyal and likes to prove it. I would find out later that he'd waited downstairs for four and a half hours to get in and see me.

His powerful hands clenched. "This is like one of your books. Except worse."

"I'll take that as a compliment."

My fingers were at my head again, riding the rosary beads of the secondary suture scars. I noticed Chic watching me and lowered my hand.

He looked concerned. "How you holding up?"

I stared up at the ceiling until my vision got less watery. "Scared shitless." A rush of panic constricted my throat, reminding me why it was better not to tackle the fear head-on.

He seemed to be considering his next words. "I been in jail, but nothing like this. Your shadow must be 'fraid of its shadow."

I rubbed my eyelids until my heartbeat no longer sounded like a scaffold drumroll. Then I said, "Make sure April's okay. She hasn't visited me. Not in the hospital, not here."

"You haven't been together so long."

"I suppose it is a lot to handle."

Chic raised his eyebrows as if to say, *Ya think?*

I couldn't talk about losing April while maintaining a stiff upper lip, so I asked, "What news from the front?"

"Usual shit. CourtTV, three-minute segments on *Five,* five-minute segments on *Three.* Reporters feeling good 'bout themselves because they remember to say 'allegedly.'"

I already knew that the prosecutor's version had infected the media's take, and vice versa. The victim had been photogenic, and the public had hooked into her the way it liked and into me the way it required. The story had taken on a life of its own, and I'd been cast in the nastiest role.

He squinted at me. "You getting *any* sleep?"

"Sure."

But I wasn't getting much. Last night I'd stayed up like Lady Macbeth, staring at my hands, staggered by their secret history. A fleck of dried blood remained wedged under my right thumbnail, and I dug at it and dug at it until frustration gave way to something like horror and I tore off the tip of the nail with my teeth. Later I dreamed about Genevieve—her pale Parisian skin, her inviting cushiony hips, lounging on my deck chair and spooning avocado curls from the dark shell, edging them with mayonnaise from the dollop she'd dropped where the pit had been. She looked at me and smiled forgivingly, and I awoke having sweated through one end of the slim pad of a pillow. The polyester sheet was thin, and I knew I was a sorry sight there in the darkness, trembling and terrified by something I couldn't put a name to.

"Can you get my condolences to Genevieve's family?" I said quietly. "Tell them I didn't do this."

"All due respect, they prob'ly don't much want to hear from you right now." He held up a hand when I started to protest. "How are those lawyers who your overeager editor found for you?"

"They seem to know what they're doing."

"Let's hope so." He withdrew a stapled document and put it in the pass-through box.

The guard rushed forward, blurting, "Let me take a look at that, sir."

Chic waited impatiently while the guard flipped through the document, searching for the blowtorch concealed in the pages. He justified himself by removing the staple from the corner.

Scrap Plan B. No flying out of here on a magic staple.

Once the document cleared security, Chic slid it through to me. A power of attorney that designated Chic Bales with broad powers over my finances and legal affairs.

"Broad powers," I said. "That include X-ray vision or just shape-shifting?"

He half smiled, but I could see his concern in the lines that pouched his eyes. "Law firm needs a two-fifty retainer. You'll have to take a second on the house."

"A third." Just contemplating the state of my finances made my temples throb. There was some bureaucratic fuss until the guard produced a notary's seal, required to validate any power of attorney. Another reality tidbit overlooked in the pages of my—I now realized woefully unrealistic—novels.

I signed and sent the document back through. Chic's eyes caught on the note I'd included. "What's this?"

"For Adeline."

"Genevieve's sister? You really think she wants to hear from you?"

He unfolded the paper without asking and regarded my adolescent script.

I didn't kill your sister.

Tell me if there's anything I can do.

I'm so sorry for your loss.

He refolded the note, and it disappeared into a pocket. His look said it all.

"You get accused and you're no longer allowed to have a human reaction?" I said.

"You are, but no one's gonna believe it. If you're sincere now, you'll get chewed up. Everyone'll think you playin' to the jury pool. You're in a game. The sooner you figure that out, the better."

"So what can I do?"

"Look innocent."

"I *am* innocent."

"Look it."

We sat in silence for a few moments, staring at each other. The guard strode over. "Time's up."

Chic's stare didn't so much as tic over to pick up the guard's reflection in the glass. "I just got here."

"You'll exit to the right. Got it?"

Chic sucked his teeth and screwed his mouth to the side. "Why, *sho'.*" And then, to me, "Hang tough. I'm here for whatever and all of it." He pushed back with a screech, and then his footfall echoed off the cold concrete walls.

The next morning I was summoned by my lawyers back down that ammonia-reeking hall to the Plexiglas Pavilion. They waited in their chairs, outlines bleached by strong morning light, one leaning forward, elbows resting on knees, lips pouched against the weight of the decisions to come, the other canted back in his chair, thumb dimpling a cheek, forefinger riding his upper lip. Both of their heads were bowed as if in prayer. Before their features resolved, I had a strong sense I was walking into the famous picture of JFK and Bobby taken when Khrushchev's freighters were steaming toward Cuba.

I understood their concern. I'd already proven less than pliable as a client. Despite their advice, I'd elected *not* to waive my right to a speedy trial. Bail had been denied, a cover-yer-ass move by the down-the-middle judge we'd drawn, cowed by mounting media fanfare. The prospect of spending maybe years locked up awaiting trial was terrifying enough to compromise my judgment on the matter. My lawyers and I had also gone a few rounds over the plea. My choices were *guilty* or *not guilty*. The temporary-insanity issue would be visited—in a second trial phase—only *if* I were found guilty.

Donnie Smith, hair tamped down from his post-gym shower, picked up right where we'd left off. "Your pleading not guilty will antagonize the judge, the public, the press, and the court. And it's that group that decides your fate. Not just those twelve people. You *have* to plead guilty to help you gain credibility on the question of impaired sanity. Given the media, Harriman's gonna try the case, and you can bet she'll mop the floor with us in the guilt phase, leave you stained. We need to get to sanity quickly, with a clean slate, and without dragging you through a trial that you are unlikely to win."

My heart felt like it was fluttering my shirt. "But I didn't *do it*. And not a single fucking person believes me."

Not the first time they'd encountered such a claim. Blank eyes. Patience, edging to impatience.

"So your position is you don't remember that you *didn't* kill her?" Donnie spoke slowly, as if to a developmentally delayed child.

I didn't answer. It sounded stupid to me, too. As before, each minute with them contributed to my growing fear that I had no defense. And that if I didn't want to die in a prison cell, I'd have to admit to something I did not remember.

My frustration bubbled to the surface. "Is *anyone* trying to find out who really did this? Or are they all too busy playing trial games like us?"

Donnie and Terry glanced at each other uneasily.

"*What?*" I said, worried. "What's that look?"

"LAPD turned over something troubling yesterday in discovery," Donnie said. "Genevieve called you the night of the murder at 1:08 A.M., approximately twenty minutes before her murder."

"I was told that already."

Donnie removed a sealed LAPD evidence bag from his briefcase. It contained a CD. "And she left you a message."

"Is it bad?" I asked. No answer. Agitated, I stood, walked a tight circle, sat back down again. "That's why they changed my voice mail access."

Donnie popped the CD into his laptop and clicked a few buttons.

The familiar voice, back from the dead, was haunting. "I wanted to tell you I'm with someone new. I hope I hurt you. I hope you feel this pain. I hope you feel so alone. Good-bye."

It took me a few moments to recover from hearing Genevieve. I sat there with my heartbeat pounding in my ears and my lawyers staring at me with calm concern. Her voice, the accent, those nuanced pronunciations. But the invasiveness of the message's presentation also unnerved me. The cops had heard Genevieve's last words to me before I had. The message—like the rest of my life, frozen by the prosecution and available to me only secondhand—hammered the final nail into the coffin of my rights and privacy.

I didn't remember hearing Genevieve's message that night, of course. The bitterness of it clashed with where I thought she and I had left things between us, but she'd been moody and difficult at times, so the tone was hardly shocking. Under no circumstances could I imagine it making me want to harm Genevieve. But, I realized with mounting dread, the message would play nicely to a jury primed on photos of her abused body.

"This shores up motive even more," Donnie said gently. "So we need a simple version to sell to the jury. Temporary insanity's your only way out of this. It's clean. It's self-evident. It's supported by the facts. *The brain tumor did it.*"

I returned his exasperated stare.

He pressed on. "We lay out the facts, you'll walk out of here. You can worry about the rest of it from your own bed someday." He studied my expression, finding something in it he didn't like. "We play this wrong with what we have stacked against us . . ."

The thought of hard time made me feint fetal, my shoulders hunching, my shoes lifting an inch or two from the floor before I stopped my knees' rise to my chest. In the movies, no matter what, prison is the same. You go in scared, and they call you "fish" and bet cigarettes as to how long it'll be until you cry. You cell with Bubba, and he breaks you in, and then you become hardened, dead inside, and you barter for candy bars and have to shiv some guy in the shop or his buddies will gang-rape you, and then you get gang-raped any-way just for good measure.

"You're a crime writer," Terry said calmly. "Allow us to help you see how this will read to a jury. Let us take you through it again."

And they did, right from the sordid beginning. I sat in my hard little chair, dry-mouthed and stunned by—as they call it on TV—the preponderance of evidence. I'd known the elements, of course, but hearing them edited together into a tale of my murdering Genevieve was chilling. When my nerves settled, I had room for a single lucid thought.

I'm fucked.

My righteousness about the plea would have to dissolve under the pressures—and realities—I was facing. I could offer a gut sense of my innocence and little more. Nothing felt more important than staying alive, than staying free. Not even announcing to the world that I was a murderer.

When they finished, I wanted to give the answer I'd been rehearsing in my head but found myself frozen. I folded my hands on the pitted wood and stared at them, and then I heard myself say, "I won't plead guilty to a murder I don't think I committed."

The attorneys' heads swiveled to face each other, their worst fear realized. They appeared as shocked as I was by my decision.

"With all due respect," Terry said, "how can you still think you didn't?"

"Because I would know in my bones if I had."

Out in the hall, the guard cleared his throat loudly. Terry scratched his hair in the back, fingernails giving off a good scraping sound. The sun inched higher in the window, making me squint against the glare.

Donnie finally punctured the swollen silence with a sigh. He bounced forward, slapped his knees, and rose.

"So what now?" I asked.

"We argue each phase like your life depends on it." He looked up from loading papers into his briefcase. "Because it does."

I hunched against the cold under the sheet, eyes on the blank wall opposite. A discoloration stained the concrete a few feet up, a splotch and then the trickling fallout. It couldn't have come from anything benign. I thought of the men who had occupied this cell before me, who'd slept their restless sleep and dreamed their lying dreams.

Wudn't me.

Some motherfucker set me up.

I'm *innocent.*

A guard approached, slipped an envelope through the bars. "You got a letter."

I retrieved the envelope from the floor. My name, in a feminine hand. I sat back down and opened it. A piece of paper, torn to shreds.

ll your sister.

Tell me if

I didn't ki
so sorry for
I can do. I'm
there's anything
your loss.

The scraps of my note to Adeline slipped from my hands, scattering across the floor. One in particular stared back at me: *your loss.* I didn't notice my slow-motion deterioration to the concrete until it was pressed against my cheek, my body curled around my knees. I remained more or less in that position until the next morning, when they summoned me to court.

L.A. had sweated out a whole year without a celebrity murder trial. I was neither a household name nor, as far as I knew, a killer, but the forces of the market had converged to make me both. Opening arguments had started sixty days from the second arraignment, time enough for me to lose weight, grow sallow and shaggy, and look otherwise convictable.

A few minutes into the trial, I knew that my lawyers were right and that it would end disastrously. As promised, the rising-star prosecutor—sharply dressed Katherine Harriman accessorized with sensible low-heel slingbacks and a father who'd jetted in from Chicago to beam proudly from the front row—Swiffered the floor with me, the jury sailing to their verdict after only an eight-day trial and an hour's deliberation.

I'd been convicted. The only question now was if I'd slide off with a not guilty by reason of temporary insanity. Through the beginning of the sanity phase, the only way I could slow the quiet breakdown I was undergoing was to detach. I quickly learned that—like the other players—I had to devote my attention not to the ingredients of the trial but to its sugar glaze.

And I had the support of my friends, who, my lawyers were pleased to note, comprised a nice demographic skew. Chic tapped his chest with a fist whenever I caught his eyes. From time to time, Preston would glance up from whatever manuscript he was editing and offer a supportive nod. He had a stack of pages that went with him everywhere like a King Charles spaniel, under his arm, peeking out from his bag, perching on his thighs when he sat—more than once when the courtroom hushed, I could make out the distinctive sound of his scribbling. And April, bless her, had shown up that morning as promised, even enduring the requisite walk of shame along an appointed stretch of public sidewalk while reporters mobbed her. It was clear we no longer had a future together, but I was deeply grateful she'd done me this final turn.

More than anyone else, though, Katherine Harriman commanded the court's attention. She played to the jury now, doing her best to ignore my brain tumor, which Donnie had ingeniously left floating in a jar on the defense table. It looked menacing in the brackish waters, an unexploded hand grenade. I'd suffered the humiliation of sitting before it for opening arguments and more. I pictured it inside my head, latched onto my brain, operating me like a subservient robot. I was, I'm embarrassed to report, scared of a wad of brown tissue.

And why not? The expert witness for the home team, a white-haired neurologist with a dignified bearing, had just identified it as a left anterior temporal ganglioglioma. There was much discussion of ventricles and glands, designed, I assumed, to cow the jurors with Medical Science. Ganglioglioma? Even the repetitive syllable seems tacked on to intimidate. Despite the malignant look of the word, gangliogliomas are okay as far as brain tumors go. After resection, patients enjoy a survival rate that approaches 100 percent, and we don't have to smell colors or taste music. The temporal lobe, the court learned, is involved in our processing of memory, thus my inconvenient blackout. Conditions like mine have been known to lead to schizophrenia-like psychosis, delusion, and episodic aggressive behavior.

"And what causes this impressive constellation of symptoms to kick in?" Harriman asked midway into the cross, angling a bright cheek toward the carefully selected men who constituted Jurors Three through Seven.

"Of course the tumor must reach a—if you'll pardon the expression—critical mass, where it's begun encroaching on essential structures," our neurologist said. "But as for the tipping point? The addition of a few more cells. A constriction of blood vessels. Because the temporal lobe is intricately tied to emotional response and arousal, there is plentiful evidence that once a patient has reached such a fragile state, the final mental break can be triggered by an emotionally intense event." The doctor polished his glasses on a monogrammed handkerchief. "While there's much that we know about the brain—"

"There's so much more that we *don't* know," Harriman finished with an accommodating grin.

During the six months before my surgery, I'd been no stranger to migraines, certainly, even a few that had blotted my vision. At first I'd presumed the usual suspects—stress, computer monitor, dehydration—but then I'd blacked out over the washing machine, coming to after fifteen lost minutes feeling little more than a rise in my stomach and liquid detergent dripping across my knuckles.

"But isn't it true that most people with this type of tumor don't cross the line into psychosis *at all*?"

The neurologist replied, "Erratic, violent behavior is not uncommon, espe—"

"Perhaps you didn't hear my question. I asked if it was true that most people with this type of tumor *never* cross the line into psychosis."

"Statistically speaking."

"Is there another manner of speaking that better answers a medical question like the one I posed?"

There was not.

"Is there a *single* medical precedent that you can cite for a person"—she'd shrewdly dropped "patient"—"with a left anterior temporal ganglioglioma committing murder?"

The doctor rolled his lips, his face bunching. "No."

In quiet concert, Donnie, Terry, and I exhaled. Katherine Harriman did not. "Do most individuals with a left anterior temporal ganglioglioma experience postoperative retrograde amnesia?"

"Most do not, but when paired with acute stress, more than thirty percent—"

"So it is possible that an individual with a tumor such as the defendant's could be perfectly rational right up until surgery?"

"A lot is possible. The body is amazing, and constantly defies our expectations. The brain, more yet. The mind, even more than that."

"So that's a yes?"

"It is."

"And is it *also* possible," Harriman continued, wheeling on me and piercing me with a top-shelf stare, "that a very clever individual, someone much like our defendant, might use all these conditions that you've so generously laid out as smoke cover for a premeditated plan?"

As my lawyers leapt to their feet with objections, Harriman remained perfectly still, a slight smile tensing her lips, her eyes never leaving mine. She was articulate and sharp, attuned to the inherent ridiculousness of matters. Her calm unnerved me. There was much murmuring and disorder in the court, and the judge nodded to the bailiff, who called for recess.

After we returned, the onslaught continued. Our witnesses. Their witnesses. Detective Three Bill Kaden assumed the stand, every bit as sturdy as he'd been in that moment when I'd returned to consciousness. Bristly mustache, thick wrists, golf shirt under a blazer. Scrappy, chinless Ed Delveckio watched from the gallery and nodded along

with Kaden's testimony, twenty courtroom feet and one rank sepa-
rating him from his senior partner. The boning knife made an appearance, stained nearly to the end of the handle, swinging crudely
in an evidence bag. I did my best not to break down or react with
anger.

Next up was Lloyd Wagner, a criminalist who'd lent me his
time on several occasions to process fictitious bodies and who'd responded with the lab team to Genevieve's house. Yet another disturbing spillover from my prior life. We got along well, and I had
found him alarmingly adept at helping me massage plot elements, so
much so that on occasion I'd brought him whole scenes to put his
skills to work on. Dressed in his dated court suit and holding a dupli-
cate knife taken from my very own kitchen, Lloyd offered me an
apologetic little nod before displaying on a dummy the forcefulness
of the plunge that had yielded the stab wound. I found myself, along
with the jury and audience, wincing at the viciousness.

After Lloyd's performance the voice mail Genevieve had left for
me the night of her death was given yet another airing, issuing from
Katherine Harriman's laptop.

A respectful silence for the voice of the dead. "I wanted to tell you
I'm with someone new. I hope I hurt you. I hope you feel this pain. I
hope you feel so alone. Good-bye."

Of course, Genevieve *hadn't* been with someone new, at least no
one she'd told her friends or family about. Her not-so-deft manipu-
lation wasn't devastating to me from where I sat now, though the
prosecution asserted that it had been on the night of September 23.
The defense asserted privately that the message made Genevieve less
sympathetic and publicly that it had provided the final jolt of head
pressure to initiate my ganglioglioma's interference. Given my lack
of criminal history, Donnie argued, the tumor was the *only* logical
explanation for my behavior.

On day five of sanity, cutting through any calluses I thought I had
built up, Genevieve's family made their eagerly awaited entrance. Her

mother, long of bone and broad of bosom, requisite Hermès scarf draped across her clay-court shoulders, rode the arm of her husband, ever dapper in a bespoke suit. Though they carried themselves with characteristic elegance, there was a hollowing in their cheeks, a nearly imperceptible erosion in posture, that betrayed their crushing loss. At Luc's other side strode Adeline, her fair face flushed to overtake her freckles. Though they stared at me with unmitigated hatred, the reality of their diminished presence, Luc's quavering hand touching the hard wood before he sat, undid whatever self-protective remove I'd managed. Their appearance, timed just before I was to take the stand, had precisely the effect on me Harriman wanted. My throat tightened, my lips jumped, and I leaned forward on the table and pressed both palms to my face as if to hold it together. My reaction was likely taken by the jury as shame, but it was worse than shame. It was the final roosting of Genevieve's loss, a woman whom I had loved, perhaps not wisely, but had loved nonetheless.

Donnie asked for a recess so I could get myself together to take the stand, but the judge denied the request. My heart still pounding, I climbed those three short steps to the birch witness stand and raised my right hand, finally able to take in the faces of the gallery without peeking furtively over a shoulder. There was a heightened intensity to it all, yet also an apologetic ordinariness. Reporters in their good suits, cameramen with their digital gear, the court stenographer pretending not to chew gum.

Donnie questioned me gently and with great empathy. When her time came, Harriman strolled toward me, relaxed, a text open in one hand like a psalmbook. She'd removed the dust jacket, so I didn't know what was coming until she read, "'We all have an ex-lover we want to kill. If we're lucky, we've got two or three.'"

The book snapped shut like a turtle's jaws, startling the jurors in their seats. "Do you believe that?"

"No," I said.

"You wrote that, did you not?"

I acknowledged that I had.

"So you don't expect us to believe what you write?"

"Of course not," I said. Terry gave me the patting-down hands, so I proceeded, more obligingly. "The protagonist, Derek Chainer, says that. An author doesn't necessarily endorse the views voiced by his characters. I create characters who are not me and—on a good day—breathe life into them."

"So you write things you don't believe?"

"I try to let the characters express their own opinions."

"Just a way to sell more trashy novels in supermarkets?"

"And airports."

She smiled. Just two friends bantering. "How about this line? 'I believe, in my darkest heart of hearts, that when fate and passion align, every last one of us, from the pulpit crier to the bus-stop blue-hair, is capable of murder.'" She circled closer to me. "Is that your belief, or merely the expressed view of a character?"

There was a gallows silence, an electric sense in the air that, as they say, it all came down to this.

I said, "I believe that anyone is capable of anything."

My attorneys crumpled in a fashion that might have been amusing under different circumstances, and Harriman's eyes got bright and excited.

"So you believe right now, when you're allegedly sound of mind, that you could very well be capable of committing the unspeakable act for which you've been found guilty."

"*Capable,* yes,"—and here I had to raise my voice to speak over her cutting me off—"just like you."

"Except, last I checked, Genevieve Bertrand didn't break off an engagement to *me.*" Harriman nodded away the judge's reprimand, one hand raised in a mea culpa.

Stories, no matter how bad, are L.A.'s lifeblood. I'd bet that Ms. Harriman, like every prosecutor I'd met within Dolby distance of the film studios, had been asked at one time to be a consultant for a one-hour drama. Or she'd had a writer like me tag along for a trial to pester her with questions. A cousin's husband, perhaps, who needed a few minutes on the phone so he could make that third act of his script sing. Many a time I'd been that guy, that sheepish eavesdropper to the hue and cry of the Angeleno justice system. I'd dealt with cops who watched too much TV about cops, so they acted like the cops they watched on TV who were imitating real-life cop advisers. Narrative and crime—a twirling snake with its tale in its mouth. *Wudn't me. I was just minding my own bidness when . . .*

A few hours later as I listened, rapt, to Katherine Harriman's closing argument, it dawned on me just how skilled a storyteller she was. And this, she claimed, was my story.

On the night of September 23 at 1:08 A.M., roused by a ringing phone, I'd slid from my bed, leaving April there, asleep. As I'd listened to the voice-mail message left by Genevieve Bertrand, all my resentment and bitterness had congealed into a plan. I'd driven over to her house, a hobbler stuck in a canyon fold off Coldwater. I'd retrieved the key from under the potted philodendron on the porch and entered, turning left to the kitchen, where I'd taken the boning knife from its oak block. I'd drifted up the flight of stairs to Genevieve's bedroom. Awakened by my prowlings, she'd met me halfway across her white carpet, where I'd thrust the blade through her solar plexus on the rise, evading her ribs and piercing her heart. She'd died more or less instantly. Afterward I'd held and rolled her body around in its fluttery silk gown, like a cat batting a wounded mouse. For the finale, panic-stricken by the crime I'd just perpetrated, I'd had a mental break, a complex partial seizure that, when the cops and paramedics arrived, secondarily generalized into a grand mal. I'd fallen on top of the body and seized almost continuously until I'd reached the Cedars-Sinai ER, where they'd run IV Ativan to calm my thrashing. A CT had revealed the stowaway nestled into the anterior reaches of my temporal lobe, as well as some hemorrhaging, and I'd been whisked into surgery, awakening at breakfast time with a stunningly opportune justification.

Katherine Harriman thanked the jury for their time and attention, smiled disarmingly, and sat down, immersing herself in paperwork so she wouldn't have to acknowledge Donnie as he began his closing.

"Our *clever* killer, our plotter of murder most foul, could come up with no scheme better than this? He snuck over to Genevieve Bertrand's house and then . . . *what?* Decided to leave the front door wide open? So both Westec *and* the neighbors would call the police, you see. Because he *also* planned precisely *when* he was going to have a seizure. He held back until just the right moment, you see. This man, this clever man, thought it would be beneficial for his ganglioglioma to swell that extra millimeter right there in Ms. Bertrand's bedroom, sending him into a *grand mal seizure* so the police could find him in his compromised state, establishing evidence for the insanity plea he knew he'd require during the trial he knew he'd have. Certainly the most logical approach for a clearheaded individual, don't you think? Well, happily, his elaborate plan paid off. Because he definitely fooled *me.* I've had the duty of trying over thirty murder cases in my career, and never—and I mean *never*—have I been more certain of a client's compromised sanity at the time of an incident than I am today."

As Donnie continued, vehement and passionate, I felt a surge of affection, something even like love, for this man who had, for a fee, taken on my cause and argued it as his own. When he finished forty-five rousing minutes later, he sat, practically panting adrenaline, and marshaled his papers into the stretched maw of his briefcase.

After the jury filed out, I reached over, squeezed his neck, and said to him and Terry, "Regardless of how this thing goes, I want you to know I appreciate what you did for me here."

We clasped hands for a moment, all three of us.

The second verdict came back three hours and nineteen minutes later.

4

The kitchen floor beneath my bare feet felt as cool as the stainless-steel handle of the chef's knife. Through the dark I stared at the blank slit in the knife block where the boning knife should have been. I'd closed the sliding glass door—had I locked someone in with me? My heart revving, I looked through the doorway at the trail of marks I'd figured for footprints. The last few were visible on the carpet before it gave over to the flagstone entry.

Not dirt, as I'd thought.

Blood.

I had a moment's lapse into terror, genuine kid-in-the-dark terror, before I recalled that I was an adult and had no options except to outgrow my mood and handle business. Firming my grip on the chef's knife, I eased through the doorway into the entry. No one peering down at me from the upstairs railing that lined the catwalk from stairs to study to bedroom.

The footprints hadn't ceased at the foyer flagstone, though they were harder to make out against slate. But there, two steps up on the carpeted stairs, another bloody C. I gazed up, the staircase fading into the dark.

Tamping down my fear, I followed. Every other step bore the mark.

I reached the top of the stairs. The footprints continued straight into my bedroom. I moved forward, knife held upside down along my forearm, blade out, as I'd learned from an expert knife fighter while broadening Derek Chainer's repertoire. I reached the threshold. Bracing myself, I swept inside.

No one was there. But on the carpet at the foot of my bed, the boning knife gleamed. I moved forward, crouched over it. The skin of my right foot was smudged, just above the little toe and extending down my outstep. I reached down, noticing that the pads of my fingers also bore dark stains. Smears on the boning-knife handle. And on the blade's edge at the tip. My head swam a bit.

I raised my foot, noting the distinctive, if now faint, C mark left behind on the carpet.

My own blood. My own footprints.

I turned on the lights, set down the chef's knife, and returned to the boning knife on the floor. A jagged print of blood on my left thumb matched a mark left on the stainless handle. The blood on my fingers from, I assumed, touching the cut on my foot, also left predictable marks matching my grip.

My fingerprints. On my boning knife.

I washed my foot in the tub. For all the blood, it was a humble cut. A clean incision, no more than an inch long, about a thumb's width back from the base of the little toe. A Band-Aid took care of it.

My head still felt unusually foggy—ganglioglioma, back for a holiday sequel? I tried to tease apart which concerns were reasonable and which weren't but found my perspective momentarily shot. Was someone running me through a rat maze? Either I was driving myself insane or someone had gone to a great deal of trouble to ensure that I would. I sat on the tub's edge, hugging my stomach and shuddering, until compulsion drove me around the house, flicking on light switches, searching for a body, an intruder, Allen Funt and his *Candid Camera* crew.

Checking for signs of a break-in, I examined the security rod for dings and the track in which it sat for scrapes in the paint, but both were unmarred. I'd sleepwalked downstairs and opened it myself? Why would I have gone outside?

I returned upstairs and stared at my bed, dumbfounded. A few smears of blood on the sheets, the same sheets in which I'd just dreamed of Genevieve's house. A bizarrely vivid dream. During which I'd sleepwalked downstairs, retrieved the boning knife, returned to bed, and cut my foot? Why? Couldn't I find a more productive way to punish myself?

The dream flooded back, in all its significance, and I felt a jolt of excitement. I couldn't know if I'd gone temporarily insane, but I could verify something I might actually know. If Genevieve's sprinkler was in fact snapped and the saucer broken, then I wasn't completely hallucinating. At least I could determine whether I'd retrieved a fragment of the night Genevieve had been killed.

I got dressed and went downstairs. In my hybrid Guiltmobile, I checked the odometer, as if it could answer any of the riddles I was failing to work out. I started a mileage column on a pad in the glove box, so I'd know if I took my addled brain for a spin in the future.

Driving along Mulholland on a sliver of moonlight, I felt I was doing something illegal. I probably was.

I slalomed down Coldwater, slowing for the sharp turn past the bent street sign. And then there I was, in my dream, driving up the sharp grade. The streetlight, filtered through a wayward branch. The too-narrow street, laid out in the days before three-car households slopped spare SUVs to the curb. Sweat rose on my forehead, as if complying with the script. Maybe I was dreaming now. Maybe I'd created—and was now re-creating—this whole thing.

The hairpin came up fast, my tires giving their mandatory screech, and Genevieve's house looked down at me. From atop its perch, the house seemed daunting—backed snugly to the hillside, stilts shoved disapprovingly into the earth as if my car were a rat, it a Great Dane sizing up the situation.

I climbed out, my door dinging. At the edge of the lawn, the crushed sprinkler stopped me short.

I want this not to be true. I want it not to have happened.

I had not known the sprinkler to be broken, except in my dream when my Highlander jumped the curb. Which meant that it had not been a dream.

God, oh, God, I was alone in that Highlander. I came up this walk alone. I found the key alone. There was me and only me.

I headed up the slope, the pavers loose under my shoes, rocking in their beds and freeing up trickles of dirt. I knew what I'd find, but I had to confirm it.

The boards creaked when I stepped onto the porch. The house was quiet and, I hoped, empty. What possible excuse could I stammer out if sister Adeline appeared at the door?

The split-leaf philodendron waved at me from its terra-cotta pot. I wiped my palms on my jeans and crouched, pushing back the spouts of leaves to peer under.

A zigzag crack marred the clay saucer, a lightning bolt almost reaching the lip.

Not a dream.

A piece of my missing past.

5

Driving home in a stupor, I tried to process the ramifications of what I'd just discovered. If my dream was right, as the sprinkler and saucer seemed to indicate, then I'd arrived alone at Genevieve's house. That didn't look good for me. But the same questions remained. Why *had* I gone over there that night? Had watching someone *else* kill Genevieve tripped my brain-tumor blackout? The old frustration simmered below the surface. Why hadn't *anyone*—the cops, the prosecutors, my own lawyers—looked with serious doubt at anything except my sanity? Hadn't we all jumped in late in the plot?

I'd pored over the murder book that Homicide had turned over during discovery, but nothing in the investigative notes or police report pointed elsewhere—none of the dead ends or dropped leads that compose the frayed edges around every reconstructed picture of a crime. It was too tidy an account, an investigation that had its mind made up from the outset. I also had my mind made up from the outset, though my argument had the advantage of no evidence and greater implausibility—as I'd come to think of it, Occam's Hacksaw.

A glimmer of hope cut through my exhaustion. If I had recovered one memory from the night of Genevieve's death, then I could recover others. Which meant I could get at the truth, no matter how ugly it was shaping up to be.

My cell phone rang, startling me, and I screwed in the earpiece, wondering who would be calling at midnight.

Donnie's voice greeted me. "Where've you been? We've been trying you all night. Terry finally tracked down your cell-phone number."

"I'm okay," I said. "Just went for a drive."

"Sometimes the first night home can be tough."

I regarded my hands gripping the steering wheel. "Can't imagine why."

He picked up my tone and laughed. "Need some company? Terry and I could swing by."

"Thanks, but I think I'm okay."

"Well, if there's anything you need."

"Actually . . ." The idea sprang up, surprising me, though it had been lurking just beneath awareness all along. "I was wondering if I could get my hands on the case files."

"We won the case, Andrew. You're free of all that now." There was a pause, and then he said, "You're writing a book?"

"Just trying to work through what happened."

"What do you say you take a night off? Even Katherine Harriman is out having a drink. One of our paralegals just spotted her crying into her martini on the Promenade."

"Katherine Harriman doesn't cry. And certainly not in public."

"And neither should you. Not tonight anyway. Listen, Terry and I have encountered this a lot with our acquitted clients. They rework the trial like worrying a loose tooth, trying to find . . . I don't know, absolution. They don't find it there. Let me give you some advice: Let it go. Get back to your life."

I reached my turn. Right to my house, left to the freeway. I veered left. "I'd like those files, Donnie."

His breath blew across the receiver. "Well, they're yours, Andrew. We're certainly not gonna keep them from you. We'll need a day or two to make copies."

"Thank you."

"Anything else?"

"Yeah," I said. "Which bar did your paralegal see Katherine Harriman in?"

Coyly set a half block back from Santa Monica's heavily trod Third Street Promenade, Voda serves a hundred-plus labels of vodka and the one grade of caviar that counts. With its black-suited doormen and reserved seating, it likes to believe it's exclusive, but the management isn't above siphoning in tourists when the upholstered booths aren't filling up. Past the bouncer, who hesitated, recognizing but not placing me, were imported bottles, protruding on stone ledges from the wall, and plenty of glossy men and women, also available for consumption. Candles, Hawaiian protea blossoms, and flagstone waterfalls completed the confused tropical-gulag motif.

Harriman was at the black lacquer bar, slender legs crossed. Tapping an impaled pickled onion on the rim of her Gibson, she watched me approach without so much as a lifted eyebrow.

I dropped into the swivel chair next to her and ordered a Brilliant vodka on the rocks, which I sniffed and left on the cocktail napkin. She ignored me as if ignoring men were something she'd spent a lifetime perfecting, and so we sat and watched the water trickle down the flagstone as I worked up my nerve.

"I knew about my brain tumor." The words, finally spoken, continued to resonate in my head. "My health insurance had lapsed. I was waiting on another script deal to get my Writers Guild coverage back. I'd had migraines for six months, then a short blackout. I went to a private provider in Ventura so if the tests *did* reveal something, it wouldn't go on record as a preexisting condition. That's why nothing showed up in any of the medical records you subpoenaed."

I didn't add that my failure to act hadn't been just about the money—though the money had played a considerable role. I'd stalled because I'd had a book deadline and an upcoming tour and a new relationship. And, like anyone else, I was terrified. When a surgery is elective, when do you make that firm decision to let a team of people carve around inside your brain? How do you choose the day? What if you don't wake up? Or worse, what if they make a mistake and then you *do*?

A few days after I'd blacked out over the washing machine, I'd seen a neurologist, who'd given me the unhappy diagnosis. The doctor had urged me to get the surgery, but I'd told him, protected under the veil of confidentiality, that I was willing to take the gamble and wait. The trial had provided me ample time to relive his answer. *Are you willing to gamble the lives of the family in the minivan you crash into when you black out behind the wheel?*

Harriman lifted the onion off the plastic spike with her teeth, and as she crunched, I wondered whether she'd respond. Finally she said, "How much was the operation going to cost?"

"Sixty-two grand."

"And how much was your legal retainer?"

"Two-fifty."

She snickered—she couldn't help it—and it took me a moment to realize she was laughing at us both.

"Well," she said, "I'm sure you'll get plenty of screenwriting deals now."

"Yeah, I figured this would be an effective career strategy."

"There is something compellingly naïve about you. Even earnest." She made a face, then signaled the bartender for another drink. Not her second.

"How so?"

"What you just confirmed is no thunderbolt from on high. We'd considered it, of course, did some investigating."

"Why didn't you just ask me when you had me on the stand?"

"Because we weren't sure, and even if we *were* right, you would have lied."

"Why do you assume that?"

"You wouldn't go to a doctor off record to cheat an insurance company if you were an honest guy."

"Fair enough. But I also wouldn't have lied under oath."

"Well, you'll have to forgive my skepticism for not wanting to stake my case on your integrity." She took a healthy sip. "The prosecutor can't just accuse a witness of lying. It's not recess at elementary school. Putting out the kinds of books you type, you ought to know that. I would need to present evidence or testimony that *refutes*. And your lawyers never gave me a target. They're overpriced, by the way. But hey, what do I know? You won. Sort of." She gave me a big congratulatory smile. "Of course, if your honest-guy conscience had piped up, say, yesterday . . . who knows if we'd both be sitting here?" She flicked the rim of her glass with a polished nail. "Why today, Danner? And why find *me*? You looking for forgiveness?"

Her tone made clear what her position on that would be.

"No."

"Then why are you on about this? You got off."

"The verdict is irrelevant."

"Yes," she said. "It is. 'Not guilty by reason of insanity' sure as shit doesn't mean 'didn't do it.'"

"But here's where we are. You didn't convict me. Maybe you should have."

"Well, I'm sure any self-respecting second-rate crime novelist knows you can't be tried twice for the same crime."

"I . . ." My hands itched to grip my drink, but I kept them still. "I remembered something. From the night of Genevieve's death. I checked it, and it was right."

"Lemme guess—it exonerates you."

"No," I said. "The opposite. I remembered driving over there. I was alone in the car."

She touched her fingertips to her open mouth, feigning immense surprise.

"I think I can help get to what happened that night," I said. "I still want to know if I plunged that knife into Genevieve's stomach. And you can help me find out."

She laughed. "Do you know why I tried you, Danner? Market pressure. If you were a nobody, you would've pled your way down to a traffic ticket and walked before trial. But because, for whatever reason, this city decided to cast you as a celebrity defendant, we had to do something about our celebrity trial record, which—you may have noticed—is less than spectacular."

"So getting convictions is all you care about? Aren't there some cases where you actually want to know the truth?"

"The truth? The *truth*? When you're a trial lawyer, you learn something in a hurry. You're supposedly questioning potential witnesses, but you're rehearsing them and you know it. Once a witness has told you the version of the story that you've helped them arrive at, you get them to retell it over and over. And eventually that story— the story you've all shaped—it *becomes* the truth. And if you're not careful or if you're careful enough, the truth will include things that weren't there to begin with. And that's what you're gonna have happening here, only worse. You might want to retell the story of the night of September twenty-third in your head a thousand times, but it was being interpreted before you supposedly woke up. You can never arrive at the truth." She finished off her drink. "You know why? The facts are the raw material, not the finished product. And if you go looking for truth, you're just gonna wind up chasing your tail. You'd do better to search for absolution." A quick wave of her hand. "But not here."

I threw down a twenty and slid off the barstool. "Thanks for your time."

She didn't bother looking up from her glass. "I'll bill you."

It was past one by the time I reluctantly returned home. I wished there were something else I could do, somewhere else I could go. It struck me as I entered the darkness of my kitchen that I didn't want to be alone with myself. During those chill jailhouse nights, I'd imagined plenty, but I hadn't imagined that being labeled not guilty *only* by reason of insanity would leave me feeling like I'd rather die than live inside my own skin. I had to live with a lot more, too. Despite my neurologist's warning, I'd chosen to take the risk—for myself, for that family of four in the minivan, for Genevieve. The cost of my selfishness sickened me.

I scrubbed the blood from the carpet as best I could and washed off the boning knife. Then I went back upstairs and lay in bed. 2:13 A.M. Only four more hours until daybreak. Then what? What life would I live?

I studied the ceiling, listening for sounds in the house. I tried to sleep, but every time I drifted off, I snapped to, worried what might happen. Or, perhaps, worried about what I might do.

A little past three, I got a digital camcorder from my office and a tripod from the garage and set them up in the far corner of my room, pointing at the bed. I hit "record" and climbed back under the sheets. Now if I turned into the Incredible Hulk, I'd have documentation. Or if the Hillside Foot Cutter broke in and went for the other pinkie toe. Maybe I should wear galoshes prophylactically. Maybe I should check myself in somewhere. Maybe I should ask Katherine Harriman for a date.

I stared at the watching lens.

Where do you hide when you scare yourself?

6

Exhausted, I sat at the wobbly kitchen table early the next morning, eating stale Smokehouse Almonds and picking through my mail. I'd failed to sleep, finally dragging out of bed to come downstairs. I'd been unable to shake off last night—the dream memory or the nonintruder. The implications of both continued to haunt me.

A hospital bill stuck out from the mound of mail, catching my eye, and I opened it to find a twelve-thousand-dollar anesthesia charge. The memo at the bottom informed me that, since I had no insurance, I should have requested a county hospital for my surgery. During my next amnesic psychotic break, I'd be sure to ask for a detour to the ER at Wilshire and Crack Central. Or—here's an idea—maybe I'd make a decision next crisis go-round before it constituted a calamity for me and a fatality for someone else.

Through the north-facing bank of windows, the sky looked bruised and wet, the smog dampening twilight. Gus, my fat, arthritic squirrel, hobbled across the back deck. It was a miracle the coyotes hadn't gotten him yet. He cocked his head, regarding me with something like sympathy, then raised his little paws as if in Jewish complaint.

"You and me both, bud," I said.

I continued flipping through the mail. From my agency a handful of surprisingly robust royalty payments. Three marriage proposals, photos enclosed, one from an attractive housewife in Idaho. Bank statements and medical claims and flyers from tree trimmers.

The return to the banalities of life was jarring. My reality—crumbs on the kitchen table, mortgage-refinance mailers—was not how I'd imagined it would be. What *had* I expected? Me with my scarlet *M,* slinking around colonial New England, disgraced and outcast, subsisting on forest grubs?

What I wanted was an unromantic drunk, a liquid haze, an alcoholic salve, a wake-up-in-your-own-vomit-beside-the-Jack-in-the-Box-drive-through bender. I was familiar with it, the sublime indulgence of self-destruction. When you've got nothing to lose, you've got something to gain. Thus the fuck-the-world fix. Thus the meek classmate who surprises you at your ten-year with newfound confidence and fifteen pierces crowding his pale features. Thus my and Charlie Manson's marriage proposals. Given that the prospect of marrying Mrs. Sue Ann Miller of Coeur d'Alene was, for the time being, unpalatable, I wondered at my next move.

I had a pretty significant choice to make. Lie down and die. Or don't.

I removed the cell phone from my pocket and dialed. As I waited for Lloyd Wagner to answer, I recalled that little nod he'd given me in court before he'd ripped into the dummy with my boning knife. He'd felt bad, but he'd had a job to do. I didn't begrudge him that. I'd tagged along with Lloyd at the forensics lab, even to a crime scene or two. He and I had shared a few meals as he'd helped me work through various plot points. He had an elongated face, wavy blond hair, and a kooky grin that he showed rarely. A rum-and-Coke guy. Early riser. He was a little cold, as befits a criminalist, though I'd always thought we had decent chemistry. Most important, he'd bagged Genevieve's hands and feet, dusted for prints, analyzed the DNA. I got his voice mail on his cell, so I tried him at home. His wife was ill, some kind of late-stage cancer, if she hadn't already died.

Answering machine. How old-fashioned.

After the beep I said, "Hi, Lloyd. Andrew Danner here. I know it probably seems pretty weird, me calling you, but I'm, I guess, free. I'm wondering how I might reconstruct the night I . . . drove over to Genevieve's. I figured you'd be the person to ask. We never got to talk, of course, about the evidence, but I'd like to get your unfiltered opinion. I think—I hope . . . I think I was framed. Unless I'm still temporarily insane, which I might be. I . . . well, I could use your advice. Please give me a call."

I hung up and paced a tight circle around the kitchen. I withdrew the boning knife from the block and studied it as if it had something new to tell me. Then I dialed again.

The line rang three times before the familiar voice said, "Hello?"

I said, "I'd like to see you. Just for a few minutes before you leave for work. Can you do that?"

The pause was so long I thought April had hung up. Then she said, "I can do a few minutes."

I realized I was still gripping the knife, so I slotted it home. Then I thanked her and headed out.

I threaded through the Encino hills. The Ike-'n'-Mamie houses, set behind oval lawns, flashed one after another in my headlights before fading back into the early-morning gloom. Idling across the street from April's house, I called again. Aside from the dim glow behind her bedroom curtains, the house looked dead.

When she picked up, I said, "I'm here."

The lights clicked on, broadcasting her path as she made her way to the front of the house, then the entry blinds swiveled. "So why don't you come ring the doorbell?" she said through the phone.

"I didn't want to startle you."

"Okay. Well, come on."

As I stepped onto the porch, the door jerked against the security chain. She laughed self-consciously, freed the chain, and beckoned for me to enter. We sat on opposing plush white couches straight out of a tampon commercial.

She appraised the scar on my head. "Any rashes from the Dilantin?"

"Meds have been fine." I shifted on the cushions, unable to get comfortable. "I wanted to thank you for coming to court for me. I think it made a difference, and even if it didn't, thank you."

"You're welcome. I'm glad you got acquitted, and I'm sorry you went through what you went through."

Despite her impassive expression, she sat rigidly. She was wearing a linen skirt wrinkled at midthigh and a halter with straps that tied at her nape, accenting her throat, splotched red from a nervous blush that refused to fade. She stayed awkwardly on the edge of the cushion as if ready to flee, her eyes darting, uncomfortable. And why not? What was she supposed to say?

"I miss you," I said.

Her gaze dropped to her lap, and I felt suddenly cold, exposed, aware of the notch in my hair. Was she afraid of being alone with me? Or was I projecting?

It had been hard on her. Press camped on her lawn, helicopters at night. The cops had tossed her house, emptied trash cans on the floor, even come by her office with a warrant. She'd waited five days to visit me in jail, which pretty much told me where things were headed. She'd been concerned for me, apologetic, but that had only made her leaving worse. She'd reminded me that we were just starting out, not even engaged yet. It was a lot to overcome three months into a romance.

I thought about those bluish gray morning hours when I'd stir and she'd be there beside me, how I'd curl around her form and drift back to sleep. When the road is smooth, how easily we forget that we need people. That we actually *require* them. I hadn't touched April since before the murder. I'd viewed her through ballistic glass under the watchful gaze of an armed correctional officer and, now, across a stretch of dated white carpet. All I could think about was the warmth of her body while she slept and how I could no longer take for granted that I'd feel it again. Of course, I couldn't take it for granted then either. I just did.

Her stress was palpable, and it struck me hard that I'd brought this to her life.

"I'm sorry how this has affected you," I said.

She wound the hem of her shirt around her finger, then unwound it. "Listen, Drew, I'm—" Her voice wavered, and she stopped.

"Don't worry. I understand that you don't need to have anything more to do with this."

She glanced at her watch. "Then you just came by to thank me?"

"Yes, and . . ." I realized I was fussing with my hands and set them in my lap. "Can I ask something of you? One thing?"

She couldn't hide a touch of wariness.

"Take me through that night again?"

"What . . . why?"

"Because you're the only one who can. Coming home, I'm trying to piece together those missing hours, but all I've got is this breakfast bowl and a cracked saucer—"

"Drew, what are you talking about? The trial is over. You're free. You should see someone, start putting this behind you. At least get some sleep. If you don't mind me saying so, you looked better in jail."

"I'm hoping a few answers will help me sleep."

"Or they'll lead to more questions."

"Right," I said. "But at least this time they'll be the *right* questions." I waited as she studied the wall over my head. "Please, April. I won't bother you again."

She drew a sharp breath. I waited for the sigh, but it didn't come. Instead she said, "It's like I told you in jail. You worked that day. I came over around six. We went to dinner. Fabrocini's."

"Did we run into anyone we knew?"

"No. Then we came home. We made love."

"Where?"

"On the couch. With the view."

"Did anyone call?"

She shook her head. "And then you had another migraine come on. Bad one. Laid down, lights out, the whole thing. I read with a booklight so I could stay beside you. But there was nothing different from any other time it's gone like that. You went to bed normal . . ."

The unspoken part of the sentence dangled. *And woke up a killer.*

She uncrossed her legs, crossed them again, tugged at her knee with her laced hands. "I woke up alone in your bed at four A.M. when the cops showed up."

She was a deep sleeper, slow to wake. I imagined her confusion at the empty space beside her in the sheets. Maybe she'd called for me in the bathroom. The insistent second chime of the doorbell. Disorientation giving way to concern, concern to fear. Bare feet on the carpet as she felt her way through the darkness into the hall. The police lights shining through the frosted insets of my front door and rising through the open foyer, setting the second-story ceiling awash in blue and red. What a long walk that must have been down the curving stairs.

"You don't remember a phone ringing late at night? And I didn't talk to you after I supposedly listened to Genevieve's message?"

"I don't remember anything."

"I can empathize," I said. "Thank you, April. For everything."

The words rushed out of her, as if they'd been pent up. "If you'd been more honest with me about the brain tumor, we could have prevented this."

I tried to answer, but my throat was dry, and I had to start over. "I was scared."

"Right. You were scared. And you chose not to tell me. So that tells you what we didn't have."

I couldn't convey how badly I wanted to take it all back, so I just nodded once, slowly. She rose, and I took the hint. I thanked her—I had much to thank her for—and she gave me a hug at the door, squeezing me tight, then turning away quickly so I couldn't see her face. "Take care of yourself, Drew."

I said, "I'll do my best."

7

Desperate for sleep, I lay on my bed, willing myself to doze off into another fragment of lost time. But my internal clock had decided to wake up and pay attention to the fact that it was 11:00 A.M. I went downstairs, sat at the kitchen table with my stale almonds and a glass of pomegranate juice, and took in the view. I was still acclimating to what daytime felt like when it wasn't filtered through bars.

After April's, I'd gone on my first light-of-day outing—down to Whole Foods to get groceries. I'd found people surprisingly warm. An old woman with a tennis visor gave me a surreptitious thumbs-up from Dried Fruits. The clerk, shuttling my groceries into com-postable bags, leaned forward as we waited for the receipt to print and said, sotto voce, "I'm glad for you." I knew I was dealing with a skewed sample—those who didn't think I was a drooling lunatic were more likely to approach—but these quiet, kind exchanges more than made up for the drubbing I'd received from my favorite morning-talk-show hosts.

My cell phone rang.

Chic said, "What are you doing?"

I picked an almond from a fold in my shirt, popped it into my mouth. "Writing."

"How 'bout some bar-bee-*cue*? Get your mind off the human fucking condition."

"No thanks."

"I'll pick you up in twenty minutes."

"Sure," I told the dial tone, "that'd be swell."

Chic drives a cherry red Chevy pickup, so big that riding in it you feel like a Playskool figurine. I'm officially six feet tall, ever since I fudged the extra inch at the DMV when I turned sixteen, but Chic looms over me. And requires more vehicular headroom.

Onetime first baseman for the Dodgers, he'd made the All-Star Team two years running, but that was before The Pop-Up. After that, he opened a chain of rib joints, which he'd named Chics Stics. He forgot the apostrophe and went without the *k,* and it took off from there. Branding genius, homegrown.

On the Chevy's tailgate is an elaborate sign, CHIC's STICS, featuring an apostrophe I added with a Magic Marker one day while he was distracted by a flat tire. That his truck still bears a Dodgers license-plate frame says more about the man than I ever could.

His driving—slow and steady—matches his personality. Chic has not a smugness but the relaxed, found-his-priorities demeanor of a recovering alcoholic. Someone who'd lived hard and found it not to work, who now knew what mattered and what was a waste of energy. We'd met in those rooms five years ago when I'd hit "reset" on my life, and we'd gravitated to each other immediately. Despite almost running his marriage into the ground a time or twelve, the requisite string of away-game affairs, the massive swings in fortune, he was still with his high-school sweetheart. He wasn't overwhelmingly handsome, except when he smiled. And he had a sweet, soft laugh, the kind that drove the road girls wild. At least before The Pop-Up.

He'd played as the nineties rolled in, just before athletes started making tycoon money. And though he was sure of his talents, he'd be quick to tell you that he hadn't started either All-Star Game in which he'd played, that he'd crumbled with his best years ahead of him. Aside from the infamy, he now led a peaceful life with his family in Mar Vista, a bedroom community tucked between Santa Monica and Venice. Close enough to the beach for the salt erosion but too far for a view, it had, like much Westside real estate, gone from middle class to upper in a hurry over the past decade. When his restaurants had taken off, Chic could've upgraded to a place in Brentwood or the Palisades, but instead he'd bought his neighbor's house, torn it down, and made a giant yard for his eight kids, complete with a mini baseball diamond.

Angela met us at the door, baby clasped to her side, sobbing toddler clinging to her leg, three or four various-size kids flashing in and out of view behind her as they circled the kitchen table playing chase or death tag. "Drew, Drew, *Drew,* Drew, *Drew, Drew, Drew.*" She angled a cooking spoon, wet from baked beans, to the side and offered up a delightfully smooth cheek for me to kiss, which I did gladly. "Boy, we prayed for you till this here floor got *tired* of our knees."

A few of the Baleses spun off from the typhoon and collided with my knees, shouting my name. I rubbed their heads. "Ronnie, you grew."

"That's 'cuz I'm Jamaal."

"Where's Ronnie?"

"Over here."

"I thought you were Keyshawn."

"Ain't no *Keyshawn* in this house, Drew."

And so the game went.

Somehow juggling three children and a platter of fried boneless chicken thighs—if this were fiction, I'd wimp out and make it something else, but chicken it was—Angela hustled us through to the side door. We sat at the picnic table in the middle of what would have been the neighbor's front yard. I watched her, as I often did, with awe. To me she was the Great Mother, a beautiful woman with soft curves and a ready grin, always pregnant or nursing or laying cornbread on a just-wiped table. We ate lunch. Buckets of sweet potatoes, trays of corn, sliced sourdough off the cutting board.

Angela pressed the tops of her breasts, grimacing. "I'm engorged. I need a mouth."

I said, "Don't look at me."

Frowning her amusement, she threw a blanket over one shoulder as Jamaal handed off the baby.

Chic buzzsawed through a plate of baby backs, shrapnel flying. He paused to belch, and Asia, chin level with the table, said, "Don't forget you can't do that when you start kindergarten."

"Okay, baby." Chic pointed at Ronnie's plate. "You gonna eat all that?"

Ronnie shielded his plate with both arms. "Uh-huh."

"All right, then. You don't finish, I gonna make you clean the toilets with your toothbrush."

"Nuh-*uh.*"

"Just you wait and see."

Ronnie went back to picking at his plate. Finally he slid it over to his father, who crowded him in the crook of his elbow and kissed him, leaving a greasy stain on his forehead that the other kids groaned about. Angela sat the baby in her lap, biting off his fingernails and spitting them into the bougainvillea. It was cool and the air smelled of jasmine, and I looked over at Angela and said, "Thank you."

She winked at me and rose, signaling that the clearing phase had begun. The ambulatory children helped, then were dispensed to their rooms for naps or reading or setting fires.

Chic and I sat at the picnic table, drinking O'Doul's and counting the passing cars. We got to fifteen before a middle-aged guy in a construction truck bellowed, "You're a fuckin' choker, Bales!"

Chic and I waved as we'd practiced many a time, the beauty-queen hand pivot.

A one-game playoff to determine the NL West had taken place up at San Francisco a few years before I'd met Chic. The Pop-Up. I'd cursed at it live, and thousands of replays had kept it fresh in my mind ever since. Bottom of the eighth, Dodgers in the field, up by one. Runners at the corners. Tie game. Robbie Thompson hits a towering pop-up, two outs voiding the infield-fly rule. Bales is under it, waves off the second baseman. An eternity as the ball fights swirling Candlestick winds. Uribe, circling from first, is halfway down the third-base line when the ball nicks Bales's glove, strikes his thigh, and dribbles into the Dodgers' dugout. The Men in Blue go three up, three down in the top of the ninth and lose the pennant. Chic goes out drinking and doesn't come back for two years.

I said, "At least now I can keep you company in the ranks of the despised. I feel like the tuba player in high school."

Chic smiled. "High school. Worst six years of my life."

"Does it ever get to you?"

"Nope."

"Really?"

"Course it does, Drew-Drew. But then I remind myself: Everyone carries a burden. It's about how gracefully you elect to bear it. Don't you read the Good Book?" He snickered, worked something out from between his teeth. "My burden's making a fuckload of money, then becoming one of the biggest goats in the history of Major League Baseball. So I made a fool of myself in front of twenty million people. Nineteen-plus of who I don't know and never will." He shrugged. "Beats getting gang-raped in a Rwandan torture camp."

I conceded the point.

"What I did ain't no J-O-B. Yours ain't neither. There's no *need* for our so-called services, and no sick baby gonna get cured by a page-turner or an opposite-field line drive." He paused, his thick arms straightening in an air swing. "Pretty as it may be. What I provided can't even be construed as a luxury. Lamenting that I been marginalized? Hated? Shit, I'd rather work on my barbecue sauce. 'Cuz you know *that* takes a brother having his head on right."

"But I didn't just drop a pop fly," I said.

"Oh, now you *know* what you did or didn't do?" He flicked a kernel of corn off his knee. "James wrote a project last week about the environment. That drunk-ass *Exxon Valdez* captain, spilled eleven million gallons of crude oil in that sound up there. *Eleven million.* Killed about a kazillion birds and otters and shit. The government said—and the government, in my humble GED opinion, is overly optimistic—that it'd take thirty years to clean up. That puts it out till, shit, 2020. And I'm pretending to help James write this muthafucker until Angela finishes with Asia in the bath, and the whole time I'm wondering, how's *that* poor muthafucker get up in the morning? So after James goes to bed, I look him up. He's an insurance adjuster in Long Island. Wakes up every day, drinks his coffee, and goes to work like the rest of us sorry sacks. He got moufs to feed. And I say, good for him." He looked over at me and said, "What's wrong? This is supposed to be uplifting."

"I knew about the tumor. For months." I looked for shock or condemnation in his face but found neither. "I was too scared and too strapped to do anything about it. I kept it secret because I was worried that when I got health insurance again they wouldn't pay for the surgery if they knew it was a preexisting condition."

"So?"

"*So?*"

"I didn't hear no lawyer ask you if you knew you had a tumor. You didn't perjure yourself. And, far as I know, *thinking* about defrauding an insurance company ain't a crime. I doubt you would've had the nerve to go through with it anyway."

It was just a skip to a wicked irony, one that had contributed to my insomnia these past months. Genevieve may have died because of my brain tumor, but her dying had likely saved my life.

I said, "This makes me guilty even if I'm innocent."

"No, it don't make you guilty. It makes you *feel* guilty. It makes you guilt*ier* if you actually did it. But whatever way it happened or didn't, I got your back."

"Even if I'm *guilty*-guilty?"

"If you're innocent, you don't need no help, do you?"

I didn't trust my voice to thank him, but he saw it in my face.

He winked and took another pull of near beer. "They say a real friend is someone who helps you move. The neighborhood I'm from, a real friend is someone who helps you move a *body*." He cocked his head, training his brown eyes on me. His curled lashes, vaguely feminine, didn't match the rest of him. "Now, how 'bout you fill me in on what's *really* going on?"

I told him about the previous night's dream and the cut on my foot and driving to Genevieve's. "I can't live with this," I said. "I wake up and I don't know where I've been. I set up a goddamned digital camera in my bedroom to watchdog myself. I'm checking my odometer to see if I left the house. The obvious explanation is that I'm insane. But I know I'm not insane."

"Or maybe you a *little* insane, like the rest of us."

"You think I cut my own foot?"

Chic shrugged. "First day back in the world, you up in your head like you are? I'd lay odds on *yeah*. Especially with all this secret tumor business—should be clear why you obsessed. But I'll tell you this: If someone *is* messing with you? Then this is only the introduction."

"Why's that?"

"They're doing it for a *rea-son*. And given you're not a politician or Donald Trump, someone's doin' a lot of work to get . . . *what?*"

He ran his massive palm over his hair, shaved tight to his scalp with a silly line cut diagonally in the front like a part.

"So which do I hope for?" I finally asked. "That I *am* being fucked with? Or that I'm losing it?"

"What's behind Door Number Three?"

I blew out a breath. "I can't stop picking at this, but at the same time what if I don't like what I find?"

He finished his O'Doul's, musing powerfully as only Chic can. Then he said, "Face everything." He tossed the empty bottle and hit the open trash can ten yards away. "One day at a time."

We drove back to my house in silence, Chic reaching over once or twice to squeeze my neck. I was halfway up the walk when he whistled through his teeth. He was at the curb, truck running behind him. "I know it's been circled around, but no one ever says it dead on." He licked his lips, not looking away. "I'm sorry this happened to you."

As he headed back around the truck, a passing jogger flipped him off.

He waved.

8

That night I sat and watched commercials. Just commercials. I wasn't up to sustained drama. The usual high-stakes action ensued. Soap products busied themselves fighting grime. Closet messes overwhelmed frazzled housewives. Animated fungi rooted under toenails.

My cell phone vibrated pleasingly in my pocket, and I dug it out. Preston asked, "What are you doing?"

"Lying around listlessly. Bemoaning an unjust universe."

"I'm in the neighborhood. Drop by?"

"No?"

"See you in ten."

Forty-five minutes later, the doorbell rang. I yelled, "You have a key!"

Preston came in, glanced around the family room. "The drawn curtains. The dirty dishes. The ragged clothing. How about we rewrite this scene?"

Preston is a better friend than he seems. He'd come to see me in jail second, after Chic, browbeating the rookie guard into extending visitor hours. Though he wasn't a smoker, he'd lit up behind the Plexiglas, I'd assumed, out of regard for the ambience. Trying to repress a cough, he'd shot smoke past the crest of his bangs and remarked, "They don't really make a Hallmark card for this one, do they?"

In his interior forties, Preston has intense blue eyes and a square jaw that flexes out at the corners when he's working to a point, which is often. He'd been my editor for all five of my books, and I'd yet to find him wanting for an opinion on any matter trivial or life-threatening. Infuriatingly resolute, unusually hands-on, overly involved, he seems to live through the books he publishes. He loves make-believe, but the set of his features showed a heightened thrill at now being in the real-life-of-it-all.

His head-tilted appraisal of me continued. "How do you feel getting out?" He seemed to have shape-shifted already—into the streetwise confederate with a hard-boiled mouth.

"Off balance." I shrugged. "My horoscope says it's because Jupiter's in my twelfth house."

"That *is* bad," he mused. "Once, growing up, we had a possum in our outhouse." Preston grew up in an academic family in Charlottesville, and now and then he lets a yokelism slip into his conversation. Owning apartments in Manhattan and West Hollywood on an editor's salary doesn't square with outhouse and possum references, but if you took away Preston's affectations, there'd be no one left to argue with.

He looked around, folding his arms, helpless against the mess of my house. "I suppose you seem to be holding together, given the circumstances," he conceded.

"My suffering has ennobled me."

He pursed his lips and regarded me as if perhaps that weren't true.

I said, "Thanks for getting my mail. Not to mention cosigning the mortgage refinance."

Preston waved me off—no time for niceties—then nodded at the Band-Aid on my foot. "What happened there?"

"I cut myself with a boning knife."

"Naturally. *Why?*"

"Because I'm a nutcase."

"Why don't you give me the backstory?"

He feigned patience as I filled him in on the bizarre events of last night. When I was done, he said, "Let me make a cup of tea." He disappeared into the kitchen, then called out, "Do you have a lime?"

"Try the fridge."

He returned a few minutes later with a glass of ice and the bottle of Havana Club he'd smuggled back from an ostensible research trip to Cuba and given, also ostensibly, to me as an oh-look-it's-contraband souvenir. He kept it hidden in my kitchen so other guests wouldn't access it. Sitting on the long arm of my sectional's L, he sipped his rum. I noted, with some irritation, he hadn't offered to bring me anything.

"Aren't you supposed to be in New York?" I asked.

"I extended my office leave." A sly grin. "I'm editing out here for the next few months so I can be supportive." He tapped his manicured nails together. "Look, Drew, I'm not gonna lie to you. I don't know if you did it or not. But I do know one thing: If I were you, and if I had a *modicum* of doubt as to my guilt, I wouldn't be sitting around."

"You'd do what?"

"Investigate."

"Get me forensics, a blood panel, and sat footage of the canyon."

"Don't be a smart-ass. You can't afford it. You may be free, but the public views you as a murderer. You're tarred with that brush, and, unlike O.J., you can't just retire to a golf course and live off your bloated retirement accounts. If you accept the verdict as delivered, fine. Start not drinking again. But if you *don't* accept that verdict, you have to get away from that tumor, dig down into what happened, and exonerate yourself." He crunched ice thoughtfully. "The story you should be working on is the one that's working on *you*."

He took another swig, cubes clinking musically against the glass. Unable to manage his own life at all, he was happy to micromanage mine. Would he micromanage me right into a padded room? I settled back in my chair, studied the smooth white ceiling.

He continued, "Harriman effectively painted you as *the killer*. But this insanity nonsense *might not* be the real version of events. And if not, you have to find *your* story. The *real* story." His eyes gleamed. He was Excited By The Possibilities. "Maybe you *didn't* do it. Maybe someone *did* break into your house. Maybe there *is* a furtive *Gaslight* plot to mess with your head. We don't read the books about the nine hundred ninety-nine times something goes as expected. We read those about the one time it goes wrong. Or strangely. Or extraordinarily. And there are enough oddities here that this"— he pointed at me—"could be the case." He stared at me, but before I could respond, he was going again. "This is your *life*. What have you done to explore this since you've been home?"

"I looked around the house, checked my e-mail and PalmPilot to see if I could piece anything together, talked to—"

"Oh, well, I'm *riveted*. Did you do lots of tortured sulking, too? Play the saxophone in the dark?"

My face was burning. "I tried to keep sulking to a minimum, but yes, I may have sulked some. Moderate darkness. But no moody wind instruments."

"What did you do today?"

"Opened the mail. And I ate yams."

"You ate yams?"

"At Chic's house."

He threw up his hands as if that said it all. "Do you want to make progress or do you want to be angry?"

I thought for a moment. "I want to be angry."

"What would Dirk Chincleft do?"

Preston has various unflattering nicknames for Derek Chainer. That's the good thing about editors. Wit.

"Dirk Chincleft is a homicide detective," I said. "He has official leverage. I don't have leverage."

"Come on! You're stuck in the first act, and you're not driving your narrative. You know better. You impact the plot. Or the plot impacts you."

"This isn't a fucking story."

He leaned forward, jabbing a finger at the floor. "*Everything's* a fucking story. And you're letting this one languish. What you need is something to kick down the front door, come barreling into the plot, crashing into the story. Make you *react*. Make you *act*. But in the likely event that that *isn't* gonna happen, you need to uncover what happened. If you're not afraid to." His gaze zeroed in on me; he'd sensed perhaps that he'd flicked a vulnerability. "A writer's job, perhaps more than any other, is not to be afraid of possibilities."

"But I *am*." I hadn't realized it until I heard it out loud, even from my own mouth. I was afraid of what I'd discover, and that fear had stalled me out.

We'd veered into The Writer's Feelings, uncomfortable territory for Preston. He broke eye contact, gathering the strap of his bag, his intensity suddenly dissipated. He stood and dusted his pants. "I hate to sound L.A.-loathsome, but I've got bikram yoga."

"Yoga with the Muppets?"

"Hot room. Hundred and five degrees." Master of the last word, Preston paused at the threshold to the living room. For once his expression was sincere. "Dirk Chincleft wouldn't take it lying down."

The front door closed neatly behind him, and the dead bolt set with a smug click.

I'd never imagined that freedom would feel so constraining. If I'd been convicted, I'd have had the benefit of lurid prison tales, stoic last words as they strapped me into the chair. Preston was right about one thing: I was at a narrative dead end. I contemplated my options. None seemed appealing, so I stomped upstairs, echoes of Preston's oppressing me more with each step. Where do you go when the case is closed and the courts, the cops, the press, the public, and maybe even you believe you're the killer? In real life? Fucking nowhere, that's where.

Or maybe, if you're lucky, you go to sleep. Which is what I was finally going to do.

I took two steps into my bedroom and froze.

My brain tumor was gone. Save my clock radio and bedside lamp, the nightstand was empty. No glass jar, not even a lingering drop of formaldehyde.

My skin tingled with electricity.

The last time I could remember seeing it was just after I'd come in from smoking a cigar on the deck. Had I hidden or disposed of it while in my foot-cutting trance? Panic congealed at the back of my throat, constricting my breathing. I ran my hands through my hair, hard, feeling the ridge of scar tissue against my left palm.

I threw back the comforter and looked under the bed. The nightstand drawers held only their usual contents. I searched the cabinets of my bathroom next, flinging bottles and cold-medicine boxes onto the counter. I tore apart my office, tugging and slamming drawers, digging through the trash can. The guest room downstairs was next, then the living room. Charging into the kitchen, I caught sight of a gleam in the sink.

A curved wedge of thick glass.

I drew near. The familiar screw lid, a collection of shards. No ganglioglioma.

I'd been in the kitchen today only to grab the can of almonds. Had I glanced in the sink? Probably not. How about last night, after I'd followed my own bloody footprints around? Had I looked? Not closely.

I picked out the glass debris and set it on the counter. After staring at the rubber mouth of the disposal for a moment, I shoved up my sweatshirt sleeve and pushed my hand gently through. Keeping a nervous eye on the light switch that could set the chopping blades in motion, I groped around, dreading what my tumor might feel like. Slick and firm? Moist? Kernels of glass pinched my fingers. I explored thoroughly but found the disposal empty. Had I run it last night, flushing the tumor for once and for all? Or had my stalker kidnapped it to drive me further into the state of paranoia in which I'd taken up residence?

From its latched wooden box, I took a twenty-year Warre's, resting in its place the remains of the shattered jar. Then I gave last rites, pouring the full bottle of port into the maw of the garbage disposal to which the tumor may have been committed.

Exhausted and mystified, I trudged back upstairs, crawled into bed, and finally dozed off.

At 4:00 A.M. my house imploded.

9

The boom jerked me upright with a cry, and then I heard a screech of heavy objects, the shriek of broken glass. A deluge of manpower rushing inside. Pounding boots up the stairs. In my post-slumber haze, the intruders seemed like rising devils, I like a dumbstruck Faust. For a moment I was back in my cell, phantom voices drifting up to me.

Stupefied, I stared at the door, which flung violently open, admitting a stream of figures decked in black and armored with goggles, vests, and assault weapons of some kind. Dark gloves seized my right wrist and ankle and ripped me from bed.

"Stay the fuck down!"

"See the hands, see the hands!"

My limbs spread as if by their own volition, and hands frisked me, not hard to do since I was wearing only boxers. A ghost imprint of white block lettering floated in front of my eyes, though my face was mashed to the carpet. LAPD SWAT.

I jerked my head to the side so I could breathe. Detective Three Bill Kaden appeared offset, Ed Delveckio peering over his shoulder. Kaden pushed a finger into my cheek until it ground against my teeth.

"You're fucked now," he said.

As Kaden led me, cuffed and hastily dressed, past the cops already rifling through my possessions, down the stairs, over the scattered shards in the entryway from the front-door glass insets, I registered a certain foolishness, a retroactive shame about how screwed I'd been before I'd even known it. While I'd drooled obliviously on my pillow, scenarios had been drawn up, positions chosen, a battering ram readied. My heart was still jerking in my chest. Being on the wrong side of a raid? Not as much fun as you might think.

I saw newspapers spinning in to fill the screen, headlines shouting NEW EVIDENCE IN BERTRAND SLAYING. But wasn't I protected under double jeopardy?

I said, "I assume you have a warrant."

Bunched beneath Kaden's fist, the document appeared before my face. I was being arrested for murder, though the warrant didn't name names. That would be, I assumed, my job.

Kaden threw me in the back of an unmarked sedan and climbed into the driver's seat. Delveckio sat in the passenger seat. My neighbors were on their front steps or at the windows.

"You could have just called," I said. "I would've driven in. I've always cooperated." A few more blocks in silence. My alarm was finally ebbing, giving way to outrage. I cleared my throat. "I say, 'What's this about?' and you say, 'I think you know, punk.' Then I say, 'I want to talk to my lawyer,' and you say, 'As soon as you're booked.'"

The backs of their heads did not respond.

We were on the freeway now, flying toward downtown. The first time I'd ever been on the 101 without traffic. The freeway, usually bumper to bumper, was deserted, postapocalyptic.

I was not surprised, some fifteen minutes later, to see the Parker Center through the windshield. Home to Derek Chainer. And to LAPD's elite Robbery-Homicide Division. A glass-and-concrete testament to fifties architectural cost-effectiveness, Parker's rectangular rise blocked out the emerging sun.

I was steered upstairs to an interrogation room. They kept the door open, cops coming and going with papers and whispered updates. Once again I felt disoriented, nervous, shoved out of my rightful place. I knew these halls. I knew this building. I'd researched men like these and written about them in flattering fashion. After my first book came out, I'd taken the buddy-buddy tour with the public-information officer, watched a real-live interview from the other side of the one-way mirror. What a distance between that side of the glass and this.

"Why am I here?" I said.

Kaden said, "Take your clothes off."

"Okay, but it's fifty bucks up front, and I don't kiss on the mouth."

"*Off.*"

I glowered at him. "Not until I talk to my lawyer."

"After we search you."

"In case I'm secreting a bazooka up my ass?"

"You can keep your boxers on."

I kicked off my shoes, and Kaden stared at my bare feet and said, "Stop. Band-Aid off, please."

I complied. He snapped his fingers at the door, and a guy came in with an oversize Polaroid and took a picture of the slice in my flesh while I stood on one foot.

I finished pulling off my clothes, and they made sure I had no other scrapes or slashes. As I dressed, the photographer withdrew and closed the door, leaving me with Kaden, Delveckio, a table and chair, and a shiny mirror on the wall. The lights were hot, and someone had brought me coffee. My job was to drink it and get jittery and have to take a leak and spill all my secrets so I could get to the can. I could've been more compliant if I knew what my secrets were.

Delveckio nodded at my foot. "Looks to be a fresh knife cut, wouldn't you say?"

"You talk, too?"

"Answer the fucking question," Kaden said.

"Yeah," I said. "It looks like a fresh cut. Now, what the hell's this about?"

"Got a little careless?"

"Doing what?"

"You tell me."

I palmed sweat off my brow. The hot overheads were working. "I might have had an intruder two nights ago. I think someone broke in when I was sleeping, cut my foot."

"Sure thing," said Delveckio. "Easter Bunny maybe?"

I glared at him. "Not in January. I was thinking tardy elf."

"Why didn't you call the police?" Kaden asked.

"You guys haven't exactly been sympathetic."

"And this . . . mystery assailant cut you and you slept through it?"

"I was really out of it. My first night home. I woke up just after, I think. Guy might've even still been in the house, but then I wasn't sure—"

Kaden placed a thick hand on my chest and shoved me so I fell back into the chair. He kicked the table so it slid over and stopped right in front of me. I was now seated at the interrogation table. Neat trick.

"Where were you last night between ten-thirty and two A.M.?"

Last night?

"Okay," I said, struggling to keep up and failing. "Okay."

Delveckio handed me my coffee, an oddly civil gesture, despite his motivation.

"Getting smarter, aren't you?" Kaden said. "Moved the body this time. Washed it down with a bleach solution."

I believe that anyone is capable of anything.

I felt a flutter-beat of panic. "Is it April? Is she all right?"

They stared at me, arms crossed, spread stances, Delveckio a skinnier version of the big guy.

"Tell me she's okay," I said. "You already dragged me here. No need to add insult to injury."

Delveckio reached over and cuffed my head. Openhanded but hard. "You're a piece of shit," he said. "*That's* insult to injury."

My chest felt tight. I couldn't move enough air through it. "Just tell me this isn't about April."

Kaden set down a crime-scene photo on the table in front of me. I shuddered so hard that coffee spilled over the Styrofoam lip and scalded my knuckles. Woman on a coroner's slab, familiar deep gash in the pit of the stomach. But not April.

A great hope fell over me like a blanket of light. Two bodies, same MO. If I hadn't killed this woman, I likely hadn't killed Genevieve. My name could be cleared. My relieved exhale was cut short by a renewed understanding of my situation. Interrogation room. Parker Center. Logically, the prime suspect.

"I didn't do this. No *way*. You think I . . . what? Slipped while stabbing her in the stomach and cut my bare foot?"

"You undressed to make sure you didn't get any spatter on your clothes," Delveckio said. "Manipulating the body, holding the knife, mistakes happen."

"Come on. That's hardly concrete evidence."

"Oh, you want evidence?" Kaden asked.

Here we go again. Déjà fucking vu.

"We found a plastic drop cloth in your trash can. Like for, say, the trunk of your car."

My breath left me in a silent cough. I didn't know anything except to keep fighting. Blindly. And take it on faith that I wasn't a murderer, let alone twice over.

"Why would I leave it in my own trash can?" I said.

"You wouldn't," Delveckio said, "You burned it first. But you missed an edge. And it's sporting residue matching the adhesive from the electrical tape binding her wrists."

I couldn't manage a response.

Kaden laughed at my stunned expression, though there was no amusement in his eyes. "Framed again, huh? One-armed man on the grassy knoll?"

"I didn't do this," I said quietly.

"That's odd, because the killer duplicated every specific. The precise angle of the stab wound. The positioning of the body. The way the head was turned, hair down over the right eye. Not exactly the level of detail we put out for the six o'clock news."

My thoughts bled one into the next.

"Here's the kicker," Kaden continued. "That little piece of unburnt plastic drop cloth we found in your trash can? It had some more surprises for us. The victim's blood. Your blood. And as for your bleach bath? Missed a few spots. Your hair under a fingernail. Traces of your blood on the pad of her foot."

I cannot have done this. It's impossible that I did this last night.

"As far as we can determine, there is only one connection between the victims," Kaden said. "And that's you."

I pointed at the body in the photo. "I don't know who that woman is. Why would I kill her?"

"You're trying to tell us you didn't do this, and you've spent the thirty-six hours since your release digging around in the mud of the case you were just acquitted for? Stalking Katherine Harriman. Trying to get ahold of the key criminalist from the investigation. You're giving new meaning to returning to the scene of the crime."

He nodded at Delveckio, who walked to the corner, reached up, and unplugged the security camera pointing down at us. Kaden set both hands on the lip of the table, leaning over so his face was a few feet from mine. He shoved until the ledge of wood struck my lower ribs and sent me and my chair skidding back with it. The table hit the walls on either side of me, trapping me in the corner. "Decent-sized fella like yourself might be feeling a touch cramped right about now. Get used to it. Because that's your cell size *for the rest of your life.*"

Kaden stepped back. Pacing, he cuffed his sleeves up past his wide forearms. "Let's pretend I'm playing bad cop. But see, this game is different. There *is* no good cop. This is bad cop–bad cop. Delveckio and I, there's no one we hate more than killers of women. We watched you slip off once. We're not gonna do it again."

I glanced at Delveckio. Considerate of Kaden to make room for him under the macho umbrella. With his thin frame and watery eyes, Delveckio was not the most threatening figure. Kaden, on the other hand, looked ready to jam his fingers through my face and use my head as a bowling ball.

He continued, "We're willing to rough you up. We're willing to snap fingers. We're willing to crack ribs. And we're willing to testify how we had to because you were belligerent and violent. We'd rather not, but we will. You can go through it or you can skip it, but either way you're talking, and you don't have a brain tumor to save your murdering ass this go-round."

The crime-scene photo had skidded off the table into my lap. Upside down, it looked even more grotesque. Blood and severed flesh, without orientation.

The familiar sickness started in my stomach, dampening my skin. The sweat-stained hospital sheets. The voices echoing off my cell walls. The scabs had lifted to reveal the same horrible scene. Where was I? What had I done? I felt a sudden caving-in of my resolve. The utter demoralization of long-awaited defeat, of laying down arms and giving in to the inevitable. Maybe I *had* done it. I could not exactly claim to remember the last time I'd encountered a body under similar circumstances. The evidence, Genevieve, my mental lapses— it was too much.

Where were you last night between ten-thirty and two A.M.?

Home alone. Out cold. Yeah, right.

Bill Kaden, looking none too affable, advanced on the table, and I opened my mouth to offer a shaky admission of I-knew-not-what when like a thunderbolt a realization rocketed down, straightening my spine, jerking my fists against the pitted wood.

"The camcorder!" I cried. "I recorded myself sleeping!"

10

They kept me alone in that interrogation room for an hour and forty-five minutes. For the first while, I sat on the chair with the crime-scene photo, which they'd thoughtfully left behind to keep me company. On the back was printed *Kasey Broach, 1/22, 2:07 A.M.* The detectives had wasted no time in getting to me. When I couldn't take the gruesome picture any longer, I had little to do but stare at my warped reflection in the mirror. The distortion amplified the way my hair bristled above the scar line, or maybe that was how it really looked.

My camcorder was digital, with a 120-hour memory, which meant that it had been recording seamlessly since I'd set it up, capturing me snoozing, changing, gargling. For better or worse, it would hold the answer. Me, dozing peacefully. Or sleepwalking into a murder.

After a while I moved the table and chair back to the middle of the room. As I paced, I caught myself inadvertently running the pads of my fingers along the line of my hidden scar. At the hour mark, I told the mirror that I was going to urinate in the corner if someone didn't take me to a bathroom. A moment later the door popped open and a sullen rookie led me down the hall, then brought me back.

Kaden and Delveckio finally returned, carrying chairs and looking dyspeptic. At least Kaden did; from what I knew of Delveckio, that was just his normal expression. Reading their faces, I felt nothing short of elation. *Wudn't me. Wudn't me.*

They sat opposite. The folder in Kaden's lap carried a sweat mark from his hand.

"We saw the footage," Kaden said. "The lab seems to believe it wasn't doctored. No glitches in the continuity."

I blew out a breath that kept going. The relief was so intense it made me light-headed.

Kaden was talking. "But you could've had an accomplice. Or maybe the coroner's time of death was inaccurate. You were off the tape for just about all of the afternoon and the early part of the night."

"I have alibis. I was at a friend's for the afternoon, then my editor came over."

"This still doesn't play right," Kaden said. "Why's an innocent guy—an innocent guy that all the evidence at the crime scene just weirdly happens to nail—set up an airtight alibi?"

"Because I thought I might have chopped my own foot in my sleep, and I was worried I was losing my mind."

Kaden laughed. "'Losing'?"

"Let's start this over." I extended my hand. "Drew."

Kaden stared at my hand like he was about to spit on it, but after a moment he nodded. Delveckio grudgingly followed suit.

"Okay. You don't like me, and I'm not particularly fond of you guys." I glanced at Delveckio. "Especially you."

"Why especially me?"

"That insult-to-injury thing was lame. Kaden may posture more, but he cuts a more impressive swath, so I figure he's entitled to it. But"—I paused for effect—"you've both got a case weighing on you. Maybe two. I'm stuck in this investigation. Uniquely so. I'm here, and I'm not lawyered up. So take advantage of the situation."

"You know what I like even more than smart-ass Hollywood types?" Kaden asked. "Reopening cases I already closed."

"If my case is closed, who killed Kasey Broach?"

My using her name set him back a moment, but then his eyes pulled to the crime-scene photo between us. "I don't know, Danner—someone who has your exact hair, exact blood, and uses your trash can. So guess who we're coming after when we figure out this digicorder crap and have probable cause again?"

Probably not the guy who framed me.

I stared at Kasey Broach's corpse, wondering what, if any, was her connection to me. Or to Genevieve. Maybe there was a connection between Broach and the surviving Bertrands. Or maybe she'd been killed merely to set me up. Who had a motivation to see me locked up? That is, aside from the detectives right in front of me. *Had* Genevieve been seeing someone new, who didn't think I should be driving the streets with impunity? Maybe Luc Bertrand had hired someone to bring me down by any means possible. Hard to believe with his droopy blue eyes, but hey, so was a brain tumor. My mind continued to spin, reeling in an agent I'd fired, a guy whose nose I'd accidentally broken on the basketball court, a bizarre letter I'd received from an anonymous reader after *Chainer's Link*.

"How can I help you look into this?" I asked. "Where do you start?"

Delveckio said, "We don't have anything we can disclose at this point in time."

"Did Genevieve and Kasey Broach have anything in common?"

"Grieving parents. Devastated younger sisters." He shook his head. "I did the advise-next-of-kin for Adeline. I wish I'd borrowed your camcorder first so I could make you watch her reaction."

I resisted giving him the reaction he was looking for. "So you haven't found *any* connection between the victims?"

His grin faded, and the skin tensed around his eyes. "Just you."

Kaden stood to leave, Delveckio rising on a slight delay.

"You find anything unusual in her bloodstream?" I asked.

They halted. Kaden pivoted, slowly. "Why would you ask that?"

"Two nights ago I felt really hazy when I woke up. I thought it was brain-tumor fallout or stress. But maybe I was drugged so someone could cut my foot." I leaned back in the chair, folded my arms. "Take my blood."

Delveckio raised his eyebrows at Kaden, who took two solemn steps back to his chair and sat. "Why'd you wake up so quickly, then? If you were drugged?"

"Dunno. I have a pretty good tolerance from my misspent youth. Can we run my blood?"

Kaden fished a cell phone from his pocket and dialed. "Kaden here. Get me Wagner." He rose and walked out of the room.

"Lloyd Wagner's on this case?"

Delveckio looked peeved to be stuck with me. "Of course. He worked the first murder, didn't he? Isn't that why you called him? You knew him from your trial and figured you could harass your way in?"

"I knew him before. He's helped me on some projects."

"Yeah, well, I think it's safe to say he's not interested in helping you anymore."

Kaden's voice hummed through the walls, but I couldn't make out the words. Delveckio did his best not to make eye contact with me.

I asked, "On the footage did you notice . . . did you see me move anything from the nightstand?"

"Huh?"

"Something in a jar?"

"I was hoping this could get weirder."

"Did you?"

"No."

So my tumor had already crawled off by the time I set up the re-corder. Which meant it had likely vanished around the time my foot had been cut. Another oddity to toss on the heap.

Kaden returned. "Would've cleared your bloodstream by now."

I asked, "What would have?"

Kaden shifted from one foot to the other, giving me the stone-wall.

"Come on. If I may have been drugged, at least tell me what I could've had in my system."

"Xanax and sevoflurane. Alprazoblah-blah—that's Xanax—is shorter-lasting. The other, too. It's a knockout gas. 'Rapid elimination from the bloodstream,' the man says."

"So how'd you catch it in Broach?"

"Quick response. Patrolman radioed in the body. We heard that it looked similar to Genevieve Bertrand, called in the cavalry so no one would trample evidence. Our criminalist had dropped a trace-evidence report at Rampart, was just a few blocks away having a burrito. Hot-assed it over to the crime scene. They always draw blood right off."

Delveckio licked his dry lips. "Plus, Broach's metabolism wasn't working so fast when we found her."

"Why give someone Xanax if you're gonna knock them out?" I asked.

"You wouldn't," Kaden said. "We're thinking she took it before bed."

"So she was grabbed in her sleep?"

"Signs of a struggle."

"The sevoflurane didn't do the trick?"

"Or was given to her later."

"Take her kicking and screaming and subdue her after?" I asked. Kaden shrugged, so I added, "What kind of struggle?"

"Sheets dragged off the mattress, stuff knocked from the nightstand, alarm clock lost its battery at ten twenty-seven."

"How old-fashioned."

"A battery-operated alarm clock?"

"The clue."

"You have a suspicious mind."

"Let's make use of it."

"We're not gonna invite a key suspect to dick around in our investigation."

"You don't need to invite me anywhere. Just let me look at photos from the scene. See the body, how it was left. Maybe something'll trip my memory."

"Memory of *what*?" Kaden eyed me, then tapped Delveckio on the knee with his file. "Let's go."

"Whether you believe me or not, I don't know what happened the night of September twenty-third. And whether you believe me or not, I want to know if I did it. You need answers. You're professional interrogators. I assume you're capable of getting what you want from me without giving up what you don't want to."

Kaden stared at me, then chuckled and tossed the file on the table, the papers spilling out. I spread them across the surface. They were laser printouts, pretty good resolution, with multiple duplicates of each shot.

Kasey Broach's naked body had been dumped under a concrete freeway on-ramp. She lay on her back, chin tossed up and to the side as if she were trying to flip the hair from her face. A nasty abrasion mottled her right hip, and the skin looked split on her right cheek. Her wrists were bound with tape, her ankles with white rope. Around her, weeds pushed up from cracked asphalt. The skeleton of a fence remained in the background, chain-link sloughed from three remaining posts. A beater of a coupe sagged on slashed tires, windows smashed in, roof dented down to the headrests, hood dense with bird shit. Behind it on the sloping underbelly of the ramp, a graffiti artist had abandoned a work in progress.

A close-up showed Broach's arms spotted with marks where flies had started their work. For some reason they underscored her death. So helpless, incapable of swatting a bug feasting on her.

I stared at Kaden. "'The killer duplicated every specific'? Of Genevieve's murder? Are you kidding me? He kidnapped a woman, drugged her, moved her body, stripped her, bound the wrists and ankles, and dumped her in a public place."

"There are an alarming number of similarities," Delveckio said.

"As for the differences? We usually see an upward evolution as a killer grows more experienced, learns from prior mistakes."

"You neglected to mention that earlier, when you were busting my door down. Why do you think she's naked?"

"Growing bolder," Kaden offered, studying me closely. "Could be part of a growing fantasy."

"Or he stripped her for the bleach washdown," Delveckio added, "which meant he knew we'd analyze the body for trace and foreign biologicals."

"And? Was she raped?"

Delveckio shook his head.

"What'd you find?"

"Aside from your blood and your hair?" Kaden flipped through his notepad. He tapped his pen to the paper. "Ah, here it is: None of your fucking business."

"Bruising at the wrists and ankles would indicate she was bound before the fatal stabbing, no?"

The detectives exchanged an irritated glance but didn't respond. Crafty detective work, keeping me in the dark like this.

"The Sevoflurane. She was kept alive. Unlike Genevieve. Points to sadistic tendencies?" I returned their stares. "Blink twice if I'm getting warm. How about the abrasions on the hip and cheek? From being thrown out of the vehicle?"

Delveckio gave me the sour face, but Kaden just grinned his amusement. "You know, we got some experience with bodies," he said. "Maybe even as much as you." His cell phone chimed, and he glanced at it, then nodded at Delveckio and stood. "You're not our partner. You're not a cop. You're a fucking writer. And, according to your *first* verdict, a killer. When we require your help, we'll question you."

As they gave me their backs, blocking the mirror's view of me, I slid a handful of printouts from the table down into my lap. The move was purely, bizarrely instinctual.

Stealing evidence from an interrogation room in Parker Center. I was setting new standards for bad judgment.

Kaden paused at the door, his grand exit stymied, and came back for his photos, minus a few duplicates. He stepped into the hall beside Delveckio and nodded at one of their underlings, out of sight. "Get a full statement. Then kick him loose."

The door slammed shut, and I was alone with my reflection and crime-scene photos stuffed down my pants.

11

C hic dropped me off, nodding and touching the brim of his cap. "Will that be all, Miss Daisy?"

"You people are so well mannered." I hopped out.

My trash can had been upended beside the house, garbage strewn along the side run. My sneakers crackled across the bits of glass in the entry. Two nights home, two intrusions. In my head I replayed the groggy house search after I'd awakened with the cut on my foot. Had my assailant been in the house with me? Or had he already slipped away? Had he approached from the street or hiked up the slope? I examined the sliding glass door for smudges that I might have overlooked in the darkness, then walked out onto the deck and peered over the railing as if I could distinguish lightly trampled ivy from untrampled ivy. Back inside, I followed the washed-out blood footprints upstairs. The tape was of course missing from my newly cracked digital camcorder, a disappointment since I'd wanted to preserve for posterity my oh-shit face the instant before I'd been proned out by ninety-seven SWAT members. I guess future Danners would have to content themselves with late-night reruns of *Hunter Pray*.

In my office the cops had left the drawers open, files and bills crammed back out of place or tossed on the floor. My mound of unread mail had been re-sorted, and they'd helpfully opened the items I hadn't gotten to yet.

I took a steaming shower, the jets doing their best to blast Kasey Broach's pallid face from my memory. Her curled hands, like fleshy claws. Her exposed arms spotted with insect bites. What would she have thought if someone had pulled her aside in third grade, or tenth, and told her that someday she'd wind up dumped under a freeway in Rampart? I thought about my so-called tough morning compared to the morning her family was still having, and it became startlingly clear that I had little to bitch about. I thought about the hot water I could still feel, the air I could still breathe. About Chic and Angela and Preston. How I had the right to remain silent and the right to an attorney and a jury that intelligently weighed my culpability. I was alive. I was free. I was healthy. What I felt was not guilt—no, not that—but, oddly, gratitude. And the inkling that from gratitude, not from anger or even guilt, could I pull myself out of where I'd landed.

I toweled off. A Post-it note on my mirror, written in Chic's childish scrawl, quoted Eleanor Roosevelt: *You have to accept whatever comes, and the only important thing is that you meet it with courage and with the best that you have to give.* Chic had sent me home from my newcomers' meeting with it. It had fallen off and been retaped countless times.

Face everything. One day at a time. I could do that. I could do better than that.

The purloined crime-scene photos, rescued from my pants, sat on the counter beside my toothpaste tube. As I'd pointed out to Preston, I had no official leverage. But I had something in place of that, beyond my peculiar skill at thinking through mayhem, beyond my friends from various bizarre walks of life, beyond my list of contacts oddly suited for . . . well, this.

I had a story. Or at least the beginning of one.

But—as I'd asked myself last night—where to go from here? I stared at those pictures of Kasey Broach, dimpled from their illicit journey, and wanted to know why her corpse had intersected with my life. I clicked through my PalmPilot's consultants list, compiled over the course of Derek Chainer's career—Navy SEALs, cops, deputy marshals, assistant DAs, coroners, hard-boiled PIs, soft-boiled security guards, firemen, criminalists. Grabbing a pad from my night-stand drawer, I wrote down those who could bring relevant knowledge to bear. Beneath it I made a list of all the people who hated me or might want to do me harm. *The Bertrands. Genevieve's fictional lover. Kaden and Delveckio.* A thought interrupted the scribbling: I'd arrived in this unenviable position because I'd cut a corner. I'd cut plenty of other corners in my life. The question was, which ones could be catching up with me now?

The doorbell rang. In my towel I greeted the messenger from my lawyers' office, who bore my case files. Amazing the service a quarter mil will buy you.

The discovery process entitled me to the murder book LAPD had assembled in preparation for my trial—full insider evidence for Genevieve's case. I set it on the kitchen table, which wobbled its appreciation, and flipped through.

The inserts were familiar and foreign at the same time. They seemed from another phase of my life, though my final verdict had been handed down just the day before yesterday.

Dragging his considerable haunches across the deck, Gus paused to point his black marble eyes at me. He disappeared into the ivy an instant before a swooping hawk aborted its dive to land on the deck rail. One squirrel step ahead of the reaper.

You impact the plot. Or the plot impacts you.

I pulled one of my novels of suitable thickness from my vanity shelf and rammed it beneath the kitchen table to even out the legs. I dressed in sweatpants and a ripped T-shirt I'd had since college, picked up the trash that LAPD had left alongside the house, swept up the entry, taped over the shattered panes in the front door, and vacuumed up the broken glass.

I circled my desk, sat down, shoved the armrests of my chair out a click, grabbed a Bic pen and slid it behind my left ear. My notepad I placed to my left. I set the murder book to my right, beyond the mouse pad, and removed the lab records, police reports, investigative notes, and coroner's report and spaced them evenly across my desktop.

Dirk Chincleft ain't got shit on me.

I'd done the first wave of research. I knew the characters. I had a premise. I'd unearthed a few leads. So I pulled up to my desk and did the only damn thing I'd ever done passably.

I wrote.

I woke up with IVs taped to my arms, a feeding tube shoved through my nose, and my tongue pushed against my teeth, dead and thick as a sock. My mouth was hot and tasted of copper, and my molars felt loose, jogged in their beds from grinding. I blinked against the harsh light and squinted into a haze of face, too close for casual—a man straddling a backward chair, strong forearms overlapped, a sheet of paper drooping from one square fist. Another guy behind him, dressed the same—rumpled sport coat, loose tie offset from open collar, glint at the hip. Downgraded to bystander, a doctor stood by the door, ignoring the electronic blips and bleeps. I was in a hospital room.

With consciousness came pain.

12

I woke bright and early, with a renewed sense of purpose. My home telephone line was still dead, so I retrieved my cell from the office. I called the coroner's office, talked to a clerk I'd paid in the past to smuggle me sample reports, and asked him if he could get me the Broach autopsy.

He said, "You're a murderer. Fuck off and don't ever call me again." Then he hung up.

I went downstairs, made a $138 cup of espresso, and toasted Gus on the back deck. "You and me, we're just players in this crazy game called life."

Gus, a discerning critic, scurried up the Mexican fan palm at the edge of the lawn.

I called a DNA analyst I knew in the medical examiner's office. She didn't take my call, though I heard her stage-whispered rebuff through the admin assistant's imperfect clasp over the mouthpiece.

My first manuscript had received seventeen rejections before a sale. I figured the odds here to be slightly better. I returned to the murder book and rechecked all the names of cops, criminalists, coroners, and clerks, even deciphering the scrawled signatures at the bottoms of the chain-of-custody forms. The only familiar name was the one I'd started with. Aside from the detectives, Lloyd Wagner would know Genevieve's case better than anyone, having handled everything from recovering my voice-mail messages to matching the knife with the wound. And he'd processed Kasey Broach's body as well. Given our rapport, I hoped that if I could talk to him for a few minutes, I might convince him to give me a little of his time.

I got his voice mail at the lab and on his cell and his answering machine at home. Given that he'd reported my last message to the detectives, I didn't want to leave another. I closed the phone, rubbed my temples, drank another cup of espresso to wash down my Dilantin.

If I couldn't get someone inside the case, I could at least try for someone with an inside track to the case. Cal Unger, my main consultant when it came to matters Chainer, was a divisional detective out of the West L.A. Station. His job had none of the glamour—if such a word can be used in this context—of the cases hooked by the Robbery-Homicide Division downtown. RHD detectives pulled serial killers, bank robbers, and media-intensive cases like mine. They had citywide jurisdiction, better resources, and sharper suits. Cal—a Coors man all the way—had closed some key divisional cases and had been bucking for a promotion to RHD for a while now. It was not lost on me that of the myriad hours he'd given me over the past few years, most of them had been spent talking about Robbery-Homicide.

Cal and I had an unspoken agreement: He wouldn't stiff-arm my questions, and I wouldn't write an unflattering portrait of someone closely resembling him. So he indulged me, and I respected his talent and toughness, and nothing had yet turned up in print to make LAPD's public-information officer put a boot up his ass. There was an undercurrent of tension, to be sure. Cal always squeezed a little too hard when demonstrating a choke hold on me, and he was certain to evince a certain veiled disdain for my job, stemming from, I guessed, the fact that we both knew that if he was really hard-core, like Bill Kaden, he wouldn't be talking to a writer or partaking vicariously of a fictional RHD detective's exploits. Cal fell into that camp of cop consultants who were generous with their time yet continually decried entertainment bullshit, how this dumb-ass novelist had called a revolver a pistol and this sellout TV actor had referred to his Glock .357 Magnum. They'd bust my balls in the squad room, and I'd smile and nod along, knowing that once the others weren't around, once we were alone in the car heading to lunch or driving a patrol, they would clear their throats sheepishly and pitch me a script idea, something about burned-out cops and missing little white girls or even, sometimes, about the bad-ass power of Jesus.

Despite all this—or perhaps because of it—I liked and respected Cal. He was handsome and well proportioned and could wear a pair of sunglasses like Eastwood wears a scowl. Some people exude coolness, and Cal was one of them. Like Lenny Kravitz or Bono, whom you could listen to with impunity anywhere, in any company. A hard-to-find quality. No matter how much you might secretly enjoy Kelly Clarkson, you still roll your windows up at the stoplight when she's on your radio. Not Cal, though. Cal was Bono. You'd never have to roll your windows up on Cal.

I called his desk. Voice mail. Tried his cell phone. He picked up mid-order: "And a double-double, no onions." And then, at full volume, "Unger."

I hung up. He was where we often met for lunch—In-N-Out Burger in Westwood.

I glanced at the clock: 10:32 A.M. Getting an early start on his caloric intake. His shift had probably begun at seven, taking a report from a hysterical Bel Air divorcée about a stolen tanning bed. Big black market in those, I'd heard.

I shot down Roscomare into Westwood and found Cal sitting at one of the brightly colored tables. A line of palm-tree tiles decorated the wall at his back. His partner, a young cop I didn't recognize, picked at some fries. Not In-N-Out's strong suit, fries.

Cal's gaze swept over me and registered nothing. I introduced myself to the new kid—Sam Pellicano—and looked over at Cal, who still had not spoken. "I'm sure you've heard about my case," I said. "Things aren't what they seem. There's another story here, and I'm trying to get to the bottom of it. I'd really appreciate your help."

Cal wiped the space on the table in front of him, though he'd left behind no crumbs. "Here's how it went down," he said. "You knew the captain's cousin because you hooked him up with an agent once. Captain put you in touch with the PIO. The call went around—who's gonna get stuck with this one? We curse L.A. I get hosed because Captain's pissed that his niece has a crush on me. The PIO tells me to be nice, let you swing from my ears now and then. I let you pretend you know a thing or two because you use the right forensic terminology and you've got a few cop buddies who hang out with you for your money and your bullshit. I take you on ride-alongs. I laugh at your jokes. You pick up the tab at lunch, take me to the occasional movie screening. You got a house in the hills with a nice deck to smoke a cigar on. That's why I put up with you."

Cal slid on his sunglasses in preparation for leaving. My reflections in the mirror lenses looked chagrined and foolish.

"You're a murderer now," Cal said. "Which means that I don't have to pretend to like you anymore. Or help you." He slid out of the booth, and I had to step back so he could stand. Sam looked impressed, like this was the coolest thing he'd witnessed in his whole fifteen years.

"I think guys like you are exploitive bastards," Cal continued. "You dream up terrorist cells and serial killers, and you feed off real people's fears and live large doing it. Doesn't enough shit go wrong in the world without you glorifying it? You played around in the dark, and you don't like what you came out with. No concern of mine. Not anymore."

"Okay," I said. "Done being morally superior in front of the new kid?"

"For the moment."

"Then we'll just pretend we both forgot your one-hour-drama concept you told me about. The one with the detective who works too many overtimes tracking the—wasn't it the Red Glove Killer?—and his wife just don't understand?"

Cal pushed past me, knocking my shoulder. Sam looked concerned, unsure whether to step up on me with some tough-guy face time or scurry after the scoutmaster.

"The boys at RHD are too busy asserting their own superiority to take a fresh look at these murders," I said after him.

Cal pivoted, mouth jerked left in a scowl. "Kaden and Delveckio? Boy, I'd sure love to show up those fancy detectives from Homicide Special. If only I had a crazy novelist to give me an in."

Sarcasm aside, he'd been following the case, as I'd bet he had.

I withdrew the pages I'd rolled and stuffed into my back pocket and held them out. "This is the case to date. From *my* perspective. If you were smart and ambitious, you'd realize you have an exclusive line into a major investigation."

"I'm neither." But he was staring at the sheaf of paper a bit too hungrily for someone who'd just eaten a double-double.

"Take it anyway. It's only twelve chapters. You can read it in the bubble bath. I'm gonna come bother you in a while for something or something else and you'd best have done your homework so when we're smoking cigars on my nice deck you can look sufficiently foolish about all the conclusions you jumped to."

I swung the rolled pages so they tapped Sam in the chest, and, looking confused, he took them. I walked out before he could throw them at me.

13

I leaned back in my chair and put my feet up on my desk, bleary-eyed from focusing on court transcript pages, indecipherable signatures on evidence reports, and grainy newspaper photographs of yours truly. My focus remained jumpy, half on the page, half in my head, an agitation of unfinished thoughts. It was only a few minutes past five, but already the sun had dipped below the row of palms cresting the west canyon ridge. Backlit fronds, even after my twenty years in L.A., made me pause with admiration.

Imports like the rest of us, palms had been brought to Los Angeles centuries ago by Spanish missionaries. I'd read that they were dying out here, the latest wave nearing the ends of their hundred-year life spans. Local bureaucracies had determined that broad-canopy trees better fought auto emissions. Vegas casinos had driven prices beyond municipal reach. Falling fronds bugged the yuppies, scratched up their MINI Coopers. Tree-trimmer saws spread deadly fungi. But despite it all, the palms were hanging on. With their discreet roots and flexible trunks, they're survivors. They don't come down in storms. They bow with the wind. They crawl along shady ground before goosenecking north into sunlight. They're scrappy and tenacious and beautiful and useless, like most anything that survives in Los Angeles. I hoped they'd endure. Imagining L.A. without palm trees was like picturing a lion without fur.

I tried the lab for the fifth time, and miraculously Lloyd picked up. After I said hello, his voice got tight. "You can't call me. Especially here."

"I've been looking into a few things. About the Broach case. I need to talk."

A pause indicated I'd piqued his curiosity. "Don't come here."

"After work?"

"Janice isn't doing so hot."

"I'm sorry to hear things are bad."

I could hear him breathing into the receiver, and then he said, quietly, "Thank you."

"I'm sure you don't need any more on your plate, but I would really appreciate a few minutes of your time. Can I make it easier? I'll come to you, pick up dinner, whatever."

I heard some muttering in the background. Then Lloyd's voice changed and he said to me, "Yeah, okay, Freddy. I'll get on it tomorrow. I was just leaving." Then he hung up.

I swung by Henry's Tacos en route to Lloyd's house in North Hollywood, then stopped at a liquor store and picked up a bottle of Bacardi 8, his favorite, and a two-liter of Coke. He lived off a dead-end street threading behind an overgrown park, in a big old Valley house with build-ons, rambling halls, and a barn gate guarding a gravel driveway. I slipped the rusty latch and headed down the unlit drive. The house was rotated away from the street, affording from within a good view of the park but making it inhospitable, offering up only the seemingly private kitchen door.

Lloyd was in the detached garage just past the house, fussing over the equipment in the rear of his van. Floor-to-ceiling industrial shelves crowded the van and a backed-in car hibernating beneath a black cover. I approached, and he started at my greeting. The van, as always, was crammed with endless equipment and oddities. Fingerprint tape lifts. Garden loppers for cutting ribs. Colored dental stone for casting impressions of shoe prints. I'd once spent a morning driving around with him while he'd collected seventeen brands of motor oil, trying to match a stain left where a getaway car had idled.

He was stuffing various vials and pill bottles into a knapsack, and he paused wearily at my approach. "She's on more pain meds than I can keep track of," he said, as if continuing a conversation.

"Thanks for seeing me, Lloyd. With everything you have going on."

The van's rear door, which rested heavily against the sleeping car, whined when he swung it shut. I followed him in. I'd been here before, picking him up, dropping off manuscripts, but this was my first time inside. The house was dark, a few lamps illuminating splotches of kitchen and family room. Dishes overrunning the sink, clean plates and bowls stacked on the counters as if no one had the energy to lift them into the cabinets. A swirl of crocheted blankets on the couch, bed pillows mixed with the cushions. The air felt humid from recent cooking. A portly woman sat in an armchair, watching a Spanish talk show and sipping a cup of tea.

"Hullo, Meester Wagner."

"How'd she do today?"

"She do fine. She do jess fine."

Lloyd handed her a roll of bills, and the woman rinsed out her mug in the sink, nodded warmly, and plodded out the door. There was no car out front and no bus stop for blocks.

Looking around made clear why Lloyd had blown off the first message I'd left him. With everything he was contending with, the last thing he needed was a maybe-psychotic murderer dropping by.

"I'm sorry for the mess. Janice is an only child, both parents passed. We don't get much help." Lloyd lowered his head, pausing as if to catch his breath. "Make yourself at home. I'll be right back."

He squared himself toward the hall but remained frozen for a moment, gathering his will. At the end of the long, dark corridor, a seam of light showed beneath a doorway. Lloyd shrugged the knapsack strap up into place and headed toward it.

I cleared a space on the kitchen table and unpacked the food. A fall of light as the door down the hall opened, and I heard murmuring and the soothing rush of medical equipment before the sounds were cut off by the closing door. I got a few glasses from the counter, filled mine with water. A toothbrush leaned from a cup by the dish-soap dispenser. By the door a lone Birkenstock stood out from a mound of shoes, bearing the stain of a woman's foot, a simple image I found distressing. I thought about the second car out in the garage, unused. Lloyd probably didn't have the heart to sell it yet.

There were several TV trays on the floor by the couch, and I cleared them to the kitchen, washed them off, loaded one with tacos. I folded the blankets on the couch, stacked the pillows, and poured Lloyd a drink. Pictures of him and Janice were everywhere—hung on the walls, magnetized to the refrigerator, framed atop bookcases. Wedding portraits with awkward Lloyd, all big ears and blond curly hair, clinging to Janice's arm as if he still couldn't believe he'd landed her. Janice smiling from a lime green Gremlin, her feathered hair poofing beyond the frame. The standard fifteen-year anniversary shot, arms around shoulders, before the Eiffel Tower. I'd never met Janice, but I noted with some sadness that the most recent picture of Lloyd was at least five years old. She'd been dying since I'd met him.

I turned off the TV and sat in the reading chair, listening to the house creak, imagining Lloyd's split life, divided between the couch and the bedroom. How he probably stayed out here to breathe a little easier. How he'd shored himself up to make that walk to see his wife. How he probably spent his nights creeping from this end of the house to that seam of light.

Staring down the dark hall, I realized that I feared, greatly feared, what that bedroom might look like.

Fear of death. It's what we share. We ward it off in ineffectual ways, practice brushing against it, swimmers in dark waters. The obsessive bodybuilder. The weekend stunt pilot. The pool-hall slut. We drink too much. We put off surgeries. We whistle past old folks' homes. When it comes down to it, we all fear what's behind that door at the end of the corridor. That's why I write dark little potboilers. To pretend I'm poking at death with a stick. That's why people read them on subway trains and airplanes and think they're facing their deepest and darkest.

The seam in my head, the seam in Genevieve's lovely pale skin, the seam beneath that door. All cracks in what we think we're holding together. I'd never felt so attuned to the vulnerability around me, the chinks and fissures. They're everywhere. You just have to pause. And look.

The hall lightened briefly, and then I heard Lloyd's approach. I handed him his drink. He set down his knapsack, sank into the couch, took a gulp, and emitted a sigh. "Thanks, Drew. This is nice."

"Tacos and Bacardi. Old family recipe. How's Janice?"

He waved me off. "It's back. Other breast now. Third time through, make or break."

"Where's she being seen?"

"Cedars."

"I've heard they have a great onc team." The longer my remark hung in the air, the more hollow it seemed.

The glow of the lamps blacked out the nice view from the back windows. Lloyd finished his drink and said, "Pour you one?"

"I'm still on water."

"Oh, yeah." He filled his glass again, unwrapped a taco, took a bite, and set it down. "I'm real sorry for what you've been through, Drew, but I'm not allowed to talk to you. You're a suspect."

"I haven't been charged. I produced proof that I had nothing to do with—"

"I heard."

"Look, Kaden and Delveckio already revealed a fair amount to me. I just want to talk through what I already know. We can start with Genevieve, even. I have the murder book, the trial's over. No way for you to misstep there."

Halfway through his second rum and Coke, Lloyd blinked heavily, suggesting a nod. "Don't you remember it all from the trial?"

"It's blurry. I'd like to hear it again from you."

There was an awkward pause, and then Lloyd said, "Pretty damning, Drew."

"You thought I was going away for it?"

"I couldn't imagine a jury convicting you with a brain tumor in a jar, but the *evidence* . . ." His long fingers gripped the mouth of his glass, tilting the dark liquid beneath. He contemplated the rum mix. I knew how that silent conversation went.

I said, "Your report showed that Genevieve had no defensive wounds, no skin beneath her nails."

"Katherine Harriman argued that's because she knew you."

"But Katherine Harriman, unlike me, didn't know Genevieve. Genevieve was tough to surprise, especially if she was up out of bed with an intruder in her bedroom. She wouldn't be one to embrace the knife. If she'd seen the blade, she'd have gone down clawing and biting."

"It was a forceful thrust. Death would have been pretty much instantaneous."

"Prints on the knife?"

"Besides Genevieve's and her kid sister's? Just yours."

"Suspect profile?"

"You know, the usual. Left-handed male, hundred eighty-five pounds, diabolical gleam in the eyes."

"Left-handed from the angle?"

He glanced at the watch on my right wrist. "Uh-huh. Slight slant."

"Male?"

"Power behind the stab."

"Body moved?"

"Yeah. A bunch." Another awkward pause. "By you. Your seizure started as a complex partial. Not the thrashing kind, more of a break in consciousness with automatisms—lip smacking, repetitive finger movement. People can walk around, even. Complex partial seizures have been used as a defense in shoplifting cases, though that's pushing it. But you would've been functional enough to manipulate Genevieve Bertrand's body. Until your seizure generalized into a grand mal."

"Would I have been able to stab her in that state? The complex partial?"

"Not likely. I agree with Harriman that your break probably occurred *after* the murder." He studied my face, then said softly, "I'm sorry, Drew."

I sat back, rubbed at the soreness in my eyes with the heels of my hands. "I had a dream my first night home. I was driving over to her house that night. In a frenzy. She kept a key under a plant pot on her porch. I cracked the clay saucer getting to it. When I woke up, I drove over to her place." Would I tell him the rest? Could I? Lloyd's house was so still I thought I could make out the faint sigh of hospital equipment from the other end. "The saucer was cracked. It wasn't cracked the last time I remember seeing it. I think I dreamed a piece of memory. I think I'm starting to put together fragments of what happened that night."

He frowned severely, taking this in. "What do you mean when you say you were in a frenzy?"

"I was sweating a lot. Feeling panicky."

"Do you recall any unusual smell?"

The band of skin at the back of my neck went cold. My voice tangled in my throat, so I nodded.

"Bitter? Like burning rubber?" Lloyd didn't have to wait for an answer; he could read my face. "It's called an olfactory aura. They often occur just before seizures."

I remembered hearing about auras, but I hadn't put the information together with my dream. "Can I ask you about something else?"

"The question is, can I answer?"

"I want to know about sevoflurane," I said.

Lloyd pulled on his glasses, as if they helped him think better, and said cautiously, "What about it?"

"You found traces in Kasey Broach's bloodstream."

"Kaden and Delveckio revealed that to you?"

I couldn't tell if he was shocked or angry. "The night of the dream, when I woke up, I was really groggy and I had blurred vision. I also had a cut on my foot—I think someone might have knocked me out and stolen blood to frame me."

Lloyd let out an unamused cough of a laugh. "Drew—"

"Just hear me out, Lloyd. I did some research on sevoflurane today. It's a perfect drug for that. Easy to inhale, quickly induces anesthesia, nonpungent odor. It leaves the bloodstream quickly, so it's hard to test for. No strong aftereffects, so I wouldn't know I'd been drugged."

"Did you know?"

"Well, the killer had a running start, because I mostly figured I was insane to begin with. But here's the thing—sevoflurane also produces amnesia."

"So you're thinking . . ."

"I'm thinking the gas dumped me back into the same memory wasteland of brainspace as my tumor did. It helped me retrieve part of that night." My voice was loud, excited. Lloyd started to say something, but I held up my hand. "I found out sevoflurane also gives a 'good duration of action,' but I think I woke up early. I might have seen the intruder in the street in front of my house, which means I came to sooner than he wanted. I'm wondering why. Maybe I have a higher tolerance from my checkered past."

"It would be the opposite, actually. If there's liver damage, it would make you *more* sensitive to sevoflurane. But you're stacking an awful lot of assumptions here. Even your memory loss, to begin with—you can't know what caused it. The tumor? The surgery? The anesthesia?"

I mused on this a moment. But there were too many moving parts to get a handle on now. "How's it administered? Sevoflurane?"

Lloyd shifted on the sofa, swirled his drink around. "Face mask."

"I figured. So maybe I woke up because it was imperfectly administered. Maybe at my house the *killer* wore an oxygen mask and let the gas loose in my bedroom, near my face, while I slept." I snapped my fingers, leaning forward. "Remember, there were signs of a struggle in Kasey Broach's bedroom."

"Kaden and Delveckio told you that, too?"

"Broach would've woken up when the killer pressed the mask over her face, but he figured he was strong enough to hold her down until the gas took effect. She's a petite woman, looks—what?—a buck ten?"

"A hundred and thirteen pounds," Lloyd said quietly.

"Right. But I doubt he'd want to take his chances waking me up by pressing a mask over my face. So he released the gas into the air while I was sleeping."

"Do you have any proof you can hang this theory on?"

"Not a scrap. Maybe this points to someone with medical expertise. Is it hard to get? Sevoflurane?"

"It's controlled, but not like an opiate."

"Can you tell from Kasey Broach's blood level how *long* she was kept unconscious?"

"Nearly impossible to determine."

"Can you tell *when* my DNA got on her body? Or the plastic drop cloth?"

"There's no way to put an age on DNA. Only that it was there during analysis." Lloyd held up his hands, thin fingers spread. "Let's hold on a minute. Slow down. You're not working off facts—"

"How else did my DNA get on Kasey Broach's body?"

"For the record, we didn't get you on DNA. This isn't a TV show—we need at least forty-eight hours to DNA type. We did a traditional ABO. You're AB negative, which puts you with less than one percent of the population."

"They SWAT-raided me off *that*?"

He rooted in his knapsack and came out with a report, which he tossed at me irritably. "The hair follicle. I matched the cuticle and medulla with a known sample we had for you."

"How about these?" I pointed at four samples farther down the page. "These don't match."

"That's because one's mine and two are from Ted McGraw, who helped me examine the body." He studied my expression and shook his head. "A simple contamination during processing, happens all the time. Don't go putting poor Ted in the conservatory with the candlestick."

"How about the fourth hair?"

"Unidentified. No match in the databases. We're holding it, but it's probably nothing. Frankly, I'm surprised we didn't pick up more strays, the way the wind was blowing."

"So one hair for me, one for Mr. Mystery. But *my* door gets the battering ram."

"Between your hair, the blood-type match, and the similarities to Bertrand's body, Kaden and Delveckio were ready to make a move on you. At this stage you're the only link between the victims." Lloyd's gaze was steady. Not judgmental, not accusatory. Just steady. "The blood DNA comes back tomorrow. I wouldn't hold your breath that it'll exonerate you."

"It *could* be someone inside. Kaden and Delveckio said the killer posed the body like Genevieve's, in ways that weren't released to the press. And a cop—or detective—might want me to go down for Genevieve's killing."

Lloyd looked at me as if I were paranoid, which I was. "So badly that they'd murder an innocent girl? Come on, Drew. Crime-scene photos leak." He leaned over and snatched the paper back from me. "Unlike criminalist reports. Plus, given the trial, there were a lot of lawyers and reporters poking around the Bertrand case files. The specifics were hardly kept as state secrets. Kaden and Delveckio were probably just trying to rattle you."

The crime-scene photos I'd stolen reinforced Lloyd's point. Kaden had grown touchy when I'd pushed for more information on what they'd gotten off the body. *Ah, here it is: None of your fucking business.*

I led him a bit with my next question. "What about the other key piece of evidence?"

"The rope? It's an all-cotton brand used for bondage. Probably bought at an erotic specialty store."

"Why tie rope around the ankles but tape the wrists?"

"Easier to transport a body. Easier to throw it out a vehicle. No limbs flapping around."

"No, I mean, why use different restraints on the same body?"

"You ever bind someone's wrists with rope?"

"No. Have you?"

He guffawed—I'd forgotten about his great, unruly laugh. "No. But it's difficult. You can squirm your hands free easier than you can your feet."

"So why not use electrical tape on both the wrists and ankles?"

"I don't have an answer for you, Drew. But we're looking into it. This and more." He set down his glass and yawned. I could only imagine his exhaustion—working long days, caring for his wife every spare waking hour. He walked me to the door. "It goes without saying that you can't mention to anyone—and I mean *anyone*—that I saw you today."

"I won't. And don't worry—you didn't tell me anything that hasn't already been disclosed to me." I felt like a heel. This was a guy who, when asked to confirm an autopsy detail for me, would fax me a two-page essay. Now he'd stepped away from work and left his dying wife to help me, and I'd manipulated him, then lied about it. Not the first time I'd lied in pursuit of something I wanted, but I told myself I wouldn't let it come back to bite him in the ass. We shook hands, and I said, "I'm very appreciative that you took the time to talk with me. I know you're on overload."

He nodded, pausing in the doorway while I walked up the gravel drive. He didn't seem eager to head back down that hall. I got to the gate and turned around, and there he was, still silhouetted against the faint light from the kitchen.

"Leave it alone, Drew," he called after me. "This isn't one of your books."

I raised a hand and slipped through onto the street.

The hell it isn't.

14

I stared again at my latest chapter, now pockmarked with Preston's notes.

Someone was out to get me. Someone had broken in to my house, drugged me while I slept, stolen my blood, and dripped it onto a corpse. Creeped out, I rose from bed and moved room to room, inspecting the doors and windows. ~~All secure.~~ Then I checked the garage, the closets, behind sofas and under beds.

~~I was alone in the house.~~

I'd covered over the shattered panes in the front door with acrylic packing tape. Though guarded by shards and tape, the apertures ~~may~~ might have been big enough for someone to reach through to the dead bolt a few feet below. Before returning upstairs, I layered over the windows yet again, figuring that if I left my bedroom door open, I'd be able to hear the tape being peeled back by an intruder.

I lay atop my sheets, sweating despite the January chill, images and conversation snippets crowding my mind. The crime-scene photos, spread across the interrogation table like an opulent feast. Kaden and Delveckio freezing me out of the investigation. *We don't have anything we can disclose at this point in time.* Cal's offering me only a denunciation and my own image

Use something here that's not a cliché.

Why not hammer a piece of wood across the holes? We're talking about your life—let's not be fastidious about the architecture.

I went to one of those meager, inopulent feasts just last week. It pisses me off that they call them feasts, y'know?

Why did you go to Cal without any concrete goal? Go to people when they're required for something—as with Lloyd—or else the plot drags. And you'll unnecessarily deplete human resources you may need later.

Point in time? Why must these guys talk like Dragnet? Their self-important language is embarrassing, since the narrator seems not to notice it.

reflected back from his mirrored lenses. Preston's in-
~~cessant heckling.~~ ^*incisive observations*^ A writer's job, perhaps more than
any other, is not to be afraid of possibilities. What
was I afraid of? What was I still not considering?

Perhaps that there were more variables in play
than I cared to look at. The fact that I hadn't killed
Kasey Broach hardly retroproved that I was blameless
in Genevieve's death. Though I could count few people
I knew who would have been willing and able to kill
another woman and frame me for murder, perhaps an
unhinged member of the TV-watching public—a crusad-
ing vigilante, a pushed-too-far militiaman obsessed
with society's deterioration, an angry husband who'd
lost his wife to a similar crime—had gone after me,
seeking vengeance.

Someone was out to get me. And now I was out to get
him.

You're focusing on yourself because you've heard the movie-trailer voice-over tell you "This time it's personal" about a thousand times. Open yourself up to more narrative possibilities. This might center on you without being about you. Life is fucked up enough—you generally don't need diabolical plots. They just happen. Factor in the 310 area code, you got more coincidences than a Dickens plot.

I glanced up from the red-marked pages. Preston was sprawled
on my sectional, editing some other victim and looking characteris-
tically pleased with himself.

"I'm in the 818 area code, actually. Just over the crest."

Preston's eyes flicked over to me. "I was giving you the benefit of
the doubt." He finished his morning cup of rum, leaving it on the
coffee table for the housekeeper I could no longer afford. He fanned
himself dramatically with the manuscript pages, then cast them
aside. "It's hot in here."

"You're menopausal."

He rose, took my pages from my hands, and flipped through them,
failing to suppress a chuckle at one of his edits. He slapped the sheaf

against an open palm. "There's gotta be a story that incorporates all these elements gracefully. We need a development meeting." He glanced at his watch. "I have a lunch reservation for three at Spago."

"Three?"

"I thought you might invite Cal Unger. We require him for brainstorming."

"You just wrote not to bother him unless I have a—and I quote—'concrete goal.'"

"But this is social."

Preston had met Cal once at the book-launch party for my third Chainer novel.

"He's not gay, Preston."

"Of course not. Gay is a level of self- and political awareness. Which he lacks. He's just got tendencies."

Preston thinks everybody has. Which makes sense, since he works in publishing and splits his time between the Village and West Hollywood. When we would go out, we frequented West Hollywood restaurants, after which he'd drag me to one of those young West Hollywood plays by a nouveau–West Hollywood playwright featuring a troubled gay English-major protagonist where all the straight characters—especially the football players—wound up being gay after all, harboring secret, shameful crushes on our fragile yet intrepid hero.

"Whatever tendencies he's got, Herr Brokeback, they don't tend in your direction," I pressed. "I understand that your parents' naming you Preston Ashley Mills pretty much sealed your deal in one fell swoop, but, nature or nurture aside, the guy is named Cal Unger. I'd say that cuts the odds considerably that he smokes pole. Not to mention the fact that I need to wait for a more graceful reestablishment of diplomatic ties. I'll invite Chic instead."

"The *ballplayer*?" This last word he lent an intonation generally reserved for "chlamydia."

Preston had also met Chic at the book-launch party for my third Chainer novel.

Despite his objections, he headed for the phone. "I'll tell them we'll be running late. And I'll have them install a salt lick at the booth." He picked up the cordless. Stared at it.

"They're too busy providing excellent service to hook up my phone. Which apparently certain editors responsible for my mail didn't bother paying—"

Disrupting the late-morning air, sailing over my fence, came sounds of the young trumpeter at practice.

I've got a CRUSH on YOU, sweetie-PIE.

Preston's eyebrows met. "The hell is that?"

"Gershwin, I think."

All the DAY and NIGHTtime, hear me SIGH.

Preston despaired. "We'll call from the car."

The woman with the custom license-plate frame in the Jag ahead of us had one thing to tell the world, and that was that she went zero to bitch in 2.7 seconds. We cruised down Cañon, passing several hundred thousand dollars' worth of Bavarian engineering, long-legged women with boxy shopping bags, palm trees studded with rope lights. The rope lights served two purposes at once: They were pretty at night, and they were slick, slick being significant in that if squirrels tried to scale the trunks to nest in the fronds, they'd slip and crack their little squirrel skulls on the pavement below. That union of aesthetics and ferocity, if nothing else, defines Beverly Hills. The five-hundred-dollar porcelain curios, the reservation-only boutiques, the bejeweled cat collars.

As we coasted along, Preston pointed to a prominent window display of my books at Dutton's. At least when a bookstore cashed in on my infamy, I got a cut.

L.A., for the most part, is in on the joke that is itself. It's superficial as hell, sure, but it also knows how to enjoy it, unlike those Des Moines moms who read celebrity rags on their way to church so they can tut-tut and shake their heads, or those Ivy Leaguers who'd never admit they enjoy *People* more than Proust but who, while waiting for the dentist to mend a scrape in their enamel, will sneak a peek at the glossies to check out this singer's weight gain or where this royal couple honeymooned. Here, superficiality is our business, and we all—*all*—believe we're in on the show.

Some visitors find L.A. an insider's city. The contrary is in fact true. Anyone can get access. The only catch is that you have to bring something interesting to the table. That's the ticket of entry. It doesn't have to be depth, or conversational skills, or even necessarily talent. You can be the best hairdresser and sit down at a mogul's table between a Hollywood madam and an opera director. If you're the best hedge-fund manager on your Bel-Air block but a bore, fuck off with a smile, pal. Go back to Manhattan and complain about how shallow L.A. is.

Shallow it is, but also captivating, if you can just hold on to your sense of humor. Every now and then, an earthquake will crack the city open, just to ensure that things stay interesting, or someone will threaten to blow up LAX, or raging fires will sweep through the West Valley and everyone will lionize firemen for a week. Santa Monica waters will turn toxic. A mercury scare will put everyone off sushi. Carbs will be vilified, or Pilates, or the caloric content of Jamba Juice.

Four cars backed up on the side of the parking ramp by the restaurant, wringing out a last few seconds of cell-phone reception. We valeted. Threading through the tables, we found Chic in the rear, arms spread across the back of the booth. "I just *love* me some smoked-salmon pizza."

Preston scowled at Chic's sarcasm, and we slid in on either side. I dropped the documents I'd assembled onto the tabletop.

Preston craned his neck toward the wall of etched glass that set off the kitchen. "I wonder if that Latin guy is our waiter."

"He's got a wedding ring," I said.

"Puh-*lease.*"

"He's eyeing the tits at eleven o'clock."

"Overcompensating."

"Before you start making the love that dare not speak its name, how 'bout we order?"

Chic glanced up uncomfortably from his menu. "Just so you know, I'm not gay or anything."

Preston aimed a withering look at him. "Honey, we wouldn't have you."

When it came time to order, Preston did his best with eye contact and inquiring about house favorites, but the waiter just gathered our menus uneasily and left.

Still unaccustomed to being in public after my media searing, I carefully glanced about. One table over, two guys in suits and another in sweatpants babbled about German financing and festival circuits. Beside them, women either too old or too rich to care if they were overheard discussed estrogen supplements. A harried woman dined with kids who, because of their scowls and designer jeans, were apparently more worldly than she was. Directly across from us, a well-dressed guy hunched over his plate, and then his entire party peeked over at me not as inconspicuously as their manner suggested they'd intended. I shifted uncomfortably.

Chic clued in to the situation first, of course, and smiled at me gently. "This, too, shall pass."

Preston said, "Let's get down to story."

While we ate our upmarket appetizers, I recapped the latest advancements. As usual, I'd stored a Bic pen behind my ear for taking notes, but I mostly doodled.

When I was done, Preston cleared his throat. "Get off the serial-killer kick. They're not so compelling."

"Just because they don't pique your interest doesn't mean we're not dealing with one. We have two bodies with a similar MO."

"As you pointed out to Detective Point-in-Time, there are noteworthy differences."

"Or"—sometimes, with Preston, one did best to forge ahead—"I could've become the poster boy for a copycat killer, who then elected to frame me."

"Which would mean that you *did* murder Genevieve."

The baldness of Preston's remark caught me off guard. I felt an almost gravitational pull toward defensiveness, toward denial of both kinds. The shrewdly decorated shrimp plate suddenly looked meaty and unappetizing.

"You can't know," Preston offered. "Not yet."

"Maybe I should take sevoflurane again and find out."

Preston stirred his drink lazily with a straw. "We don't even know for sure that you've taken sevoflurane *once*, Drew. I don't think we need to be breaking in to medical offices on the slim chance that if you inhale it again, it'll put you back into the September twenty-third part of your brain."

Chic said, "Frame or no frame, fastest way to get to the bottom of this is to figure out the connection between the victims, or between them and you. The boring, unobvious shit you won't be able to uncover."

"Do I hire a private detective?"

Chic shook his head, disappointed as usual, at my inability to get things done correctly. "I know a hacker, database guy. Phone bills, gas bills, airline tickets—all that shit. Half of it's online for a price, and the half that ain't . . . well, let's just say that won't stop him. He tracks down people who skip on alimony."

"Deadbeat dads?"

"Don't be sexist, Drew-Drew. I used him last to find a woman who moved up and out on one of my nephews. He can cross-reference like a muthafucker comin' up with an alibi. Also, we need a list of all the people you've pissed off."

I removed the list I'd been working on, and we batted around a few more names, but I couldn't find any that seemed believable murderers, or even break-in artists. My neurologist, driven mad by the fallout from my noncompliance? Katherine Harriman's old man, disgraced on kielbasa-and-Bulls night, back to administer Chi-town justice? Adeline Bertrand in a ninja suit?

Finally Chic got fed up with my lack of known lethal adversaries and jumped topics. "The second body," he said. "Why rope on the ankles, tape on the wrists?"

"Tape is easier on wrists. Rope can be tricky." Preston averted his eyes, sipped his drink. "You said the cotton rope is a specialty bondage item. We could look into which places stock it around L.A."

"Let the police do the procedural shit," Chic said. "That's what they're good at."

"What are we good at?" I asked.

A long pause. "Not the procedural shit."

"I think the rope's a red herring," I said. "I think he used it to throw investigators off the trail."

The people across from us whispered a bit more, and then finally the well-dressed man stood and headed toward me. Chic said, "Handle it with a smile."

The man approached. "You're Andrew Danner, aren't you? I just wanted to let you know I'm sorry for what you went through. I don't know much about it, but I think you caught a bum break."

"Thanks very much."

We shook hands. Before leaving, he glanced over at Chic. "Nice hands, Bales, ya donkey."

He returned to his table. Preston and I got busy eating to hide our smiles as Chic nodded, egging us on. Our main courses arrived, and, my humor and appetite back, I took a few moments to indulge in my agnolotti with mascarpone. When I looked up, Chic was studying the crime-scene photos. The top one, presumably the first taken, showed Kasey Broach in peaceful repose. With no sign yet of cop or criminalist intrusion, her body seemed dropped into the composition by an ambitious graphic designer. Her bare flesh and the white film of bird shit on the hood of the abandoned car were the only smears of light in the dark scene.

Chic said, "Where'd you get these?"

I'd neglected to mention them when he'd picked me up from Parker. I told him I stole them from the interrogation room.

He whistled his admiration, then turned one print sideways, appraising the graffiti artist's terminated composition on the ramp's underbelly. "That's some serious spray work."

Preston said, "Let's focus on the body."

Chic slid a second photo out from the sheaf, this one showing a number of officers standing around or squatting by the chain-link. A hexagon outlined with police tape now staked off the corpse. Feathers dusted the spray-painted concrete, stuck to the ramp. The camera flash had brought out the glitter of shattered beer bottles.

"Lookie here," Chic said. "Our first real lead."

Preston, peering over Chic's shoulder, shrugged.

"It tells a story, Story Man, you just ain't reading it."

I seized the photo and scrutinized it. "I don't see it."

Chic slid out from the booth, bringing me with him. "Then lemme show you."

15

There was no chalk outline, no bloodstain, no sad tendrils of crime-scene tape to commemorate the body that had been here less than seventy-two hours before. Just the crumbling asphalt, the beat-down coupe, and me and Chic. Vehicles hummed overhead. The ground smelled of urine and beer. The sun was in its descent, and Rampart was no place to get caught after dark. Chic spread his arms wide.

"Wah-*lah.*"

"Wah-lah *what*?"

Chic pointed at the cloud of elaborate spray paint brightening the bottom of the freeway ramp. The artist had stretched the proportion of the piece to fit the rising concrete so that when viewed straight on it looked as if it were in normal perspective. Even so, I wasn't sure what it was. Explosions and protuberances and bubble letters, all impressively three-dimensionalized. The piece had been left unfinished, the right half fading off into gray concrete. Feathers stuck to the lower fringe, dried into the paint.

"Oh," I said. "*Oh.*"

I followed Chic over a trampled section of chain-link.

"Cops got here in a hurry, right?" he asked. "And the criminalist?"

"That's what I was told. Nearby having a burrito."

"Patrolmen see the body. Criminalist shoots the picture, captures how it is before everyone fucks up the evidence, all that. Then what's the first thing they do?"

"Secure the scene."

"Secure the scene. Which means they check this here shadow." He ducked into the dark triangular recess where the ramp met ground. An outburst of pigeons, spooked from their nighttime roosts atop the supporting beams, disrupted the relative quiet. Chic stumbled back toward me, waving his arms, pigeons squawking around his head. He'd gotten more than he'd bargained for. His retreat detracted from the solemnity of his account, but he brushed himself off, picked something off his tongue, and continued, unfazed.

"Cops scared up the pigeons. The stray feathers got stuck to the paint." Chic beckoned for the crime-scene photos and showed me the one that had captured Broach's body before the crime scene had been blocked off—no feathers yet in evidence. "Which means the paint was still wet. And *that* means"—a finger raised with academic emphasis—"the tagger was at work spraying the ramp that night when he was interrupted." He flicked his head at the painting's terminated edge. "What makes a tagger run? A car. What's the first car that showed up, scared him away?"

"The killer dumping the body."

Chic's wide grin broke across his face. "We got ourselves a maybe witness."

I stared at the coupe's hood, white with droppings. "The Case of the Telltale Bird Shit."

"In-fuckin'-deed."

"How do we locate the spray painter?"

Chic indicated the colorful work overhead. "You're looking at his signature, Colonel Sanders. That's what a tag *is*."

We'd fallen into familiar roles. Chic was one of my most useful rough-draft readers, adept at inlaying street logic to a character's motive or transforming a run of dialogue into alleyway patter. I watched him chewing his lip, another adviser turned accomplice.

He held his eyes on the graffiti an extra beat, as if committing it to memory, then said, "Lemme poke around on it, call some of my brothers."

Spread throughout Los Angeles were about twenty-seven of Chic's gold-incisored brothers, who appeared in various guises to fix a car, bartend at a party, unload a new flat-screen. Most, like him, were Philly transplants. A few he might actually have been related to.

The breeze swirled up debris, knocked from the beams during the pigeon eruption. I crouched over a fallen nest, larger than I would have thought. Inside was a ring of stiff plastic wrap, about twice the circumference of a beer holder, still boasting a Home Depot price sticker.

I no longer heard the whistle of the wind, the cooing of the displaced pigeons, the cars overhead. I no longer heard anything but the pounding of my heart.

It was wrapping for a roll of electrical tape.

16

The door swung open, and for a moment there was nothing but darkness, a curl of pale hand on the knob, and the incessant chirping of crickets. Then Lloyd stepped forward into the throw of light from the outdoor lamp and said, "The hell is this, Drew?"

"It's a *clue*." I held the to-go bag aloft. "Inside a doggie bag from Spago."

Unimpressed, Lloyd checked his watch. It was only six-thirty, but it was as dark as midnight, and I guessed he'd had a long day. His worse judgment got the better of him, and he said, "Wait here."

I stood on the porch for maybe five minutes while I heard him moving in the house, a soft, feminine voice answering his. Some shuffling, and then a door closed.

He opened the door again and beckoned me in. We sat in the same places, he on the sofa, I in the reading chair. The TV tray on the floor was still laden with tacos. Only one was unwrapped, missing the bite I'd seen him take. Down the hall, the same strip of yellow light glowed beneath the bedroom door. It was as if no time had elapsed since last night, as if no time ever elapsed in this house.

I caught him up on my Rampart adventure, ending with the electrical-tape wrapper I'd found in the fallen pigeon nest. His expression vacillated between shock, anger, and annoyed admiration.

"Jesus, you're really on this, aren't you?"

"Of course I am, Lloyd. Four months of jail time, a murder trial, and two dead women, one of whom I cared about quite a bit. The stakes are fairly personal here."

He eyed the restaurant bag, still unopened. "And what do you want from me?"

"I want you to dust it for prints."

"Look, Drew, offering you some facts is one thing. But running a print?"

"Tell me you're not curious."

"We don't even know it's our guy's. It could be trash that blew in from somewhere else. Or got picked up by a roaming pigeon."

"Could be."

"And what, the guy was so stupid he left a wrapper with his fingerprints lying around near the body?"

"The cops—or you—found a burnt plastic drop cloth in my trash can, maybe for lining a car trunk. Maybe he taped Broach inside his trunk, left the wrapper in there. It could've stuck to her body when he dumped her, then blown free."

But Lloyd wasn't to be dislodged from his objections. "And besides that, we've got no chain of custody for the evidence. There's nothing to keep a lawyer from saying you brought this in from somewhere else."

"I'm not just looking to put someone away." The comment hung self-righteously in the stale air.

"We'll need to if you want to exonerate yourself. Isn't that what you're driving at?"

"I just want to find out what happened"—I caught myself—"what's *happening.*"

His stare had not left the bag.

"Tell me you're not curious," I said again.

He clasped his hands, let out a sigh that originated from somewhere deep inside him. "I'm curious."

"Remember when you lifted my DNA from my toothbrush to

show me how it worked? What's the difference here?" I opened the bag and tilted it so he could look inside. "It's not like the cops found this evidence. It would've been lost anyway. I happened to find it lining a pigeon's nest."

"Pigeon nests are unlined. But they're big trash eaters, pigeons. It has a ridge of adhesive residue—there." He pulled the pen from behind my ear to point. "That can be sweet. The bird probably mistook it for food and brought it to its nest."

The range of his knowledge, as always, staggered me. He knew virtually everything's intersection with crime. How swollen the maggot. How rare the dry-cleaning mark. How ripe the blowfly egg in the mouth cavity.

"Why don't you just dust it?" I said. "No point in arguing if there's not even a print."

I'd finally handed him the rationale he was looking for. He went out to the van and returned with a laptop and a case that opened into shelves and levels, like a tackle box. Down on the carpet, he set to work and within minutes managed to raise a single print—a fragmentary ridge on the curved outside of the stiff wrapping, right beside the Home Depot price sticker. He sat back on his heels.

"Should have enough points for a match."

I couldn't tell if he sounded regretful or excited. Probably a combination.

I said nothing. Sometimes I actually know when to keep my mouth shut.

After a few moments of internal deliberation, he reached into his case and removed a tape lift, a clear adhesive strip the size of a small cell phone. He peeled it off its backing and applied it to the dusted area, then returned the strip to its backing, locking in the print in two dimensions. He disappeared into the rear of the house and returned with a digital camera. He shot the tape lift and uploaded the image into his laptop. When he angled the screen away from me so I couldn't see him input his password, I felt a surge of excitement. We were going to the fingerprint database.

I waited silently as he tapped away, pictures of him and Janice grinning back at me everywhere I looked. A wicked reversal on Dorian Gray—all that wellness preserved behind glass while the real thing languished in a back room.

Lloyd's eyebrows rose and quivered. I resisted the urge to ask, and finally he spun the laptop around. A booking photo stared woefully out at me, a guy with deep-set eyes, a thinning pate, and a square jaw. Richard Collins. His birth date put him at thirty-one, but he looked at least a decade older. He'd gone down on two possession charges, the last three years ago, but he had a clean record since.

My first to-the-investigative-moment glimpse of Genevieve's or Broach's possible killer. I was disappointed that Collins didn't look more formidable; he seemed like a workman who'd do a shitty job on your house and not care when you wouldn't pay him.

"Who's this guy to you?" Lloyd asked.

I'd been asking myself the same question. Had my path crossed Richard Collins's during my days of wine and roses? Had I dated his sister? Elbowed him aside in a cocktail lounge?

"I don't know. I don't recognize him."

"Well, if he's been trying to frame you, it's a safe bet he recognizes you."

"Now what?"

"You hand it off to a detective."

"You can't run with it?"

"This isn't like on TV. The criminalist doesn't solve the case. Even if I *didn't* have my hands full." Lloyd placed the tape lift and a computer disk containing the digital photo into a Ziploc and said, "Anyone can take it from here. And don't tell them I ran it for you, or the secret handshake guys'll get after me."

His step seemed a little lighter as we headed out. Despite the caveats he'd offered to brake my excitement, he, too, felt the exhilaration of circling a suspect. I was winning him over, one selfish demand at a time.

My shoes crunched on the gravel driveway.

"Good luck, Drew," he called after me. His tone was uncharacteristically upbeat, but when I turned around, the door had already closed behind him.

17

"This is a fingerprint lifted off a piece of evidence found at the Kasey Broach crime scene. It belongs to a convicted felon, Richard Collins. As a free citizen, I am going to his residence to ask a few questions. I think you should accompany me."

Cal stared back at me through his screen door, cigarette dangling from the corner of his mouth. He wore a wife-beater that showed off thick shoulders marked with Calvin and Hobbes tattoos that had probably been a good idea when he was eighteen and drunk. The tape lift and computer disk, visible through an evidence bag, made a far more dramatic impression than the Spago take-out bag had the last go-round.

He palmed the screen open. "You out of your fucking mind?"

"Pronounced so by a jury of my peers."

"You have no peers, asshole. Talk."

I gave him a full account, leaving out Lloyd. His silence indicated his interest. Or he'd fallen asleep with his eyes open.

When I finished, he asked, naturally, "How'd you run the print?"

"I just recognized the whorl pattern. Don't you?"

He grimaced, entertained by my wit. "You sure you didn't leave that fingerprint yourself? In a mystically induced trance, of course?"

"I'm currently certified one hundred percent brain-tumor-free."

"Aside from your overactive imagination."

"My overactive imagination didn't produce this." A shake of the bag, in case he'd failed to notice it.

"The chain of custody is shot—"

"Fuck chain of custody. It's been blowing around there all week because your colleagues didn't find it. This isn't about making a case right now, it's about asking some questions. Which I'm going to do."

He tried to take the Ziploc, but I pulled it back.

He said, "Give it to me. I'll look into it."

"Look, pal, you had a chance to play RHD detective when I came to you yesterday, but you were too busy bemoaning violence in the media. So this is now a citizen's investigation. I'm going to visit Mr. Collins, and there's no law that can stop me from doing so. If you'd like to come, I think it might be beneficial to your career."

"You said you were a free citizen. Let me remind you, you're a *relatively* free citizen." He held out his hand for the bag, but I kept it. "Determined fucker, aren't you?"

"Are you driving or am I?"

He stared at me for maybe ten seconds. That's a long time to be stared at, especially when you're staring back. I bet he regretted not having his tough-guy sunglasses to complete his expression. Finally he stepped aside from the door, letting it swing open in unspoken invitation. On the couch behind him, I could see the well-thumbed pages of my manuscript.

He turned, walking away. "Let me grab my badge. It'll impress Mr. Collins."

Christened the Ronald Reagan Freeway in '94 by nostalgic legislators, the 118 runs unglamorously through the north San Fernando Valley to Simi. Cal stared out his car window as Granada Hills rolled by in a blur of strip malls and tract housing. We'd stopped by the station for him to rescan the print. When Richard Collins and his Northridge address had popped up on the computer screen, Cal had glanced over at me and said, deadpan, "Nice eye, Danner."

We took in the passing view, indistinguishable from one mile to the next. Away from the city, beyond the fringes of manufactured cool, these neighborhoods lacked even the glamour of the urban wastelands, the Crenshaws and South Centrals and Comptons, where dead presidents change hands and bullets crackle and tricked-out Escalades brighten dingy blocks. I wondered if the people out here resented the blandness. The year-round sun, beach access, and just-right humidity ensure they don't even get to suffer.

Maybe that's what had made Richard Collins murderous. An address at Corbin and Parthenia.

After a while I realized that something more than the scenery had soured Cal's mood. "Why so cranky?"

A pause as he considered whether we were friends again. "Annoying date. This broad could be from one of your books. If you wrote horror."

"*That* annoying?"

"'When Patches meows like this, she's saying she's hungry. When Patches meows like *this,* she's saying she loves me.'"

I laughed. He didn't. "Nothing doing with the ex, huh?" I asked.

"She's remarried. To an agent. He's got a punch-me face, and he's named Jeremy. *Jeremy.*" Cal shook his head.

I decided not to ask any more questions.

We exited the freeway and pulled up on an apartment building that looked like every other apartment building we'd passed. He climbed out, but I sat for a moment, the reality of the situation sinking in. We were going to knock on the door of a man who might have killed two women and set me up. I wondered what was keeping my fingers from the door handle. A cold blade of doubt in the base of my spine. What if we discovered that Collins was our guy but that he'd framed me for only *one* murder? What if the Bertrands' hateful courtroom stares proved to be justified?

Cal came around the car and leaned over my open window. "Lose your nerve?"

I shook my head.

"Maybe you should. We knock-noticed a guy last year who crapped in his hands so no one would want to cuff him."

"What gets someone to that place?"

"Daddy put out cigarettes on his forehead. Mom didn't shower him with affection. Too much Black Sabbath before puberty." Cal straightened up. "Sometimes there is no good reason. Sometimes people are just fucked up."

Yeah, I thought, but reasons are more interesting.

He started for the stairwell, and I had to move to catch up. His hand darted inside his jacket, unsnapping the break on his shoulder holster. One of Apartment 11B's windows overlooked the floating hall. The pane was shoved back a few inches, but the curtains were drawn.

Standing to the side of the jamb, Cal knocked with the butt of his flashlight. "Richard Collins? LAPD. Please open up."

A clattering inside, perhaps a chair falling over.

"Open up, please. We just have a few questions."

"The hell you guys want?"

"Sir, open this door *now*." Thumping footsteps across the room. "Last chance, then I'm sending in tear gas." Glancing over at me, Cal shook his head reassuringly.

He strode down the hall, lifted a fire extinguisher from its mount, and returned. He pulled the pin and tossed it to me across the door, then loosed a carbon-dioxide blast through the window's gap. A shriek, and then Collins stumbled into the hall, arms raised.

Cal spun him against the wall and frisked him. "Let's go back inside."

The apartment smelled of pot. As Cal stood Collins up against the wall, I strolled around the front room. A table had been pushed into the corner by the alcove kitchen. A fork protruded from a pot of re-heated SpaghettiOs. A chair lay overturned, resting on the bright orange button-up shirt that had been slung over it.

"I didn't do anything, man. I can't have a third strike. I can't."

Cal asked, "Where were you the night of January twenty-second?"

To his credit, Collins looked baffled. "I don't know. When was that?"

In the sink, shoved halfway down the disposal guard, was a dime bag. I glanced up from the sink, and Collins was looking over at me, terrified.

"Thursday, three nights ago," Cal said.

"I was working."

"Between ten-thirty and two?"

I walked over and righted the chair, pulling up the still-hooked shirt with it.

"*Working*, man. You can check my time card, talk to my manager. I'm a stocker. I work nights."

"Where?"

I looked at the familiar logo stitched into the button-up's fabric at the breast. To say I felt chagrin would have been a significant understatement. Cal looked over and caught sight of the uniform just as Collins said, "Home Depot."

Cal chuckled once, but it caught fire and he doubled over, hands on his knees, laughing.

Collins said, "Wait a minute. What's going on?"

From the kitchen I asked what was, in hindsight, a stupid question: "You remember selling anyone electrical tape?"

"I don't work the floor. I just unload. Electrical tape, sure. Crates of it. Listen, if you talk to my manager, please don't tell him about my record. I lied on the application. I'm sorry. I couldn't get a fresh start, not with the drug charges."

"Don't worry about it," Cal said.

Collins was still staring at me. "I'd be so fucked if I got a third strike. Twenty-five to life. I got child support I gotta pay. I been clean for anything that matters. I been clean."

In my fervor I'd made a big leap, transforming Collins from pot-head to savage killer. In doing so, I was ready to fuck up his life worse even than mine, and he didn't have a handy brain tumor to get him off the hook. Pretending to wash my hands, I let the water push the Baggie of marijuana down into the disposal.

"Don't worry about it," I said.

Cal didn't talk to me as we walked back down the stairs to the car. Before leaving he'd gotten the Home Depot manager on the phone and confirmed Collins's hours the night of January twenty-second. I'd taken away one piece of information, but it came loaded with so many variables as to be nearly useless. *If* the wrapping had come from the killer's electrical tape, then he'd bought it at the Home Depot in Van Nuys. *If* he'd shopped close to home, that would make him a Valley boy. Two *ifs* weren't going to advance the home team's cause significantly.

We climbed into the car. I expected Cal to yell, but he just looked over and smirked. "Don't quit your day job."

Lloyd called me on my cell phone as I was driving home from Cal's. "How'd it go?"

I told him.

"Ouch," he said. "Sorry to pile on, but the DNA tests came back from Broach's body and the drop cloth we found in your trash. It's yours. Not that it undermines your alibi, but I just wanted to give you a heads-up."

I thanked him and hung up. Heading home reminded me of my damaged front door and Preston's note about the dangers it might leave me vulnerable to. I called information and got one of the alarm companies I'd seen advertised on metal posts shoved into neighborhood flower beds.

"Sorry, pal. Can't get someone in to wire you until Tuesday, maybe Wednesday."

"You sure you don't work for the phone company?"

"Sorry?"

"Never mind."

I gave him my address and made an appointment. Then I called Home Depot, figuring they owed me one or I them, beeped my way through an elaborate menu, and left a message for the door department that of course stood no chance of being returned but left me feeling as if I'd fulfilled due diligence in addressing my editor's notes.

Richard Collins. Professional electrical-tape handler. Don't quit your day job indeed.

I decided I'd give myself the rest of the drive home to feel discouraged. But I blew my deadline. I was too worn down for a cigar on the deck, so I plopped into my reading chair, mulling over my missteps. After a while I tired of myself and clicked on the TV.

Humidity was low, terrorist chatter was high. Another day in America. Guess what was reairing on TNT? *Hunter Pray.* Sure enough, there was Johnny Ordean, wearing an ill-fitting priest's collar and holding a scumbag's dripping head above a rank toilet bowl. *"Cough it up or we go another round on the baptism."*

Good God.

The resultant gurgling spurred my thumb to action. A seductively named hurricane was ravaging the Georgia coast. Newscasters were emboldening the terrorists. A teen singer had been in a fender bender at Fairfax and Le Brea, and a news unit was there to capture each cracked taillight and curse word.

While I'd been occupied, public attention had moved on.

I punched the button and sat in the relative darkness. There is no silence quite as plaintive as that of an empty house when the television turns off. Now that the media were no longer mistreating me, I felt left out.

The back cushions on the couch, strewn by Preston, jarred loose a recollection of Genevieve. Before we'd watch a movie or an opera on PBS, she'd pull apart the whole damn couch like a kid building a fort, and rearrange it to her liking, which usually entailed transforming it into a faux-suede nest, elevating her like Cleopatra on the barge. From her regal perch, she studied me now with those imploring French eyes.

"I'm working on it," I said. "Everyone has setbacks. Remember Waterloo?"

She vanished at the ring of my cell phone.

"Who's the mack daddy?"

"Barry Bonds?" I guessed.

A sound of disgust. "Chic Bales, that's who."

I told him about Richard Collins, the innocent, pot-smoking Home Depot felon.

"Don't despair, Chicken Little. I got us a spray artist. We ride at first light."

After the call I stared at the couch, but Genevieve wouldn't reappear. I didn't blame her. I was lousy company, and I might have shoved a boning knife through her rib cage.

Upstairs I dozed sporadically, finding myself wide awake at 1:00 A.M. The Genevieve hour. Each whistle of the wind was a screen being slit, every creak in the house a foot set cautiously down. Turning on the lights before me, I retrieved spare cuts of plywood from the garage and hammered them across the broken windows in my front door.

Back in my bedroom, I lay in the darkness, surrounded by familiar shadows.

You have to accept whatever comes, and the only important thing is that you meet it with courage and with the best that you have to give.

I'd looked stupid. It wasn't a first. I'd spent the evening spinning my tires. Not like I had anything better to do. I'd played a card with Cal I could've saved for later. So what? I had more up my sleeve. Tomorrow could bring a graffiti-artist eyewitness, another body, a rise in the ocean that left us all breathing through snorkels.

For Genevieve, for Kasey Broach, for myself, I was committed. I was in the plot. After blood, sweat, and tears would come an ending, favorable or not.

For the first time since I'd awakened in that hospital bed, I slept soundly.

18

I met Chic in a part of Compton that had been revitalized, meaning the crackheads looked better fed.

He leaned over my window and said, "Genevieve's father invested in a company that owned a boutique that Kasey Broach once bought soap at. They bought car tires from the same wholesaler, Broach in person, Genevieve through her mechanic at Lexus."

"What's that give us?"

"Nuthin' worth marking on the scorecard." He grinned. "Database guy is good at digging stuff up, not necessarily *good* stuff. We'll see what else he comes up with. I don't think there's gonna be much between the two of them—it's a connection between Broach and *you* that would smell like pay dirt to me. If it links Genevieve, too, trifecta." As we crossed the street, Chic flicked his chin at the warehouse up ahead. "That's our boy's art studio there."

"Art studio?"

"That's right. And don't go embarrassin' me and callin' it graffiti."

"What do I call it?"

"Aerosol art."

"Naturally."

We entered to find a large woman behind a reception desk, blowing on a set of fingernails that doubled the length of her hand. She looked up, eyebrows raised as if we'd shoved in on her in a changing room.

"Engelbert Humperdinck here's lookin' for Bishop," Chic said, jerking his head in my direction, "but he didn't want to come down alone because he's afraid you all might put him in a cannibal pot."

"One o' them black ones?"

"Uh-huh."

"Lemme go get it." She pushed back from the desk and disappeared through a metal door. Her voice came amplified through the walls. "Bish! Folks here to see you!" We couldn't make out the response, but we heard her say, "Then sit reception you *own* damn self."

She reappeared, holding the heavy door for us to pass through. She eyed me as I passed. "He a cop or a buyer?"

"He a writer," Chic said.

She snorted. "Which restaurant?"

We entered the warehouse proper. Aside from a desk in the far corner, several cardboard boxes, and a rotund naked black man, the room was empty. The man was giving us his generous backside, facing an enormous canvas, marked with splotches, that was strapped to the far wall. Paint dripped from his fingertips, streamed down his broad calves.

I looked at Chic, and he shrugged. We crossed the vast space, admiring the blown-up photos adorning the walls—distinctive graffiti art on trains, billboards, even a few cop cars. The cardboard boxes were full of spray-paint cans, tips and nozzles, night-vision goggles flecked with backspray.

Chic cleared his throat, but Bishop didn't turn around. He bent over, plucked a roller from a pan of purple paint, and ran it from his shins to his neck. Emitting a bass roar, he charged forward and flung himself against the canvas, leaving a large purple mark. He took a few steps away from the wall, wiped himself down with a wet towel, and pulled on a pair of velour sweatpants.

"Interesting technique," Chic said. "Seems like . . ."

"Bullshit?" Bishop said in a great rumble of a voice. "Course it is. But it fetch me three grand at the gallery. If you could get that for a Rorschach of your nutsack, tell me you wouldn't."

I said, "If I could get three grand for anything involving my nut-sack, I would."

He laughed. "You gentlemen lookin' to buy?"

"Actually, just a quick question for you." I unfolded a copy of the freeway ramp graffiti from my back pocket. I'd pulled some Kinko's magic, blowing it up, zeroing in so as to leave the body out of frame.

Bishop glanced at it and said, "Wudn't me."

"I know the feeling," I said, "but we're not cops or prosecutors, and we don't care that it's illegal."

"No, I mean it *wudn't me.*" He gestured grandly to the surrounding photographs. "See the 103 tag? Lower-right corner, every time?"

I studied the photos. The numbers resolved, almost as in the posters at the mall that you squint at for twenty minutes before being awarded a 3-D image or a migraine.

"That 'cuz I came up on 103rd in Watts." Bishop tapped the copy in my hands. "Ain't no 103 there. Beside, I don't use no Amazon Green and Metallic Periwinkle. That ain't Bishop's palette. This some toy done bite my piece."

"Translation for the white guy?"

"I'm a fame writer. That's why y'all knew to come find me. But this a toy writer, a kid comin' up. He bite my work—copy my shit—to show props."

"Do you recognize which kid made this graffi—"

Chic cut me off. "Aerosol art?"

"Course. That his name right there, fool." Bishop flicked the paper in the upper-left corner. Hidden in the puffs and bubbles of color were two letters, rendered in abstract hypercalligraphy. *WB.* "West Manchester Boulevard, by the Forum in the 'Wood. That where *he* came up. Inglewood. Junior do good work, bombs freeway ramps and long-term storage joints. No stencils or airbrushing shit, squiggles the tail on his Qs."

He'd pronounced the name soft, Latin style: *Hoon-yore.*

"He Mexican?" Chic asked.

"Ain't no racial issues in the graf community. We about the *art*."

"You know where we can find him?"

"Yeah. Boy send me fan mail." Bishop plodded over to the little metal desk and dug in the drawers, sending candy-bar wrappers fluttering to the ground. He pulled out a crumpled letter from a drawer full of correspondence. It contained a Polaroid shot of a rolling storage door that had been transformed into a spray-paint wonderland. The letter read:

> *Dear Bish,*
>
> *I think your the best there is. Heres a piece I did like your job on the Metro Red. Its not as good but someday I hope to tag as good as you. When I get older I gona tag the white house right on them pillars. Ha ha ha. Maybe when I off probation I could meet you and here your stories.*
>
> *You da man!*
>
> *Junior Delgado*

I flipped the envelope over. The return address listed a place called Hope House with an address on West Sixth. I pulled the Bic from behind my ear and copied the address in a black-leather detective's notepad Cal had given me years ago.

"I gotta go meet with a distributor at the restaurant," Chic said. "Think you'll be safe visiting Junior without a big Negro holding your hand?"

"Dunno." I looked at Bishop. "Wanna hold my hand?"

Bishop smirked. "I'm spoken for."

19

A guy with gang tattoos across his throat flew down the handicap ramp on a wheelchair and veered toward the van parked beside my car. I'd called Preston on my way over, and he'd googled Hope House for me. It proved to be a residential placement facility—social services–speak for a group home—just above MacArthur Park. It was a six-bedroom house, two kids per room, with overnight staff. Last stop before juvy for problematic Angeleno youth.

I climbed out of my car. The guy was laboring to get out of his wheelchair and into the driver's seat.

"Give you a hand?" I asked.

He turned. The lettering on his baseball cap read THERE BUT FOR THE GRACE OF GOD GO YOU. "Yeah, I came all the way down here, and I don't know how to get in my fucking van."

So far I was a hit.

The house was a dilapidated two-story—peeling paint, crooked shutters, the whole deal. I walked into a whirlwind of motion, young teens flying out of rooms, screaming at one another, tumbling over the broken-down play structure in the backyard. A Hispanic counselor paced, biting her nails, phone pressed to her ear. "His PO has *not* shown up, we're short a driver, and I have to bail Patrick out, so I can't take him."

She hung up, blew a sigh. "Are you my driver?"

"No, I'm looking for Junior Delgado. I need to ask him—"

"*Just*"—her hands flew out, then she caught herself and finished in a gentler tone—"go wait out back. You'll have to talk to Caroline Raine—she's our clinical therapist. She's upstairs dealing with a contraband issue. She'll be down in a sec, but this isn't the best day. Grab a cup of coffee." She pointed to a row of homemade mugs hanging from wooden pegs. "Might be a while. Wash it out when you're done."

Refueling on caffeine, I strolled out back and sat on the lip of a planter filled with dirt but no flowers, next to a kid who looked about as animated as James Taylor. "You know where Junior is?"

"Dunno, man." He got up and trudged away. My presence had offended him.

It struck me how much movies had colored my view of kids' homes. Here there were no long-lashed Latin boys with smooth skin, no girls flashing million-dollar smiles from beneath dirt-smudged faces, no eager minds waiting for a role model, a state-sponsored music program, a whimsical mathematics instructor. Just a lot of baggy shorts, Converse sneakers, and scowls. The play-structure slide had rusted, and two of the monkey bars were missing. I thought kids like this probably deserved something better to play on, but they seemed to be making do.

A Down syndrome kid sat in one of the cracked rubber swings, holding his head in his hands and weeping. "I waa ma mama."

A boy in a lime green sweatshirt weighed in. "You killed your mom, retard."

"I know. I know."

I thought, *I will never complain about anything ever again.*

A scrawny Latin kid, maybe fifteen, wore a Lee jacket, bell-bottom jeans, and PRO-Keds. He looked like someone Fat Albert had sat on. When he turned to huddle with a co-conspirator, I saw that the back of his jacket was custom-painted. Aerosol art, I believe the term is.

"Junior?"

He strolled over, sat down beside me, and straightened out my pronunciation of his name.

"Sorry. Is this your work? I'm not a cop, just an admirer."

He glanced at the folded paper and smiled. "Yeah, thass me."

"Painted it last Thursday night?"

"How you know that?"

I pointed to the pigeon feathers stuck to the concrete. "Paint was still wet. And this picture was dated. What time were you there?" It took me a moment to read his hesitation. "Don't worry. I won't tell anyone you snuck out."

"Late. I'd guess from, say, eleven forty-five to ten to two."

"How sure are you?"

"More sure about the ten-to part." He showed off an impressive Sanyo. "My watch beeps on the hour. I got a beep when I was biking home, 'bout halfway."

The time stamp on the first crime-scene photo had read 2:07 A.M. Which led to my next question. "Why didn't you finish your piece?"

"Got interrupted."

"By a car?"

"Uh-huh."

"Did you see what kind of car?"

"I see *everything,* homes." Sensing my eagerness, he fixed his brown eyes on me. "Ms. Caroline say it okay for you to be here?"

"Didn't say it wasn't."

"Uh-hunh. You seen her yet? I mean, laid eyes?"

"No."

He grinned wolfishly.

"Why?" I asked.

"Excuse me, sir."

I turned to see a woman standing over me. Her face, at first glance, was like a shattered, beautiful mask. Scars divided it, one starting at her hairline, curving around her temple, another beginning under her eye and bridging the bumps of her lips, splitting the edge of her mouth.

I dropped my coffee mug. It was probably due more to the zealous glaze job on the ceramic than to shock, but either way the effect was the same. I felt like a prissy Jane Austen heroine, teacup trembling on saucer as gossip came back from the ball. My mortification grew with each embarrassing arc the intact part of the mug described on the concrete, and Junior's stifled laughter didn't help.

"I'm sorry," I said, "I lost my grip."

Her expression revealed nothing. The indentation in her lips didn't align, and the path of the longer mark seemed equally haphazard. The scars were faded, the color blending, the skin slightly dappled in places from what I guessed were healed-over grafts. She was graying, but not by the strand or lock. All her hair had dulled slightly to a dusty sandalwood. It was lank, taken up in a twist around a pencil. Her features, glimpsed through the damage, were stunning. Icy green eyes, delicate mouth, lovely bone structure that accented her cheeks.

I offered my hand. "I'm Drew Danner."

"I recognize you from your murder trial."

Junior looked at the boy in the lime green sweatshirt, who mouthed, *Hells yeah.*

"Junior, go to your room please."

"Ms. Caroline—"

"Now."

He hustled. I would've hustled, too.

"What do you want, Mr. Danner?"

"I'm trying to figure out what happened to me. I just had a few questions for Junior."

"So you thought you'd come out here and interview one of my boys without getting approval from me?"

I forced a smile. "Be nice to me, I had a brain tumor?"

"Not gonna work here, buster."

"Drat."

"Clean up your mess and leave."

She left me on the planter. The remaining kids laughed at me, the

Down syndrome kid included, and the boy in the sweatshirt stuck out his tongue. I wanted Junior's description of the car that had interrupted his spray-paint job, but could see no acceptable way to get to him. Now.

I collected the ceramic shards in my palm and found a trash can a few steps up a hall. From the other room, I heard Caroline's and the counselor's raised voices.

"Judge Celemin has had it. He misses another appearance, he's going straight to the hall."

"What can we do, Caroline? I have to bail out Patrick—now—and the driver flaked. It's okay, there's nothing—"

"No, it's *not* okay. I didn't double-schedule staff, and now he's gonna wind up in the hall because of me."

I left them to the joys of charitable enterprise.

I was pulling out when a bang on my window startled me upright. Caroline Raine gestured for me to roll down the window. I had the sense that when Caroline Raine suggested you do something, you did it. She thrust a document onto my steering wheel. "Here. Sign this. No, here. Now you're a Big Brother. Through our facility. Take Junior to court—you're already late. It's just one hour out of your day, and you'll save him from juvenile hall."

I pictured the book jacket: *Tuesdays with Junior*. "Are you kidding me?"

"You can question him all you want on the way. Not that it'll get you anywhere."

"How do you know I'm not some psycho?"

"Clinician's eye."

"I was up for murder."

"By reason of insanity is pretty tame compared to these kids. Junior'll eat you for lunch."

"After what I've been through," I said, "I'm probably toxic. I think I can handle a kid with some attitude."

20

"So you got interrupted?" I asked. "By what kind of car?"

"Quit pushin' me, homes. I got court. I always get nervous when I got court."

"How often do you have court?" That got the look it deserved. "What for this time?"

"Sprayin', what else?" Junior fiddled with the radio, started bopping to a beat that made the windows rattle. "What's *your* story, homes?" he shouted. "You stared down a murder one?"

I adjusted the volume and told him, asking myself the whole time what the hell I was thinking recounting all this to a bored juvenile delinquent. The repetition, like rewriting, helped me clarify the holes and weaknesses, the detours requiring further investigation.

When I finished, Junior surprised me. "Thass fucked up, homes. You know what you need? You need you a *dog*."

"A talking dog who solves crimes?"

"Someone broke into your house, cut you up and shit. A dog would protect you, homes, watch your back. I had a Doberman-rotty mix. You had a dog like that, you wouldn't need to worry 'bout *shit*. Not in your castle."

I conceded that it wasn't a bad point. We pulled up to the Eastlake Juvenile Courthouse. I glanced at the graffiti patterns on the back of Junior's jean jacket as he climbed out. "Given the grounds for your appearance, you think you might want to leave your jacket in the car?"

"No way, homes. I gots to repre*sent*." He kicked out a leg, showing off a white PRO-Ked. "This and my kicks, this my old-school tagger gear."

My watch put us forty-five minutes past the court-appointed time. "We're late."

"Don't worry about it," Junior said, skipping along. "Judge Celemin *love* me."

Judge Celemin glowered at us, black robes gathered high on his shoulders like a vulture's wings. "So pleased you could join us, Mr. Delgado. I trust you weren't too put out trying to make it here?"

Junior beamed. "Not at all, Your Honor."

The judge shifted his predacious attention to me. Given our tardiness, the public defender had moved on to another case across the corridor, but Judge Celemin had demanded that "Mr. Delgado and whoever was responsible for his transportation" appear regardless. "This is the second time Mr. Delgado, at the tender age of fourteen, has violated his probation by being apprehended in possession of spray-paint cans. You're his Big Brother?"

I found myself sweating. "Guilty as charged, Your Honor."

"You might want to think about the quality of the moral instruction you're imparting."

"I have in fact been giving that a fair amount of consideration lately, Your Honor."

"Surely your own recent experiences have taught you what the Sixth Amendment affords, Mr. Danner?"

I drew a complete blank. I used to have a great fear that I wasn't as smart as I thought I was. And it had been a great relief to discover that I was correct. Still, no professed grown-up wants to come up short on a topic taught in sixth-grade social studies. You get a certain distance from your schooling and you realize to your chagrin that you are that illiterate asshole who can't find Maryland on a map or name the planets in order. "I assume it's not the right to arrive late to court."

"Your guess is correct, Mr. Danner. Now, Mr. Delgado was down to his last shot here and elected to show up late, so I'm afraid I'm going to have to—"

"It was my fault," I said resignedly. "I got caught up with . . . an appointment and picked him up late."

An appointment? Light on your feet, Chandler.

And I'd thought that Judge Celemin's expression could not have evidenced more revulsion. "Well. You will return tomorrow at the same time with Mr. Delgado's attorney, and we will settle this matter definitively."

"Tomorrow's a bit hard for me, but I'm sure someone else can—"

"What in the sentence I just said implied to you that I was inviting a discussion?"

"Nothing, Your Honor."

"I need an adult's guarantee that this minor will be here tomorrow."

"Me?"

"You are an adult?"

"Some might take issue with that, Your Honor."

"I among them. But in the flawed justice system, Mr. Danner, we must work with what we have. As for your busy day tomorrow? I hate to inconvenience you. I'm an hour behind on my docket, so I know how difficult it can be when one's schedule is compromised."

Junior chuckled the whole way out to the parking lot.

"Spit it out."

"How 'bout we go to the movies, Big Brother?"

I screeched the car over and said, "I'm done playing this game.

You're gonna tell me about the car you saw or I'm dumping your ass out here."

He glanced around. "Nice neighborhood." Still, he looked uneasy. "Okay. I was tagging the bridge when I saw some headlights. I hauled ass."

"But you saw the car?"

"Brown Volvo. One-a them wagons. Dent on the front wheel well. I could see 'cuz the paint was flaked off."

"Which side?"

He looked at his hands, made an L with his thumbs and forefingers. "Right side."

"Old Volvo, new Volvo?"

"I just recognized the ugly-ass shape. A Volvo's a Volvo, homes."

"Good point. Did you see the license plate?"

"Of course."

"Of *course*?"

"When you bombing and a car come up on you, you always check the plate. See if it's the pigs. *E* with a circle around it at the beginning of the numbers stand for 'exempt.' That's how you can tell an unmarked cop car." He smiled, pleased with himself. "But there wudn't no *E*. This one started with a seven. That's all I can tell you, homes. Lucky seven."

"Did you see the driver?"

"Hayell no. I didn't stick around. I bolted when he was busy parking."

"Anyone else around?"

"Yeah, a convent of nuns was coming through. I like to do my tagging with lotsa witnesses around."

"Where'd the Volvo park?"

He pointed to a spot off the photograph. "Down here."

I recalled a dirt apron under the ramp on that side. Which could mean tread marks from tires or shoes.

"I want you to show me. How do I get to the ramp from here?"

We listened to music, Junior's head lolling back against the head-rest. "Turn right here. Left. Now right. Okay, stop."

I was at a curb in front of a row of tiny houses. "Where are we? This isn't the ramp."

Junior hopped out and jogged for the nearest front door. "Just come inside a sec."

I scrambled after him, swearing at him in a manner unbecoming a Big Brother.

I banged through the screen door. Junior was standing in the dim and cramped entryway, whistling around his fingers.

"This my cousin's," he said by way of explanation.

From the back of the house strutted a peacock of a man. Black suit, broad-brimmed black hat, black tie, black shoes—one twist of the ethnic dial and he could've been a Hasidic diamond merchant. He turned his somber face to Junior, his mouth twitching.

"This is Hector," Junior said.

Hector said, "Get your fucking dog outta here."

"Thass why we here, homes."

"Don't 'homes' my ass, Junior. Knock the ghetto crap. All you *ni-ñitos* forgetting your brown pride." He headed for the door. "I'm going out. That bitch better be gone by the time I get back, or I'm hauling her ass to the *pound*." He shot his cuffs and left.

I said, "*Oh,* no."

Junior opened the back door, and a Doberman-rottweiler mix padded in, rope leash dangling from her bull like neck. "Get you one of these, no one *ever* gonna fuck with your house again. Look at her. Ain't she beautiful? Name is Xena. The princess warrior. She a vicious killer, homes."

"I don't need a vicious killer."

"Look, look." He tugged on the rope. Xena growled.

"I don't need a Xena. I just want to see the ramp."

"Want something to eat, homes?"

"We're going. I want to see the ramp."

"Ain't gonna show you the ramp unless you take Xena."

"I'm not taking Xena."

"You gonna let a perfectly good guard dog die when you need one?"

"I don't need one."

"You said you did."

"I was being nice!" I yelled.

Junior took a step back, and he rubbed his head. "I can't let Xena die." His eyes were wet now.

"Oh, Christ," I said.

He hugged Xena around her neck and started crying. "They gonna *kill* you, Xena." He was rocking and holding his dog, who'd accommodatingly slumped over to complete the pietà. "They gonna take you to the pound and inject you with *poison*."

This went on, with minor variations, for several minutes.

"All right," I finally said. "I'll take the goddamned dog."

He smiled and jumped up and down, and I remembered he was fourteen. Then he held out his hand, palm up. His tears had stopped with a single twist of the spigot.

"What's this?"

"This a top-notch guard dog you getting here. Fitty dollars."

"I gotta *pay* to rescue Xena?"

"Hayell yeah." Junior smiled. "She a princess warrior."

I gave him my best Big Brother grin. "No. Fucking. Way."

Xena stood on all fours in the backseat, sticking her head between us. The broken streetlights around Rampart did little to check the evening's arrival.

Junior asked, "Can we stop and get some spray paint?"

"I fear that would be defaulting on my role-model obligations."

He sucked his teeth and slid down in the seat, arms crossed. "You a writer, homes. What would you do if *your* art was illegal? Stop doin' it?" We pulled under the familiar freeway ramp, and he glanced around. "Is *this* shit legal? Taking a minor to fuck wit' a crime scene?"

"A minute ago you were a cross between Beelzebub and a Ginsu-knife salesman. Now you're a minor?"

He didn't answer. He didn't have to. His point was stronger than my retort.

"Look, if you get more spray paint, you'll violate your probation and wind up in deeper trouble."

"I don't care. I like probation. I get to stay at Hope House. Ms. Caroline's fly. I don't want to leave. Free food and board, and I can still spray."

"I think you might be missing the point."

"'Point.'" He blew out his breath in disgust at my ignorance.

He skulked over and showed me where the brown Volvo had pulled in. The dirt had been fanned by the wind and trampled by in-numerable feet. I was disappointed, but still happy with the lead Junior had given me. A brown Volvo, dent in the right front wheel well, license number starting with seven.

Back in the car, Junior let Xena lick his face while I called Lloyd, getting voice mail for his work and cell and the answering machine at home. I was just getting ready to pull out when there came a hard rap on my window and a flashlight beam in my face.

I rolled down the window and found myself looking down the wrong end of a pistol.

21

The cop kept the pistol trained on Xena, who was obliviously scratching her jowls on Junior's armrest.

"Can I help you, Officer?"

"Let's see some ID."

I handed over my ID. He looked at it warily, then moved his flashlight from my face to Junior's. "How old are you?"

"Fourteen."

The flashlight came back to blind me. "Are you aware that this kid is underage?"

"Oh, wait. No, no, no. I'm his Big Brother."

"Sure you are. And I'd imagine you have some documentation to that end?"

I could picture the expression on Preston's face.

"No, I don't. The signed paper is at Hope House, this boy's placement facility."

"Phone number, please."

I looked at Junior, and he rattled off a number. The cop disappeared back into his squad car. Between Xena's satisfied growls and Junior's giggling, surprisingly still audible despite his hand clamped over his mouth, I tried to formulate a game plan.

Before I could, the cop reapproached. "There was no answer." He stood back from the car, gun drawn and pointed at the princess warrior. "Is that your dog, sir?"

"Yeah," I said wearily. "It's my dog."

"Get out and leave her in the vehicle. Both of you."

I looked back. A large man was aiming a pistol at my head, and Xena was slobbering happily all over my headrest.

"Some guard dog."

Junior shrugged. "I trained her to respect authority."

I turned back to the cop. "Look, if you'll just let me call—"

"I did call, sir. There was no answer. Please step out of the vehicle and put your hands on the roof."

"You're kidding me."

"Yeah, I'm in a real jokey mood."

I got out of the Highlander and complied. Through the window I watched the dog curl up contentedly in the backseat.

"Down, Xena," I said.

The holding cell at the Rampart Station was surprisingly clean, despite a permanent olfactory overlay of vomit. I was, of course, kept separate from Junior, lest I corrupt him further.

After an eternity Caroline Raine's face appeared through the bars.

I'd never seen a prettier sight.

"You're a bad influence," she said.

I peeled myself off the sticky bench. "You're just figuring that out?"

We dropped Junior off at Hope House, and then Caroline took me to pick up my Highlander. I let Xena out, and she trotted over to a throw of weeds, squatted, and peed.

Caroline asked, through lips pursed with amusement, "Isn't that Junior's dog?"

"She a princess warrior, homes." I whistled Xena back into the Highlander.

Caroline looked around, shivered in the night breeze. "There was a murder here the other night."

"Yep. I was framed for it. Elaborately. But I had an alibi this time."

She nodded slightly, a tough woman to shock. "Which was?"

"I camcorded myself while I was sleeping."

"You have a lot of strange habits."

"It's a longer conversation. Let me buy you dinner."

She laughed uncomfortably. "Like a date?"

"Like a thank-you."

She looked immensely relieved. "There are some fine culinary choices in the area." She pointed up the street. "Pepe's House of Gastric Distress?"

"Just my speed."

Caroline sipped a beer while I nursed a ginger ale. The remains of burgers and chili cheese fries lay on the table before us, weighing down grease-stained paper inside red plastic baskets. A few stragglers at the bar, an empty pool table, the Stones reminding us from the jukebox that we can't always get what we want. We'd caravanned a few miles to a less downscale section of town. I'd left Xena dozing happily in my backseat, guarding the Guiltmobile with her vicious killer instincts.

Caroline had brought a persistent curiosity to bear over the meal. She maintained direct eye contact, maybe a therapist habit, but it didn't make me as uncomfortable as I would have thought. I fielded one sharp question after another about my trial, my theories, my ongoing investigation, and how it had wound up with me and Junior in the clink.

"That is one smart kid," I said.

"Junior was left in an alley as a baby with the umbilical cord still attached. He's a lifer in the system, and it's taught him quite a few tricks." She took another pull of Corona. "He's very taken with you. Maybe you should see him. After tomorrow's required court date, I mean."

I shrugged. "Might be good for me to do something for someone else."

"I don't trust anything that doesn't have selfish motives. Be a Big Brother to him if you want to. For you."

Her face had hardened. I studied it, trying to decipher the mood shifts, a skill I had honed during my years with Genevieve. I had a tough time not staring at the scars. Their lines were clean, if jagged, leading me to guess they'd been inflicted by a blade, probably the result of an attack. I ran a risk, I realized, of fetishizing Caroline's face, of finding it fascinating in its own right. Aside from the obvious damage, her skin was smooth, well tended with lotion. I would have bet that she had taken pride in her skin once; maybe she was astute enough to still appreciate its appeal. Her body was lean, but she had curves overlaying the muscles in the right places, a variation between hard and soft that seemed to match her personality. She was a few years older than me, having already closed on forty, but her hands, wrinkled in the palms, were the only part of her that showed her age. They looked soft and forgiving, more fragile than the rest of her.

I glanced around, mostly to stop examining her.

On the sole overhead TV not tuned to ESPN1, 2, or 12, Johnny Ordean appeared, rerun in his usual role, Detective Aiden O'Shannon. A stage-named Jew from Brooklyn playing an Irish Chicago cop on the backlot at Fox. Welcome to Hollywood.

Johnny and I had one of those 310 friendships—I pretended to flutter around his flame, and he kept me programmed into his cell phone in case I accidentally wrote something else that his agents could package.

Detective O'Shannon crouched over a mangled corpse, eating a—get this—hot dog and holding up an ejected bullet casing with a bent paper clip. The closed-captioning read, with appropriate humorlessness, *HUSTLE THIS TO FORENSICS THE CASING NOT THE HOT DOG.*

Caroline followed my gaze. "Isn't that the guy who played whatever they turned Derek Chainer into for that crappy film?"

"You've read my stuff?" I was thrilled.

"Of course I've read you. Why do you think I watched the trial?"

"Perverse curiosity?"

"That's why I read you, too." When she smiled, the scars straightened, and the indentations carved through her lips aligned. The damage hardly disappeared, but it grew significantly less pronounced. The wounds had been inflicted when she was scowling, or weeping, or screaming, and somehow a smile simulated those conditions enough to bring back the original lines of the blade. "You never played into the trial. You didn't turn into a trained seal. I bet it was difficult not to."

"It was a learning experience all the way around."

"What'd you take away from it all?"

"I can smell auras."

"Really?"

"My Spidey-senses are tingling right now, in fact. And your aura smells a little like"—I leaned over the table, sniffed her delightful head—"wet dog."

"*Wet dog?*" She wasn't smiling.

"Yeah. Pekingese, maybe."

She backhanded my shoulder.

"I thought you liked me for my sense of humor."

"I don't like you. But if I did, it would be for your vast infamy."

"It'll fade. Time heals all wounds."

"No," she said. "It doesn't." She studied the tips of her hair.

"Uh-oh."

"What?"

"You're Engaging in Private Grooming Habits. If I'm to believe *Men's Health,* that means you've lost interest in this conversation."

"*Men's Health?*"

"Yeah. Sorry 'bout that."

"Despite prevailing scientific wisdom, it doesn't mean I've lost interest. It means I'm uncomfortable."

"Because . . ."

"I work now. I don't go to dinner with men I don't know."

Laughter over by the pool table drew our attention. At one of the bar tables, a musclehead with twinning ear pierces nuzzled his spectacular girlfriend. Blond hair, blue eyes—she was a recessive-gene showcase. They looked young, likely in on fake IDs.

"What I'd give to have a tape of me in college," Caroline said. "The past always seems so glamorous, once you pass it. Yet here we are, stuck in the ever-unglamorous present." She watched the young couple kissing. "Remember that age? Everything you felt, it was the first time anyone had ever felt it. Like you'd discovered emotion." The longing in her voice was palpable. "You can't burn that way your whole life or you'll burn out, but it's still a loss when it fades away."

The guy stood up. His T-shirt read IT AIN'T GONNA SUCK ITSELF.

"Ah, yes," I said. "Young romance."

Caroline laughed, and the guy stopped and gave us his best glare.

"Right," I said, "you wear that shirt and you don't want people to look at you."

Scowling, he continued outside, tapping down a pack of smokes. The waitress came over, and I tried to pay, but Caroline insisted, a bit too firmly, on splitting the bill.

After our change arrived, Caroline said, "When I first started at Hope House, we realized we weren't getting traction with certain kids because we didn't understand some of their reactions, their hardwiring. So I implemented home visits—for the counselors. To see where these kids came from. It gave us a better understanding of how to deal with them in other contexts." She paused to finish her beer, leaving me unsure where she was going. "You knew Genevieve, but all you have of Kasey Broach is a body in a photograph. If you want to figure out how to fit her in, you need to see where she lived, meet her family."

"And say what? 'I'm a suspect in your daughter's murder and I'd like to ask a few questions'?"

She shrugged. "You're creative. Presumably." Her eyes darted over to the pool table. "Wanna play?"

"You hustling me?"

Again with the beautiful smile. "I'm not very good."

Two and a half minutes later, I watched as she leaned over to draw a bead on the fifteen, her second-to-last ball on the table. I had six solids remaining and little of my barroom dignity. I'd discovered that Caroline Raine had a whole vocabulary of laughter—the victorious whoop, the confident chuckle, the under-the-breath snicker.

"Is the fifteen feeling skinny? I think it's feeling skinny." Off her shot she threaded it, impossibly, through the one and the five and lined up for the nine. "The jeweler is in," she pronounced before cutting it to the side pocket on a backward vector I'd seen only in Paul Newman movies.

She circled the table, chalking her stick. Witty T-Shirt was still tied up on the pay phone, but his girlfriend's chair blocked Caroline's angle.

Caroline asked, "Would you mind letting me take this shot?"

"We were here first," the girl said. "And I already moved once. I'm not gonna keep dancing around the table."

"It puts you out that much to scoot four inches to your left?"

The girl flashed a fake smile onto her unreasonably pretty face. "Likes: water sports, long walks on the beach, kittens. Dislikes: pushy chicks with fucked-up faces."

Caroline colored everywhere except her scars; the contrast was severe. She set down the pool cue and turned to me. "Let's go." She took a few steps toward the door, then stopped and looked back at me intolerantly.

I paused next to the girl. On the table beside her Smirnoff Ice were photo proofs of her in various cutesy poses. She or her boyfriend had circled several with a red grease pencil, selecting prospective head shots.

"I know you," I said quietly. "You lucked into a decent set of genes, and you think that constitutes a contribution to the world. You don't really want to act—you're just lazy, and you want to be looked at and get your rent paid doing it. You booked a mouthwash commercial and a print campaign for TJ Maxx, and your agent thinks you're the next big thing. In a few years, you'll give up on leading lady and convince yourself you'll get cast as the wry best friend or the sitcom wife. Another excuse to do more nothing for another decade. In the long meantime, maybe you should reflect on what entitles you to be cruel and smug besides high cheekbones and the word of people paid to flatter you."

I didn't see her boyfriend coming until the fist loomed over my right side. I jerked away, and the blow glanced off my jaw, and then I heard a thud and a barstool toppling, and I finished reeling to see Caroline standing over the guy, holding one twisted arm captive, foot at his jawline, applying pressure to drive his face farther into the worn carpet. His girlfriend's mouth hung open, one hand curled over her perfect teeth. She'd turned white. Maybe she was a good actress after all.

Caroline glanced up at me. "Ready to go?"

I nodded. She released him. This time I followed her out to the parking lot. We paused between our cars. Xena was at my driver's-side window, snub tail wagging.

"You're a second-rate writer with a first-rate mouth," Caroline said.

I looked for a snappy comeback—I would've even taken on-the-nose—but I had writer's block and my jaw hurt. I touched it gingerly.

Caroline sighed, annoyed by her concern. "How do you feel?"

"Embarrassed."

"I meant your jaw."

"It's embarrassed, too."

"I bet." She crossed her arms. "What important lessons did we learn here?"

"Don't play pool with a woman who calls her cue Charlie?"

"One: This girl can take care of herself. Two: Don't start a fight you can't finish."

A few cars blew by, honking, until one veered off down a side street. Condensation wafted through the screen from the barroom kitchen.

"It wasn't your prerogative to get pissed off in there," she said.

"You asked what I took away from the trial. I suppose I countenance spitefulness less well."

"I know that game, too. I used to go around with my big bleeding heart, attuned to human frailties. The overweight girl, no rings, who nods a little too earnestly when people talk, eager to be useful. Little old lady at the bus stop, plastic bag shielding her purse in case it rains. Middle-aged immigrant working the counter at McDonald's. And then I realized I was riding the Projection Express and figured I needed to reserve some of that concern for myself."

I thought about her self-berating carrying through her office door. *No, it's not okay. I didn't double-schedule staff, and now he's gonna wind up in the hall because of me.*

She seemed to read my mind. "Not that I'm any good at it. But I did figure out one thing."

"Which was?"

"You can't get through life, which is this—shit—this fragile enterprise without getting damaged. You just don't. Not if you're a feeling person. Not if you don't have your head buried in the sand. *Everybody's* fucked up. Some of us are just in on the joke. And when you don't want to see that in yourself, you see it in others."

She climbed into her car and started to back out, then rolled down her window. "That's what you don't understand in that pulp you churn out. Everyone's a good guy. Everyone's a bad guy. It just depends how hard you're willing to look."

22

I knocked again on the hemlock-wood door, then peered through one of the frosted glass panes. Though I'd picked up Preston out front many times, I'd never actually been inside his condo, a balconied two-room floating among the billboards of Sunset. It occurred to me that I'd always had an image of it—Milanese furniture, stone bathtub, faint whiff of sage hand soap.

The door opened face width. For an instant—even from this close—I mistook Preston for someone else. His hair, usually flared so carefully over his forehead, lay limp against his head, and he was unshaven, his stubble sprinkled with gray. I could see the lapels of a bathrobe—he hadn't left all day?

Mortification flickered across his features.

I tried for a joke to put him at ease. "I didn't tell you I was picking you up for a black-tie at the Beattys'?"

His face was tense; for once he wasn't sure what to say. He cleared his throat, eased the door farther open. "I've been editing. No time to get my face on." He said it with a defensive edge, and it occurred to me that in the years I'd known him he'd never extended an invitation for me to drop by. He always seemed so comfortable marching into my house with his own key that I'd assumed the informality ran both ways.

"Bad time?" I asked. "I could—"

"Well, you might as well come in *now*." He stepped back, and I followed him down a brief, dark hall into the main room. The furnishings were hardly threadbare, but I was shocked by their ordinariness. A standard couch. White-tile kitchen. An antique credenza with hairline cracks, a ding or two away from a garage sale.

Preston returned to the tiny table by the window, sat, and gestured to the other chair. The table, stacked with shuffled sections of the *New York Times,* wasn't really sized for more than one person. Preston set aside Arts and went back to the soggy bowl of cereal I assumed was his dinner. A bare leg poked out from the fold of his bathrobe.

The whole scene was so banal, so unfabulous, so decidedly un-Preston. I'd never seen him unshaven. I'd never seen him not nattily attired. I'd never seen him eating food bought at a grocery store. It was a perfectly ordinary scene in a perfectly nice condo, but it was also somehow a breach in my view of him and how he kept himself, and this we both sensed. Nothing had happened—nothing at all—but the awkwardness was pervasive.

"So?" he asked. "What's so urgent it couldn't wait for me to barge in on *you*?" He didn't lift his gaze from the bowl; his heart wasn't in the joke.

I pressed forward. "You'll get a kick out of this. That kid—Junior, right? So I found him at Hope House. . . ."

But the surroundings continued to distract me. Sodden coffee filter on the counter. A lonesome glass in the sink, awaiting the dishwasher. Manuscript sheaves, bearing Preston's editor-red scrawl, had colonized most of the condo's flat surfaces. The thought of him in here alone, only these chunks of text keeping him company, seemed oddly dismal. Had I expected him to edit during cocktail parties?

Atop the crammed bookshelf by the TV, bookended between two heavy mugs, sat a row of my hardcovers. The closest thing to a display in sight. Preston always badgered me so much about my writing that I'd forgotten that maybe he liked it. The possibility that he valued me more than he let on oddly diminished my view of him. A trust-fund editor more articulate than I was, he'd taken a gamble on me five books ago, and I hadn't really updated my underlying view of him since. Though we'd become good friends, if not intimates, in my hidden thinking he'd always remained part of the unscalable edifice of New York publishing, and I felt a devotion to him for giving me that first hand up. I knew, of course, that I was an opportunity for him then and especially now. But perhaps I represented a more profound opportunity than I'd thought. Like the rest of us, Preston was busted in his own lovely way. But maybe he was also ordinary like the rest of us. Maybe he needed me as much as I needed him.

Preston had said something.

I refocused. "Sorry?"

"I said, 'Yes, you found Junior . . . ?'"

I forged back into the story—Xena and the cop and the jail cell—but I couldn't convey the maddening hilarity of it. Preston humored me with a faint smile and the occasional nod, but we were both distracted and aware that the surface exchange had become a charade.

When I was finished, I said lamely, "You gotta meet this kid." I riffled the edges of the nearest newspaper section until the noise grated. The air felt unvented, claustrophobic. I was eager to get out of there, impatient to start looking into the vehicle ID Junior had given me. Finally I said, "I gotta get over to Lloyd's. Tell him about the Volvo. I just thought you'd get a kick out of the other stuff."

"Sorry to disappoint."

"You never disappoint, Preston."

He summoned a smile before rising to see me out. "No," he said. "Of course not."

23

L loyd sat at the kitchen table, head bent, arms folded on a place mat dotted with crumbs. I'd informed him of my tentative vehicle ID at the door, and he'd taken a few steps back and sunk into a chair.

"Unbelievable," he said. "You came up with a make, color, distinguishing body damage, *and* the first license-plate number?"

"Should I go to Kaden and Delveckio with it?"

"Let's think this over." He stood and poured himself a rum and Coke. I noticed that the bottle of Bacardi 8 I'd brought him two days ago was nearly empty. He was wearing sweatpants and a T-shirt, and the blanket on the couch was thrown back. In the background a talking head chattered mindlessly about avian flu, predicting calamity and ruin. "You don't know for sure that the Volvo belongs to the body dumper?"

"No. The witness split before he saw anything. It's possible that another car could've come along after, but we're talking a pretty narrow time frame here between when my witness left and when you snapped that first crime-scene photo."

"Either way it'd be worth talking to the Volvo driver. Either he's our guy, or he likely saw something." Lloyd sucked an ice cube from the glass, crunched it loudly. "How reliable is your witness?"

I tried to imagine Kaden and Delveckio taking Junior seriously.

Lloyd read my face. "Then we should load the deck. Let me run the info in the morning, see what I find. I can't check for a wheel-well dent, obviously, but with everything else? You've given me some great search criteria. If I come up with a strong suspect, you'll be better armed bringing it in to Kaden and Delveckio." He aimed a forefinger at me. "But no mention of me."

"I haven't implicated you in anything. And I won't."

A moan, cracked with dehydration, floated down the hall, and then a faint cry that I realized was his name being called.

Lloyd jerked to his feet and jogged back into the house, his steps sped by panic. The voice had been startling—frightening, even—and I found myself standing at the mouth of the hall peering down its length. The bedroom door was closed as usual, but through it I heard Lloyd's voice, raised with concern, and the sound of bottles clinking. I was unsure whether I should slip out, giving them privacy. I had, after all, barged in late and unannounced on a Monday night after another unsuccessful round of calls to Lloyd's various numbers. Persistence and self-centeredness—useful traits for a writer, but they didn't make me the most considerate name in the Rolodex. As a penance I tidied up the kitchen, trying to make headway against the avalanche of housework that confronted Lloyd each morning.

I stacked the dishes, wiped the counters, and gathered the loose trash—stale tacos included—into several grocery bags, all the while thinking of Caroline's comment about trusting selfish motives. Lloyd likely wouldn't notice, but the thought of leaving him with a clean kitchen made me feel better. I finished and resolved to go.

I had my hand on the doorknob when I heard Lloyd's voice behind me. "I always thought death was beautiful."

I turned, and there he was, holding a tray loaded with dirty teacups, bowls filled with uneaten food, and a crusted washcloth. His back was slightly stooped, as though the tray were pulling him downward, and his eyes looked sunken and weary.

I released the doorknob, took the tray from him, and set it by the sink.

"I don't mean it in a creepy way," he said. "The colors, if you detach yourself. Burnt oranges and greens and deep blues. Like an autumn bouquet. It's beautiful, death." He looked up, his expression blank, dazed. "But not dying. No, dying's quite awful."

"She okay?"

"Her line worked its way out. Blood spray on the sheets, her clothes, the floor. It happens."

He shuffled over a half step and slid into the kitchen chair.

I said, "Do you want me to go? Maybe you want to be alone?"

Lloyd picked at the edge of his place mat. "And the clothes that are comfortable. That provide . . . access." He blew out his cheeks. "Terry cloth. Polyester. I should design elegant deathwear. I'd make a fortune."

I eased into the chair next to him. He stared at his place, me at mine. We were like two dinner companions with nothing to eat.

"She's wrapped up in the awful business of dying. Moving her car registration into my name. Signing off on the pension. I keep begging her to stop. She needed some bridgework done last month, four grand. She looked at the dentist with this . . . this resigned expression and asked, 'Can it hold?'" He shook his head and covered his eyes. His face contorted into a sob, but no sound came out, and when he removed his hand, there were no tears. "'Can it hold?'" He shook his head. "She said it's because she doesn't want to go through the pain in the ass of it—who wouldn't avoid the dentist?—but she's from New England stock way back, spends money like she's opening a vein. I'll be fine, money, but she's worried. And I just . . . I just want her to have a new dental bridge, Drew. That's all I want. This woman deserves that. She's forty-two. Forty-two. Nineteen when she married me. You'd think twenty-three years was a long time, but it feels like . . ." He made a whisking sound through his teeth, as if shooing a cat, then shuddered off a thought. "I'm rambling. I'm rambling."

With a shaking hand, he poured himself another rum, upending the empty bottle into one of the trash bags, and added a splash of

Coke. He pinched crumbs on the table into a stray napkin. Why? What did it matter? How did *any* of it matter to him? Rising when his alarm clock bleated. Picking out clothes. Filling up his gas tank. The mundane business of life. And yet he endured, he and Janice, staring into the face of it day after crushing day. What choice did he have? What choice did she?

He noticed me watching him and crumpled up the napkin nervously, as if he'd been caught doing something shameful. I wanted to tell him that it was okay, that he could poke all he wanted at those crumbs, left behind like the ghost footprint in the Birkenstock.

At some age it occurs to you that this aging thing is for real. That you've done both loop-da-loops and there's only the corkscrew left before you have to disembark. The ride doesn't last forever—no shit—but there's one definable moment when the cold, hard fact of it hits you in the gut. Mine was the summer when I was thirty-three, a Sunday night after another lost weekend. I was the age of Jesus and had accomplished relatively little by comparison. Through a haze of shower steam, I'd stared at myself in the mirror and noticed a new web of wrinkles suspending each eye. I'd sat on the brim of the tub, head thick with last night's booze and the crushing weight of the obvious. The reality had been there all along, like the key to a well-crafted mystery, but I'd averted my eyes, tuned out, drunk myself into mind-numbing stillness.

Now's the slot for the painful confession, though mine is as banal as those crumbs I deployed to such grand literary effect. After my mother's third stroke, when she was teetering at the cliff edge, ravaged in mind, her face caved in on itself like that of someone two decades her elder, when the nurse gave me that final solemn nod, *Now is the time, Drew,* I froze outside her door. I couldn't go into her room. The thought suddenly, powerfully, terrified me. She likely wouldn't have recognized me anyway—it'd been weeks since she had—but that proved scant consolation. My father, bless him, never judged me. Not a flicker of disapproval in his eyes then or in the year and a half he lived after. That day, outside my dying mother's room, he kissed me on the forehead and left me in the corridor, gripping the silver-lever door handle as if I were going to get it together and enter the room at any instant, though I knew I wouldn't. With my head pressed to the door, shamed beyond description by my cowardice, I heard that blipping monitor smooth out into a flatline.

"Lloyd," I said, "I am so goddamned sorry for what you two are going through."

He nodded his thanks quickly, an uncomfortable tic, and sipped his drink again. "When I was a kid, I always thought I'd learn to reconcile it. Another thing I'd pick up along the way. Maybe that's why I . . . the job, you know. But then, with Janice—well, I never did. Learn. You never do. You can't, maybe. It's always there, and no matter how close you think you are to it, you're never ready."

"Listen, when this . . . If there's anything—"

He cut off my awkward reach of affection, not ready to concede the worst-case. "We have a shot." He spoke quickly, though his voice wobbled. "One more round. We have a shot."

He rose, and I followed suit, and we walked the two steps to the door that dumped out from the kitchen to the gravel driveway, the patch of venetian blind jiggling as I tugged the knob.

"You have to understand. Hope is all you've got. That's it." He gripped the doorframe and tilted his face into shadow, so it wasn't until he spoke that I realized he was crying. "I'm sorry," he said, "I'm sorry."

I stood there struck by the incredible limitation of the language I claim to have a passing knowledge of, saying, "It's okay," at intervals like a coach with a Little Leaguer who'd scraped a knee.

Finally he pulled back, covering his face and apologizing still, drawing the door closed quietly behind him and leaving me to the crickets sawing through the chill night.

24

My cell phone tap-danced on my nightstand beside my alarm clock: 7:02 A.M. Lloyd's words came fast, excited. "Two rapes, a molest, and an indecent exposure."

I sat up against the headboard, grinding my eye with the heel of my hand.

"I got a suspect for you," he continued. "Check your e-mail—looks like a spam piece, subject heading 'Real Rolex Watches.' Print the attachments only. They'll be untraceable. Then call me back. At the lab."

I padded into my office, opened the attachments, and printed a few copies. Leafing through the pages, I dialed the lab on my dead home line before snapping out of it and doing a second take on my cell phone.

Lloyd said, "Top document gives you registrant information for all hundred and fifty-three brown Volvos with a license beginning with seven that the DMV has on record for L.A. County."

I scanned the list eagerly, looking for names I recognized. My breathing had quickened. Had one of these people intended to put me away for a murder I didn't commit? Had one of them sunk the knife into the soft flesh above Genevieve's navel?

"Flip to the next doc," Lloyd said. "Those are photos and rap sheets for the five individuals from the first list who have a criminal record."

Four men and a woman, all with the pallor and frizzed hair unique to booking photos, gazed from my monitor. None I recognized.

"Four are just penny-ante stuff," Lloyd continued, "but one I like. I like this guy a *lot*."

I knew which one before Lloyd said the name. Morton Frankel. A low shelf of a brow shaded dark eyes. Flared nostrils, angular cheeks, cropped hair. Thin, well-tended sideburns extended past the bottoms of his ears, ending in points. He wasn't smiling so much as baring his teeth, which seemed just slightly too long, as if his gums had receded. Ropy muscle sheathed his neck; he'd flexed as the photo was taken. His bearing and grooming seemed purposely refined to convey menace.

Who the hell was this guy? And if he *was* the killer, why had he gone to such elaborate lengths to bring me down? How was he connected to Broach and Genevieve? And what the hell did he have against me?

"This guy's right off the movie poster," I said.

"Arrested in '99 and '03 for the rapes. Acquitted once, the other he pled down to a battery—he put a hooker in the hospital. Did some time there, his second brief stint. He was a person of interest in another rape investigation in '05, but there wasn't anything to hold him on. Questioned again last year on a missing girl, never held. As you can see, he's got a lot of affection for women."

I thought about the unidentified hair found on Kasey Broach's body. "No DNA on record?"

"Just prints. He's a machinist, drawing a salary right now from Bonsky Forge and Metalworks in Van Nuys. But look at his address. He lives downtown, not ten minutes from the Broach dump site."

"And the electrical tape was bought at the Van Nuys Home Depot, by his work."

"There you go. He's got the diabolical gleam in the eyes, too."

"That he does. Rasputin himself."

Though I had only the thinnest of circumstantial evidence, I couldn't help but put Morton Frankel in Genevieve's bedroom. This was the face that she'd glimpsed through her last panic flash, approaching her in the night? *That* face in her peaceful bedroom with the vanilla candles and fluffy duvet? It seemed impossible, profane, even. Had he been obsessed with her? Or had he killed her to work out an obsession with *me*? What continued to plague me most was the thought of Genevieve's fear in that final instant before the knife tip found her heart. A terror that Katherine Harriman, my redoubtable prosecutor, might have called unimaginable. But I could imagine it all too well. Would Morton Frankel have made it worse— Genevieve's last moment alive—than if it had been me in that room? I prayed that she hadn't suffered at his hands, that the struggle had been as brief and merciful as billed. The thought of him watching me while I slept made me actually shudder. This man, with pointed sideburns, crouching over my sevoflurane-slumbering form with a boning knife?

Lloyd had been talking.

"Sorry, what?"

"I said, this is my ass on the line. I'll deny sending you this to the bitter end."

"I will, too. Getting it from you, I mean."

"Hand it off to Kaden and Delveckio. I can't without answering questions of how I closed in on it, which means I would implicate you, which means I would implicate myself. Get it?"

"I get it."

"I'm sorry about last night—"

"If there's one thing you don't have to do, Lloyd, it's apologize."

There was a long silence, and then he said, "I have to go."

I couldn't take my eyes off the booking photo. There was something unquestionably perverse about Morton. Something unreasonable about his very appearance. He made for much better cackling-villain material than Richard Collins, the Home Depot stoner. Maybe Frankel murdered women for the thrill of it. That would explain the lack of obvious connections between Genevieve and Broach. But it wouldn't explain why a random serial killer would want to frame me.

A scrape at the door startled me—I'd forgotten I was a proud dog owner. Xena ambled in, squatted, and urinated into a box of *Hunter Pray* DVDs in the corner.

I'd let her sleep on a mound of pillows in the kitchen, figuring the flagstones to be impervious to accidents. Then again, glossy jewel cases probably held up pretty well under dog urine, too. I mopped up as best I could and went downstairs, Xena slobbering at my side. Since I didn't have any dog food, I pan-fried some hamburger meat, adding salt, pepper, and a dash of curry as befitted a princess warrior. Xena seemed quite pleased with the results.

Gus had been MIA for a few days. The coyotes had probably caught up to him at last, poor guy. Before letting Xena out, I checked the backyard one final time, then offered my missing squirrel pal a toast with my glass of pomegranate juice. I went upstairs and showered. Preston arrived just as I finished dressing, and Xena unleashed her inner killer on him, nuzzling his crotch and licking his hands in threatening fashion.

We made and broke eye contact, neither of us eager to acknowledge my drop-in the previous night. Were we going to discuss it? Discuss what?

Preston brushed past me, rubbing his palms together eagerly. Business as usual. "Got more pages for me?"

"Better. I have a suspect."

He detoured through the kitchen, returned with a rum on the rocks, and plunked onto the couch, oblivious to the two dirty glasses he'd left on the coffee table in his prior house calls. Xena curled at my feet, licked herself vigorously, then fell asleep. As I brought him up to speed, the gardeners arrived. Xena failed to rouse when the team of five masked men, wielding hedge trimmers and weed whackers, carved up my backyard.

Preston thrilled at the photo of Morton Frankel. "What an antagonist! He even *looks* like one. But Mort? *Mort!* Why can't he be *Cyrus?*

Or *Bart*? Who names their kid Mort? Only Jews with a dead Mort somewhere."

"Like in the attic?"

"You know what I mean."

I got Preston my latest pages, and he set them in his lap and leaned back on the couch. I detected an underlying sadness. Or, having seen his digs—as lonely as mine—was I projecting?

"Listen," he said. "I, uh . . ." An unusual hitch. He cleared his throat and started again, more formally, "I don't do so well when I'm . . . I suppose I do better when I'm out. And skip the obvious jokes. It's a part-time condo, if that. Just for me, really. I'm not actually here that much that it makes sense to do a whole thing. I don't even take dates back. People pawing around. It just feels too invasive."

"Invasive," I said. "Right."

Leaving Preston on my couch reading my latest pages and Xena trying to bite the stream of air from the floor vent, I gathered up my untraceable documents and my various theories and went in search of a detective.

"Since I wasted your night last time, I figured I'd give you first crack at it."

I waited through the pause. I'd caught Cal at home, readying to forge into another day of Westside crime. Someone had kidnapped a poodle from a Brentwood nail salon, which meant that Fifi had wandered off but the owner wanted police help in retrieving her. Ethics bow before toy dogs. I looked down to plug in my headset, almost sending the Guiltmobile flying off a Mulholland ridge.

Cal said, "Listen, as much as I'd like to get on this—fuck, do I want to—and as much as I appreciate your cutting me in, you're gonna have to bring it to Kaden and Delveckio. I can't dick around anymore. My captain caught wind of our Starsky-and-Hutch stunt and came down pretty good."

Thus the poodle assignment.

"I didn't tell him you were there, though," Cal said, "though it might come out soon. Figured you got enough balls in the air, and I was the dumb-ass with the badge."

"Shit, I'm sorry. How'd your captain catch wind of it?"

"Richard Collins is pressing charges."

"*What?*"

"The whole fire-extinguisher thing."

"I'd wondered whether that was within departmental regs."

"I saw it on TV once. *Aiden's War.*"

Johnny Ordean's show. Served us right.

"Tell Richard Collins that I used my cell-phone camera to take a picture of the pot he was trying to wash down the disposal. And sent it, Web-time-stamped to my computer at the very minute we were inside his place."

"He *was*? You *did*?"

"Yes. No. But it won't be worth his risking a third strike to call the bluff."

Cal exhaled—a relieved sigh. A lawsuit would've killed his chances of getting to Robbery-Homicide. "You know I love you, Drew. Listen, you're not doing such a shitty job here. About the Richard Collins angle? We all step in it, as I proved. That's how investigations proceed. Like writing, I'd guess. You fuck up and keep trying until something hits."

"It'll hit for you, Cal. You'll make RHD."

"Yeah, right after I collar the poodle." He laughed. "Listen, I know I was a dick when you first asked for help. I was pissed I was stuck in West Latte Division and you murdered someone and didn't even call me first."

"Next time," I said, "I'll be sure to."

.   .   .

Kaden set a brick of a fist on the papers I'd placed on his desk. "Where'd you get these documents?"

"They're illegal for you to have," Delveckio said. "This is confidential information. Just like the case files your buddy Cal Unger's been quietly digging around for."

"Cal has? When?"

"Right. This is news to you."

It was. Cal had just told me that since getting busted he'd stepped off the extracurricular investigation. He put in a request for the case files before then and hadn't told me? Or was Delveckio lying? As LAPD detectives, both were certainly in pole position to dick around with evidence. Why would Cal be secretive about seeing the case files? Because he was gunning for a promotion or helping me out but had to cover his ass since he was out of his jurisdiction. Or for more ominous reasons. What had he said to me when I'd first tracked him down? *I think guys like you are exploitive bastards.* But his name wasn't on the Volvo list—I was sure of it. Was I paranoid? Yes. Wrong? Maybe. I made a note to have Chic get Cal's information to the database privacy invader. Next I'd be getting the guy to investigate Chic. And then himself.

"Now," Kaden said, his tone snapping me back to the cool Parker Center air, "how 'bout you tell us where you got the DMV records?"

"You know I can't tell you that. So can we skip this part and figure out how to use what's here?" Leaving out Lloyd's involvement, I'd explained to them twice already how I'd arrived at the DMV registration list and the suspect photos. Frustrated, I leaned back in the folding chair before Kaden's desk and peered around the squad room. I'd drawn a few looks of recognition and disdain on my way up and as I'd moved through the halls.

Kaden angled his computer monitor away from the glare of the bare windows. "What's the witness's name again?"

"Junior Delgado."

He hammered on the keyboard, then shook his head as if he'd found what he'd suspected all along. "Kid's got a rap sheet longer than my dick."

"So does my Aunt Hazel. Come on, Kaden, who do you expect to find wandering beneath the Rampart freeway overpass at two in the morning?"

Kaden fanned off my comment with a hand. "We'll look into it."

"When?"

"We have about a hundred leads, most of them from more reputable citizens than Hoon-yore Delgado."

"And none of whom were there that night."

"And none of whom were located and interviewed by a suspect in the case."

"So my information is tainted."

"Of course it is, asshole. We've got no corroborating reports of a brown Volvo anywhere in either murder investigation. And this *minor*"—a finger jab at the screen—"seems like someone who'd be easily led by the nose."

I laughed. "Interview him. I beg you."

"We will."

"When?"

Kaden threw down his pencil. "You're an amateur, so you don't see how many assumptions your guesswork rests on. Brown is the second most common Volvo paint job behind that shit yellow. There are a hundred and fifty-three brown Volvos with licenses starting with seven in L.A. County. Great. You know how many there are in the *state*?" More hammering on the keyboard. "One thousand two hundred ninety-one."

"How many are owned by convicted sex offenders?"

"How many of the victims in this investigation were sexually assaulted?"

"How about your theory that the killer evolved?" I tapped Frankel's sinister booking photo. "The forensics line up. He's a hundred eighty-five pounds—"

"Just like you."

Delveckio leaned back so his thin shirt stretched across his narrow chest. "And you maintain that Morton Frankel doesn't mean anything to you?"

"I told you already," I said. "I don't know the guy. I think the question is if I mean anything to *him*. And it's easy enough for us to find out. One strand of hair from this guy could prove our case."

"Prove?" Delveckio repeated. "Us?"

"The unidentified hair found on Broach's body might have nothing to do with anything," Kaden said. "Dumped bodies pick up hairs. Or it could be a plant, like your hair supposedly was. That's what you don't get. It's *never* neat. And even if it is, it's not just about evidence. It's about building a case."

"Look at the guy. A jury'll hate him."

"Not probable cause for a seizure warrant to force him to surrender a DNA sample. Frankly, there's not much from a legal perspective to differentiate him from the other satisfied Volvo owners on that DMV list."

"Morton Frankel is a felon."

"Let's just forget the *non*felons who drive Volvos," Delveckio said. "Guys too smart to get caught, we ain't interested in *them*."

"I assume you have to start somewhere. And a car registered in L.A. County to a felon who lives around the block from one of the crime scenes seems like not a bad place."

Kaden settled back in his chair and said, "Oh. I get it."

Delveckio: "What's that?"

"This isn't a real conversation, Ed. We're in a script. Characters."

Kaden feigned amusement. "We're the cops who bumble around with their bureaucratic agendas and investigative oversights so the vigilante hero, the average-guy-in-peril, can pursue the clues and solve the case without the inconvenience of competent law enforcement sharing a city with him." He leaned over his desk, anger rising to the surface. "What you found was a felon who drives a Volvo. Congrats. I must admit, a rare demographic. You know why you like that lead? More than, say, the all-cotton rope found on Kasey Broach's wrists that only ships to three erotica—and I use the term loosely—stores in Los Angeles? More than the two thousand one hundred and sixty hours—three months, right?—of security footage we're reviewing from one store? More than the credit-card transactions we're sorting through from the other two? More than the shipping records from those dildo shops? You know why you like your brown Volvo more than the electrical tape on Broach's ankles, which was part of an irregular lot sold discount to Home Depot and shipped only to the Van Nuys store and one on Cave Creek Road in Phoenix? More than Broach's and Bertrand's phone records, which, cross-referenced, reveal overlaps to at least two establishments? More than the FedEx guy who delivered packages to both women two months apart? More than the pool guy who services a complex two blocks over from Broach's place and did a dime at San Quentin for slitting his sister's throat? You like Morton Frankel more because he's *yours*. Because you found him. Now, despite the questionable combination of Junior Delgado and Andrew Danner as generators of this particular trail, we *will* look into it, certainly and absolutely. This and the other hundred and fifty-two Volvo owners on the list, which—you're right—is where we should and will start. But we're not gonna drop everything we're working on this instant because we're so darn bowled over that you found a clue."

His anger, cold and rational, had put me back in my seat. "Did you do that *before*?" I asked. "Check messengers to Genevieve's house? See if any of her neighbors had criminal records?"

Kaden glared at me. "We knew you did it. We didn't give a shit to beat the bushes. We gave a shit to *convict*."

I stood, leaving them the documents, pissed off at Kaden for his last crack and for raising so many goddamned good objections before it.

Kaden reached across the desk and grabbed my arm. "You're in the real world now," he said. "Watch that you don't get yourself killed."

I pulled my arm free.

Delveckio swiveled in his chair to watch me pass. "Oh—and, Danner?" He met my look evenly, his red-rimmed eyes detached and calm. "Don't leave town."

25

I eased my car through the packed parking lot of Bonsky Forge and Metalworks, up one row of vehicles, down the next. In the market for a brown Volvo. My tires rattled across the plane of crumbling asphalt, faded back to dirt in patches. Pollution smudged the building's concrete blocks. The only windows were casements set high under the eaves, but from the edge of the lot, through a fence and a rolled-aside warehouse door, I could see the men inside. They labored over blade wheels and soldering torches, curved masks shielding them from sparks fanning up at their faces. The whine of machinery, even at this distance, made my dashboard rattle.

Kaden had been right about one thing: My guesswork *did* rest on too many assumptions. I needed to gather more facts.

Like, say, whether Frankel's brown Volvo had a dent in the right front wheel well.

I finished my second tour through the lot—no Volvos of any color—then drove the surrounding blocks to see if Frankel had parked off site. No better luck there. Maybe he'd left the state. Maybe he'd burned his car to eliminate evidence. Maybe he'd sold his Volvo four months ago to his poker buddy, the Zodiac Killer.

I could walk into the factory under a ruse and see whether I could spot Frankel. But there were two problems: the welding masks and the fact that if he was my guy, he'd recognize me as much as I would him. And if there was one thing I didn't want, it was Morton Frankel with the pointy sideburns knowing I was sniffing his trail.

I called information and had them put me through to the factory office.

"This is FedEx," I said. "I have a delivery for a Mortie Frankel that I need him to sign for. Is he in today?"

Gruff voice—"Hang on. Lemme check the board." Rustling. Screeching machinery. "Yeah, he's here."

"I'm stuck in traffic in Burbank. How late will he be there today?"

"They knock off at three." He hung up before I could thank him for providing excellent service.

A genuine lunch whistle split the air. I drove back to the parking lot and watched the men spilling out into the weedy side yard to eat. They sat on cable spools and rusted machinery and had metal lunch pails with thermoses. I watched more emerge from the gloomy interior, lifting their face shields to reveal red, shiny faces. I was losing hope when a thick form stepped out into the midday glare. He was facing away, but the vibe off him was electric, and I wasn't surprised when he turned. He swiped a palm across that hard brow and flicked a spray of sweat to the dirt. Flapping the front of his blue overalls to move air through them, he exchanged a few words with another worker.

There was maybe fifty yards between us—parking lot, fence, brief throw of yard—but I felt as though we existed in separate bubbles, he with his tools, beat-up overalls, and sparks, I with my leather driver's seat, notepad, and tinted windows. Suddenly sweating in my air-conditioned Highlander, I stared at him. Had this man stood in the dark of my bedroom the night of January 21, watching me sleep? Had he drugged me, taken my blood, and plucked a hair to leave beneath the cold, dead fingernail of Kasey Broach? And if so, why?

There was something fascinating about Frankel—looking at him was unsettling, but I couldn't take my eyes off him.

Please be a killer so I'm not.

It dawned on me that Kaden had been right about something

else. Frankel *was* mine. He was my suspect, and he would be until he wasn't.

I watched those teeth tear into a sandwich, watched his jaw flex as he chewed.

See you later.

26

C hic staggered beneath the pop-up hit by his eldest son, Jeremiah, screaming, "I got it! I got it!" to call off his various children wielding mitts of all sizes.

He snared the ball in a basket catch, then let it flop free. His brood groaned and hurled gloves at him and piled on as he laughed at his self-parody, rolling on the grass of his extended front lawn and covering his head protectively. Grabbing ankles and wrists, I pulled the kids off him, calling them by all the wrong names.

Angela came out, her glare sending the children—and almost me—scrambling to wash up for lunch. She bore a tray of drinks for the workers who were lazily assembling a high-end play structure to the left of the baseball diamond. Complete with corkscrew slide, rope ladder, and mini rock-climbing wall, and topped with a fake tree house, the contraption made the play set at Hope House look like a heap of scrap metal.

Angela served the workers, then turned to her husband. "Baby, take Drew on down to the truck and get me some queso blanco."

"We having soul *comida*?" I asked.

She nodded. "And, baby, pick up a gift for Asia's lil' friend from camp. They brought her the Polly Pockets when they dropped by, 'member?"

We headed off on foot, sourcing the distant chime of the Mexican-food truck as Chic filled me in on the latest from the database guy. He'd unearthed a number of the overlaps between Genevieve and Broach that Kaden and Delveckio had referred to, and a few others that sounded irrelevant. Broach and I both belonged to 24 Hour Fitness but worked out at different locations. We both had checking accounts at Wells Fargo. Stop the presses.

"And there's one other tidbit—nothing that shudders the heavy bag, but worth poking at." Chic pouched his lips. "Your boy Delveckio bought his life-insurance policy through the same broker as Adeline." He reacted to my face before I could say anything. "I knew you'd go spinning on this like you did with the Cal Unger thing"— though he'd agreed to look into it, Chic had been understandably skeptical about Cal as suspect—"but it's probably nothing, like everything else. Question, though—what's a rich girl like Adeline need a million-dollar life-insurance policy for?"

"Genevieve had one, too—they were each other's beneficiaries. Their father read in some in-flight magazine that people with life insurance live longer and take fewer risks."

"Ain't that like buying a Subaru because you hear people with low blood pressure own 'em?"

"I thought so, but Luc plays golf with Warren Buffett, and I use the driving range off I-5, so whose advice are you gonna take?" I rolled my lips over my teeth, bit them. "I don't like this Delveckio overlap at all."

I pictured the detective in the interrogation room, his weak features set in their best approximation of anger. *I did the advise-next-of-kin for Adeline. I wish I'd borrowed your camcorder first so I could make you watch her reaction.* I repeated his words to Chic, who shrugged.

"Don't you think it's weird he referred to her by first name?" I asked. "And why mention her at all, let alone so emotionally? And now we've got a million-dollar life-insurance policy in the mix."

He gave me the slow-down hands. "It's a big city, but the right demographics cut it down to size. So they used the same insurance broker. So the fuck what?"

I was embarrassed to have no answer. Plus, how would Delveckio fit with Frankel, my lead horse? Like Cal, Delveckio ran across Mort Frankels every day in the course of doing business. Frankel could be a hire. Or, given the paucity of connective tissue, both cops could be red herrings. Delveckio and Genevieve's kid sister used the same insurance broker. Any more salient than my sharing a gym with Kasey Broach?

Chic interrupted my thoughts. "Hard to imagine Delveckio having an affair with Adeline—I've met her and seen him, and that match only works if the finances tilt the other way." He sucked his teeth, an old Chic standby. "And even if they was? What they need another million for anyway? If there *is* a hook here, it ain't the broker, it's a step removed. The cat who *referred* them to the broker, that kind of stuff. Until then it's just another L.A. overlap. So we'll keep chasing the digital trails and focus on whoever put that sheen on your forehead when you first drove up. And that was . . . ?"

I was convinced Chic was Sherlock Holmes in another ethnic incarnation. I told him about Morton Frankel and asked him to put his guy on him to see if and how he connected with the other living and dead players in our evolving drama. Chic of course lifted an eyebrow at the new name and listened pensively while I yammered on about the case developments.

"What you gon' do next?" Chic asked. He seemed to have been expecting my silence, and nodded. "Call me when you need it."

We ducked into the corner store and picked up a plastic braid set for Asia's friend.

"That's how it works," he said. "They buy crap for your kids, then you buy crap for theirs. It's supposed to show you're caring."

My cell phone rang, and I tugged it out of my pocket and answered.

"You'll be here at one-thirty, correct?"

It took me a moment to place the voice as Caroline's.

Junior's court date. Oh, yeah.

"*Hello?*" she said.

"I'm just . . . I'm sort of tangled up today. More than usual, I mean."

Caroline said, "Last I heard, your presence was court mandated."

"There is that."

"Get him there, then you're off the hook. But you'd better not screw this kid over with what's at stake for him."

From my brief experience of jail, I knew it was no place for a fourteen-year-old who cried over his dog going to the pound.

"I agree," I said.

"Trust me, you don't want to go to war with me."

"No," I said, "I think I enjoy you too much."

I hung up as Chic ran down the food truck. His shapeless jersey, from an obscure minor-league team, drooped to midthigh. Together with his unlaced black high-tops, it made him look as if he'd raided the closet of one of his sons. We strolled back together in silence, the sun coming off the pavement in waves.

"The lady psychologist?" he finally asked.

"Yeah."

"You like her?"

"A lot. She's a bit hard-edged, though. Moody, too."

"Always easier to take somebody else's inventory."

"What do you mean?"

"I listened when you talked about her earlier."

"Thanks for the clarification."

He smiled his broad Chic smile, proud of himself, pleased with the world. "This life leaves you behind, Drew-Drew. There's no way around it. Everyone. The singers, the actors, the shortstops all look younger than you. Okay, fine, you can get used to that. But then you take a ten-year nap and you realize that you're pushin' forty and Jimi Hendrix was twenty-five when he recorded 'Purple Haze.'"

"Twenty-seven when he died."

He tapped his temple. "You was always gonna be the one guy

who'd do it different. Live up to your i-dee-lized self. Wudn't gon' get stained by mediocrity or domesticity. Keep reachin'. Keep fightin'. Have that affair with Sue from Accounts Payable. There's them and us, and then there you are. Beer gut." He tapped his washboard stomach. "TV watcher. Coupla rib joints. Slow-growth mutual funds. It hits you you ain't gonna raise no monument or have your mug stamped on a coin. You're you and you can't avoid it. But I tell you this—when it quiets down, when you're done fussin' over how you miss the big paychecks and your shot at the Hall of Fame or wherever I was gonna wind up if I kept up a lifetime .302, the one thing you got is that woman next to you in bed. None of it matters. Nuthin'. Monogamy been tough on me—I never denied it. You give up the smile at the stop sign. The locked eyes in the elevator. Movie romance—marriage ain't never that good. It ain't never that good, but it's better, too. It's been ten years since I stepped out on Angela, and I ain't never gonna step out on her again. Because I'm not afraid anymore 'bout what's passin' me by."

Chic's wisdom, as usual, came in baffling guises. I'd kept up with about half of what he'd said. His alteration between first and second person, while seemingly as sloppy as his free association, struck me as no accident.

Before I could not respond, a yellow Camaro passed us, then locked on its brakes and reversed back to us speedily. A guy with thick hair and a track suit hopped out. "Chic? Chic Bales?"

Chic eyed him warily, accustomed to the drill. "The one and only."

The guy ran over, jiggling happily beneath his clothes, and embraced Chic. "I *love* you, man."

Chic patted his back. "Giants fan?"

"That's right. Thank you."

"Glad to give something back."

The guy did a double take at me, then frowned at Chic. "Nice company you keep." He climbed into his car and screeched off.

We returned to a picnic table literally bowing under the weight of the food. The workers were packing up at the curb. My gaze pulled from the laden table across the expanse of the yard to the newly erected play structure, and I couldn't help note the contrast between here and the cramped little space at the back of Hope House. I wandered off from Chic toward who looked to be the foreman.

"Hey," I asked, "how much does a play structure like that cost?"

"The Romp-n-Stomp? Thirty-five hundo."

"I'd like you to send one to this address." I jotted the Hope House address in my notepad, tore the page, and handed it to him. Tucked into one of the credit-card slots in my wallet, I kept an emergency check, which I unfolded and filled out.

The guy asked, "You want to write down a message, something?"

"Naw, say it's an anonymous donor." The guy shrugged and climbed into his truck. I saw a shadow and turned to find Chic standing behind me. "We don't want it tainted," I said.

Chic stared at me knowingly. "Right." As we headed back, he added, "You don't got no money."

"I got more than those kids."

"Still."

"I'll sell my cappuccino maker."

"Huh?"

Angela was waiting for us at the table. She kissed Chic on the neck. "How's my Drew?" she asked.

"Contemplative," Chic said.

"Hi," I said, "I'm right here."

We sat elbow to elbow, mowing through tortillas and chips. But I didn't feel relaxed and safe as I usually did at the Baleses' table. Every time I'd get distracted into a teasing match or a domestic squabble, Morton Frankel would seep into my thoughts. The gloomy factory interior, lit with flames and sparks. His dangerous eyes. Those too-long teeth, like fangs that he didn't have to bother to sharpen up.

Occasionally swatting a child's reaching hand, Angela listened quietly as I told her about the four days since I'd seen her last.

"That Junior," she said, "he sound like a nice boy."

"For a multiple offender."

"And the woman in charge of him? Ms. Caroline. He lucky to have her."

"She might be too smart for her own good."

"I know, baby." Angela shifted her attention to Jamaal. "Tell your daddy what you wanted to tell him."

Jamaal said, "Okay okay oka-oka-oka-oka—"

"Deep breath," Chic said.

"I want to go out for the team next year."

"Nuthin' wrong with that."

"Soccer. Not baseball."

Chic dropped his fork.

"And the scars," I added quietly, to Angela. "I'm not sure I could get used to them."

"I know, baby." Angela's eyes didn't leave her husband.

Chic looked over at her, and she nodded once, slowly. With admiration I watched him gather his composure, his jaw grinding left, right, and then he said, through a strained smile, "Nuthin' wrong with that either."

Jamaal came around the table and hugged him from the side, and Chic got him in a headlock and pretended to smack his head into the picnic table. Angela stood to clear.

I said, "I think I might ask her out."

Angela rested a hand on my shoulder. "I know, baby."

Chic walked me to my car. I rolled down the window, and he leaned in. His eyes snagged on Frankel's booking photo on the passenger seat. "Careful on this next move, y'hear?"

I rested my hands on the steering wheel, studied my thumbs. "Kaden was right—I think like a writer. But this is the real world."

Chic patted my forearm, drawing himself up. "It's all the real world, Drew-Drew."

27

"Hi, Big Brother."

"Hello, Junior," I said for the fifteenth time.

"You mind if I turn on the radio, Big Brother?"

I finally caved. "Would you stop calling me that?"

Clapping, Junior fell against my passenger door, weak with laughter. He wore a sweatshirt with the hood raised over his baseball cap in case we needed to pull over and rob a 7-Eleven.

"Just look at the damn printouts before we get to court."

I'd zipped home after lunch at Chic's to feed Xena scrambled eggs with diced bell peppers. She'd shown her appreciation by crapping on my hearth. Once I'd cleaned up after her, I'd hopped on the Internet and printed out pictures of Volvo wagons through the years. Junior's attention was a scarce commodity, but we'd already determined that what he'd seen was clearly not one of the recent not-your-mama's Volvos. He couldn't distinguish between the 200s, the 700s, and the 800s, but he was pretty sure it hadn't been a 900 series, with the rounded corners, introduced in '91. Though it spanned too many years to be particularly helpful, the range of models he liked included Morton Frankel's 760.

"I tole you, homes, all this suburban shit look the same to me. Now, if it had some *rims*"—bouncing in his seat—"yeah, boy, then I tell you who, what, where, when, and *why*."

"And you're sure the cops haven't called you yet?"

"Hayell yeah, I'm sure. You think Ms. Caroline gonna lose the message if the LAPD come callin' for my ass?"

She hadn't been there when I'd picked him up. "Will she be back when I drop you?" After he shrugged, I cleared my throat. "She's . . . Do you know what happened to her? Her face, I mean?"

"What happened to yours?"

Fair enough.

"Course I know." Junior studied me with his smooth brown eyes. "Oh, homes. Oh, *homes!*" Now with the elbows-out dance bump. "Big Brother and Ms. Caroline sittin' in a tree. K-I-S-S-I-N-G. First comes love, then comes marriage—"

I screeched into a parking space and hopped out before the baby carriage's arrival. We were, thankfully, on time, but Judge Celemin wasn't. Or at least he pretended to be running late, his occasional glances an indication that he was taking pleasure in making me and Junior wait on the uncomfortable bench in the rear of the courthouse.

I checked my watch again—2:15. Forty-five minutes to quittin' time for Morton Frankel. I assumed he'd come home for a post-work shower, and I wanted to be parked by his apartment to see what he drove up in.

The judge bumped a few more hearings ahead of ours and then dragged through some paperwork. By the time he called Junior up—the public defender materializing as though he'd been summoned electronically—and tacked three more months onto his probation, it was ten till.

I hurried Junior back to the car. He seemed pleased about the ruling. "I don't *never* want to leave Ms. Caroline. She the *shiznit.*" He eyed me. "Ain't she?"

Frankel's place was close to the courthouse. I wouldn't have time to take Junior back and get there in time. I drove quickly, letting Junior distract himself by working my radio like a video game. The ploy only lasted so long.

"Where we going?"

"I'm having you neutered." I slowed in front of a run-down three-story complex on a street spotted with fabric stores and taquerías. Five black teenagers squatted on the strip of brown lawn next door, hugging their knees and rolling dice. In the brief parking lot, the space corresponding to Frankel's apartment number was empty. I cruised the neighboring blocks looking for a Volvo.

Not the ride of choice in Lincoln Heights.

At ten past I cruised up to the curb opposite the complex and threw a few quarters into the meter. The air smelled of car exhaust and boiling hot dogs from the cart parked up the sidewalk beside a bus stop. I was concerned that the teenagers might spot us after a while, but they seemed engrossed in their game.

"This that guy's pad, ain't it, homes?"

A pickup truck rolled to the front of the complex. Morton Frankel tapped the driver—a worker I recognized from the yard—on the shoulder and climbed out. Junior noted my rigid posture but didn't say anything. Frankel walked up the unenclosed staircase, reappearing on the second floor. He swung open his door, threw his jacket and lunch pail inside, and headed back down. Reaching ground level, he started walking toward us.

Before my heart rate could get up a good head of steam, Frankel cut left up the street. Junior blew out his breath. I reminded myself that fourteen-year-olds, no matter how nefarious, also get scared. Stalking a rapist with my juvenile delinquent, I guessed, would knock me from contention for Big Brother of the Year.

Once Frankel was up the block, I pulled out after him.

"Where's his fucking car?"

"That's what I'm wondering. Maybe he's taking the bus."

"This L.A., homes. Nobody take the bus."

"Not everybody has a Huffy."

"Stay further back, homes. Don't you watch no *T.J. Hooker*?"

"I was watching *T.J. Hooker* before you boosted your first car."

"*Boosted*? The word, Grampa, is 'jacked.'"

And so on.

We followed Frankel another few blocks before he turned in to a body shop. I parked across the street by a rental-car lot—plenty of vehicles for the Guiltmobile to blend into. Mort disappeared into the office, a prefab shack. He emerged a few seconds later, rolled a cigarette, and smoked it.

One of the garage doors slid up, and out coasted a brown Volvo wagon.

For an older car, it was in great condition. A few cracks in the paint, but perfectly clean. Clearly Frankel took a lot of pride in his 760. Or he was taking care to keep it free of evidence.

A mechanic with arm-sleeve tattoos hopped out, and Mort gave him a handshake and a shoulder bump. You keep an old car looking that good, you'd better be friends with your mechanic. The guy walked Mort to the right front wheel well and ran his hand over the perfect curve. Mort followed suit, then nodded, impressed with the work.

Why fix the dent? Because he loved his car? Because he wanted to eliminate a potential identifier? Because he'd dented it dragging Kasey Broach's corpse inside?

He pulled a checkbook from his back pocket, leaned over the hood, and signed.

With his left hand.

A hundred eighty-five pounds, left-handed, diabolical gleam in the eyes. Just like me, but with a better gleam.

I stared at his close-cropped brown hair.

I just need one strand. Like you took from me.

I drove back and reclaimed my old spot across the street from the complex. A few minutes later, Mort pulled in to his parking space, slid a Club security bar onto the steering wheel, cranked the window down a few turns, and disappeared into his apartment.

I slapped Junior's knee. "I gotta get you back."

"Thass it? Homes, you gots to get your *evidence.* You gots to break in to the car, see what you can find."

That was my plan, but I wasn't about to tell Junior. "If I find anything, the cops can claim I planted it to get my own ass off the hook."

"Thass why you need me. I'm a *witness*. Plus, you can't argue with no *hair*."

Hearing my own thinking spoken back to me by a fourteen-year-old was a powerful indication that I needed more sleep. "Why'd he leave the window down?"

"He don't keep nuthin' worth nuthin' in there, and he don't want no one to break a window to find that out. And it ain't worth cutting through a Club to steal no old-ass Volvo. Now, go check the headrest."

"Thanks, but no."

"*No?* You gots to have ethics, homes."

"Ethics? Breaking in to his car would show I have ethics?"

"Yeah. Like I won't tag no trees or Lutheran churches. *Ethics*. You got a stone-cold killer out there, and you the only one knows who, and you too bitch-ass to pluck a hair off the headrest?"

"What if the cops come?"

Junior checked his watch. "It's shift-change time at the Hollenbeck Station. Streets are clear of cops."

"How would you know that?" I waved him off. "Never mind. I'm an idiot." I stared nervously at the black teenagers still playing dice on the lawn a few feet from the parking lot. "Those guys just watched him pull up. They'll know I'm not the owner."

"What would you do in one-a your books?"

"Create a diversion."

He snickered. "Like light a fire?"

"No. Something clever."

"Hows about this?" Before I could stop him, Junior climbed out of the Highlander and onto the roof. I scrambled out, looked up to see him cupping his hands around his mouth. *"Yo! Why's there so many niggers up in here?"*

He leapt from the roof, seeming to bounce on the sidewalk, and took off up the street in a sprint. I leaned back against my car as the five young black men blew past me in angry pursuit.

Diversion. Clever. Right.

I stole across the street to the parking lot, keeping a nervous eye out to see if the commotion would draw Frankel from his apartment. Ducking through the Volvo's open window, I scoured the headrest. Not a single hair. The interior looked freshly vacuumed. Of course—they'd given it a cleaning at the body shop. I reached down and popped the trunk, taking a deep breath before lifting it open.

No blood puddles. No remnants of plastic drop cloth. No stainless-steel boning knife. The worn carpet bore lines from the industrial vacuum.

I slammed the trunk and turned for my car when I looked up and saw Mort filling his doorway, staring at me over the second-floor railing. I jerked back, startled, the soles of my sneakers scraping asphalt.

Whether he'd caught a clear look at my face or seen me at his open trunk, I couldn't tell. He came off his step, moving toward the stairs. I walked a few paces up the sidewalk away from him as if continuing on course, pretending to talk on the cell phone. The adrenaline surge left my senses heightened. I listened for his approach, waited to feel the vibration of his charging footsteps rising from the sidewalk. I sensed him behind, shadowing me maybe twenty yards back.

You're in the real world now. Watch that you don't get yourself killed.

When I risked a glance back, he'd turned off down another street. Keeping a full block between us, I followed. He got to the corner and paused, looking in the window of a clothing store. He took a pen from a slit by his breast, tugged something from his back pocket, and jotted on it. I crossed the street so I could make out the window display while keeping my reflection out of view. Mannequins draped with sequined dresses and cheap suits, a few broken down into inhuman segments and left floating in a mound of uncut fabric to the

side. Mort gazed back up through the window, transfixed. A few of
the mannequins were bare-chested or naked, stiff and pale like the
dead. Was he admiring the smooth, waxy skin?

Whatever he was holding slipped from his hands. He took a step
back, still admiring the contorted human forms, then vanished
around the corner.

I waited a few minutes before approaching. He'd dropped a
matchbook, the creased cover sporting a skull and bones. I crouched,
picked it up, thumbed up the flap.

Jagged writing on the underside.

I SEE YOU.

I rose sharply, breath firing in my throat. A movement in the window snared my attention. Standing among the posed plastic bodies,
his leering face a few inches from the glass, was Morton Frankel.

28

Mort pulled back from the window, knocking aside a mannequin, and jumped off the display ledge, running for the door. I bolted.

Dodging honking cars, I sprinted across the street, tangling up with a pissed-off biker on the far side. Mort was at the curb, waiting for a break in traffic. I yanked my cuff free from the bike chain and ran up the street. A bus was just starting to pull out from a stop. I drew beside it, banging the side and yelling. It stopped with an angry hiss, rear doors yawning. Mort hurdled the biker and kept coming.

Afternoon commuters overloaded the bus. I shoved through them, tripping over paper bags and knees, waiting to hear the doors suck closed, but they held open on a lethargically timed delay. Horns bleated; the bus was nosed out into the slow lane.

I stumbled up to the front, the bus driver now joining the protests. Through five or six arms dangling from straps, I saw the rear doors begin to slide closed.

A thick hand snaked into the gap, blocking the rubber bumpers.

As Mort pried the rear doors apart, the front ones opened in unison.

I ducked down, slid off the front stairs on my ass, spitting out onto the curb in time to see Mort's boot vanish up into the bus. The doors snapped shut with a pneumatic wheeze, and the bus veered out into a stream of traffic.

Standing, I dusted myself off. The bus passed, Mort's face a blur through the smudged side window. He caught sight of me and moved to the rear, bucking like a dog in shallow water. He cleared the people on the back bench as if parting curtains, leaning forward menacingly, breath fogging the glass.

I stepped out into the now-empty lane, meeting his gaze as the bus accelerated through the intersection.

His lips moved. *I see you.*

"I see you, too," I said.

As I jogged back to the Highlander, my phone vibrated in my pocket.

Junior said, "I'm at the corner of Daly and Main. Gas station."

I was more relieved than I would have thought possible.

"How'd you get this number?"

"Ms. Caroline."

"What'd you tell her?"

"That you leave me to get chased by a buncha black guys so you could break into a murderer's Volvo." He laughed. "Juss kidding, homes. I say I wandered off to get me some eats."

I hopped into my car and headed to pick him up. He'd managed to run nearly three miles. I found him sitting on the concrete wall by the bathrooms, smoking a cigarette. He was new to the game, still working on a cool-looking exhale. I parked and walked over. I debated telling him how worried I'd been, but it would have been awkward for us both.

"What happen?" he asked.

I told him.

"Big Brother got some *moves.*" He held up his hand, and we high-fived. "Even if he is old."

"I'm thirty-eight."

"Like I said." He tapped the pack of Marlboro Reds against the heel of his hand awkwardly, a trick he'd probably just picked up.

"When I was a kid, my grandfather caught me smoking and made me finish the whole pack," I said. "Every last one. I got so sick I never smoked again."

"Yeah? Any other a' them folk tales you got to tell?"

"No. But why don't you give it a go?"

He shrugged. "'Kay." He teased out another cigarette and held it up ceremonially before lighting it. He went after it quick and hard, the cherry lurching several millimeters a pull. He finished, lit the next off the butt.

After he'd smoked two more, I asked, "How do you feel?"

"Great."

The next three cigarettes he seemed to enjoy even more.

"How about now?"

"Million bucks."

By the ninth he'd mastered the French inhale. By the thirteenth he was blowing smoke rings. He crushed the fifteenth on the wall between his knees, paused to stretch his arms happily to the sky, then lit up another.

I climbed up on the wall, sat next to him.

"Bum one off you?" I asked.

Caroline looked me in the eye as if she were sizing up an opposing boxer. Her index finger moved from her chest to mine. "There's no chemistry here."

"It's just dinner," I said.

She crossed the shag rug and settled behind her desk, as if she felt better with a large object between us.

I peered at the photographs on the bookshelves. Group-home kids of all ethnicities lined up for the Matterhorn, like a carefully cast Disney brochure photo. A crew of counselors around a campfire, kids sprawled in the foreground and across laps. On the side of the desk, there was a picture of Caroline laughing, arm around a black kid in his early teens. She was younger, her face unmarred yet by injury, and her beauty was radiant. I pointed at the picture. "Who's that?"

She slammed the photo flat and slid it into a drawer.

I said, "I meant the boy."

She flushed. Her collar fluttered from the pivoting fan. With quiet dignity she reached back into the drawer, removed the picture, and propped it up again. "That was J.C. I had a lot of jobs before this one."

I checked my watch. "I called Kasey Broach's apartment manager this morning. If his answering machine is to be believed, he's available only from six to six-thirty. To implement the Caroline Raine home-visit rule, I've got to get moving. I'd love you to take up my invitation to dinner tonight, but your deliberation is getting unflattering, and I'm fragile."

Her lips twitched—not quite a smile. "Don't invite me to dinner because you think it's doing me some favor." She stared at me evenly. "I'm just fine on my own."

"Yeah, you seem great—the picture of well-adjusted, just like me. That's why I think you and I could use each other." I walked over, paused by the door. "Eight o'clock?"

She gave me a faint nod.

The counselor with the bitten-down fingernails stood just outside in the hall, pretending to tidy up the telephone table.

She looked up as I passed. "You hurt her, I'll kick your ass."

"I hurt her," I said, "I'll help you."

29

Kasey Broach's family moved through the open doorway of Apartment 1B to a U-Haul and back again, toting lamps, trash cans, cardboard boxes. Strong family resemblance in the parents and the younger sibling, whom I recognized from the news. They moved in automated silence through the powerful beam of the truck's headlights. Now and then one would halt along the brief path from truck to door and lean against a post, bending over as if catching lost breath.

Frozen meals thawed in a translucent trash bag by the doorway. Kasey's father paused to dump in an armload of toiletries—fraying toothbrush, faded razor, half carton of Q-tips—while his daughter wound a telephone cord around the base unit before stuffing it into a salad bowl. The logistics of loss. The awesome minutiae.

The 110 rattled along behind a vast concrete barrier a half block away. A group of kids ran around the dark street, waving toy guns that looked real enough to get them shot by worn-down cops. Their laughter seemed to mock the somber procession of surviving Broaches.

To see the apartment, I wouldn't require the harried manager's goodwill after all. What I required was perhaps more nerve than I could muster. This was an opportunity that my trial had robbed me of having with the Bertrands. A chance to speak to the bereaved and offer what little anyone could under such circumstances. For a moment I hated who I was for how it would taint my approach here. And I hated my ulterior motive, a seamy lining to a dark cloud.

The mother, a stout, well-put-together blonde, glanced over at me a few times, and I realized I must be creeping them out, watching behind my car's tinted windows with Kasey's killer still at large.

I approached, keeping a respectful distance. "Mrs. Broach? I'm—"

"Yes." She paused, a stack of dresses, still on their hangers, draped over her arm. "Andrew Danner. I recognize you."

"I'm so sorry to intrude. I know it's quite odd, my coming here and . . . and . . ." The hallway light over Kasey's door had been broken recently, judging by the bits of glass kicked to the side of the jamb. The coldness of such preparation made me shiver. That's why the Broaches were using headlights for illumination now—because the killer had broken the hall light in anticipation of dragging out their daughter's unconscious body.

"Well?" her husband said from behind me. "What *are* you here for?"

In the distance, the street kids shouted back and forth in prepubescent sopranos. "I got you! I shot you *dead*!"

A small choke came out of nowhere, seizing my throat, shocking me. I pressed my lips together, trying to find composure.

Mrs. Broach dropped the dresses on the ground, stepped forward, and embraced me. She rubbed my back in vigorous circles, infinitely more effective than I'd been when Lloyd had broken down. She was soft, slightly damp with perspiration, and smelled nicely of conditioner. For a moment she blended into my own mother, April, Françoise Bertrand, cooing accented forgiveness.

I pulled back, blinking against the headlights, and said, "I don't even know how to begin. Except to say that I'm so sorry for what happened to Kasey. And I'm sorry this happened to you."

Kasey's sister—Jennifer, if memory served—stood in the doorway, chewing gum and swiveling a lanky leg on a pointed toe. The news stories had made much of the fact that she was a freshman in high school, which put almost two decades between her and her big sister. Jennifer looked as if she wanted to cry but had no more energy for it. Somehow she summoned it, pressing her hand to her top teeth and hiccupping out something between a moan and a sob.

"Come on inside," Mr. Broach said.

We went in, stepping over half-packed boxes and strewn clothes.

Mr. Broach looked around and said gruffly, to himself, "How do you know what to keep?"

They sat on a couch that had been shoved away from the wall, I on a large overturned earthenware pot. Where to start?

"I was a suspect in your daughter's murder," I said.

Mrs. Broach said, "We know. Bill told us."

Bill Kaden. Right.

"He said you still *are* a suspect," Mr. Broach said, "but I don't think you did it. I watched your trial. That tape you made showing you sleeping the night our Kasey was killed? Bill thinks it implicates you more. I think the opposite." He looked at his wife. "We understand how you could have gotten to the point of questioning yourself."

Here we were, just a couple of old friends dismissing the notion I'd murdered his daughter.

"I appreciate that," I said.

"I'm simply stating my opinion. We certainly don't presume to judge."

Mrs. Broach sat sideways on a hip, tilted over her daughter, one hand smoothing Jennifer's hair behind her ear. "Kasey's in a better place now. Joshua 23 says God keeps all promises. *All* promises. One way or another."

"I'm glad you can find some peace in this. I doubt I'd have your strength."

"We have experience," Mr. Broach said. Then his eyes watered, and he coughed into a fist. "We lost our boy, too, five years back."

I must have looked stunned.

Mrs. Broach picked it up. "No, no. Tommy died of leukemia."

Some people get it with both barrels, can barely catch their breath before fate reloads. And others skip through life stepping on the heads of others, swinging the world by its tail.

Jennifer was staring at me. "Did you do it?" she asked.

"No. I did not."

"How about the first? That French girl you dated?"

"I don't know. I don't believe I did." I parted my hair, showed the seam of scar tissue. "But I can't know for sure until I work out what really happened."

"So that's what you're doing?" Mr. Broach asked.

"What I've been through . . . I think maybe I could help find out more about your daughter's death. I've been looking around, and I've found a few leads."

Mr. Broach said quickly, "Have you told the police?"

"I'm sharing everything with them as I go. But they're working the case day and night and have a lot of leads of their own, too. So I figure I might as well stay involved, see that nothing slips between the cracks."

"How can we help?"

"Well," I said, looking to each of them, "can you tell me about Kasey?"

"Oh," Mrs. Broach said, "we can do that."

She spoke first, detailing Kasey's habits and lifestyle, but soon they were all chiming in with small memories, smiling. A box of tissue circulated. The man in 1A had been out the night of her death, but Trina Patrick had been home in 1C. She'd been watching a game show, volume up loud, augmenting the experience with a table red, and had heard nothing. I asked about Morton Frankel and brown Volvos and recent boyfriends, and we all grew politely frustrated at our inability to get traction.

Mrs. Broach leaned into her husband, and he held her. "She was a wonderful girl. Sunday school. Youth group. Some trouble in her teens, but who didn't have that? Her job worked her hard, but she still found time for outreaches, short-term missions. Always had a hand out for others. Her brother, when he was diagnosed, they run the test on family members, you know? None of us matched." Mrs. Broach waved a hand to encompass the three of them on the couch. "But Kasey did. She was Tommy's angel. She went in time after time, shots in the hip, needle this thick, never complained, not once." Her fingers were trembling, and when she spoke again, her voice cracked. "We had three children. We've still got one. We're blessed." She pressed her face to her daughter's and squeezed her hard around the shoulders. Jennifer wore an expression I'd seen once in a photo of a makeshift raft that had come apart en route to Florida. A Cuban girl bobbed among the flotsam, clinging to a tire, the sole survivor and not sure that she wanted to be.

"Do you mind if I take a look at Kasey's room?" I asked.

Mr. Broach, tending to his wife, waved his assent.

Kasey's furniture had been broken down, and maybe half of her possessions had been boxed, though there was no discernible order to the packing process. A picture of Kasey with her brother, thin and bald, was taped to the inside of her closet door so she'd see it every morning as she dressed. Her mattress leaned against the wall, the unhooked headboard and slats propped against it. I closed my eyes, imagined Morton Frankel approaching the bed through darkness, toting a canister of sevoflurane and a face mask. Kasey's brief, terrified struggle before the gas took effect. The Volvo he could've parked right out front where the U-Haul was now. I walked over and fingered down the blinds, noting the motel-style proximity of parking spaces to doorways. Five steps through darkness and he'd have had her passed-out body in the back of the wagon. It would've been easy to time so no one would notice.

On the windowsill a cluster of key chains the size of a fist pinned down a petite monthly calendar. I flipped through. It was unused, purchased, I guessed, for the cheesecloth-filtered pictures of wildlife at play. In the midst of the key chains and charms, only three keys—car, apartment, mailbox.

A silver thimble hooked to the ring caught my eye.

I plucked it from the tangle, letting the other baubles swing.

A recovering alcoholic's reminder that even a thimbleful of booze counts as a slip.

The tiny bathroom had already been packed up. I searched out the box of meds and dug through it, finding little more than Aleve, Tylenol, and various antacids.

No Xanax.

A recovering alcoholic wouldn't want to mess with benzos. Yet the autopsy had revealed Xanax in Kasey's system.

I walked back out. The Broaches were doing their best to get into packing mode again, but clearly our conversation had thrown them off.

"Kasey was a recovering alcoholic?" I asked.

Mrs. Broach flushed—not a favorite topic of discussion. "Well. As I said, she had some problems in her teen years, right after Jennifer was born. We got her help."

"Did she ever slip?"

"We just celebrated with a twenty-year cake."

"Do you think she would have ever taken Xanax?"

"Not a prayer of a chance. She wouldn't touch my Black Forest cake, not even with the cherry brandy cooked off."

In the kitchen Mr. Broach dropped a coffeemaker, and the pot shattered. He looked down at it blankly.

A potent three seconds passed before his wife said, "What were we going to do with it anyways?"

"I've put you behind schedule," I said. "Would you mind if I helped?"

Mr. Broach said, "We wouldn't mind that at all."

For the next hour, as the whine of traffic diminished and the kids chased each other around the street, whooping and screaming, I helped pack and load. We made decent progress.

I came out with a halogen floor lamp and a framed Matisse print to find Mrs. Broach sitting on the ground, running her thumb over a white-ribbon barrette that had fallen from a bag.

Mr. Broach paused before her, helped her to her feet.

"I think that's enough for tonight," he said.

We finished loading the stuff by the U-Haul, and he turned to shake my hand.

"Maybe they're wrong about you. With Genevieve Bertrand."

"I hope so," I said back to him.

Mrs. Broach smiled sadly at me. "You take care of yourself, Andrew."

Jennifer offered me a wave from the U-Haul as they pulled out, and I stood and watched until the taillights were two distant eyes in the darkness. The kids circled with their crew cuts and ten-year-old voices, yelling about stickups and screeching imagined injuries. Their toy guns emitted electronic blips and blasts, red lights blinking deep inside the barrels.

I was almost to my car when I noticed that one kid's pistol was deadly silent, nothing inside the bore but a circle of shadow. I jogged a few steps after him.

"Hey," I called out. "*Hey.*"

He pivoted with a crooked grin and said, "Bang bang, you're dead, buddy."

The gun he was pointing at me was real.

30

I put my hands in the air. "All right, I'm sticking 'em up, buddy. Don't shoot."

He smiled, showing off a gap between his front teeth. All fun and games.

I watched his little finger tighten around the trigger and said, "Wait! Lemme give you my wallet first."

Shuffling forward, I dug in my pocket and produced the pitifully light leather billfold. It distracted him just as I hoped, and I snatched the gun out of his hand, grabbing the barrel from the side and twisting it out and free. He stared at me, rubbing his wrist, stunned. "I was just playing."

"This is a real gun."

A shitty .22, to be precise. I nosed back the slide—no round in the chamber. Lucky thing, or someone would be bleeding out on the pavement right now. I dropped the magazine. A hollow point peeked out from the top, spring-loaded and ready to go. I reseated the mag and thumbed the safety on.

"Where'd you get this?"

"I didn't steal it. I didn't. It was in my trash." He pointed to a row of houses backing on the parking lot. Garbage cans lined the rickety wooden fence, awaiting pickup. "I found it. On my property. It's mine."

I turned the pistol to check the serial number on the frame above the trigger and was not surprised to find only a stripe of gouged metal. "When?"

The other kids circled, scared but keeping a good distance. A boy in an Angels cap ran off toward the row of houses.

"Dunno. Coupla days ago."

"The night the cops were here?"

"Day after. They weren't looking for this, though. A lady got kidnapped from right there. That's why we're all playing together now. Buddy system."

"You talk to the cops about this?"

He shook his head, scared. I looked across at his house. The kid in the Angels cap was returning, tugging at the hand of a big man in a flannel shirt. Through a back window, I could make out trophies and baseball pennants.

"You see anything the night she was kidnapped? Out front here? Around ten, eleven?"

"A car was there a little while." He pointed at a parking space to the left of Kasey's door—her car would have held the front slot. "Then it was gone. That's all. I was up watching TV, so I didn't even see nobody."

"What kind of car?"

"It had a big butt on it with windows."

The best description I'd ever heard of a Volvo. I opened my door, digging through printouts. "What color was it?"

"Brown, or black even. It was hard to tell, 'cause there was no light."

I handed him a picture of a Volvo 760. "Like this one?"

"Yeah." A dirty fingernail tapped the printout. "Like that one. Now can I have my gun back?"

"Can I help you?" the man in the flannel shirt shouted, advancing quickly.

"He was playing with a gun."

"My boys can play with whatever they damn well please."

"A real gun."

"Where's my ten-year-old son gonna get a real gun?"

"It's not, Daddy. I swear."

The man continued at me aggressively. I didn't want to fight a father in front of his son, so I chambered a round, aimed straight up, and fired. The boom sent the kids sprawling on the concrete and the man back on his heels, crouching, arms raised over his head.

"It's a real gun," I said.

Their scared reaction didn't make me feel good about myself. Not even close.

The kids stayed down on the ground until I drove off.

"Remember for *Chainer's Law* you showed me how to restore a serial number that had been filed off?" I raised my shirt, showing the pistol snugged in the front of my jeans.

Lloyd stared at me across the pristine sheet of butcher paper that covered his lab bench. "You want to blow your pecker off? This isn't a movie, Drew."

I withdrew the .22 and set it down beside the skull-and-bones matchbook, dimpling the glossy paper. Lloyd coughed uneasily and glanced around.

He'd gotten stuck processing some paint chips and was eager to get home to his wife. Given my excitement over the pistol, he'd yielded to my pressure to see him at the lab. He was working late and figured his superiors would be gone by this hour. I'd caught a few stares on my way in, but the halls were mostly abandoned.

"This doesn't make sense," he said, snapping on latex gloves. "Why bring a gun if he was planning on knocking Broach out with gas?"

"It wasn't for Kasey. Her he wanted alive and unconscious. It was in case one of the neighbors stumbled in on him or during that short unlit walk to the Volvo."

He dusted the pistol, though I was certain that five days of fetishistic fondling by the kid would have smudged over any underlying prints. Indeed, besides mine, Lloyd brought up only child-size marks, which we matched against the prints the kid had left on the Volvo flyer I'd shown him. The magazine and bullets—each of which Lloyd dusted and checked—had been wiped clean.

Using a rotary hand tool fitted with a buffing wheel, he sanded the gouged strip where the serial number had been to a mirror finish. "Wouldn't he know the neighbor's routines? Everything else about this guy points to meticulous preparation."

"But I think he was getting desperate," I said. "Needed a fix, maybe. He's thinking less clearly here—he should've picked someone who lived somewhere more secluded, like Genevieve. But for whatever reason, he wanted Broach. Which meant neighbors. Which meant he wanted a gun for backup. Once he had her safely in the car, he didn't need the gun anymore. The trash cans were at the curb, right on the way back to the freeway. He could've just slowed down and tossed the gun into one of them."

Lloyd carried the .22 over to a fume hood, beside a wire basket filled with guns, mags, pistols, and slides of all makes and models, samples for comparison. Quite a few had their serial numbers ground off as well. He donned goggles and gloves and clicked a button on the fume hood's overhang, the fan suctioning air out from the cube of workspace in which the gun rested. The acids and reagents ranged from clear to dark green; Lloyd applied them to the obliterated metal using cotton swabs, wiping gently in one direction. The acids ate into the steel, the smell keen and foul. The metal that had been deformed by the stamping process should erode more quickly, leaving us with a ghost impression of the numerals.

Focused on his task, Lloyd said, "He's got an unconscious woman in the back of his wagon and he's worried about getting caught with a gun?"

"It's not just about getting caught. I think he doesn't *like* guns."

Looking wonkish in his protective eyewear, Lloyd glanced up from the bubbling acid. "Morton Frankel," he said, "doesn't strike me as skittish."

"You might be surprised about the complexities of Morton Frankel. Kasey Broach was twenty years sober. The Xanax? I don't think she took it. I think he gave it to her."

"The killer gave her Xanax? Why? She was knocked out."

"Maybe not the whole time. Sevoflurane's difficult to regulate, and Frankel's not an anesthesiologist. Maybe she popped back into consciousness a few times—especially if he kept her under for a long period."

"Why would he care if he's a sadist?"

"Maybe he's not."

Lloyd guffawed—the broad laugh. "Come on. This hardly matches a guy who used bondage rope to bind her wrists. So now what? He was worried about his victim's anxiety? Morton Frankel with the two rapes and a molest? What kind of killer is he?"

What I knew of Mort, I had to confess, didn't match my theory. Which meant either my suspect had to budge or my theory, my character or my plot. Then it struck me—"Frankel's in a small apartment. If he brought her there, maybe he gave her Xanax in case she stirred so she wouldn't freak out and make noise before he could adjust the sevoflurane."

"That," Lloyd said, "is a valid hypothesis." He steered the boom-mounted lamp down to a hard oblique angle to pick up contrast on the gun, and used water to rinse off the acid. "I'm getting something."

I leaned to squint at the emerging characters, lighter than the surrounding steel, but he moved me back from the rising fumes.

"Wait a minute," he said. "These aren't numbers. They're letters."

"How is that possible?"

He applied a bit more acid, trying to get the final edges to resolve. "He could've gouged off the number entirely, so no restoration could be performed, then stamped letters on and scratched it down again."

Easy work for a machinist.

Lloyd took off the eyewear and threw it on the lab bench. "Looks like our boy has a sense of humor."

I stepped around and peered down at the frame of the .22. Brought to the surface of the gouged metal, a simple message.

NICE TRY.

31

The .22 pressed reassuringly to the small of my back, I coasted down from Mulholland, leaving a message for Bill Kaden, Detective Three.

"Morton Frankel just got his car back from the shop today," I said. "He was getting a ding on the right front wheel well repaired. He caught me following him around, and we almost got into a fistfight, but I gave him the slip. Then I figured out Kasey Broach didn't take Xanax, and I found a kid who gave me an additional sighting of a brown Volvo, putting it at Broach's apartment the night of the murder. He lives in the westernmost house backing on the parking lot. Tell his father I say hello. Oh—and I also have a gun the same kid found in his trash can the day after Broach was killed. I had it thoroughly and professionally processed. There are no adult prints, no nothing except for a hidden greeting where the serial number used to be. 'Nice try,' it says. So I'm hoping all this is sufficient to move Mort up on your lengthy list of priorities. Go interview him. Pluck a hair out of his misshapen skull and run it against the unidentified sample you took off Broach's body. Whatever. But keep him from coming here. If he's our guy, I'm guessing he saved the MapQuest directions from last time he drove over to carve up my foot. If he shows up again, I'm gonna shoot him. And I have a gun with a serial number scraped off, so you'll never trace it to me."

The beep cut me off.

There. It was out now. If Delveckio turned out to be involved in some way—admittedly a long shot—my keeping his partner informed might bring the heat. My instincts told me Kaden didn't have anything to do with some frame-up. And my instincts were right at least 30 percent of the time.

A coyote trotted down the slope ahead of me, an escapee from a noir novel. He lunged up a neighbor's hillside, his white-gray coat blending into the fog.

Not surprisingly, Kaden called back in a minute and a half. *"What?"* he said.

I pulled into my driveway, parked, and filled him in on the day's adventures.

When I finished, there was a speechless pause. "How'd you get the pistol processed?"

"I know a guy."

"Okay, this has been nice and diverting so far, but now I've hit the wall. If you tangle in this investigation any further—"

"You will arrest me for obstruction of justice."

A pause. "That's right. Ed and I are gonna come see you tomorrow, and we're gonna take the pistol and back you out of this case or—"

"Throw my ass in jail."

"It would be a mistake to take this as a bluff, Danner."

"Why don't you come get the gun tonight?"

Kaden covered the mouthpiece for a murmured consult, then said, "We're outside Morton Frankel's apartment."

I felt a surge of excitement at having managed to get the proper authorities, or at least authorities, on what I hoped was the proper trail. If Delveckio and Frankel knew each other already, would Kaden pick up on it? What would he do even if he did?

"Is he there?" I asked.

"He is. We're gonna take him in for interrogation."

"Break him."

"We will. We're gonna sit on his pad for a few hours first."

"Why wait?"

"See if he gets up to anything. Plus, they're softened up when you wake them."

I recalled SWAT crashing my house at 4:00 A.M., dragging my discombobulated ass from bed.

"I doubt Mort softens significantly."

"Either way he'll know we're keeping an eye now."

"I'll sleep soundly."

"Try not to murder anyone while you're doing it."

Now that I knew Frankel was taken care of for a few hours, I called Caroline, apologized for running late, and asked if she would like to come over. She agreed hesitantly, which I took as progress. I would've liked to have cooked, but my excursion to the crime lab had left me short on time, so I cruised down the hill to Simon's Café. The eponymous owner, dapper, gray-haired, and with a black mustache, is everything you want a chef to be. A septualingual Moroccan export by way of Haifa, he makes a borek of three blended cheeses that, with its pickled lemon garnish, will make you speak in tongues. I ate at Simon's last with Genevieve, a late-night dinner that left us stumbling, food drunk, into the warm Valley air afterward.

Diners are used to people-watching in L.A., and I took note of the heads rotating to observe my entrance. I approached the counter, mindful of the whispers, and paid for my order.

The familiar restaurant effaced the ten months since I'd seen Genevieve to what felt like hours. Our split, though not nasty, had been sharp with unspoken resentments, and we'd barely spoken afterward. It occurred to me that Genevieve had likely changed in my absence, the accelerated transformation people make after a breakup. The Genevieve I knew may not have been the one who died. A talk-show shrink I watched once ventured that people either get healthier or sicker emotionally as they grow older. They never stay the same. Under the conditions of this psychological parlor game, which route had Genevieve gone?

As I left with my to-go bags swinging about my knees, a woman met me at the door. Her face, wrinkled severely, looked more anguished than angry. "You shouldn't be on the streets."

I smiled politely. "How else will I find Nicole Simpson's killer?"

I zipped home, leaving the packages on the kitchen counter and walking through the house clicking on lights and whistling for Xena.

The shredded remains of several of my throw pillows were strewn through the living room. Tufts of stuffing had settled about the carpet and in the fireplace.

My house had been searched? Again? For what?

A strand of toilet paper ran from the powder room, across the entryway and living room, disappearing into the dark family room. I drew the pistol and turned on the light. The couch itself had been massacred, the suede torn to pieces. I followed the toilet paper around the ottoman to where Xena lay, snoring contentedly, the end of the two-ply strip in her drooling mouth.

I lowered the gun, surveyed the damage. "Glad your fangs work for something."

She awoke at my voice and scrambled to her feet, licking my hand, then followed me around contritely as I cursed and picked up the larger clumps of fabric.

As I plated dinner, I called Hope House and got Junior on the line.

"I gotta return Xena."

"You can't return no *dog*."

"She chewed up half my house."

"Homes, she just upset you leave her all day. You gots to think of your responsi*bilities*."

I paused from setting the table. "My responsibilities?"

"Thass ride. I come talk to her, homes. Thass all you need."

"I'm dropping her off. First thing tomorrow."

"Where? Here? I can't do nuthin' with her."

"Then we'll take her back to your cousin's."

"That wasn't my cousin."

"Of course not. I'm coming tomorrow morning. With the dog.

And we're dropping her somewhere or I'm taking her to the pound." I hung up and looked at Xena. The ropy strands of saliva dangling from either jowl made her look doleful. "I'm just bluffing. I would never take you to the pound."

As I was lighting the candles on the table, my phone rang.

Junior said, "Look, homes, you wanted to know about Ms. Caroline. I tell you about Ms. Caroline."

"What about her?"

"Her face. I heard my probation officer tell the story. I was in the hallway, but he leave the door open. Ms. Caroline used to work in a *prison*. Assessments, all that. I guess she was on the rapist ward when a riot broke out in another wing. Guards took off to help. They did a lockdown but forgot she was in there. Trapped in with a buncha rapers. For *days,* homes. They pulled a train on her, cut up her face good. You know what a train is?"

My throat was dry, so the words stuck at first. "I do."

"She was barely alive when they found her. But she lived. That's how tough Ms. Caroline is." His tone changed—back to the cheery fourteen-year-old. "*Now* will you keep Xena?"

"Good-bye, Junior." I stood over the table, the match burning down to my fingers. I shook it out and sat, watching the smoke curl and dissipate. The doorbell rang.

I took a moment, smoothed my shirtsleeves, and answered.

Caroline stood at the edge of the porch, gazing up at the house's exterior. She wore jeans and a black button-up with cuffs, the pashmina thrown across her shoulders matching her eyes as if the designer had pulled the color from them.

She looked at me, her smile vanishing. "You found out what happened to me." She leaned in close. "There's a change around the eyes. Like pity, but worse." She turned and started walking away.

I caught her at the curb, already in her car, about to swing her door closed.

"Let's make a deal," I said.

She stopped but kept her grip on the handle.

"Let's for one night suspend all awkwardness and nervousness between us. Let's just put it on hold and eat and talk and see what that feels like."

"Easy enough for you."

"Let's not be arrogant."

"You're a fine one to talk."

She closed the door. I knocked on the window.

"If you drive away, you're gonna feel bad," I said. "It's just a familiar brand of bad."

"I like my brand of bad."

"So it's gotta go this way, huh?"

She seemed to collapse into anger. "You want to play Prince Charming and rescue me from my tragic predicament? Well, I would say get in line, but I've scared away the rest of the line. And I'll scare you away, too. So why don't we just skip it and save ourselves some time?"

"*Hey,*" I said, sharply enough that she jerked back to face me. "I know what it's like to have people afraid of you. So drive off, fine, but don't kid yourself into thinking you're the only person drawing the wrong kind of stares in public."

She squealed out from the curb, and I had to step back to keep my foot from getting run over.

I walked inside. Xena cocked her head, regarding me quizzically.

"Sometimes grown-ups fight," I told her.

I blew out the candles. Recorked the wine. Started to clear the dishes when the doorbell rang. She was holding her hands clasped at her stomach, as if it hurt, and her face was flushed except at the scars.

"Do you mind if I come in?"

"I'd love you to."

She came, not bothering to take in the view, and sat at the table. I took the chair opposite her.

"The facts are always less scary," she said. "More containable."

"When you can find them."

"What did you discover? About me?"

I told her.

She said, "It was a correctional institute, not a prison. An interview room with a door that didn't lock. There were three of them. Men. They were territorial toward the others, kept them out. It wasn't days. It lasted two hours and forty-two minutes." She kept her gaze unflinchingly on mine, reading my face. I did my best not to show any reaction but probably failed. She leaned forward so I could feel her faint breath across my cheeks. "Hey," she said, "at least I got syphilis out of it."

I studied her for a long time, thinking how she'd like to have me go running around my living room with my arms waving over my head.

Instead I said, "How about a drink?"

"I'm not going to talk about it with you. Not details. Not broad strokes. So don't think we'll get cozy and I'll get all cathartic. Off-limits. Got it?"

"Yes."

"I'll have that drink now."

I worked the cork free, poured two glasses, and handed her one. "In case you're more pretentious than you look, I should tell you it's a flinty, soil-driven sauvignon with a rich finish." I buried my nose in the glass, inhaled the fumes.

"This is delicious." She looked around, as if for the first time. "Spectacular view."

"You're not allowed to be gracious. I won't recognize you."

She bared her teeth at me. I retrieved the plates from the kitchen counter, and we dug in. We both had some trouble with the designer utensils, food dropping back to our plates before it reached our mouths. Finally she held up a MOMA fork, one tine separated by a gap. "I'm not adept at using this."

"But isn't it pretty?"

"It's a fork. It exists to convey food to the mouth."

"In our case clearly not." I spun my fork around, regarding the design. "These really *do* suck, don't they?"

She was smiling now, broadly. "You have something easier? Garden trowel, perhaps?"

"Chopsticks?"

"How about Ethiopian bread?"

"I'll check the Mirte stove. In the meantime . . ." I took our forks and tossed them into the trash compactor. I found some plastic utensils, still bagged from my last round of takeout, and we reapproached our plates more successfully.

"This is amazing," she said. "What is it?"

"Israeli salad. Watch out—it just launched a counteroffensive against the Wiener schnitzel."

"I'll send in the couscous."

"Keep it up and I'll drop a Big Mac on your ass."

"Aren't you going to taste the wine?"

A flash of memory, six years new—Mustang slant-parked in the bed of hydrangeas off my front step, radio blaring, me standing on the steaming hood hoarsely shouting Morrison's voice-over on "The End" with a blonde wearing butterfly barrettes.

I said, "My name is Andrew Danner, and I'm an alcoholic."

"Then aren't you supposed to keep all booze away from you?"

"I need to keep an eye on it so it doesn't sneak up on me."

"Like the Israeli salad."

"Precisely."

"How's sobriety?"

"Ruins my drinking."

"What kind of alcoholic were you?"

"I was one of those guys who never knew when the party stopped, or that it had. As long as there was booze and anyone else still drinking, I kept going. Pig at a trough. Sorority binger confronting Twinkies. I wasn't one of those drown-the-pain lushes. I just loved alcohol." I shuttled more couscous onto my incredibly effective plastic fork. "If you believe that, my former shrink would be unimpressed with you."

"Last one to leave a party," she said. "You didn't like being alone with yourself?"

"And a writer. The irony thickens." I swirled my wineglass, watched the maroon legs streak the crystal. "I guess if life was easy, it wouldn't be as much fun."

"Sure it would."

"The Cliché Buster claims another victim. I guess I've been regurgitating that dandy since my childhood."

"Good childhood?"

"Am I on the clock, Doctor?"

"Yeah, but you bought dinner, so I'll only charge half."

"I was a replacement child. My parents lost a daughter a year before I was born."

"That's supposed to be difficult."

"My folks must've skipped that chapter."

"Not bad?"

"I was cherished. My feet didn't hit the ground until I was five."

"Passing you back and forth."

"Exactly. And you?"

"I lost my mom recently." She took a sip of wine. "We were very close. My dad's great—lives in Vermont. Gonna be remarried in the fall."

"Two stable childhoods. How refreshing. And here we are, forty-ish and single."

Despite my flippancy, the remark cut her deep. Loudmouth *moi* of the thoughtless aside. I stood to clear, imploring her to sit. She watched as I dumped my glass of wine down the sink.

"Why buy expensive wine if you're just going to pour it out?"

"I said I was an alcoholic, not that I had bad taste." I scrubbed and loaded while Caroline sipped and looked at the view. We engaged in some small talk, which was surprisingly enjoyable. She lived in West Hollywood, on Crescent Heights. Hated cats and shopping. Brown belt in judo, reached it in just three years. I'd forgotten how warming it was to have company.

The rest of the objet d'art forks joined their mates in the compactor, drawing a laugh from her.

I asked, "Would you mind handing me that equally affected trivet?"

"Do I have to do *everything*?" Smiling, she set down her glass and brought the trivet over to me.

"Why don't you sit on the mauled couch in the family room? I'll join you in a minute."

"Junior's dog?" She waited for my reluctant nod. "Where is she?"

"I put her in a decompression chamber upstairs."

She started for the other room, and I said, "Hang on."

She turned back. The pashmina she'd draped over her chair, and her black shirt had loosed another button, revealing a dagger of smooth flesh. Delicate clavicles, lovely, slender neck. The notched-down lighting demoted her scars to impressions—pronounced, to be sure, but there was a kind of beauty to them as well. They accented the composition of her features like war paint, bringing to them a hyperdefinition, added force, added grace.

"You look spectacular."

She tried to repress her smile, a shyness I hadn't thought she possessed. "This from a tumor-addled alcoholic suffering from temporary insanity."

"Nothing wrong with my eyes."

As she turned away, I caught a smile in her profile. When I finished, I found her in the family room, facing the bookshelf filled with my titles.

She turned at my approach. "Where's *Chain Gang*?"

"Propping up the kitchen table."

"Are you working on a new book?"

"Every minute. I lost the divide between my life and my writing."

"You're living an investigation?"

"A story. We all are, but this segment of my life has a pleasing structure to it."

"Maybe that's why it happened to you."

"I don't believe in intelligent design."

"Sure you do." She waved a hand at the book spines in all their eye-catching glory.

It took a moment for me to catch her meaning. "I believe in narrative. But I don't believe there's a reason for everything and that matters work themselves out for the better."

Tell it to Lloyd and the wedding picture hanging in that dark hall.

Tell it to the Broaches, sorting through Kasey's half-used toiletries and frozen dinners and white barrettes.

Tell it to me, waking up in that goddamned hospital bed with Genevieve's blood dried under my nails.

Caroline was looking at me, studying my face, so I continued. "I don't deny design, no, but I believe you have to craft your own and it's hard work and there are no guardrails."

"So what happens when you veer off course?"

"You wind up with wasted years or a shitty first draft. Neither of which is particularly consequential."

"It's not the randomness of life that holds meaning, Drew. It's our response to it. Say your wife gets hit by a bus. You could spend the rest of your life bewailing an unfair world, or you could decide to start an orphanage."

"Or a home for people paralyzed by incompetent bus drivers."

"If you choose to start your merry home for impaired and guilt-crippled bus drivers, then you've given a senseless event meaning. You've given it its place in a story. No merry home, no story. No story, no meaning."

"No meaning, no growth."

"People don't change much, not as adults, but this thing, maybe it gave you a shot." She licked her lips. "I was forced to change."

"For the better?"

"I don't know. I'm smarter, I think, but also maybe worse off."

"According to you, it depends on where you go from here."

"Exactly. But am I up to it?"

"Inquiring minds want to know."

"I don't know. I don't know if I'm up to it." She was trembling, arms crossed, fingers nervously working a thread that had come loose in the stitching of her shirt. For a moment I thought she might be cold, but then she said, "You drew back the first time you saw me. On the playground at Hope House. I disgusted you. It's the only pure response you'll have. You don't get another true reaction to my face."

"I wasn't disgusted. I was surprised."

"Great. Romantic."

I reached gently for her shoulders, and she let me take them, and then I pulled her to me. The indented scar split her lips at the edge, the flesh soft and warm. I drew back, and for an instant she kept her eyes closed, her head tilted, mouth slightly ajar.

She opened her eyes, pale green flecked with rust.

"Surprised?" I asked.

"Surprised."

"Disgusted?"

She shook her head. A few lines raised on her forehead. "I can't stay with you. I'd like to, but I can't."

"Can I walk you to your car?"

As we crossed the front step, she took my hand in a bird bite of a grip. A tentative hold, didn't last three strides. The air was wet, sweet with night-blooming jasmine. We were awkward at her car—which side the head goes on for the embrace, me holding the door for her, not sure if I should lean in to kiss her again. I tried, but she pulled the door closed and I stepped back quickly. Her face had darkened with concern, and she fiddled with the stick shift, then said, "That was the nicest time I've had in a while," as if that were something extremely troubling.

"Me, too."

"See you around, Drew."

She pulled out. On cue, the neighbor kid started his brass serenade.

Out OF the TREE of LIFE, I just picked me a PLUM.

Whistling along, I went upstairs and freed Xena from the master bathroom. There was no upholstery for her to masticate, but she'd gotten into the bath mat pretty good and, for good measure, overturned her bowl of water.

She followed me to my office. I pulled my notepad from my back pocket and set it on the desk to the left of my keyboard. The loaded .22 I placed beside it. Tools of the trade.

How times had changed.

I fell into my chair, elbowed out the armrests, slid a Bic behind my left ear. Eighty pounds of Doberman-rottweiler curled on my feet. The house was quiet, the windows black rectangles pinpricked by the lights of the Valley below. A small plane blinked its way from Van Nuys Airport off into the night. My fingertips found the raised bump of my surgical scar and then the shallow indentations of the keyboard letters.

Right now Kaden and Delveckio could have Morton Frankel under the hot light. Maybe answers were being spilled—what had been done to Genevieve, to Kasey Broach.

To all of us.

Or maybe it wouldn't be so easy. Maybe the interrogation would yield more questions, more vagaries, more dead ends and broken trails. Maybe Morton Frankel was really just a nice guy with a dented Volvo who didn't appreciate being treated like a plot device.

I faced the blank page. Waiting, like me, for chaos to be forced into order.

32

The voice came at an inappropriate volume through my cell-phone headset. "We're at your house. Where the hell are you?"

"Kaden?"

"And what's wrong with your home line?"

"I'm waiting for Pac Bell to deliver excellent service."

In the backseat Xena belched. Junior giggled—yet another break in the glumness he'd been attempting to convey since I'd picked him up to bring his dog to the new home he claimed to have lined up. He was way too talkative to sulk effectively.

"Where's the gun?" Kaden asked.

"Upstairs on my desk."

"Where are you?"

"Returning a dog."

"Smart, dipshit."

"I figured you wouldn't want me to leave a .22 in a manila envelope on my porch."

"We want you to be home to give us the damn gun."

"It's noon. You told me you were coming by in the morning."

It had been hard for me to shake a sense of dread at dawn. I'd been out of jail a week to the day and still woke up panicked that I was encased by cinder blocks. In hopes of lightening my mood, I'd set out a breakfast bowl of pistachios on the deck for Gus, but he hadn't shown, tied up, no doubt, in a coyote's digestive tract. Stranded like a tramp in a Beckett play, I'd returned to my computer and pounded wrathfully on my loud keyboard, a clackety holdover I'd preserved for precisely such moods.

Chic had called before I'd left, saying word had come back from the cheap seats that Morton Frankel wasn't known as a thug-for-hire. Merely as a vicious criminal. I felt better about talking openly with Kaden and Delveckio and worse about being me.

"We were busy," Kaden said.

"With Frankel?"

"No—interviewing the kid who found the gun. We questioned Frankel last night."

"And?"

"You'll be shocked to hear he said he didn't do it."

"He alibied?"

"Sleeping alone. Which, if he wasn't carving up Kasey Broach, is reasonably what he'd be doing."

"Can't you take a DNA sample? Just one hair?"

"Sure, right after the covert CIA chopper drops him off at Guantanamo Bay. It doesn't work that way, clown. You need what we here in nonfiction refer to as 'probable cause.' And a brown Volvo ain't enough to make a judge sign on the dotted. Now we need that gun."

"I'll run it over to Parker when I get home."

"You bet your ass you will."

"How hard did you press him? Frankel?"

"Hard." A rustle as he started to hang up.

"Hey, Kaden? When you unplugged the security camera in the interrogation room with me, that was just bad-cop posturing, right?"

I heard the whistle of wind across his mouthpiece. "Sure thing, Danner."

I ducked out of the headset, almost knocking my pen from its perch behind my ear.

Junior's mouth picked up right where it had left off. ". . . and they drop off this *mad* jungle gym, homes. Got ladders and bars and shit. The retarded kid went apeshit, pissed hisself down the twisty slide.

Dude say it was donated by some rich a-hole, didn't know what to do wid' all his money."

"Sounds like an a-hole, all right."

"Turn here. Now get over a lane."

"How much farther?"

"We almost there, Big Brother. Left here. Now right. Go straight. Okay."

We were at Morton Frankel's apartment complex. I glowered at Junior.

"I been thinkin' . . ." he said. "Homeboy who you followin'? You need a hair." He pointed across the street at Frankel's apartment. "That's where the shit would be."

"I'll just ring and ask him politely."

"Hel*lo*? Workday."

"Maybe not after he spent the night getting questioned. And besides, how am I gonna get inside his apartment?"

Junior slapped his chest with both hands, insulted. "What the fuck?"

"No. *Oh*, no."

He hopped out.

"As your Big Brother, I am ordering you to get your juvenile-delinquent ass back in this car."

He sprinted across the street. The light changed, and I had to wait for a string of cars before I could follow. I took the steps two at a time. Frankel's door rested open, kissing the strike plate, and Junior was leaning against the wall beside it, pretending to buff his fingernails on his Lakers jersey. A pick dangled from his lips. I grabbed his arm and dragged him back down the stairs. He complained and swore all the way to the car. I opened the passenger door and deposited him roughly in the seat.

He looked at me sullenly. "I was just tryin' to help."

I tossed him the keys. "Keep an eye on the street and honk if you see him coming."

A two-second delay, then a grin lightened his face. "Aw*right,* Big Bro-Bro."

Leaving his chanting behind, I crossed again and climbed the stairs, a bit more cautiously. The hinges gave off a creep-show whine when I knuckled the door open a few inches. The strip of visible room looked empty enough. A puddle of sheets on a mattress. No bed frame. Alarm clock on a shoe box turned on its side. The drawn blinds left the air dim and unvented. I pressed a shoulder to the door, widening my field of vision a few degrees. Of course the furnishings budget had gone to a big-screen TV and a Barcalounger—maroon, with a remote-control pouch and a cup holder hole-punching one plush arm.

A quick jog, a hair plucked from a brush or comb, and I'd be on my way. Easing inside, I took in the odor of curtain dust and tired plumbing. I kept the door cracked behind me, leaving no barriers to a hasty retreat.

Despite the sparseness and the moldy smell, the place was kept neat—cardboard boxes stacked in one corner, lintless carpet, countertop scrubbed clean. The drip of the kitchen sink was maddeningly loud.

Open facedown on the floor behind the mattress, a paperback of *Chainer's Law.* Heart pounding, I stared at the familiar cover, my name lettered in vibrant red. After all the searching and digging, at last a concrete link between me and Morton Frankel. I lifted the book, looking for marked passages. He'd reached page 24. A receipt slipped from the book and fluttered to the floor. I picked it up. *Chainer's Law,* $7.99 plus tax. The purchase date? Today.

Having recognized me yesterday, he'd started a bit of research of his own. Or was this ongoing study, further indication of his fixation on me? Standing here, violating precisely the kind of privacy rights I paid lip service to during more convenient times in my life, I was forced to consider again if I was making headway or only confronting obstacles I'd thrown in my own path—the Heisenberg uncertainty principle of plotting. I was lost in my own story, banging the labyrinthine walls of my investigation.

Setting the book back in its place, I didn't bother telling myself to stop. What's the use? I never listen.

A brief hall, broken by a coat closet and a metal footlocker, led to the bathroom. Keeping the lights off, I made tentative but steady progress. Pairs of shoes along the far wall, lined almost decoratively. An adequate oil painting of a farmhouse in a shaft of purple light. A few wire hangers bent and stuffed into a grocery bag used as a trash can. The footlocker blocked the hall, dust streaks indicating it had been recently moved. I paused over it, took in the fat padlock dangling from the clasp. Maybe Frankel had pulled it out after last night's visit with Kaden and Delveckio, a reminder to dispose of whatever was locked within.

A bead of sweat ran down my ribs before my shirt caught it.

I crouched and gripped the footlocker, which tilted accommodatingly, its contents sliding with a rattle. After tugging at the padlock idiotically, I continued into the bathroom, rattling the shower curtain back on its rings to make sure I was alone. The mirrored medicine cabinet revealed a toothbrush tilting from a coffee mug. The drawer under the sink held a gaggle of disposable razors, a *Hustler,* a spare bar of soap, and, way in the back, a kelly green comb.

I removed the comb, angled it to the light. Not a strand of hair. I checked the drawer, then sink. Nothing, save flecks of dried soap and toothpaste.

A spot of color at the threshold stabbed at my peripheral vision.

I turned little by little, like an animal before a predator's gaze, concerned that a sharp motion would draw attention.

Just beyond the doorway in the hall, a matchbook.

Skull and bones on the cover.

My mouth had gone dry. There was no way I would have stepped over the matchbook without noticing. Even focused as I was on the drawers, the cabinet, the promise of a comb.

Moving with excruciating slowness, careful that my shoes not so much as squeak on the linoleum, I took a step forward, kneeled. Plucking the matchbook off the floor, I spread it open.

I STILL SEE YOU.

A thump to my right, and a blinding strike knocked me flat on the floor. Seconds stretched out, the sharpness of the pain lending everything intense clarity. The floorboards, sprayed with my saliva. My pen, looming large before my left eye, rolling away into normal perspective. A workman's boot, laced loosely across a stiff leather tongue.

I had one instinct only—do not get caught down.

I'd barely registered the wood grinding my cheek when I sprang up as if off a bounce and squared myself, vision swimming, desperate to fix on something despite the motion and the throbbing of my head. Then I heard the low tick of a chuckle, and Morton Frankel stepped forward into focus, opening a folding blade and letting the spring flick it closed. The coat-closet door was open behind him.

Without hesitation I charged. You don't need courage when you have familiarity with self-destruction. Once you've had a quart of Gran Patrón pumped from your stomach, you don't expect God, or fate, or yourself to be much concerned with your preservation. So it wasn't courage, not exactly. More like readjusted expectations about the warranty package.

I knocked his knife hand wide with a sweep of my arm and drove my forehead down into his nose. I missed but caught his chin, and then he wheeled and stabbed the knife back at my side, and I caught his wrist awkwardly, and we fell. There were no direct punches, no clean kung fu angles, just glancing blows, grappling, and almost instantaneous exhaustion. In the tight space, we kicked our bodies around, fighting for position, walking the walls in a thoughtful sort of slow motion as our clothes twisted and our breathing grew harsh.

Methodically, he gained position on me, driving a knee into my side, leaning over me and turning his sweaty wrist in my grip, trying to free his knife hand. Our faces stayed close enough to kiss, a drop of perspiration threatening to fall from the tip of his nose, those bared teeth grotesque in close-up. The bitter scent of his skin—factory grime and chemical soap—pervaded the narrow hall. He got the bar of his forearm across the bridge of my nose, prying his knife hand free. My flailing shoe caught the footlocker, jammed it against the wall for resistance, and I shoved, flipping onto my stomach and trying to take his arm with me.

His knife hand popped loose.

I was on my stomach, Frankel straddling my back with both arms free, the knife lost from my field of vision. I scrambled on the floorboards but was pinned, so I bucked to keep him off balance. Each unguarded instant seemed an impossible duration.

His knee braced against the wall, setting his weight. A sharp intake of breath and a whistle of fabric as he drew an arm back for the plunge.

My escaped pen spun lethargically across the floor. I lunged, straining, getting it at my fingertips. Closing the plastic Bic into the vise of my fist, I rotated and jammed the uncapped point into the meat of Frankel's outer thigh. He let out a hiss, his swipe thrown off by our twisting momentum, the blade embedding in the wall and releasing a puff of drywall dust. I jammed the heel of my hand north, cracking his nose, the pain raising him to a bent-legged hover. Shoving free, I hooked his ankle with a foot, knocking him down onto his ass. His hands, bloodless from the pressure, gripped his thigh around the pen. As crimson blotted the white leg of his Dickies, I leaned over him, squeezed a handful of his hair, and ripped.

I ran, his fingernails scrabbling against the walls behind me as he pulled himself up. I pitched forward against the front door, banging it open, and stumbled down the stairs. Junior and Xena filled the Highlander's windows, the whites of their eyes visible across two lanes. As I dodged traffic, Junior turned over the engine and flung my door wide. Keeping my left hand curled tight to trap the protruding hairs, I fell into the driver's seat and peeled out, door slamming on its own as the Highlander hurtled forward.

Morton Frankel stood at a tilt on the second floor, two red hands curled around the railing like talons, watching us go.

33

L loyd blocked the gap in his doorway with his body as if nervous I'd muscle my way inside. A lab drone had told me he'd gone home early today, so I'd raced over after leaving an excited Junior at the curb outside Hope House. Xena, snoozing in the Guiltmobile's backseat, would live another day in Casa de Danner. Lloyd had listened to my account impassively, not budging from his post.

"I can't help you anymore, Drew."

"This is *it*, Lloyd. It all hinges on this." I lifted the plastic Baggie so he could see the six of Morton Frankel's hairs pressed inside. Four had nice follicular tags, white dots of flesh, attached to the roots. DNA treasure troves.

"We took a gamble on you coming into the lab last night, but now word of your visit's gotten around. Henderson himself was waiting at my bench this morning. I can't lose my job, our health insurance." His voice trailed off. "Things aren't good here, Drew. That's why I'm home."

"I'm sorry."

He stared at me. "I'm sorry, too. But I can't help. I'm barely staying afloat here."

"Where else can I go?"

"Go through official channels."

"You and I both know I can't do that without landing in jail."

"Have someone take a look at that eye."

"That's not gonna get these hairs run for DNA."

"You obtained them unlawfully. You broke in to his apartment. That's illegal *and* unethical. You crossed a line, Drew. It's not my fault that you can't get anyone else to cross it with you."

"This guy framed me. He knows who I am. Where I live. Which means he'll come after me. I'm in a jam here, Lloyd."

"And I'm not? I raced home today because Janice got a nosebleed that wouldn't quit. Forty-five minutes before we could get the platelets in to stop it." He dropped his gaze, unwilling to look me in the face. "I'm sorry, Drew, but Janice and I have to look out for ourselves."

The door rasped closed. I stood holding the six hairs, listening to his retreating footsteps.

"Know what happens when someone punches you in the face? It hurts. That's it. No white bursts before the eyes. No blinding flashes. It just fucking hurts."

Patiently waiting for me to finish, Chic dabbed at my swollen eye with a Q-tip dipped in alcohol. "And unlike Derek Chainer's bullet grazes along his shoulder and them pretty shiners he come down with, it gonna hurt for more than one chapter."

"Yeah, I was full of shit about that, too." My right eye throbbed as if someone were pressing a stove coil against it. The image my bathroom mirror threw back at me was not a pretty one. The skin around the eye had gone parchment yellow and had a papery look to match. Broken vessels squirmed from the lids like the locks of Medusa. A half-moon at the temple, where the flesh had split, glittered darkly.

We felt Big Brontell's approach through the floor; he'd gone down to get his gear. "What's Newt Gingrich doin' in there?" he called out.

"Moaning, mostly," Chic said.

Big Brontell entered, the first-aid box like a travel sewing kit in his massive hands. The most professionally successful of the multitude of Chic's brothers, he was a charge nurse at Cedars-Sinai Hospital and spent much of his time repairing his brethren after motocross crashes, electrical shocks, or enigmatic altercations. He looked like Chic, only Supersized.

Chic and Big Brontell's arrival had interrupted a bout of furious writing, the words flying out of me as if I were taking dictation rather than making them up. I'd almost forgotten I'd called on my way back from Lloyd's to enlist their help; when the doorbell had rung, I'd started, anticipating Mortie bearing a boning knife and a horsey grin. I'd answered the door, gun in hand, and Big Brontell had chuckled and said, "How you like *that* for racial profiling?"

The strands of Frankel's hair, preserved in the Baggie, rested on the counter by the sink. They'd been hard-won, and I wasn't going to let them out of my sight—my own paranoid evidentiary chain of custody. Chic's deadbeat-mom-and-pop tracker had uncovered nothing new linking any element of the case to Delveckio or Cal Unger—or to Bill Kaden, whom he'd tossed in for free. And he'd yet to come up with anything salient on Frankel, so those hairs, for now, were all I had.

As Big Brontell began stitching me with surprising grace and care, I kept my gaze on those six brown hairs, grasping for solutions, options, new avenues. "Why can't you have any brothers who are criminalists?"

Big Brontell said, "We got plenty who are crim*inals*."

He finished, and I thanked him and walked them down. At the door Chic set his hands on my shoulders and leaned forward so our foreheads almost touched. "You keep that gun near and call if you need me, hear?"

"I hear."

"You're splashing through dangerous waters, Drew-Drew. Might want to slow down for a time, drift with the currents."

"If I can just get one of those hairs run for DNA, I'm thinking I can close this whole thing up."

Chic smiled knowingly; I rarely said anything that surprised him. He jerked his head, indicating the sunset that was now my right eye. "Juss remember," he said, "your best thinking got you here."

34

After Chic and Big Brontell left, I couldn't make progress writing because I didn't know how to make progress on the case. I sat at my desk, staring at the
blinking cursor, caught up to my present. *← No one shall be admitted*
into the theater during the
Six hairs ready to be run for DNA, a murder case— *riveting*
maybe two—at stake, and nary a criminalist in sight. *writer's-block*
The way I'd attained the hairs—breaking and entering, *sequence.*
assault and battery—had compromised me, leaving me
vulnerable to arrest, lawsuits, and psychopath retali-
ation. I could hardly claim self-defense for the pen
stabbing when I'd put myself in a situation where, in
any reasonable red state, Mort could have shot me with
impunity. Lost in his own private tragedy, Lloyd was
unwilling to help. Cal had made clear he could do no
more prying on my behalf. Kaden and Delveckio hadn't
exactly adored
been fond of me *before* I'd ignored their latest round
of warnings by playing incompetent hair burglar, and
they'd likely relish the chance to get those black-
steel bracelets around my wrists again.

I clicked through the consultants list in my Palm-
Pilot, hoping there was someone I'd overlooked. If so,
how would that introduction go exactly? *I ripped some*
hairs out of a murder suspect's head and was wondering
if you could run them. This is Andrew Danner, by the
way. You might remember me from the tabloids.

Think outside the box! Get the hair run some other way. You're a writer. With
talented friends and odd experts and bizarre people you've met along the way.
Bribe a criminalist in a remote lab. Call a science teacher who heads up the
CSI society at Spoiled Brat High. Something.

Thoughts of Caroline dissolved my sense of isolation. I recalled the way she'd taken my hand briefly last night as I'd walked her out, as if she were practicing. Today's movies and billboards glorified unreason- *Right, and the Greeks carved busts of homely Athenians.* ably beautiful standards, but there was a thin line between perfection and blandness. With looks, as with personalities, I'd take striking over standard any day. ← ———————— *Jackie Collins phoned. She wants her sentence back.*

Evening mist had settled through the Valley, turning the northern hills to bruises. It had darkened in a hurry, the sun already lost behind the Santa Susanas. I put my hand on the solid grip of the loaded .22, looking for reassurance. I had promised to bring the pistol in to Parker Center, but now my black eye would raise more questions than I could answer. Plus, in light of my hallway tango with Mort, there was no way I was leaving myself unarmed. He could be belly-down on the hill right now, hidden in the ample slopes of ivy, fixing that diabolical gleam on me and awaiting an opening.

In the hall Xena snored vigilantly, working off the southwestern sausages I'd fried up for her.

My cell phone rang, a welcome distraction, and I snapped it open to hear Preston's voice. I'd left him a message encapsulating the latest.

"What's happening?" ~~he asked eagerly~~

"I don't know."

"Read ahead."

"I'm stuck." *Can you help me?*

"Of course. I'm coming over."

"Not sure I'm in the mood for your editorial attention."

~~But he'd already hung up.~~
"You may not be in the mood," he said, "but it sounds like you require it."

The cursor continued to wink at me, awaiting my
next move. *Your next move, while challenging, is not unclear: You need to get an illegally obtained hair analyzed. Here is your assignment, as dogged protagonist: How can you meet this challenge in a manner unique to you? In a way that draws upon who you are or, better, in a way that only you can?*
"Tell me about it," I said.

My gaze lifted from the pages, stained with Preston's stereotype red, to his face. "Spoiled Brat High?"

"I was going for Harvard-Westlake but blanked on the name." He drained his glass and set it down, completing his collection on my coffee table. Now that I'd felt the mood in his condo, I understood better why he dropped by at every opportunity. Stretching, he rose from the couch, not seeming to note the tufts of stuffing clinging to his pants. He turned down the volume on the evening news, which, refreshingly, didn't include me, and gathered his various stacks of papers.

He paused beside me on his way out and said archly, "I edit you hard because I care."

"I could warm my hands on your affection."

"Call if I can be of further assistance."

"Further?"

"Of course. 'Farther' is for distance."

"Never mind."

He disappeared from the room, leaving behind the bottle of Havana Club, which, down to its last drops, was no longer worth hiding. I sank into my reading chair, which alone had been spared Xena's wrath, and propped my feet on the ottoman. The news jingle gave way to a commercial for *Chain of Command*—a coveted fifteen-second spot my publisher had refused to grant me before I'd been indicted for murder. Marketing had chosen a disturbing publicity still of my face, which looked somewhere between angry and constipated, floating eerily above the cover of my most recent novel.

Next, adhering to some bizarre karmic logic, the familiar drumbeat opening of the main title sequence of *Aiden's War*. Here was Johnny Ordean tackling a street hustler, there ducking a roundhouse thrown by an unappealing Arab. Looking noticeably more svelte than he had in his role as Father Derek Chainer, Johnny stopped for a zoom close-up as he did weekly, or nightly if you had a dish.

I flashed on the scene I'd caught when I was at the bar with Caroline—Johnny crouching over a corpse, studying the bullet casing he'd impaled on a paper clip. *HUSTLE THIS TO FORENSICS THE CASING NOT THE HOT DOG.*

I shuffled through the pages, finding Preston's final note. Then I tugged my cell phone from my pocket and dialed.

Over the pulsing beat of club music, a guy with a strong Brooklyn accent: "Johnny Ordean's phone."

Ever since *Aiden's Law* had racked up enough episodes for a DVD box set, Johnny had assumed the affectation of unavailability, putting nine layers of entourage between himself and others.

"Surprisingly," I said, "I'm calling for Johnny. This is Drew Danner."

"*Andrew* Danner? The . . . ?"

"Murderer," I said. "Sure. That's me."

Animated shouting, then Johnny's voice, hoarse and loud: "Drew? That you? Crazy days, bro. Crazy days. You kill that broad?"

"Twice."

"Drastic." Johnny partook vigorously of the bad slang that seemed to sweep through L.A. every other season like a crimson tide.

"How's it going?"

"Solid. The show's kickin'. We're doing a spin-off next year."

"*Aiden's Law Omaha?*"

"Very funny, bro. It's called *Mary's Rule,* and the sister—"

"Listen, I need a favor. You still have criminalists on staff as expert consultants?"

"Yeah, a handful."

"I have a hair that I need to get run by a crime lab. It could prove me innocent." Of course, it *wouldn't* prove me innocent, but I was trying to feed him the kind of dialogue to which he was accustomed to responding. "I need to know who it belongs to."

"Like a clue?" Noticeable excitement in his voice.

"Yeah, Johnny. Like a clue. Can you have one of your guys do it?"

"Sure, I'll take it in to them, say I need to see how it works for an episode idea I'm developing. They love walking me through that stuff at the lab. When you need it by?"

"As soon as possible. It's hard for me to describe how important this is."

"Bring the hair by Flux. It's a closed party—I'll have you put on the list. I'll call one of the consultants, have him check out the hair tonight."

"You can get that done? Tonight?"

"I'm Johnny Ordean. I can get anything done."

35

F lux is the Hollywood club of the minute, trending hot with wheatgrass martinis, bamboo walls, and a bump-and-grind DJ beat ideal for ecstasy humpers, film-industry underlings, and clubbies. I paid twenty bucks to park in a space fit for a lawn mower and legged it down Sunset.

Beneath every windshield wiper, a glossy postcard hawking bad theater. At every street corner, a woman stomping her boots against the cold. Even at this hour, bodies spilled from gyms, where would-be scribblers and bit players simulated honest work. Bodies so sculpted and chiseled they seem of a different species, bodies that have endless time to devote to themselves, to do that extra six sets of ten on the cable pull that defines the inner prong of the triceps or the outer slab of the quad. I used to have a body like that, a lesser model built from a matching mind-set before both grew too weary to keep up. I walked on, taking in the night, these bits of a past persona I never quite inhabited. The tangy scent of deodorant, candy-colored iPods strapped to glistening arms, steam lifting from overheated Dri-FIT shirts like cartoon sizzle.

The velvet ropes that in other, more reasonable cities are consigned to museums and musicals sprout from the sidewalk like futuristic shrubs. Massed at the imaginary walls before the bouncers are dime-store vixens and cultivated tough guys. Everyone is in costume; everyone has a getup; it's perennial Halloween. Pearl Jam plaid, skullcap chic, scruff faces and denim vests cut to show off shoulder tats. A girl, for no reason, wears a Gatsby cap and a wide tie snaking into a 1920s vest. Even the firemen shuffling through the bars are done up and done down, T-shirts announcing their stations, blond wisps grown just long enough to curl out the bottoms of their stocking caps, models in search of calendars. They are all children, and yet they are all adults. They unpack from Jettas and Navigators and the occasional Lotus. They cross streets in packs, like wolves, sipping Vitawaters and smoking American Spirits, yammering on cell phones with customized bleats and chimes, the night lit with a psychedelic rainbow of LED screens—cotton-candy pink, toilet-bowl blue, horror-show green.

L.A. is a city of memorable faces. Even the unattractive character actors have that certain something, that exemplification of type. The others, too, lodge in the mind. The near misses. All lacking that extra *it* that would catapult them, that would mean they're not here at this place with these people, with you and me. Perky girl in a White Sox cap, nose-job-enhanced but not quite there. The wrestler who won best smile at Wichita High. The cheerleading captain who gave great backseat head in Short Hills. They come like pioneers, bringing abdominal six-packs and twenty-two waists and little else, seekers of prepackaged glory without the talent for Broadway or the balls for the service. L.A. is the edge of the American dream, the farthest your hopes can carry you before you topple into the Pacific, Icarus without water wings. And yet still they come. They come out and crowd the cliff edges, penguins above dangerous waters.

L.A. will devour them. It will crush them into inconsequentiality, grind them into a paste and smear them through the city's forgotten alleys. They will clip coupons and pre-party to save money on bar tabs. They will inhabit dojos and Coffee Beans during working hours—sunny L.A.'s businesses thrive with patronage from the idle keeping their empty audition hours open—and they'll scour online job sites for graveyard shifts that don't exist. They will get gigs as trainers and waiters and Cuervo girls, and their friends will mumble, *That's cool, that's cool.* They'll turn into third-rate entrepreneurs, making bamboo purses, designing jewelry in Reseda, marketing a blue-colored vodka in college bars. Their days *must* be open for auditions that come less and less frequently, but just when they're about to lose hope, they'll land Laura in a small-theater production of *The Glass Menagerie* and the rush and promise will fuel ungainful employment for another few years. And then, if they haven't wised up and beat a retreat to Billings or Sioux City, someone will offer them a pinch of escapism or a skin flick—not porn but tasteful erotica—and so the next downward spiral will begin. And new meat arrives by the busload. It pours out of LAX and off the freeways, chattel for the abattoir, oxen groomed for the altar.

I reached Flux, fighting through a mosh pit of wannabes mobbing the unmarked double doors. No one has a name here. They are all "dawg" and "baby doll." They gain position in the scrum by working in concert, like raptors, with the friends they'll be only too eager to drop once they book their first pilot. They call out to the bouncer using his first name, which they've researched. Their boss's brother knows the bartender, or their brother's boss knows the owner. They swell and shove politely, and a chirpy girl with a clipboard feigns exasperation through her ecstasy of purpose and rank, chiding them and distributing wristbands as if feeding chimps at a zoo. A few older women, indistinguishable from prostitutes by garb and makeup, have ceded bitchiness with their age; they can no longer compete directly. Instead they switch strategies, cooing support at the czarina working the door. *That poor girl. Look, she's all alone managing the line. You go, honey. You tell them.* Still, they do not curry enough goodwill to pass Go. The girl with the clipboard knows their type, knows that in a different life they've blown smoke in her face at a cattle call or discarded her head shot while working nights filing in a casting office.

Consigned to club-line purgatory, the crowdlings bicker and pop pills and talk loudly of embellished career developments and pretend not to be where they are, waiting outside in the bitter Hollywood night. That is where they will wait, night after night. And then one day Fame will pluck one of these poor unfortunate souls and elevate her like a priestess to the top of the ziggurat, and thenceforth, she will never know cordon ropes and lines and bouncers named Ricky, and it will make it worth it for everyone else who still does.

Chic's voice, like warning bells in my head: *Always easier to take somebody else's inventory.*

What made me any different? About how I got here? Where I'd wound up?

A shorter bus ride and a longer stain.

Then what? Envy? I thought I'd sworn off that with the single-barrel bourbon. Envy for what? The exuberance? The hopefulness? The youth? As Chic had said, life leaves you behind. By Hollywood standards I was long in the tooth, like Morton Frankel. I had a few successes under my belt and access to rooms behind some of the city's locked doors—as a writer, as an alleged murderer—in a way that others might envy, but I'd have traded it in a stockbroker's minute to be back on the other side, out in the unforgiving night, with all my solutions lying inside. I'd have traded it all to believe in the myth once again.

But instead I am here to deliver a hair.

I cut through the crowd, and it yielded to my apathy. Inside, over an ungodly remix beat, some kid covered Bob Seger without the grit or gravitas.

"Drew Danner," I told the girl at the door. "I'm with Johnny Ordean."

At both names the frontmost constituents of the throng stilled and the girl dropped the clipboard against her thigh, revealing it for the prop that it was, and wordlessly unhooked the maroon rope.

Sliced-and-diced Seger had given way to pump-and-hump rhythm. Threesomes were freaking under seizure-inducing lights. *I find me bitches left and right. I find me bitches every night.* Production-development girls in Chanel grooved in a circle, their oblivious movement an inadvertently droll endorsement of the lyrics. The club had a kind of magnetic energy that pointed to the rear corner, where indeed I found Johnny Ordean and his franchise face. Fulfilling the no-neck contingency of the entourage, his cousin sat deep in the booth, hammering cigarettes into his face one after another.

He slid out and I slid in. Johnny wrapped an arm around my shoulders, raised his brows at my vibrant eye, and gave my neck a squeeze like an old-school mobster. Playing the part, I reached inside my jacket pocket, removed the envelope, and dropped it on the table like a payoff. The envelope held a Ziploc containing a single specimen of Morton Frankel's hair. The others I was saving for a rainy day.

Johnny wound his finger in the air, a let's-get-moving gesture, and his cousin shifted the cig from one end of his mouth to the other and pressed a cell phone to his sweaty cheek.

"Fast and quiet," I said.

Johnny squeezed my neck again.

"And thank you."

"Of course, bro. What good is celebrity if you can't put it to work?"

It was, I thought, an excellent question.

36

Far from the madding crowd, I sat like a tailgater on my little rented rectangle of Hollywood asphalt and dialed my cell phone.

"I'd like to see you," I said. "I'm in your neck of the woods."

"Ah, yes," she said, "I can hear the excess in the background."

The parking-lot attendant gave me a peculiar look as I pulled out. For twenty bucks I should've set up camp for the night.

Caroline proved to live in a corner unit on the sixth floor of a recently renovated building on Crescent Heights. I tripped over some vestigial scaffolding on my way in, the doorman kindly pretending not to notice. I waited in the freshly carpeted hall while she undid a profusion of dead bolts. She double-checked me through a veil of security chains, and then the door closed on me again. More metallic unhooking and we were face-to-face.

She reached out, gingerly touched my right temple just beyond the stitches. "Have you iced that?"

Minutes later I was sitting on her plush sofa, she on the adjoining coffee table, the better to press a bag of frozen corn kernels to my eye. I described to her the nature of my disagreement with Mort. To my surprise she didn't reprimand me for Junior's role, but then, she knew him better than I and, given her profession, likely applied a stringent doctrine of accountability regardless of age.

The edge of the bag caught a stitch, and I grimaced. Leaning forward, she adjusted, and then our faces were close, the air chilled from the frozen bag. She brushed the hair off my forehead gently, and her lips parted a bit, her gaze on my mouth. I moved the bag aside, but she stood abruptly and said, "What are we doing here, Drew? I mean, why do you like being with me?"

"Your trusting nature?"

"I'm serious."

I set the bag on my knee. "Because it's the only time I don't want to be anywhere else."

She opened her mouth to say something, but instead she held up a finger and walked swiftly down the hall, and then I heard a door close and the sounds of retching. The sink ran for a while, and there was toothbrushing and gargling, and soon she returned, red-faced, reluctant to make eye contact.

I said, "If I kiss you, does your head explode?"

She said, incredulous, "You still want to kiss me?"

"I do. I also want to wake up next to you." I held up both hands. "Today, a year from now, whenever. I'm just letting you know that I find you—"

She said, "Come here." She was shaking. She took my hand and led me to her bedroom, and then she turned off the lights and stepped out of her sweatpants. She kissed me nervously, too hard, and said, "Get a condom. It's in the drawer," and as I fumbled out of my clothes, she tugged me on top of her. I moved to lift her shirt, but she grabbed my wrist, firmly, and said, "I want to keep it on," and then guided my shoulders and set her jaw in the best spirit of let's-get-it-over-with.

I kept thinking I had the angle or position wrong until it struck me that she had tightened up, locked down her body in panic until it was as though there were no aperture. We shifted and reshifted until she laughed and said bitterly, "Hey, you wanted to," and rolled over, and then her shoulders shook once, and I realized she was crying.

"I'm not crying," she said.

I lay there in the dark beside her, wanting to touch her but not sure if that was the right call.

"That moved a little fast for me," I said. "I'd imagine it felt the same way to you."

She kept on her stomach, angled away, her head lowered to the cross of her arms. Her voice was hoarse and unsteady, but gentle. "Just lock the front door behind you, okay?"

"What are you feeling?"

"Philosophical."

"That's not a feeling."

"Oh, great. This game."

"Knock it off," I said.

She was silent for a long time, and then she said, "I'm sorry. That's a reasonable question. I don't know if I'm clear enough to answer it."

"So make it up."

"How do I feel . . . ?" A car horn blared in the distance. From one of the apartments in floating proximity came Eric Clapton, an accompaniment to someone's romantic dinner. Caroline's shoulders seized a bit more, but she didn't make a noise, and then she hung her head off the bed and miraculously came up with a tissue and blew her nose, all the while keeping her face from view. She settled back into position. Her voice cracked when she spoke. "That if I'm not vigilant, undisclosed awful things will happen to me. And." A deep breath. "That I may not be brave enough to allow myself something like this."

We breathed for a while in the semidarkness, and then eventually I said, "Do you mind if I take the rest of my clothes off?"

She turned slowly, hair hiding one eye. Sheer lavender curtains filtered the faint lights from the street below. She watched me for a long time. "No."

She'd pulled me to her so furiously that my clothes were still clinging to me—one shoe, both socks, a tangle of boxers at my ankle. I stripped and she watched me, and then I lay flat on her bed, hands at my sides, and said, "Okay. I have no expectations. I'm just lying here naked so you can look at me."

She pulled her shirt back into place, sat Indian style before me, and studied me clinically.

After a time I asked, "How do you feel now?"

"Anxious. I haven't, obviously, since . . ."

"I figured."

"Can I touch you?"

"Yes."

She pressed both palms flat against my chest and leaned, as if testing my consistency. She stroked my thigh with the tips of her nails. She cupped me in her hand and said, "You're so soft."

"Not if you keep that up."

She laughed, covering her mouth as if the sound had caught her off guard. She tugged out her ponytail holder, and her lank, sandalwood hair relaxed into wisps, which brushed my chest as she leaned over me. She felt my entire body, inch by inch, a blind person learning a new shape. After maybe twenty minutes of silent examination, she lifted off her own shirt.

Her torso, too, bore the marks of the abuse she'd endured, though they were less striking, inlaid against her splendid form. A short run of mottled flesh at her left shoulder, a ridge of stomach muscle, a gnarl of scar tissue at her ribs, the swell of her breasts.

"You can touch," she said. "Me."

I lifted my hands from my sides and explored her delightful, unpredictable body. Her breathing shifted. She tilted her head, let her hair spill across her face. Falling back, she pulled me on top of her again and clutched my back. Her breath came hot against my neck. It took time for her to unclench; we moved slowly, with patience, murmuring and kissing, one vivid moment at a time. And finally we were making love. It was not without awkwardness, but it wasn't without grace either.

Afterward she clung to me, started crying, and didn't stop. She wept with the abandon of a child, until she was limp, until her face was drained to a dishwater gray. Beneath the veneer of exhaustion and terror, she looked elated.

She slung a leg across my stomach and propped herself up on an elbow, her face beside mine. "Sorry I cried."

"I don't mind. Apologize to yourself if you want to."

She lowered her chin to my chest. "I used to be good at this, you know."

"I'm told I never was."

She laughed, hit me weakly.

"They say the eyes are the windows to the soul," I said. "I do not believe this to be true. I believe the toes are the windows to the soul."

"Oh? How are my toes?" She wiggled them, showing off.

"Magnificent."

We talked a bit more and then dozed off together. At 11:32 I awoke with a start.

"What?" she said sleepily. "What's wrong?"

I sat up to try to slow my breathing.

She felt my shoulders. "Jesus, you're drenched."

My dream-memory streamed back in vivid detail, me in my car the night of, driving to Genevieve's. Alone. Running up her stairs. Alone. Finding the key. Alone.

"I can't spend the night here. The last time I spent the night with someone was when I . . ."

"You don't know."

"Exactly."

"Either way. Whatever you did or didn't do, you had a brain tumor."

"I've done or not done plenty since then."

Like when I'd awakened to find the slice above my little toe. With a clean bill of mental health, I'd followed my own bloody footprints around the house. Returned to find my boning knife, bearing my own prints, by the bed. Discovered the shattered jar in the sink and ganglioglioma gone spelunking down the disposal. What if I hadn't been gassed with sevoflurane? What if Morton Frankel had never been to my house? What if this was all my writer's mind at work on an elaborate fiction? A more convenient tale, spun for the age-old reason all escapist yarns are?

A memory hit me, fresh as a vision. Genevieve bouncing foot to foot along the cliff's edge above Santa Monica Beach, giggling manically as I shadowed her five feet off. An ingenious blackmail—should I be scared? Indifferent? Should I approach? Tourists watching with trepidation, parents shepherding their kids away. We'd gotten into a fight over something monumental—taco stand or Korean barbecue—and it had erupted as it often did. *What's the matter, Drew? I'm embarrassing you?* Embarrassment, sure, but also terror that she'd misjudge her footing, resentment at how my hands clutched the air every time she wobbled. At the time I hadn't identified the sensation hiding beneath the others like a buried ember. Rage.

I believe that anyone is capable of anything.

In addition to my own unstable self, I had other nocturnal dangers to offer. Kaden and Delveckio could come calling—after all, I still owed them a gun—and drag Caroline into the investigation. Morton Frankel could be smoking hand-rolled cigarettes in the alley below, staring up at this window right now.

"I don't trust where I am. I need to get more answers."

"Sorry," she said, "but there's only room for my issues in this relationship."

That drew a smile from me. She threw on a nightgown as I dressed. At the door we kissed. I ran my thumb along the line of one of her scars.

She asked, "What if you get to the end of this road and discover you did do it?"

"I don't know that I could live with myself."

"Drew," she said, "we're generally not given that choice."

37

I emerged from sleep calmly and knew the time before I glanced at my nightstand clock: 1:08 A.M. A menacing rumble downstairs. An unusual chill in the air, colder than the house got at night, even in January. I rolled over, rested my hand on the loaded .22.

The noise ceased, then commenced with renewed energy.

Xena growling.

I threw back the sheets, ran to my closet, and dressed rapidly. Passing the window above the bathtub, I stopped, my breath jerking out of me.

Across the street, beneath the gloomy overhang of the neighbor's carport, a man stood in the ribbed darkness, peering up at my house. He was little more than a black form—because of the interplay of competing shadows, it was difficult to gauge even his height.

Morton Frankel, finally come calling?

He stood motionless, the tilt of his head suggesting he was looking up at the very window before me. Could he see me in the darkness behind the glass?

I moved swiftly through my room and eased out onto the catwalk. Peering over the railing, I saw the security rod on the carpet, again dislodged from the slider's track. The sliding door itself I couldn't see, but Xena stood facing it, fur raised in a wolfish bristle along her neck and upper back. A gust rattled the screen door, and an instant later I felt cold air rise to my face.

I slid off the pistol's safety and hurried down the stairs, letting my shoulder whisper along the curved wall to my right. A movement at the front door, toward the top where I'd clumsily covered the shattered inset windows. Beneath the nailed plywood, on the only sliver of exposed packing tape, a slit had been cut. It had been widened to maybe six inches before whoever cut it had realized that the plywood wouldn't allow a hand to snake through and reach the inside lock. Pouched inward, the slit breathed with the wind, a weird sort of acrylic mouth.

I came around the base of the stairs. Xena must have smelled that it was me; she kept her focus on the two-foot gap where the sliding door had been pushed open. Leaves scratched along the back deck, nothing more. I drew even with Xena. Mort hadn't counted on my having a guard dog. In the slider's track, the paint was scraped where the slim jim had been slipped through to pop the security rod out of place.

I opened the screen, stepped out onto the deck, closing Xena inside so I could make silent progress. As before, the side gate clanked. Down the hill a pack of coyotes bayed, closing in on someone's pet. Straight-arming the .22, I crept around the house, moving in and out of shadow until I reached the street.

Beneath the carport nothing but my neighbor's familiar van and pools of shadow. Was I losing touch? Again? I ran over, checked behind and under the van, then came out and stood in my old spot in the middle of the street. No movement except bobbing branches and fluttering leaves.

And the distant purr of a motor.

I listened, but the sound neither rose nor faded.

Keeping to the sidewalk, I moved down the street, the noise growing louder. I made my way past two lots, pausing before the high stucco wall that guarded the corner house's driveway. The wall played with the acoustics; I was unsure if the running car was just behind it or farther along on the intersecting street.

Keeping the pistol raised before me, I leaned around the wall, but the vehicle—if it was there—was too far back to draw into my line of sight. Holding an inhale, I stepped past the wall onto the dark driveway. The outline of a facing car, maybe ten yards up the long, narrow drive, the windshield an impervious black sheet, exhaust clinging to its rear. The house was up around the bend, set back above a sharp slope. The memory of cigarette smoke tinged the air. To my right, the reliable wall, on my left, a bank of ivy.

Had the driver kept the car running for his return, or was he in there now, watching me?

Vigilant of ambush from the side or behind, I shuffled forward, aiming at the windshield, braced to run. Despite my fear and the cold, I managed to keep the gun steady, the recurrent puffs before my face an indication of how much my breathing had quickened.

A few steps revealed the car to be a Volvo. Dark paint. The license plate had been removed. Another few feet and I'd be able to make out if there was a form in the driver's seat.

The headlights flared, blinding me. The engine roared and the tires squealed, seeking purchase. The Volvo leapt forward. I fired, the bullet punching a hole in the top right corner of the windshield. Bolting left, I got in a step and was airborne when the hood clipped me. I rolled up the edge of the windshield, the driver a passing blur, and flew off the side, landing in the ivy. The Volvo skidded onto the street, through the intersection, and was gone. I lay on my back, panting, a sprinkler head dug into the small of my back. Rats rustled around me through the damp matting. After a time the crickets resumed. The neighborhood remained silent, unimpressed that I'd just fired a shot.

Pulling twigs from my clothes and hair, I again registered that hint of cigarette smoke. Crawling on the driveway, I looked for a hand-rolled butt. To the side, caught on a broad leaf of ivy, was a matchbook. Guess what was printed on its cover?

I found a twig and used it to lift the matchbook so as to preserve any prints. The matches had been used up, but written on the back side of the flap in a familiar block print, an address.

It was an address I'd be unlikely ever to forget.

38

The skull and crossbones glowered at me from the match-book, preserved benignly in a Ziploc. I paced under my kitchen lights, glaring back. Like the cigarette smoke, the matchbook struck me as a contrivance. But how was I supposed to interpret it? That Mort had written Genevieve's address when first stalking her? I doubted that matches dating back four months had only just been used up. Had he jotted the address while planning the copycat killing? Maybe he'd been using Genevieve's house as a work-shop, taking Broach there after the kidnapping to avoid leaving evidence at his apartment. More or less unoccupied, it would make an ideal safe house. My windshield kiss raised additional questions: If Mort was framing me for the murders, why run me over *now*? Because he knew I was onto him? Was he trying to take me out before I could get something concrete to the police?

I thumbed open my cell phone and dialed. Angela answered, accepted my apology, and handed off the phone to her husband.

As always, Chic sounded alert, as if I'd caught him on a morning stroll. He listened quietly. I finished filling him in and asked, "Can you meet me at Genevieve's?"

"Course. Why?"

"I don't buy the matchbook any more than I bought the bondage rope. Someone who's been this careful with evidence wouldn't pull up on my street, have a smoke, and toss a matchbook with a convenient address on it out his window."

"Unless they thought you was gonna be too dead to find it."

A reasonable point.

"I think I'm being led."

"And you gonna follow."

"Yeah. I think he planted something in that house for me to find. Something that incriminates me further. And I want to find it before the cops do and get out before the trap springs."

"Dangerous game."

"That's why I need blackup."

"Then blackup gon' be what you get."

I stood in the gutter, Chic and his brothers—two I knew, one I didn't—beside me, Genevieve's house looming over us. We'd finished checking the surrounding streets and land, and Fast Teddie had squeezed through a bathroom window with a gold-plated Colt .45 and safed the house, making sure no one was inside.

Chic nudged me. "Ready to take a gander?"

I was.

We passed the strip of lawn with its broken sprinkler, made our way up the shifting pavers to the floating porch. There the philodendron, there the terra-cotta pot with the cracked saucer.

I had been here many times in my life, in reality, in dream, in memory. This late-night visit felt like a melding of all three.

Fast Teddie picked the front-door dead bolt in about three seconds.

Chic pressed the door open, handed me a flashlight, and said, "We'll be where we're at. Keep your cell phone on."

I moved inside, closed the door behind me.

Alone in Genevieve's house.

A memory attached to every object. Baccarat candy dish, sleek to the touch. Blank spot on the side table where a Murano paperweight used to rest. Pink-and-white striped scarf slung over the banister, bearing the faintest scent of Petite Cherie. The marble tiles of the foyer were hard underfoot. The knife block stared at me from the kitchen's center island, five stainless handles and one empty slit. Thinking about that bleach wash given to Broach's body, I checked the sink and the bathtubs and strayed into the dark garage. I searched the living room and the carpeted alcove that Genevieve used to refer to as a dining room, looking for anything out of the ordinary.

Only the upstairs master remained. My legs tingled as I ascended. Adrenaline? Fear? The door had been left ajar. Even in the dim light, it was clear—a broad-ranging blob, lighter than the surrounding carpet, where industrial cleaners had bleached the beige fibers.

The bed had been made, a detail that drove my emotion to the surface. Who had pulled it together during the aftermath? Genevieve's mother? Had a thoughtful criminalist turned up the sheets before withdrawing?

I blinked myself back to usefulness and checked the closet, the sink, the luxurious pink bathtub with its inflatable headrest, touched now with mold.

I returned to the spot on the carpet and sat cross-legged.

Here Genevieve had met the curved boning knife.

Here her life had been extinguished.

Here I had sat with her body, dipped my hands into the bloody well, tumbled into seizure and blackout.

Somewhere the memory lurked, lost in the coralline whorls of my frontal lobe.

I wanted answers. I wanted a sudden flash of recognition, the thunderbolt of epiphany. Instead it was just me and the stainless quiet of a deserted bedroom.

After a few moments, I picked up on the faintest hiss. I stood, spinning to source it, wound up with my ear pressed to the built-in speaker beside the headboard.

I moved downstairs to the edge of the dining room, where a wall of fine-wood cabinets arced toward the kitchen. A picture window, the largest in the house, showed off a view of the hillside and intervals of the street below as it twisted down to Coldwater. The left-most cabinet, where through some flight of bizarre Gallic logic Genevieve hid the stereo components, opened readily under my touch, releasing a wave of electronic warmth. Glowing from the dark stack of hardware, a green pinpoint. The CD player had been left on. Playing something the night of her death? Maybe that music I'd heard in my dream-memory as I'd stumbled up onto the porch hadn't been merely in my head, like the sharp scent of smoldering rubber. The digital counter showed that the CD had run its course. I clicked "eject," the tray sliding out to offer an unlabeled disc, something Genevieve had burned from her iTunes library.

I was about to thumb the tray back in to play the CD when my cell phone chimed, breaking the tense silence. My gaze rose to the window.

Down the hill two dark SUVs with tinted windows and no running lights turned off Coldwater onto Genevieve's street, starting up the hill.

Chic's voice came rushing through my cell phone—"Get outta there."

I flew from the house, the pavers rocking violently in my aftermath. Leaping into my car, I slid Genevieve's unmarked CD beneath my floor mat. As I zoomed away from the curb, I popped in my headset, watching Chic's taillights blink on the stretch of road visible down the hillside to my left.

"Where are they?"

"A block down from me," Chic said. "Teddie just executed the world's slowest three-point turn to hang 'em up. Can't see who through the tint. You got your piece?"

I set the .22 on the passenger seat. "Yep."

"Nice and easy. You drive right past 'em heading down. The road's narrow—they'll need time to turn around. We hit the bottom of the hill, we go in five different directions."

My grip tightened on the steering wheel. I wedged the .22 in the gap in the seat break; if chaos ensued, I didn't want it sliding out of reach.

Blind turn followed blind turn, and then finally, a sweep of head-lights illuminated a thicket of chaparral on the left shoulder. I slowed, hugged the wall of the canyon, and two black Tahoes flew by, rock-ing my car. No time to see a license plate. The windows looked uni-formly black.

I was almost around the curve when, in my rearview, I saw the back Tahoe's brake lights flare. My stomach surged.

Accelerating down the dangerous road, I said to Chic, "They spotted me."

"Okay. Keep me in your ear. Tell me where you are."

I skidded onto Coldwater, sending a spray of rocks and gravel across the opposing lane, and rocketed up the hill, blowing the light to veer left onto Mulholland. "I'm heading for home."

"I'm right behind you."

The lead Tahoe nosed into my mirror, but I lost it around a turn. The light at Benedict Canyon was yellow; I saw another dark SUV waiting at the intersection and hit the gas, squeezing through as it pulled forward to block me. Three cars in pursuit? The FBI? Gang-sters? The mob? Maintaining a dangerously heavy foot, swerving into opposite lanes to shave turns, I kept my pursuers one bend of the road behind me.

Chic said, "What's your cross street?"

Approaching Beverly Glen, Mulholland added a few more lanes, opening up for the intersection.

The wind brought me wisps of sound from a bullhorn: "Your ve-hicle over *now*—" Hitting the brakes, I careened around the turn and saw the blockade ahead—six police units parked nose to nose, lights strobing, doors open, firepower aimed at yours truly. A few confused drivers cluttered the intersection behind them, starting to reverse away from whatever was coming.

When the screech of my tires faded, I heard the sirens harmonizing behind me.

I said, "It's the cops."

Chic said, "I'm gonna go home now."

In my rearview I watched the distinctive cherry red pickup veer right and ease calmly down a side street. I turned on my dome light, placed both my hands on top of the steering wheel. One of the Tahoes pulled up next to me, the dark window sliding down.

I said, "There's a loaded .22 on the passenger seat."

Over the aimed sights of his Glock, Bill Kaden said, "Yes, I believe I'm familiar with it."

39

Resting my cuffed hands atop the interrogation table, I gazed around at the familiar yellowed walls, the one-way mirror flecked with rust. It was morning, but you wouldn't have known it.

Kaden and Delveckio had had me delivered by two gruff cops who smelled of cigarette smoke and refused to acknowledge me until they yanked me out of the backseat. A few reporters had been hanging around Parker Center on a rumor an indicted gangbanger was being moved downtown for a trial. In his absence they'd been happy to capture me doing the perp walk. Upstairs I'd been left to entertain myself for a few hours. Despite the cuffs, I tried to make hand-shadow animals on the far wall. Whoever said oppression breeds creativity was full of shit.

The door banged open, and Kaden ambled in. Cuffed sleeves, shoulder holster, smelling of chalk and coffee. Behind him Delveckio blew his nose into a handkerchief.

"We found Kasey Broach's shirt in the laundry-room sink of Genevieve Bertrand's house," Kaden said.

The laundry room. I hadn't even been bright enough to stumble over evidence planted for me.

Delveckio added, "And your prints all over the house."

"Of course they are. I spent a lot of time there before we broke up."

Kaden said, "We have you on her street."

"I was taking a drive."

Kaden gripped the table, arms flexing. "Are you denying that you broke in to her house a few hours ago?"

"I'm neither confirming nor denying anything until I talk to a lawyer."

"So why don't you request one now?"

"Because we'd have to stop talking. I know you think you've got something on me. Probably something horrifying. And I want to know what it is." I was sweating through my shirt. "I can tell from the setup. Nine units pursuing me, handcuffs, the smug set of your mouth. So what do you got? My high-school prom date ten toes up beneath the bed of tulips in my front yard?"

"You don't have a bed of tulips in your front yard," Delveckio said.

"I know, but 'hydrangeas' is a mouthful." A loaded silence. I was too anxious to let it stretch on longer. "Come on," I said. "Let's get it over with."

Kaden said, "We were on our way to arrest you when an anonymous call tipped us to a break-in at Ms. Bertrand's address."

"Why were you on your way to arrest me?"

He threw down an evidence bag containing a familiar hair on the table in front of me. "This hair matches several left behind by the Redondo Beach Rapist over the past three years."

"I . . . *what?*"

"He wears a ski mask, so we've never been able to get a composite. Seven rapes and we've got nothing but the occasional strand of brown hair." Kaden eyed me. "Matches *your* hair color."

"This is bullshit. By the time we're done, you're gonna have me toilet training the Lindbergh baby with Jimmy Hoffa."

"You wanna tell me why the hell you were having *our* lab process a hair from a wanted rapist?"

"They made a match and Ordean spooked," I said, more to myself than them.

"Of course he spooked. He's a fucking TV actor. The CSI clowns consulting on his show ran a microscopic hair comparison to play show-and-tell, put it against strands from high-profile outstanding cases. It hits the jackpot, they about swallowed their tongues. Ordean said you gave him this hair. Has no idea where you got it."

"Where do you think I got it?"

Kaden reached over and pressed a thumb to the swelling around my eye. "Morton Frankel."

I jerked away, and they snickered at me.

Kaden asked, "Why were you at Genevieve Bertrand's house?"

"Someone tried to break in to my house tonight, then run me over with a brown Volvo. He left this behind." Cuffs jangling, I pulled the Baggie holding the matchbook from my pocket—they'd missed it when patting me down for hardware—and flung it on the table.

Delveckio examined the skull-and-crossbones matchbook sourly, or maybe that was just his face. The more I studied him, the less I could imagine him having anything to do with Adeline—or any of the Bertrands, for that matter. Rather, the less I could imagine them having anything to do with him. Delveckio awkwardly manipulated the bag, showing his partner the address inside.

"Who tipped you?" I asked. "That I was allegedly at Genevieve's?"

Kaden said, "An anonymous caller."

"Don't you trace incoming phone calls?"

"It came in to my private line. Not 911. Not dispatch."

"That's a very anonymous anonymous call. When you go pick up Mort, why don't you see if he's got your digits written down somewhere?"

"We can't pick him up," Delveckio said.

"The guy tried to make me Volvo meat."

"Says you."

"And the matchbook."

"This evidence"—he tapped the bag containing the hairs—"was illegally obtained."

"But not by you," I said. "So you know you *can* use it—for a warrant and to build a case. And I've been told that it's all about building a case."

Kaden glared at me. "You ever fucking relent?" He jerked his head at Delveckio, and they left me alone with my none-too-chipper reflection.

I wasn't wearing a watch, so there was no way to gauge the time. Every few hours I'd ask to go to the bathroom, and I'd be respectfully led down a hall, passing under a clock.

After my third escort deposited me back in the room, I asked if I'd been arrested, and he said, "Not yet. You're still just being questioned."

I asked, "You guys trying out a new Zen interrogation technique?" He looked at me blankly, so I added, "Don't you have to charge me or let me go?"

"Not as long as we're holding you as a person of interest."

"Person of interest," I said. "That's flattering. I think I'll call my lawyer now."

"Hang on," he said. And then, as if I'd argued, "Just hang on."

He exited, pointedly leaving the heavy door ajar. A few minutes passed, and then I heard the staccato beat of footsteps down the hall. Morton Frankel, led in cuffs, passed the open doorway, Kaden and Delveckio on either side. Catching sight of me, Frankel bucked against the detectives, elbows flaring, and glared in at me. Bruises ringed his eyes from when I'd broken his nose, and he stood stooped from my stabbing him in the thigh. A sheen covered his face, and he had sweat stains under his arms; they'd kept him under the lights. Seeming to relish the confrontation, the detectives gave him a moment.

Frankel said, "I'm gonna gouge out your eyes and skull-fuck your head."

He lunged at me, causing me to jump up. My chair clattered over. Laughing, the detectives yanked him from view, and I heard Kaden ordering someone else to get him to Booking. Kaden and Delveckio returned, closed the door, and sat opposite me. Kaden's eyes went to my knee, which was jackhammering up and down from the scare, and his lips pressed together in a smirk. From his watch it was already two o'clock.

"Good detective work," Kaden said. "At his place our boys found a rape kit in a footlocker—ski mask, flashlight, pick set, cloth gags, plastic flex-cuffs, the whole nine yards. And the boy was just sentimental enough to keep a few trophies—a scarf, bathrobe sash, bracelet." He paused, bit his lips. "Only one problem, Danner. One of his hair samples we have on record was from an attack he committed the night of January twenty-two under the Redondo Pier. Around, say, eleven o'clock. That time and date ring a bell?"

When Kasey Broach was kidnapped.

Disappointment came in a rush. I sagged back in my chair.

Delveckio gave me a wan grin. "So unless Frankel chartered a helicopter to make his rounds that evening, that pretty well puts him out of contention."

"Who borrowed his car?" I asked.

"We're looking into it," Kaden said. "But we're assuming he needed it to get to Redondo to rape Lucy Padillo."

"That was the car," I said. "The dent on the right panel, everything."

Delveckio threw the matchbook on the table in front of me. "We had the lab take a look at this. No prints, which strikes us as a bit odd, given that it *is* a matchbook. But you'll like this part even better: The handwriting didn't match Frankel's. Know whose it matched?"

Kaden smiled. "Yours."

I opened my mouth but realized I had not a single goddamned thing to say.

"You're chasing a phantom all right, Danner." Kaden unfolded a photocopy—the matchbook note next to a sample of my handwriting, pulled from a DMV form I'd filled out sometime last year.

Matching characteristics of the letters had been circled in red. At a glance it made a convincing argument.

"Block letters are the easiest to forge," I said quietly. I didn't know this to be true, but it sounded good, and I had the force of desperation on my side.

Kaden and Delveckio looked at me like well-intentioned friends about to point out that my belt didn't match my loafers.

"Right," Kaden said, "and good ol' Mort takes a crash course in forensic handwriting after his shift stamping metal."

"But congratulations," Delveckio said with false cheeriness, "you caught a rapist, helped us close a case. So you're in the clear."

He offered his hand, but I knew better than to take it.

They both chuckled heartily.

Kaden said, "It doesn't quite work that way, as we tried to explain. You refused to walk the line, and now we have you on obstruction of justice, assault and battery, a couple B&Es. We asked you nicely, we asked you not nicely, and we warned you that this would wind up in the shit. But you were too busy playing gumshoe to think we were serious. That there would be consequences. So we're gonna charge you. Because, see, we're curious why you're so desperate to hang Kasey Broach's murder on someone else. You've got your taped alibi, fine, but we're gonna connect the dots, because we know they're there to be connected. And while we're busy doing that, we're gonna leave you in general pop over in Twin Towers."

Kaden stood and gripped my arm hard at the biceps. He led me out into the hall. What was I supposed to do? Kick and scream? Fight?

We rode the elevator down, then drove across to Twin Towers. They tugged me out, me moving numb on my feet, not fully believing they'd put me in the fish tank with murderers and rapists but believing it at the same time. I was prodded into Tower One. The building's hexagonal shape, contributing to the much-touted panoptic design, turned the interior into a house of reflections, each module faced and flanked by its multiple mirror image. The smell of the building had been singed into memory, bringing me back to those infinite four months. The stained concrete, the metallic din, the echo of wall-muffled shouts and clangs. The thick air took up bitter residence at the back of my throat.

"You have to charge me first," I said, "and let me call my lawyer."

The detectives left their Glocks in the gun lockers, and we passed through the double security doors into the no-man's-land of Sheriff's deputies with their tan-and-green uniforms and holstered pepper spray. Beyond one more gate of bars, I saw the inmates circling the vast rec room, talking shit, their too-loud laughter edged with aggression. Frankel wasn't among them, but he would likely be soon. While two cohorts watched, a prisoner with a shaved head and a goatee leaned up against a skinny black kid, pinning him to a barred window. A ripple of awareness passed through the group, heads swiveling to the gate, to me behind it.

I twisted my arm free. "This is bullshit. You can't do this."

Kaden unlocked my handcuffs. The deputy nodded at a colleague behind ballistic glass, and then the gate hummed pleasantly and he drew it aside and gave me a little shove. I knew better than to turn back pleading, so I stood and faced the others. The rec room was deep, at least a hundred blue jumpsuits dotting the metal benches and hanging from the pull-up and dip bars. The air was still, uncooled, and the heat from all those sweltering, stressed-out bodies vibrated the air like a low, sustained note.

Behind me the gate closed with steel finality.

Maybe fifteen convicts drew toward me, interest piqued. A man with matching crosses branded into his forearms stepped out in front, stretching his fingers wide as if flexing them. I moved to the side, putting concrete at my back as the others spread strategically and began their approach.

40

T he inmate with branded forearms smiled, his red mustache seeming to spread, and he feinted at me. I jabbed, missing badly.

The others whistled and laughed, and someone said, "Regular Mike Tyson."

"Shit," one of the black inmates corrected, "white boy a regular Jack Dempsey, you gonna poke fun."

Another guy came from my left, and I swung hard, clipping his chin, my momentum throwing me off balance. The inmate with the brands slipped in from my right, tying me up from behind in a bear hug, his body pressed to mine, stale cigarette breath puffing across my cheek. Pivoting, throwing elbows, I tried to get in a blow, but he lifted me off my feet, and then I hit the cold concrete and saw scores of white canvas shoes shuffling in swiftly for me.

There was a bang of steel, and then the crowd dispersed, my attacker pried off me. Two deputies at his side, Kaden hauled me up and hustled me out, down a corridor, onto an elevator, where he and Delveckio stood silently on either side of me like executives getting off work. Before my breathing had slowed, they'd moved me through the lobby and out into the bright afternoon.

Kaden stuck his finger in my cheek. "Let us give you some pointed advice. You are to stay the fuck away from this investigation. Entirely. No. Let me correct. From all investigations and all LAPD activities. Understood?"

My breath was still hammering through me. "Understood."

Delveckio shoved a shoe box into my chest, filled with my personals. The glass doors glinted, and they were gone. I took a few unsteady steps and sat on a planter.

Two seconds of still, and then I began shaking violently.

People passed oblivious, discussing weekend plans, complaining about coffee.

After a few minutes, I was able to pull together my thoughts. My handwriting on the skull-and-bones matchbook? Maybe I was further gone than I'd imagined. But there was evidence, also, to the contrary. Just because you're paranoid doesn't mean they're not out to get you. In fact, it would be easier to frame someone on perpetual edge.

The night of Kasey Broach's murder, Morton Frankel had been busy raping another party. But he'd been set up as Broach's murderer, just like me. Was he the backup fall guy? Or had he been framed as the guy framing me? Was he really after me? Or was I being set up to take *him* out? There I was, hanging off the ledge in the treadmill shot from *Vertigo*.

Finally I fished my cell phone from the shoe box and punched in Chic's number.

He answered on a half ring.

"Pick me up," I said. "I've got a lot of work to do."

I'd settled considerably by the time Chic got there, but the thought of those unprotected minutes in the jail rec room still sent acid washing through my stomach.

Chic pulled up and said, "I'm getting tired of picking you up from jail."

"Pretend you're my pimp."

"Talk about your low-wage jobs."

When I explained that I had given the hair sample to Johnny Ordean, Chic just shook his head. "Come on, Drew-Drew. That's minor leagues. You know better than to entrust a piece of evidence to someone who's hysterical by *vocation*."

"What should I have done?"

"I'm sure someone knows someone in the paternity-testing biz who could've run a hair. It's quiet where it's shady. Not under the klieg lights."

Not for the first time, I wished that I had been born with Chic's sense.

We drove for a while in silence as I ran through my next move in my head.

My cell phone rang—Preston, desperate for an update. I brought him up to speed, and then Chic started talking in my free ear, so I clicked on the speakerphone.

We all started talking at the same time; Preston, of course, prevailed. "So, fine, you were framed, Mort was framed. You're missing the *point*."

"That's what I been trying to tell him," Chic said. "If Mort ain't your guy—"

"Then why'd he act so bizarrely hostile toward you?"

Annoyed by their ebony-and-ivory routine, I took a moment to respond.

But Chic didn't give me a moment. "Because homeboy thought *you* was framing *him*."

"He's on the wrong side of the story, just like you are," Preston said. "You're still not asking the key question. And that is—"

Preston and Chic, now side by side on the piano keyboard: "Who framed *Mort*?"

Chic stared at me expectantly. Static from Preston. Clearly they were better at posing questions than coming up with answers. We sat in frustration for a few moments before Preston signed off. The silence that followed felt like defeat.

My Highlander was parked on the dirt shoulder off Mulholland where it had been left.

Chic gave me a wink as I climbed out. "Call when you find what you find."

I'd left the moonroof shoved back, and the seats gave off a deep warmth. Closing my eyes, I worked every link in the case like a rosary. How was I gonna know who would have a motive to frame Mort? I didn't know anything about him. I stared at the view, the world's most expansive dead end. It dawned on me by degrees—Preston and Chic's motive approach was wrongheaded. It came down to *opportunity*.

Not *why* would somebody have framed Mort? But who *could have*?

I pictured that telltale dent on the right front wheel well of Frankel's Volvo. My mind kept realigning the data, and I didn't like what it was coming up with.

I called the hospital and asked to be put through to Big Brontell's unit.

An unreasonably pleasant clerk answered. "I'm sorry, he stepped out for a bite. He'll be back shortly."

I left my cell-phone number, which she kindly jotted down, and then I drove the remaining two miles home. Xena had pulled my high-tops from the coat closet and chewed the toes to a pulp, but last night she'd likely saved my life, which I figured worth a pair of Nikes. I reheated some taco meat and put it in her salad-bowl dish to reward her for her bad behavior. Then I went to my office and got the murder book and all the notes I'd gathered on the investigation.

I was halfway down the stairs when I stopped, went back up, and grabbed my manuscript.

For the drive across town, I twisted and turned the evidence, trying to make a pretty picture. I got a few variations on the picture, none of them pretty.

Though the four o'clock sun was strong, the lights shone at the window of Frankel's apartment, a reminder of the detectives' late-night visit. I drifted up the street past the hot-dog stand, past the fabric store with the creepy mannequins tilting in the window, and parked by the car-rental lot. Frankel's mechanic was across the way, locking up the garage. I caught him as he fastened the security screen.

"Hi, I'm Drew. I was referred to you by one of my neighbors. Mort?" I offered a hand, and he held his up in apology, grease etching the lines in the rough skin.

He had wonderfully elaborate tattoos, dragons and busty nymphs, sheathing either arm. The ink stopped in neat cuffs at his wrists. "Oh, yeah. Mortie. Sure."

"He said you do great work."

"Dings to wrecks."

"You must be good. Mortie doesn't exactly lavish praise, does he?"

"No, he don't."

"You banged out that dent for him."

"That's right."

"I got one myself. Came out to my car in the morning and there it was. Wheel well." I shook my head, galled by the imaginary scofflaw. "Just like Mort's. No note, no nothing."

"He figured some asshole smacked it with a bike."

"We park side by side. I think the guy hit mine at the same time. A week ago Wednesday."

The mechanic shook his head. "Not Mort's. His got hit just a couple nights ago. You know Mort—he brought it to me the next morning."

"You sure?"

"Course I'm sure. He dropped the car first thing Tuesday, I had it back to him by the time he got off work."

The very night I'd gotten the vehicle ID from Junior, a ding had appeared in Mort's wheel well. And there was only one person other than Junior who could've known to put it there.

Acutely aware of the breeze across my suddenly hot face, I said, "You work fast."

"He's funny about that car. You'd do better to punch him in the nose than ding it. Though I wouldn't want to punch him in the nose."

"No," I said, "neither would I."

. . .

I sat in my car, elbows on the steering wheel, face tilted into my hands. My eyes ached, especially when I rubbed them.

I needed to proceed carefully and consider every possibility. Two reasonable options remained to explain Mort's wheel-well dent. Since the first was so incredible, I focused on the other. If Junior had embellished his story about the Volvo, that would have sent me scrambling off down the wrong clue trail, narrowing the field to felons and crooks and picking one of my liking. The ding in the right front wheel well—a considerable coincidence in this scenario— made this unlikely. But I had to be certain.

I called Hope House and explained to Caroline how I'd spent the time since I'd seen her last.

She said, "When the time is right, you'll have a nice lawsuit to press against LAPD."

"Right now I need you to make sure Junior is absolutely certain about everything he told me about the brown Volvo. Put him on the rack or whatever you shrinks use."

"Thumbscrews."

I thanked her, then stopped for a Coke and a refill at the gas station where I'd solidified Junior's love of smoking. The sky was starting to take on orange at the fringe, outlining the buildings and trees. My phone rang.

Caroline said, "Junior's positive about the Volvo. He said he's offended you're questioning his memory."

"Of course he is. Tell him I'll make it up to him at the Big Brother soiree next month." I climbed back into the Highlander, turned over the motor, and peeled out.

Fifteen minutes later I was across from the killer's house in North Hollywood.

41

I parked in the shadows about a half block down, beneath the waterfall foliage of a pepper tree. Shadows scalloped the windshield, and dry leaves scraped the roof. From my vantage only the garage and edge of the house were visible.

The scene demanded a noirish cast—dramatic lighting, gloomy sky, pessimistic clouds. But Los Angeles can be an uncooperative place. The evening had darkened a few degrees, sure, but there was a pleasing uniformity to the remaining sunshine, a suburban flatness. Leftover warmth lingered, trapped in the stifling stillness of the Valley air. It smelled of mulch and frying meat. Overhead a jet droned lazily toward Burbank.

The garage door was raised, the rear of the van laid open—apparently he was midtask, though from my limited perspective I could spot no movement around the house. The van was now the vehicle of choice; he wouldn't risk taking the other car out, not again.

I didn't want to believe it—I almost *couldn't* believe it—but who else made sense? Who could've broken in to my house, taken my blood, and put it on Broach's corpse? Who could taint the crime scene with a hair that wouldn't raise suspicion? Who had been helpful as long as I was running down the wrong trail? Who had samples from which to simulate my handwriting in the matchbook? Who'd shown me Richard Collins's fingerprint match only once he'd confirmed that the lifted print wasn't his own? Who had handpicked Mort from the pool of brown-Volvo owners I'd closed in on, selected him as the felon most plausible for a murder upgrade? Who had carte blanche access to equipment and databases and throwaway pistols? Who would know precisely how to angle the blade into an unconscious body to make the killer appear left-handed? Who'd been in convenient proximity to the site where Broach's body had been dumped, in fact, because he'd done the dumping?

Caroline had said it well: *That's what you don't understand in that pulp you churn out. Everyone's a good guy. Everyone's a bad guy. It just depends how hard you're willing to look.*

I knew I'd have to approach that garage and see with my own eyes. His house, the evening, the quiet neighborhood block I was parked on—they all felt surreal, hallucinatory stand-ins for reality.

Part of my manuscript had slid off the passenger seat. I stared at the top page beside me. `We got along well, and I had found him alarmingly adept at helping me massage plot elements, so much so that on occasion I'd brought him whole scenes to put his skills to work on.`

I got out, eased the door shut, and crept along the mossy wooden fence at the front of the property line, the rambling house drawing into view. I slipped through the barn gate, my shoes crunching on the gravel driveway. I passed the blind side of the house, the kitchen door Lloyd had sagged against, sobbing, as I'd left Monday night.

Pausing, I pressed my ear to the door. The grumble of movement deep within the house. A chair screeching back on its legs?

The sun was far enough gone now that when I ducked into the garage, I had to squint to make out the far corners. The car beside the van, hidden beneath a black cover, looked like a shapeless blob. It was backed in as before, the swung-open rear door of the van leaning against it. At the right front wheel well.

I had visited this very scene before. I remembered the van's rear door, how it rested heavily against the covered car, how it complained when Lloyd swung it shut.

The complaint came again, a dream echo, as I rotated the weighty door a foot or so, letting it rest against my shoulder blade as I faced the neighboring vehicle. Janice's disused car. Gathering a handful of cover, I tugged the soft fabric up to reveal the nose of a brown Volvo. A dent in the right front wheel well. Where the metal had crumpled inward, a white seam, jagged at the edges with flakes of paint. The original coat was in view around the mouth of the indentation. Harvest Gold.

What had Kaden told me? *Brown is the second most common Volvo color behind that shit yellow.*

I tented out the cover until I saw the jagged eye of the bullet hole in the upper-right corner of the windshield. The shot I'd fired last night in my neighbor's driveway.

I stepped away, the fabric slipping silently back into place, the van's door creaking open and finding the groove it had knocked in the Volvo's frame.

Lloyd had repainted his wife's Volvo so if anyone—like Junior—spotted it at one of the crime scenes, Janice wouldn't pop up on the DMV databases. There were 153 brown-Volvo owners in L.A. County. Only problem was, Janice's car was in the system as a *yellow* Volvo.

My cell phone rang, strident in the garage's confines, scaring the hell out of me. Caller ID flashed CDRS HOSPTL. Glancing around, I thumbed the volume down to "mute," whispered, "Just a sec," into the mouthpiece, and moved swiftly up the gravel drive, casting a nervous eye on the house and trying to keep my footsteps quiet.

Safely back in the Highlander beneath the protective cover of the pepper tree, I let out a deep breath, raised the phone, and said, "Sorry."

Big Brontell's bass vibrated the receiver against my head. "Help you, Drew-Drew?"

I asked, "Can you check for me if Janice Wagner is being treated in the oncology center there?"

"No. But I will." I heard him tapping away, wondered how the keys could accommodate his giant fingers. "We had her four months ago, but not now. She was discharged for home hospice September sixteenth."

September 16. A week before Genevieve's death.

I gathered the manuscript into my lap, wanting to be sure I remembered it right. Lloyd's words stared out at me from the page: "It's back. Other breast now. Third time through, make or break."

I said, "She wasn't seen for breast cancer, was she?"

"Breast? No. For—"

"Leukemia," I said.

My head humming, I flipped through my manuscript. I didn't want to believe it, but there it was, in plain type. Motive. "I'm sorry for the mess. Janice is an only child, both parents passed. We don't get much help."

Janice had no family to act as donors. Which meant that blind luck would have to intervene to stop her from wasting away. And when it hadn't, her husband had.

Lloyd could've just killed Kasey Broach and taken the marrow from her corpse. So why risk using sevoflurane?

I asked, "You have to be alive for a bone-marrow extraction, right?"

Over the sounds of continued typing, Big Brontell said, "That's right."

Please, please, let him have killed Genevieve also. Let him have killed her and then learned afterward that he needed to keep the next one alive for the marrow to be successfully extracted. Let him have evolved as a killer so both murders could be hung on his conscience and none on mine.

Doubt tugged at me. Why would Genevieve have *been* on the bone-marrow registry? To my knowledge she had no ill relatives, and she was hardly one for invasive charity. Also, if Lloyd had killed her, my brain tumor seemed something of a convenient fluke.

"What are the odds for a bone-marrow match?" I asked.

Big Brontell said, "One in twenty thousand. Give or take. Of course, your pool is limited to people who submit to testing."

"Are there any matches for Janice's type in the registry?" I asked. "People who live in Los Angeles?"

"Lemme check." The phone shifted noisily against Brontell's cheek, and then I could hear him breathing as he typed.

I dug through the manuscript furiously, checking my memory against twelve-point font: "None of us matched." Mrs. Broach waved a hand to encompass the three of them on the couch. "But Kasey did. She was Tommy's angel. She went in time after time, shots in the hip, needle this thick, never complained, not once."

I picture Kasey Broach's blue-tinted corpse, sprawled on the cracked asphalt beneath the freeway ramp: A nasty abrasion mottled her right hip. I racked my brain to recall if a similar scrape had been left on Genevieve in the same location. Wouldn't take much to skim away puncture marks from a cluster of needle perforations, to hide traces of the extractions under a glistening wound. Had I checked? Had anyone?

What had he said at our last good-bye? "I'm sorry, Drew, but Janice and I have to look out for ourselves."

Sorry, indeed.

He was no sadist, though he'd introduced a bondage rope to throw us off course. Sevoflurane to keep them alive and pliant. Xanax so they'd feel relatively calm should they breach consciousness—a humane facet of an inhumane act. He wouldn't have wanted the victims to suffer any more than he wanted me to. He just wanted his wife to live, no matter the cost. Had he apologized to his victims as he had to me? Had he wept as he pressed the gas mask over their faces to still their thrashing? As he'd positioned the boning knife for the final plunge?

Big Brontell said, "There are two matches in L.A."

A held breath burned in my chest. I prayed silently. Let Genevieve's name be one of those two, making me innocent.

"Let's see," Big Brontell said, with a deliberateness that made me want to scream. "Kasey Broach, but she took her name off the active list."

But it would've been a snap for Lloyd to get clearance to tap the bone-marrow database, to find matches present *and* past.

My voice sounded strangled. "And the other?"

"Sissy Ballantine."

I tilted my forehead into my hand, felt it slick and hot.

"She's listed as a sibling donor," Big Brontell said. "Transplant pending."

So her marrow was being reserved for a brother or sister, which meant it wouldn't be made available for Janice. Which in turn meant Lloyd had to take the marrow forcibly from one of the two matches and kill her to cover his tracks. Kasey Broach, long inactive on the donor list and thus further afield of the clue trail, had been the wiser choice.

"Thank you very much, Brontell. I can't tell you—"

"Hang on." Then he shouted across the phone. "Get the four-points and the Haldol!" Back to me: "Gotta run, Drew-Drew. My girth is required on the psych unit."

He disconnected, and I folded the phone and set it on the passenger seat.

When I looked up, Lloyd was at my window.

42

L loyd signaled me with one hand to roll down the window. His other arm was out of view, since he was standing half on the curb, bent beneath a wayward bough of the pepper tree. As I hit the switch, I kept my eyes on that hidden hand. From the flex of his arm, he was holding something. The cell phone was sleek and hard in my fist.

"Hey, Lloyd."

A dated weave belt pinched his tan Dockers at the waist. His brickred Polo shirt he wore tucked in, though it had tugged free at one side from recent exertion. His wavy blond hair sparkled with sweat where it met his forehead and temples. "Hello. What do you need?"

I gestured at the manuscript pages in my lap, giving myself an extra beat so my voice wouldn't reveal the adrenaline pounding through my veins. "I came by to give it one more shot, see if you'd take a look at some pages for me. I was just reviewing—"

He shifted, his arm moving, and I came within an instant of smashing his face with a Motorola-fortified fist. What swung into view, though, was not a weapon but a roll of silver electrical tape, which he spun absentmindedly around a finger.

"Drew, I'm just too overwhelmed right now. I can't help you. Or see you. This is a really bad time. An impossible time."

For all the heinousness of his actions, he was speaking the truth. He certainly looked overwhelmed, worn down by grief and dismay. As if his panic bell had been rung so often so he no longer registered the clangor inside his head. Like me he'd arrived here by desperation, choosing the less awful of two scenarios. From his face I'd say he'd had his share of second thoughts.

"Right. Okay. Sorry to bug you." I tugged the gearshift into drive. "See you later."

"See you, Drew," he said softly.

I pulled away, watching him in the rearview. He stood on the curb, staring after me, then started for the house, his shoulders stooped as though his thoughts were pulling him downward.

I turned the corner, pulled over, and dialed. "Detective Unger, please."

A few moments later, Cal picked up.

"It's Drew. I'm around the corner from Lloyd Wagner's house. I need you to get here now and bring the guns. Lloyd's got a Volvo with the right dent, repainted in brown. His wife has leukemia. There are only two matches for her marrow type in Los Angeles. One of them was Kasey Broach."

I heard wood creak as Cal sat down. "Was the other match Genevieve?"

"No," I said. "Some girl named Sissy Ballantine."

"Did you say *Sissy Ballantine*?"

"Yeah. Why?"

Cal's voice got tight. "An Amber Alert just hit my desk. Ballantine was snatched outside her house in Culver City a few hours ago. Neighbor saw a guy wrestle her into a white van."

I threw the Highlander into park, turned off the engine.

Cal said, "Stay put. Do not approach that house. We're on our way."

"Get over here."

"Stay out of the house. Promise me, Drew."

I snapped the phone shut, grabbed the tire iron from the trunk, and headed back down the street.

43

As silently as possible, I approached through the neighboring hedges. The garage door had been lowered, and I could hear from behind it the screech of tape being stripped from a roll. Slowing my breathing, I eased up on the window at the side of the garage, wading through a scented hedge of juniper. A dusty set of venetians guarded the glass, but where the stiff blinds had been tweaked down, I could see into the dim interior.

Lloyd's waist and legs protruded from the back of the van. At his feet a heap of plastic drop cloth. He emerged, roll of tape in his mouth, X-acto knife in his hand. Judging from the unused material, he was on the tail end of the job.

I withdrew, peering over my shoulder at intervals. He'd left the kitchen door unlocked, and I slipped inside. Dirty dishes, crumbs, and empty jars had overtaken the counters I'd cleaned just days before, a half-eaten burrito resting atop the rubber guard of the garbage disposal—Lloyd doing his best to keep doing.

Tire iron swinging at my side, I squared off with the dark hall and the seam of light under the bedroom door at the end. Beneath the nervous ticking of the kitchen clock and the grandfather's stately tocking from the living room, I could make out the wheeze of medical equipment. I started back, the photos of Lloyd and Janice hung at intervals providing a journey through their married lives. The wedding picture, the two of them beaming and clutching like prom dates. The bumper of their Gremlin, trailing toilet paper and tin cans, *Best of Luck!* frosted in cursive on the rear window. Poolside in Hawaii, paperbacks splayed on lounge chairs, fruit-bedecked cocktails raised. I was aware of my footfall on the slightly warped floorboards, my breath firing in my chest, that strip of light growing ever closer. Threads of gray had crept into Janice's hair by the time they were snapped before El Capitan in Yosemite. Jovial smile lines textured their faces as they held hands across a wrought-iron patio table in a Venetian piazza. Most of the pictures had caught them looking at each other rather than at the lens, as if they couldn't help themselves, as if they had a secret from the rest of the lonely world.

I reached the bedroom door and set my hand on the bulbous antique knob, the white-noise hum of the medical equipment beyond drowning out the clocks, my thoughts. In hackneyed narrative tradition, I couldn't help but recall standing outside another door, fearful of entering.

Before I lost my nerve, I pushed through into the room.

The bed was across the wide space, raised unreasonably on a box spring and penned in by metal guardrails. It had been angled toward the window so Janice could take in the downward-sloping stretch of trees. The room smelled of sitting food, sweat-laced linen, and residual human waste, not quite scoured from bedpans and fabric. The overlay of antiseptic cleaner and the various monitors and IV poles sprouting up like electronic growth brought me back to the room in which I'd awakened four months earlier to discover Genevieve's blood beneath my nails.

Janice looked soft and fleshy, her baldness making her head appear unusually round. She had no eyelashes or eyebrows, her blue eyes pronounced and burning from the depths to which they'd sunk. A terry gown had fallen open at the chest, revealing bone ridges above her breasts. Her lips were moist, slack cheeks folded in on them like an infant's. A bag of crimson, frothed lightly at the top, dangled from a metal pole, transfusing what I imagined was fresh bone marrow into her veins. Syringes, pill bottles, and vials overloaded one of the metal trays pushed to the wall. From the labels, potent names jumped out at me in officious pharmaceutical print. CYTOXIN. BUSULFAN. CYCLOSPORIN. To the right, a draft sucked at a closed door.

She raised a wasted arm, dripping a sheet of loose skin, as if to fend me off, her mouth opening slowly, repetitively, shaping a word. Her voice was depleted and her lips stiff with the great effort, hiding her teeth, turning her mouth into a wavering black hole, a parody of yelling. Passing her by ignored was unthinkable. I approached, owing some respect to the deathbed. To my great horror, I realized she was trying to call her husband's name. I became suddenly, horrifically aware of the tire iron hanging by my knee.

"No," I whispered, "I'm not going to hurt you."

A rasp, so dry as to be nearly inaudible. *"Make . . . him . . . stop."*

I left her there straining on the bed. The far door opened to a brief hall, which led to another door, left partially ajar. Listening for creaks in the old house that would broadcast Lloyd's return, I moved forward on tingling legs, the dim room drawing into view. It was, I saw by degrees, an in-law suite, a narrow bedroom complete with kitchenette and bathroom. Like some condemned construction site, it had been veiled in plastic and fabric. Hunter green bedsheets were tacked over the windows and over a sliding glass door that led to the backyard. His wife, I guessed, knew nothing of the comings and goings through that rear entrance, though clearly she knew that something was not as it should be. A plastic painter's drop cloth, meticulously laid down, slipped beneath my shoes and made it feel like I was moving across ice. It had caught drops of blood, many long dried. I stepped over coils of clear medical tubing, a gas canister lying on its side. A sleek box of a machine, the size of an old heater, purred. A processor of sorts, I assumed from its labels and dials. It was at work. Jumbled on the Formica counter, cartons of medical gloves, a collection of fat syringes, coils of white cotton rope, crusty transfusion bags. There, on a floating metal tray, a curved Shun boning knife, the Japanese character standing out starkly, black against stainless steel. And just behind it on a cot, almost disguised as another inanimate object, lay a young woman on her side.

Her eyes were closed peacefully, and Lloyd, sensitive soul, had propped her head on a pillow. I watched her raised shoulder sway gently with her breaths. The skin at her left hip was peppered where a big-bore needle had been thrust through to extract marrow from her pelvic bone. The marks were fewer and more tightly clustered than I'd have thought; Lloyd must have gone in repeatedly through the same perforations, sliding the skin to reach new bone.

She lay, depleted and unconscious, awaiting the boning knife. I imagined that Lloyd, feeder of Xanax, didn't like that part and so had left it for after he'd prepped his van for her body's transport. He couldn't let her live any more than he could've released Kasey Broach after taking from her what his wife required. The soreness and resultant medical treatment would have revealed that bone marrow had been extracted, and from there it would've been a short hop to matching wait-listed patients, and to Janice. Leaving a corpse also made it significantly less likely that the marrow theft would be uncovered. I'd learned from Lloyd himself that during an autopsy medical examiners generally extract and weigh organs, examine visible wounds, and take fluid and tissue samples. They'd have little call to look for perforations in the bone beneath a divot of carefully scraped flesh. And of course there'd be no patient around to complain of deeper soreness.

Behind the processor, restored to a Pyrex jar and left on the floor like a kicked-off shoe, was my ganglioglioma. My tumor had found the killer before I had. It took me an instant to tear my eyes from the familiar cluster of cells that Lloyd, during his *Gaslight* campaign, had kidnapped and led me to believe I'd destroyed. He was probably planning to leave it at a crime scene, adding to my confusion or culpability.

I moved toward the girl. Sissy Ballantine? I set the tire iron down on the thin mattress at her side and reached for her. The girl's eyelids rose lazily.

She said calmly, "Behind you."

I spun around, nearly tripping on the flared end of a medical tube.

Lloyd filled the doorway. "Damn it," he said sadly. "Damn it, Drew."

I took a half step to my right, hoping to block the tire iron from view. If I didn't set him off, this wouldn't have to get violent. Would it? The floating metal tray pressed into the small of my back. Sissy murmured something behind me, and then her voice trailed off.

Lloyd said, "I couldn't just let her die, Drew. I couldn't. Not when I was in a position to do something about it."

My voice was hoarse. "But why . . . why did you pick *me*?"

He looked at the floor, my shoes, but not at me. "For the past two years, I've tapped in to that transplant registry every day. Every single day. And stared at those two women whose marrow matched Janice. One who'd removed herself from reach, the other whose marrow was already spoken for. Nothing I could do. By day I processed bodies, by night I watched my wife die." He rested a hand on the half-open door, swinging it slightly on its hinges. "But one night I got called out of bed. And there was Genevieve lying in her bedroom. I was stunned. The paramedics told me that you'd been taken away. That you'd been seizing. Dazed. That you were now in surgery. I went back and looked at Genevieve, that run of unblemished flesh at her hip. And it struck me how I could do this."

"So you didn't kill her?"

"I didn't kill her." His lips pressed together in a sad grin. "She was no good to me. To Janice. But there she was. An inspiration. And there you were. Scared. Paranoid. Tangling with detectives who already thought you were the killer. All I had to do was add an abrasion to the next one's hip. And then keep paying you out rope. You brought me the next twist and the next. A felon who worked at Home Depot. A hundred and fifty-three owners of brown Volvo wagons to choose a candidate from. You were so imaginative, you see." Lost in thought, he toed the tubing that snaked from behind him into the room. Finally he lifted his gaze to my face. "For this to work, I needed a Drew. And you were the perfect Drew."

Made strangely drowsy by the weight of the discovery and the soporific hum of the filter, I focused on his words. It was oddly difficult.

"I helped you write all those books," Lloyd said. "I figured you could help me with this one."

"I know I owed you," I said. "Did I owe you this much?"

He stared at me, and I stared at him. He'd set his weight forward so the door squeezed him against the jamb. I couldn't see his hands, which made me nervous, so I clasped my own behind my back, gripping the metal tray. The tire iron was out of reach, back on the bed.

"So," I said.

"So." He frowned, and his mouth twitched a little, as if on the verge of a sob, but then calm reasserted itself over his features. "What are we gonna do now?"

"Call an ambulance for Sissy. And for Janice. Some cops we probably know will come get you. We'll go in. And we'll straighten this out."

"No." He shook his head. "No. Here's how it's gonna go. I'm going to kill you. And I'm going to kill Sissy. And then I'm going to get her marrow into Janice."

A sudden heat rose to the line of my surgical scar, making it tingle and seethe. The tips of my fingers brushed the handle of the stainless boning knife behind my back.

"How are you gonna do that?" I asked.

Lloyd leaned over, reaching for something behind the door.

A wave of light-headedness washed through me. I sensed not an odor but a change in the consistency of the air. I staggered a half step, then firmed my legs beneath me. When I looked up, a gas mask stared back at me from the doorway, cylindrical filters shoved out from the jaw like insect mandibles. The door was wide open now, and I could see the canister he'd hidden behind it. His fingers rested on the metal valve atop the canister. In his other hand, he held a plastic face mask, shaped for the nose and mouth, its tube trailing back to the nozzle. I glanced dumbly at the end of the tubing at my feet, only now noticing the slight hiss it had been giving off all this time, virtually hidden beneath the hum of the filter.

Lloyd wrenched the valve, rerouting the escaping gas through the mask, and lunged. Reaching blindly for the knife, I blocked with one arm, but he managed to shove the mask over my face, and I jerked in a pure inhale, feeling my knees buckle. I flailed, striking the tray, and went down amid the metallic rattle.

My hand grasped for the knife among the folds of plastic drop cloth, finding the cold handle. As Lloyd stumbled down over me, jamming the mask again to my face, I brought the knife up and felt it press against his belly as he fell, then break surface tension with a pop. He collapsed on top of me, his gas mask knocked askew so it rode up in his thick curls. My bucking legs struck the Pyrex jar—the tinkle of breaking glass and then the schoolroom reek of formaldehyde. Lloyd was weeping with horror, his face twisted. Both of my hands, gripping the shaft of the knife, were trapped beneath his dying weight. His white fingertips, straining around the plastic, dug into my cheeks, keeping the face mask rammed unevenly against my nose and mouth.

He sputtered and collapsed, drooling blood onto my chest.

Burning rubber.

The acrid odor washes through my head, lining my nasal cavities, enveloping my brain. I cannot breathe it away.

I am driving. My dashboard clock reads 1:21 A.M.

Genevieve's house comes into view, and I jerk the steering wheel, banging over the curb, snapping the sprinkler at the fringe of the decorative lawn.

The dinging of the open car door behind me, I am running up the walk to the house, my thigh muscles burning. My flesh is clammy, pulsing with some unknown terror. I stumble onto the porch. Music swells from within.

I seize the terra-cotta pot, lose my grip, crack the saucer. Leaning the pot back again, I grasp the brass key in the grime. My hands fumble at the dead bolt. I drop the key. It bounces knee high but avoids the cracks between the decking.

My head fogged with the stench, I jam the key home, twist, and shove. Stumbling in, I bang the side table. The Murano paperweight slides like a hockey puck and shatters, millefiori segments rattling on the marble tile.

Flights of strings, thundering horns, the wrenching wail of a soprano.

Perché tu possa andar . . . di là dal mare . . .

I seem to float up the stairs, my shoes barely touching carpet.

Genevieve lies collapsed on her face and chest, knees jammed beneath her as if she'd been kneeling.

Already dead.

Blood has soaked into the white carpet around her. Her window is open, and her cream silk gown, blown back from one pale shoulder, flutters about her.

Something lets loose in my chest, and I utter a cry, running forward. I grasp her lightly at the shoulders and turn her. One arm swings stiffly on a locked elbow, striking me in the face.

The music crescendos, unrelenting.

Amore, addio! Addio! Piccolo amor!

She lolls in my arms, delicate hand curled, forefinger pointing like Michelangelo's Adam, except without a mate. A knife is sunk into her to the shaft. Sobbing, frantic, I grip the stainless tip with both hands and tug it free. She tumbles from my lap.

Blackness encroached on the dream-memory, starting at the fringes and blotting out my vision.

Through the sevoflurane haze, I heard sirens.

44

It was so late it was early, but the sky wasn't admitting it yet. A *Los Angeles Times* graced my doorstep, the first since I'd restored service after jail. Covered with Lloyd Wagner's blood, I stooped and picked it up. Maybe things were finally getting back to normal.

Above a picture of me looking pallid and displeased, the headline, behind on gossip as usual, read DANNER TAKEN BACK INTO CUSTODY.

Maybe things weren't getting back to normal.

I stepped inside, Xena bulling into me in greeting. I tugged off the stained shirt and threw it in the trash, then wandered into the family room and sat in my venerable reading chair. The TV chatterheads buzzed with the news of Lloyd's death and, of course, my involvement. They *didn't* announce that I hadn't killed Genevieve Bertrand, that she'd already been dead when I'd found her. The evidence for that particular lay locked in my unreliable frontal lobe, and, try as they might, Fox News couldn't plug in to that.

But now I could.

To a strobe-light effect of flashbulbs, Cal commanded a podium outside the North Hollywood house, detailing how they'd stormed the place to find me and Sissy Ballantine regaining consciousness in the makeshift medical suite. In the background two stalwart paramedics steered Janice out on a gurney, and we viewers were given a zoom to follow her rolling entry into an awaiting ambulance.

Her close-up was appropriate; she *was* the unwitting star of the story. I hadn't been the protagonist after all, but—like Kasey Broach, like Sissy Ballantine—a bit player. Morton Frankel, fellow fall guy, had played his role as well as I, two expendable L.A. walk-ons hitting the marks and saying the lines. I'd responded to Lloyd's preparations with a promptness and an ardor that could scarcely be improved on, calling him within hours of my release from jail, scratching at the imagined scab of my guilt until I'd raised blood. Book after book, I'd reinforced Lloyd's increasingly imaginative involvement in what had previously been dry scientific work. Some of the most diabolical killings in my novels wouldn't have been nearly as inventive were it not for Lloyd. And perhaps his crime wouldn't have been nearly as well plotted were it not for me. Or as far-fetched.

An improbable fiction? Certainly. But then, we don't want to construct the story that's most likely to be told. We want to tell the one that finds its way to the pit of the gut, like a curved boning knife.

I never would have guessed it, but Lloyd had proven a better crime writer than I was.

I turned off the tube and petted Xena's oversize head, enjoying a few minutes of blissful silence.

The telephone rang. Not my cell but the glorious, hearty ring of the landline, harmonized on a faint delay with the phones upstairs. The noise filled the rooms. It made it seem as though my house worked again.

I strode over to the cordless mounted on the living-room wall and answered.

Caroline said, "Done showing off?"

"I hope so."

"You're all right?" Something in her delivery connoted great care.

I considered for a moment, then answered, truthfully, "Yes. I am."

"You weren't answering your cell," she said. It was only then that I realized the phone had been on mute since Lloyd's house. "So I got your home line from your Big Brother form. I have something to cheer you up."

"What?"

"Me?"

"Do you deliver?"

"I do."

She hung up. Xena garishly stuck her muzzle between my legs. Jealous, no doubt.

I went to my car to retrieve the half-written book and the unlabeled CD from Genevieve's that I'd shoved beneath my floor mat.

Back upstairs I sat at my desk, placed the pages beside my mouse pad, and slid the disc into my computer, bringing up iTunes on the monitor. My screen asked if I wanted to retrieve track and album information, identifying the burned music from the online library.

I did.

While iTunes searched, showing me a horizontal barber pole to solicit my patience, I picked up my office phone to call Chic. The line bleated, indicating messages.

I dialed voice mail. A synthetic voice said, *"Greetings. You have forty-nine saved messages."*

My lawyers and I had reviewed digital copies of all the messages while preparing my case. My messages had been preserved in the actual system, too, it seemed, from when LAPD froze me out of my voice mail right up until the day SBC interrupted my service. I bleeped through them now, deleting the first several from September 22 and the day of the twenty-third. Preston, nagging me about deadlines, a missing jacket, and an anthology he'd wanted me to contribute to. April asking what time she should come over for dinner that night.

The synthetic voice spoke the chillingly familiar time stamp: *"Fifth message. Sent September 23, 1:08 A.M."*

Genevieve's damning message. I cocked back in my chair.

The softly accented voice whispered in my ear, "It's me."

A wave of heat passed through my face, setting my scar on fire. I'd heard the message countless times during my incarceration and trial. That wasn't how it started.

The computer search completed, iTunes confirming what I already knew. *Madame Butterfly—Disc 3.*

The first track began to play from my tinny computer speakers, an accompaniment to Genevieve's message.

"I wanted to tell you I'm peaceful. I'm okay, I feel okay now. I've heard you're with someone new, and I'm . . . I'm glad for you." A moist inhale. "I'm sorry. For how I hurt you, for how I hurt everyone." How fragile her voice, how delicate that French inflection. "Maybe this can be one of your stories one day. Maybe you'll understand."

From my computer Madama Butterfly wailed, *Verrà, verrà, vedrai.*

"Maybe you'll forgive me. For that and for this. I ask of you only one thing. My last request. Don't judge me. I hope you can walk around in my skin for a while. Isn't that what you do? Feel this pain. Write about it so maybe other people don't have to feel so alone."

Salite a riposare, affranta siete . . . al suo venire vi chiamerò.

"Good-bye, my love."

The click of the hang-up.

Tu se con Dio ed io col mio dolor . . .

Gently, I replaced the phone in its cradle. Her real message, so different from the altered version played ad nauseam in court. As Preston reminds me every chance he gets, it's all in the editing. Slowly, I reached over and thumbed through the ragged manuscript: Aside from the detectives, Lloyd Wagner would know Genevieve's case better than anyone, having handled everything from recovering my voice-mail messages to matching the knife to the wound.

The original message would have exonerated me, causing the

prosecution to drop the case. If no one believed I'd killed Genevieve, Lloyd would have lost his ideal fall guy. A guy whom everyone—the cops, the media, the prospective jury pool—believed guilty of murder. A guy the detectives would be eager to rush to judgment about. A guy who already half believed he was losing his mind. Lloyd knew he couldn't delete phone and caller ID records, but he could digitally reorganize the voice-mail recording, making it as ambiguous as the rest of the case, before turning it over during discovery. He'd told me himself he couldn't imagine my getting convicted, given the brain tumor. I'd be free yet tainted, available for the frame-up. A story-perfect investigation where no one would dig beneath the skin and find the hidden holes. To be sure, it was a risk, but with his wife's life hanging in the balance, he'd proven all too willing to take gambles.

I played Genevieve's message again, imagining its impact on me the night of September 23. A suicide warning, not a snotty rebuke.

What were the good doctor's words?

"Because the temporal lobe is intricately tied to emotional arousal, there is plentiful evidence that, once a patient has reached such a fragile state, the final mental break can be triggered by an emotionally intense event."

An emotionally intense event. A message from an ex announcing her intention to kill herself would likely qualify.

April, contented midwestern soul, was a deep sleeper. Unlike me, she wouldn't have been roused by the ringing phone. In the darkness of that night, I'd padded into my office, sat, and played Genevieve's message. Startled, I'd risen, my office chair toppling over.

And then, altered and frenzied, I'd hot-assed it over to Genevieve's to find her, in typical dramatic fashion, robed in her best approximation of a geisha, slumped over the blade she'd thrust into her own belly, operatic death song blasting from the walls.

Her prints had been lifted from the handle. That was to be expected—her knife, her house. My prints, from removing the knife, had been more eyebrow-raising.

She'd been right-handed, the reverse stab angling the blade as if the thrust had come from a left-handed attacker. As she'd keeled forward, the butt of the knife had struck floor, driving the blade deep enough to suggest that a 185-pound male had been behind the handle.

Straightforward enough to untangle, had I not arrived to fuck up the crime scene.

As a show of gratitude for the revelations the past hours had afforded me, I retrieved an '82 Bordeaux I'd been saving for years and drained it down the kitchen sink. I let Xena lick the neck when I was done. No need to waste it.

I wandered onto my back deck, put my feet on the rail, and stared out at the lights. All those people, all those stories.

Xena chased her stub and rolled in the brittle leaves.

I'd started out innocent and wanting to clear my conscience. I'd discovered I was not a murderer. And I'd wound up a killer.

I could live with that; as someone once told me, generally, we're not given the choice anyway. What a piece of work is man, and all that.

The doorbell rang, a deep chime causing Xena to lift her square head from the union of her paws.

I rose and walked inside.

45

I'm a free citizen, at least until my next brain tumor. Cal leaked Genevieve's voice-mail message to the press, which, on the crest of the sensationalist coverage of Lloyd's machinations, restored my name to whatever dubious standing it had achieved before the trial. My sales continue to increase.

A deputy corroborated my account of the jail recroom incident, but before I could formally file a complaint against Kaden and Delveckio, all pending charges against me were dropped. Morton Frankel awaits trial, but I have been informed that he is—as they say in the hallowed halls of Parker Center—fucked.

Sometimes Cal drops by and we smoke cigars on the back deck, overlooking the city. He's not promoted yet, but his captain's got his ear to the ground and says any day now. We talked about the case a lot, me and Cal, and then all of a sudden we didn't.

I've still heard nothing from the Bertrands, and doubt I ever will. My association with the ugliness surrounding their daughter has branded me guilty, even if I am not, and I don't begrudge them their construal of events.

Sissy Ballantine completed a swift recovery and eventually made the marrow donation to her brother. I got to meet him, a brunch that was a better idea in theory than awkward reality. His wasted shoulders poked at his vintage bowling shirt, he had the first wisps of a beard coming in, and he looked baffled and humbled by all the commotion that had happened around him. When I shook his hand, I could feel his bones clearly through the skin. Sissy followed me out and gave me a quick hug. "Thank you," she said, smiling the wide smile of the healthy, and damned if I didn't feel, for a brief moment, up to snuff with Derek Chainer.

The Broaches had lost one child, in effect, because they'd lost another years before. Think about that the next time you're feeling secure about your place in the divine order.

The home-administered chemo had emptied Janice Wagner's bones of marrow in preparation for the second transplant that never came, and there'd been nothing to replace it. About a week after Lloyd's death, she died. It's hardly justice, but not quite karma.

I guess it's life.

The Broaches granted the exhumation order, and when the coroner peeled back the abraded flesh on Kasey's hip, he'd found the bone beneath marred with barely premortem needle punctures. The photos found their way to the tabloids.

Kasey's marrow, as you may have guessed, hadn't been taking in Janice's bones. It's not a complicated business, I've been told, but complicated enough that they don't sell home kits. Lloyd hadn't gotten enough marrow from Broach's right hip alone; he'd needed to extract it also from her left, but the detectives surmised that he'd been concerned that dueling hip abrasions on the corpse would have been hard to sell.

From the beginning, the tight time frame had left

Lloyd desperate. Once Janice's bones had been ravished, he'd had to move swiftly on Broach—thus the gun and the at-home neighbors—and he'd rushed Sissy Ballantine even more. One of the doctors treating Janice had later said that Lloyd seemed to have worked out the kinks, that his chemo cocktails had put her leukemia into temporary remission, so the second transplant could very well have taken. But, of course, the rest of Sissy Ballantine's marrow—prudently taken from both sides of her pelvic bone—hadn't made it from the filter to Janice's veins. Instead it had been removed from the machine and put on ice for Sissy's brother, for whom it had originally been intended.

Janice had been sufficiently impaired to withhold and withstand keen questioning, and she'd pushed off from the dock without anyone ascertaining how much she knew about what Lloyd was up to in that suite down the hall. I believe I heard that she never even found out that her husband had died just one room away from her.

The day after her death, Cal showed me an entry from Lloyd's journal, full of tortured remorse and pleading apology, with a clarity about grief and loss that gave me a pang of empathy.

A pang.

I suppose Lloyd will draw some comfort during his long drift across the river Styx from the fact that his wife never had to find out his full story.

What was his story? As Chic would say, that's no groundballer. Lloyd was a guy like any other, I suppose, subjected to the right pressures and passions. A guy whose wife was dying in sluggish, wrenching increments. Day after day he hacked into that transplant registry and stared at those two stubborn owners of matching marrow, his brain redlining to come up with an angle—any angle—that could get him and Janice to their twenty-fifth anniversary. *Unlike* any other guy, Lloyd had an extraordinary skill set to counter those pressures. I'll still be out in my yard, or lined up at the In-N-Out drive-through, and remember some other wrinkle Lloyd had forensically smoothed from the fabric of his plan. I'd never considered the ramifications of the first time he'd called me excited about a murder scene years ago, a bizarre hot-tub death in Manhattan Beach. My greed as a writer brought me into this. I had volunteered to be his subject when I drew Lloyd into devising my stories. I always wanted my plots to be realer than I could make them myself. And I needed someone who lived it. I needed someone who'd smelled that stench. And I got it.

A story, after all, doesn't have to be true. Just convincing.

Spring is slow in coming, though you can't tell by the weather. I have a vicious killer of a dog, who attacks pillows and shoes and hardcover novels like nobody's business. I have a Little Brother who can spray-paint and pick locks well beyond his years. He takes me to Dodgers games and batting cages and, most frequently, to court when he violates probation. I still see Genevieve at times—through the steam in the shower, humming a melody, as I'm driving some stretch of road—but less often now.

This morning, at the end of breakfast, guess who reappeared out on the deck? Gus. Big grin, pouched cheeks, and buck teeth, like a smug third-grader back from some mysterious adventure and privy to secrets we'll never know. He wobbled across the deck and began assiduously chewing a hole through the garden hose. I rose and pulled back the sliding glass door. Caroline followed me out and tossed Gus a scrap of toast. He looked up at us indifferently, then scampered off through his path in the ivy.

Like the rest of us, trying to stay one squirrel step ahead of the coyotes.

Acknowledgments

I cannot sufficiently express my appreciation to Robert Crais, who encouraged my new direction from the gates and championed this book unswervingly from his first reading of the manuscript. Aaron Priest and Lisa Erbach Vance exceeded even their reputations with their skill and grace as agents. Marc H. Glick, Rich Green of CAA, and Jess Taylor, as always, provided invaluable support and input. I feel fortunate to have found an energetic and perspicacious editor in Josh Kendall; I owe much gratitude to him, Clare Ferraro, and so many others at Viking for the enthusiasm they've shown me and this novel. Thanks also to Melissa Hurwitz, M.D., Lucy Childs, Kristin Baird, M.D., Nicole Kenealy, Richard Kim, James Kryzanski, M.D., Michael Sebastian, and Maureen Sugden. Finally, Delinah, who was there for it all and not once asked me to play it safe.